THE CASE OF THE

Fabulous Fake

by ERLE STANLEY GARDNER

All Grass Isn't Green

by A. A. FAIR

Published for the
DETECTIVE BOOK CLUB ®
by Walter J. Black, Inc.
ROSYLN, NEW YORK

THE CASE OF THE FABULOUS FAKE
Copyright © 1969
by Erle Stanley Gardner

ALL GRASS ISN'T GREEN
Copyright © 1970
by William Morrow and Company, Inc.
Published by special arrangement with
William Morrow and Company, Inc.

THE DETECTIVE BOOK CLUB®
Printed in the United States of America

THE CASE OF THE

Fabulous Fake

Chapter One

Perry Mason looked up from his desk as Della Street, his confidential secretary, stood in the door of the office which communicated with the reception room.

"Yes, Della?"

"We have a young woman in the outer office who won't give her name."

"Then I won't see her," Mason declared.

"I understand how you feel about these things," Della replied, "but I think there's some interesting reason why this young woman won't give us the information."

"What sort of reason?" Mason asked.

Della Street smiled. "I think it might be interesting to find out."

"Blonde or brunette?"

"Blonde. She's holding on to a flat black bag in addition to a purse."

"How old?" Mason asked.

"Not over twenty-two or twenty-three."

Mason frowned. "Are you sure she's over twenty-one?"

Della shook her head. "You can't tell by looking at her teeth," she said, smiling.

"How about her hands?" Mason asked.

"And you can't tell too much by a woman's hands until after she passes thirty," Della explained.

"All right," Mason said, "bring her in, we'll take a look."

Della Street turned, went into the outer office and shortly returned with a young woman who was trembling with excitement as she approached the desk and said, "Mr. Mason?"

Mason smiled. "There is no need to be nervous," he said. "After all, I'm an attorney and if you are in trouble perhaps I can help you."

She seated herself across the desk from the lawyer and said, "Mr. Mason . . . I . . . I . . . I'm going to have to disappear and I don't want my parents ever to be able to find me."

Mason regarded her thoughtfully. "Why are you going to have to disappear?" he asked. "The usual reason?"

"What's the usual reason?" she asked.

Mason smiled and shook his head. "Don't cross-examine me," he said. "Let me do the questioning. Why do you want to disappear?"

"I have my reasons," she said. "I don't think I need to go into all the details at the present time, but I do want to disappear."

"And you want me to help you?"

"I want you to be in such a position that you can, if necessary, furnish the missing link which will connect me with my past life. But I don't want you to do it unless I give you permission and tell you to, or unless certain circumstances develop which will make it imperative that you do communicate with my parents."

The telephone on Della Street's secretarial desk rang and she said, "Hello . . . yes, Gertie. . . . Right away? . . . Is it that important? . . . Very well, I'll be right out."

She glanced meaningly at Perry Mason, said, "If you'll excuse me a moment," and hurried through the door to the outer office.

Mason regarded his visitor quizzically. "You're asking me to take you on trust."

"Don't you have to take all of your clients on trust?"

"Not entirely. I usually know with whom I am dealing and what the score is."

"And you are usually retained to defend some person who is accused of crime?"

"Quite frequently."

"And how do you verify the fact that your client is telling you the truth?"

Mason smiled. "You have a point there," he admitted.

"You take them on trust," she said.

"Not entirely," Mason replied. "Any person accused of crime, whether guilty or innocent, is entitled to a defense. He's entitled to his day in court. I try to give him legal representation."

"But you try to make that representation effective so that you prove his innocence."

Mason thought for a moment, then, choosing his words carefully, said, "I try to make my representation effective. I'll go that far."

Della Street appeared from the outer office, motioned to Perry Mason, and walked through the door into the law library.

Mason said, "You'll have to excuse me just a moment. We seem to have some rather important matter demanding immediate consideration."

"Certainly," she said.

Mason swung around in his swivel chair, got up, walked around the desk, gave his visitor a reassuring smile, said, "I'm satisfied it will only be a moment," then opened the door to the law library.

"What's the excitement?" he asked Della Street when he had closed the door.

"Gertie, at the switchboard," Della said.

"What about her?"

"I hardly know," she said. "You know Gertie, she's an incurable romantic. Give her a button and she'll sew a vest on it every time, and sometimes I think she even uses an imaginary button."

Mason nodded.

"She observed something about our visitor in there, or thinks she did, and perhaps you'd better talk with her."

"Can't you tell me what it is?"

"Of course I can," Della said, "but I can't evaluate what Gertie's saying the way you can—it makes quite a story."

"All right," Mason said, "let's go see what it is."

He took Della's arm, escorted her through the door which opened from the law library into the entrance room.

Gertie, at the switchboard, was sitting on the edge of her chair, her eyes wide with excitement, her jaws chewing gum in a frantic tempo, indicative of her inner nervousness.

Gertie had an insatiable curiosity. She always wanted to know the background of Mason's clients and, quite frequently, vested them with an imaginary environment which, at times, was surprisingly accurate.

Considerably overweight, Gertie was always going on a diet "next week" or "after the holidays" or "as soon as I return from my vacation."

Despite the fact there was no one in the office, Gertie beckoned Mr. Mason over to her desk and lowered her voice so that it was barely audible.

"That young woman who went in your office," she said.

"Yes, yes," Mason said, "what about it, Gertie? Did you notice something about her?"

"Did I notice something about her!" Gertie said, quite obviously savoring the fact that she had for the moment become the center of attention. "I'll say I did!"

"Well," Della said impatiently, "tell it to Mr. Mason, Gertie. After all, she's waiting in there."

Gertie said, "You noticed that black bag she's carrying with her, that she hangs on to so tightly?"

"I didn't notice her hanging on to it so tightly," Mason said, "but she has both a black bag and a hand purse with her."

"It's a kind of cosmetics and overnight bag," Della said. "In a bag of that type there's a mirror on the inside of the lid when you open it."

"And cosmetics, creams, and hairbrushes on the inside?" Mason asked.

"Not in *this* bag," Gertie asserted vehemently. "It's packed, jammed solid with hundred-dollar bills, all neatly packaged."

"What!" Mason exclaimed.

Gertie nodded solemnly, obviously enjoying Mason's surprise.

"How do you know, Gertie?" Della Street asked. "Tell him that."

"Well," Gertie said, "she wanted to get something out of the bag or put something in it. Anyway, she opened it, but it was the way she opened it that attracted my attention."

"In what way?" Mason asked.

"She turned around in her chair, her back toward me, so that I couldn't see what she was doing."

Mason smiled and said, "And the minute she did that you craned your neck, trying to see what it was she was concealing."

"Well," Gertie said, "I guess everyone has a natural curiosity, and after all, Mr. Mason, you want me to find out about the clients that come to see you."

"I was just making a comment," Mason said. "Don't let it worry you, Gertie. What did you see?"

"Well, what she didn't realize," Gertie said, "was that just as soon as she turned her back and opened the lid of the bag, the mirror at a certain angle reflected the contents of that bag so that I could look right into the mirror and see what was inside."

Mason said, "Tell me exactly what you saw."

"The whole inside of that black bag," Gertie said impressively, "was just one mass of hundred-dollar bills, all neatly stacked in piles just as they came from the bank."

"And you saw that in the mirror?"

"Yes."

"Where were you?"

"I was here at my desk by the the telephone switchboard."

"And where was the young woman?"

"Sitting over there."

"All the way across the office," Mason commented.

"That's right. But I saw what I saw."

"You say she turned her back to you?"

"Yes, very ostentatiously."

"And then opened the bag?"

"Yes."

"And when the lid reached an angle of approximately forty-five degrees you could see the contents of the bag?"

"That's right."

"Now, did she very carefully hold the lid in that position so you could continue to look at the contents, or did she open it the rest of the way so the lid was straight up?"

Gertie thought for a moment and said, "When I stop to think of it, I guess she opened it the rest of the way, but I was so startled at what I saw that I didn't realize she had opened it the rest of the way until you asked me just now."

"Then she held the lid which contained the mirror for some appreciable interval at that angle of forty-five degrees so you were able to see the contents?"

"I guess she must have, Mr. Mason," Gertie conceded. "I didn't think this all out until— My heavens, you cross-examine a person so!"

"I don't want to cross-examine you," Mason said, "but I do want to find out what happened. You must admit that if she opened the lid of that bag and then held the mirror at an angle so that you could see the contents, she must have been rather anxious for you to see what was in the bag rather than trying to conceal it from you."

"I never thought of that," Gertie admitted.

"I'm thinking of it," Mason said thoughtfully.

After a second or two, he went on. "How did you know they were hundred-dollar bills, Gertie? You couldn't see the denomination at that distance."

"Well, they . . . they looked like hundred-dollar bills, all flat and—"

"But they could have been fifty-dollar bills?" Mason asked as Gertie hesitated. "Or perhaps twenty-dollar bills?"

"Well, I distinctly had the impression they were hundred-dollar bills, Mr. Mason."

"And, by the same sign," Mason said, "looking at those bills in a mirror across the length of the office, they could have been one-dollar bills?"

"Oh, I *certain* they weren't one-dollar bills."

"What makes you so certain?"

"Just the way they looked."

"Thanks a lot, Gertie," Mason said. "I'm glad you tipped us off on this. You did quite right."

Gertie's face lit up. "Oh, I thought I had botched it up, the way you were asking those questions."

"I'm just trying to get it straight," Mason said. "Forget all about it, Gertie."

"Forget about something like that!" Gertie exclaimed. "Mr. Mason, that woman is . . . well, she's going to lead you into *something*. She just isn't any ordinary client."

"That's quite right," Mason said. "She isn't an ordinary client, which is perhaps why the case intrigues me."

The lawyer patted Gertie on the shoulder. "You're a good girl, Gertie," he said. "You just keep an eye on these clients that come in, and if you see anything unusual always let me know."

Mason nodded to Della Street and they went through the door into the library.

"What do you think, Chief?" Della asked.

"I think Gertie saw the contents of that bag, all right, and I think it was packed full of currency. But whether it was filled with hundred-dollar bills or whether it was filled with one-dollar bills is anybody's guess. I don't think Gertie could have seen the hundred-dollar denomination at that distance while looking in the mirror."

"Gertie has a wonderful imagination," Della said.

Mason nodded thoughtfully. "But," he said, "the important thing is how long that mirror was held at a forty-five degree angle; whether our mysterious client *wanted* Gertie to see what was in the black bag and report it to us, or whether she was taking something out and Gertie's quick eye managed to get a glimpse of the contents. . . . You have to hand it to Gertie for that; she can see more in a tenth of a second than most people can see after staring for five minutes."

Della laughed. "And then her mind has a computer system all of its own by which she multiplies what she has seen by two."

"Squares it," Mason said, laughing. "Well, let's go back and see our client."

Mason and Della returned to the lawyer's private office.

"I'm sorry we kept you waiting," Mason said. "Now, let's see, where were we? You wanted to have a lawyer who would represent you in case you needed an attorney?"

"That's right."

"But you didn't want anyone to know your identity."

"I have my reasons, Mr. Mason."

"I presume you have," Mason agreed, "but that makes it rather unsatisfactory as far as I'm concerned. Suppose you want to communicate with me so I can do something for you. How am I to know that I'm talking with the same person who retained me?"

"We'll agree on a code," she said.

"All right," Mason said, "what do you suggest?"

"My measurements."

"Yes?" Mason asked.

"Thirty-six, twenty-four, thirty-six," she said.

A smile flitted across the lawyer's face, then he was serious once more. "That's not much of a code," he said.

"But if I gave you the measurements in my own voice over the telephone—you'd recognize my voice, wouldn't you?"

"I'm not certain," Mason said. "I might. Sometimes voices are rather hard to place over the telephone. What would you want me to do? That is, what do you think you'd like to have me do if I should decide to represent you and you should call me over the phone?"

"Defend me," she said.

"For what?"

"Heavens, I don't know," she said, "but the people who are trying to find me are very, very ingenious. They wouldn't go to the expense of hiring private detectives when they could accuse me of having committed some crime and put the police on my trail. *That's* what I'm afraid of.

"You see, Mr. Mason," she went on hurriedly, "I'm not at liberty to tell you all of the facts, but there are certain people—that is, a certain person who wants to find me or who might want to find me. That person is devilishly ingenious. He would stop at nothing."

"It's not easy to find a person who deliberately disappears," Mason said.

"I know," she said, "and this other party knows that, too. He isn't going to waste his time and money hiring private detectives at fifty dollars a day. He'll accuse me of some crime and get the police to find me."

"And then?" Mason asked.

"Then," she said, "I'd have to defend myself."

"You mean he'd actually try to press these trumped-up charges?"

"He might. He might try *anything*."

"He would be putting himself in a very vulnerable position," Mason said. "That is, unless you *have* committed some crime."

"But I haven't."

"What do you think he would accuse you of?"

"Heavens, I don't know. Murder perhaps. He's absolutely ruth-less."

Mason eyed her steadily. "Or perhaps embezzlement?" he asked. A sudden flush of color flooded her face.

"Well?" Mason asked.

"He might even do that," she said, "but I hadn't thought of that."

"That would seem to be a logical thing to do," Mason commented, making his voice elaborately casual. "If he accused you of murder he would have to have a corpse. Whereas, if he accused you of em-bezzlement he would only have to swear that a large sum of money was missing."

"Yes," she said, and then added slowly, "I see your point."

"And just what did you have in mind?" Mason asked.

"I wanted to give you a retainer and have it so that you'd be will-ing to act as my attorney, to come to my rescue in case I should telephone. . . . No matter what it was I wanted."

"How much of a retainer did you have in mind?" Mason asked.

"Would three hundred dollars do?"

"I would say that that would be a reasonable retainer," Mason said. "Of course, after you consulted me and in case the situation became complicated, I'd have to ask for more money."

She opened her hand purse, held it carefully so that Mason could not see the contents, and took out six fifty-dollar bills.

"Do I give them to you or give them to your bookkeeper?" she asked.

"My secretary will make a receipt," Mason said. ". . . Those fifty-dollar bills look uniformly crisp."

Her laugh was nervous. "Well, I prepared myself. I don't ordi-narily carry large sums of money like this. I got these for you—at my bank."

"Here in the city?" Mason asked quite casually with a quick glance at Della Street.

"No, no, not here in the city. Heavens, no."

"I see," Mason said, picking up the fifty-dollar bills and fingering them casually.

"Just what did you expect me to do for you?" he asked.

"Probably nothing. Don't misunderstand me, Mr. Mason. You are just an anchor to windward. If all goes well you'll never hear from me again. I'll walk out of this office and out of your life."

"And if all doesn't go well?" Mason asked.

"Then you'll hear from me."

"And what will I hear?"

"I don't know. I'll be calling on you for help."

"What sort of help?"

"I don't know, perhaps advice in a tight situation."

"I can't establish a relationship with a client on that kind of a basis," Mason said.

"You mean financially?"

"In part."

"At the time I call on you for help we'll discuss additional fees. I know that you'll be fair with me and I certainly won't ask you to do anything which is unfair, inequitable or unjust."

"Or illegal?" Mason asked, with a twinkle in his eye.

She started to say "or illegal" but suddenly caught herself, hesitated a moment, then said, "You wouldn't do anything that was illegal, so why waste time talking about it?"

"Then you'll get in touch with me if you need me?"

Very definitely."

Mason said, "You can reach me at this office during office hours. During the evening you can reach me through the Drake Detective Agency, which has an office on the same floor here in this building."

"I saw the sign on the door as I walked down from the elevator," she said.

"They have a twenty-four-hour switchboard," Mason said, "and in the event of any emergency—that is, if it's a *real* emergency—they can usually get in touch with me."

Della Street handed her a card. "Here are the numbers," she said, "day and night."

"Thank you, Miss Street."

Mason said to Della, "Make out a receipt, Della, for a three-hundred-dollar retainer in the form of cash. Now, do you want this made simply to the Code Number thirty-six, twenty-four, thirty-six?"

She shook her head. "I don't want any receipt." She slipped the loop of her purse over her wrist, picked up the black cosmetics bag, smiled at Della Street, said, "Thank you for seeing me, Mr. Mason," and walked out.

Mason sat watching the automatic doorstop as it closed the door.

When the latch had clicked, Mason said to Della, "You know she put on a good act."

"In what way?"

"That we'd never see her again."

"You think it was an act?"

"I'll give you ten to one," Mason said, "that within a matter of five days that girl calls us up and is in serious difficulties—difficulties which she has already anticipated."

"No takers," Della said. "It's bad luck to take the other side of a bet with you. I'll tell you one thing, however, those weren't *her* measurements. She's nearer thirty-two, twenty-four, thirty-six."

Mason thought that over. "Padding?" he asked.

"Not that much," Della said. "She's using quite a bit, but not that much."

"Now that you mention it, Della," Mason said, "I see what you mean. So we have a client who is lying to us right at the start."

"Sailing under *false* colors," Della Street said, smiling.

Mason said meditatively, " 'The Case of the Falsified Tape.' "

"Let's hope it doesn't turn out to be 'The Case of the Costly Client,' " Della said. "I'm suspicious of padded stories, padded expense accounts, and padded clients."

"She sneaked up on my blind side," Mason said. "I should have given her more of a third degree and broken down her story. However, it's too late now. We'll ride along with her false measurements."

Chapter Two

At ten minutes after nine Mason entered his private office through the hall door, smiled a greeting at Della Street, said, "Anybody in the outer office, Della?"

She shook her head and then said, "Gertie."

"Well, Gertie is supposed to be there."

"Gertie's there, hitting on all six," Della said. "Gertie is so excited she is running around in circles."

"What's excited Gertie?"

"Your mysterious client of yesterday."

Mason's eyebrows rose in surprise. "We've heard from her again?"

"Gertie has."

"What do you mean?"

Della motioned to Mason's desk. On top of the mail was a folded newspaper, opened at the section of CLASSIFIED ADS and folded so that that the so-called "Personals" were on top.

Mason walked over to the desk, seated himself in the cushioned swivel chair, picked up the paper, let his eyes glance down the section of personal columns, and noticed the ad which had been marked in the margin:

AM HERE READY TO CONCLUDE NEGOTIATIONS
ON STRAIGHT CASH BASIS. NO CHECKS.
SPOT CASH. CONTACT ME AT WILLATSON
HOTEL. 36-24-36.

"Well, I'll be darned," Mason said. "Do you suppose that's our gal?"

"Sounds like it," Della said.

"Hang it," Mason said, "that's what comes of taking a case sight-unseen. Now, that gal is mixed up in some adventure which is going to get her into trouble just as sure as shooting. And when she gets into trouble she's going to look to us to get her out."

Mason hesitated a moment, then jerked his thumb toward the telephone. "Paul Drake, Della."

Della dialed Paul Drake's unlisted number and, in a moment, said, "Just a minute, Paul, Perry wants to talk with you."

She handed the phone over to Mason.

"Hi, Paul," Mason said, "are you too busy to come down to the office for a minute?"

"Never too busy but what the scent of new business causes me to come running!"

"Come running, then," Mason said, and hung up.

Della Street said, "Is it ethical for you to tell Paul . . . ?"

"It isn't ethical for me to tell him anything," Mason said, "not at this stage of the game—at least the way I interpret ethics. But I'm going to find out something about who this gal is seeing and what it's all about."

"Any idea?" Della asked.

Mason said, "I think she came down from San Francisco."

"Why?"

"The way she's dressed for one thing," Mason said, "plus the time of day she came in. She took a plane down, checked her baggage somewhere, probably at the Willatson Hotel, took a cab, came up here. . . . And she had probably arranged to put that ad in the paper before she ever came down here. As I remember it, it takes a day or or two to get an ad of that sort published. . . . If that's correct, she telephoned the Willatson Hotel for a reservation."

"And so?" Della asked.

"And so," Mason said, "we're going to find out a little bit about our mysterious client, a little bit more than the three measurements."

Paul Drake's code knock sounded on the corridor door of the private office. Della opened the door. "Hi, Paul," she said. "How's the digestive system?"

"Better, thanks, Beautiful. You folks haven't had me sitting up all night on cases where I've had to eat soggy hamburgers at an office desk. I've dined out on good, freshly cooked meat now for six days in succession."

"Business that bad?" Mason asked.

"Lousy," Drake said.

"Maybe we can help," Mason told him. "But this isn't a big case, it's just a routine job."

"Who's the client?" Drake asked.

"I am," Mason said.

"Oh, oh."

"He wants to find out about a client," Della said.

Drake settled himself in the overstuffed leather chair, threw his legs over the rounded arm, took out a notebook and a fountain pen, and said, "Shoot."

Mason said, "I think I let a client down, Paul."

"How come?"

Mason hesitated, spoke cautiously. "I can't tell you the details without violating the code of ethics, Paul. An attorney is supposed to protect the confidences of his client. Any statements that are made are completely confidential.

"Now then, with that in mind I want you to know that I am afraid I gave a client advice which fell short of the advice I should have given."

"Male or female?" Drake asked.

"That also is confidential," Mason said.

"Well, how did you fail this client?"

"I didn't tell the client the things the client should have known for the client's own good," Mason said. "I let the client diagnose the case and accepted that diagnosis."

"How come?"

Mason said, "Every once in a while a client wants to diagnose the case, just as a patient will come to a doctor and say, 'Doctor, I have indigestion. I want you to give me something for indigestion.'

"If the doctor simply gives the patient something for indigestion he is untrue to his profession.

"What the doctor should do is ask about symptoms connected with the indigestion. He finds out that the patient has been having pains in the chest and occasionally down the left arm, so he suspects something entirely different from indigestion. He has a cardiograph made and finds out that the patient is suffering from a high cholesterol count. He doesn't give the patient medicine for indigestion, but puts the patient on a diet consisting of no fats, no dairy foods, but high in proteins.

"The patient gets better.

"If, on the other hand, the doctor had accepted the patient's self-diagnosis, the patient would probably have been dead inside of twelve months."

"That," Drake said, "is rather elementary, isn't it, Perry?"

"I'm making it elementary," Mason explained, "because I want to show you the situation.

"This client came here and diagnosed the case and prescribed the remedy. Unfortunately, I accepted the statements at face value. I shouldn't have done that. Now then, in order to appease my own conscience, I want information."

"About the client?" Drake asked.

"About various and sundry things," Mason said. "They do not necessarily have any *direct* bearing on the situation. They may not even *directly* concern the client. But they are sufficiently significant so they concern me."

"All right," Drake said, "you've now reached your thumb by going all the way around your elbow. You want me to do a job. It's a job in which you are the client. You'll get the best service I can give and you'll get a discount on the bill. What do I do?"

Mason took the folded newspaper and handed it to Drake.

"That ad," he said.

Drake read the ad aloud:

"AM HERE READY TO CONCLUDE NEGOTIATIONS
ON STRAIGHT CASH BASIS. NO CHECKS.
SPOT CASH. CONTACT ME AT WILLATSON
HOTEL. 36-24-36."

Drake looked up from the newspaper. "That's the ad that interests you?"

Mason nodded.

"Your party evidently has three rooms," Drake said. . . . "No, wait a minute, thirty-six is mentioned twice. It may be two rooms, thirty-six and twenty-four, and then the person putting in the ad signs it thirty-six to show that that's the room where contact is to be made."

"Could be," Mason said.

Drake regarded him shrewdly. "And it could be some sort of a code," he said.

Mason was silent.

"Exactly what is it you want me to do?" the detective inquired.

"Find out everything you can about who put that ad in the paper and the person for whom the message was intended."

Drake said, "That may be a big job, or it may be rather simple. The Willatson Hotel is a commercial-type hotel. When there are conventions in town it's probably about ninety-five percent occupied. At other times the percentage of occupancy may be sixty to seventy percent. In any event there will be too many people just to go at it blind. I can find out who's in room thirty-six and who's in room twenty-four. That may not mean anything.

"The best bet is to try to get a line on whoever put the ad in the paper by making a dummy reply in the press, saying something like:

"MESSAGE NOT CLEAR. YOU CAN REACH ME TELEPHONE NUMBER 676-2211 TO CLARIFY. AM NOT WALKING INTO ANY TRAP REGARDLESS OF TYPE OF BAIT USED."

Drake made a little gesture and said, "Of course, that's just off the top of my head, Perry. I'd have to work it a little more carefully than that. I'd have to be subtle, but even so the chances are that there'd be some false note in the reply which would alarm the quarry and let your client know that some outsider was checking."

"Well," Mason said thoughtfully, "I don't know as there's any reason why a situation of that sort should be fatal. . . . It might send the client back to me and then I could . . ." His voice trailed away into silence.

"What's the matter?" Drake asked. "Can't you phone your client at the Willatson Hotel and—"

"I didn't say I thought the person who put this ad in was my client," Mason said. "The client may well be the one to whom the ad is addressed."

"In other words, you don't know where to reach your client?"

"Come, come," Mason said, "you haven't been reading your decisions of the Supreme Court lately. Before I can be questioned I have to be advised of my constitutional rights and given an opportunity to consult a lawyer. . . . I've given you a job to do. Get busy and do it."

Drake thought for a moment and said, "This situation has overtones which intrigue the hell out of me, Perry, but, after all, you said it, you've given me a job to do. It's up to me to get busy."

Drake heaved himself up out of the chair. "When do you want reports?" he asked.

"As soon as you have something definite to report. No matter how trivial it seems to you, give me a line on it."

"Day and night?" Drake asked.

"It's not exactly *that* urgent," Mason said. "Let's say day and evening."

"Okay," Drake said, "day and evening it is. Any limit as to the number of people I can put on it?"

"Don't go over five hundred dollars until you have asked me," Mason said.

"With your discount," Drake told him, "you can get quite a bit of investigative work done for five hundred bucks. . . . I'll be in touch, Perry."

Mason and Della Street watched the detective out the door. Then Mason heaved a sigh, picked up the pile of papers on his desk, and said, "Well, Della, we've done all *we* can do. I guess now we'll get to work."

"How are we going to enter this on the books?" Della asked. "You take in three hundred dollars, you pay out five hundred, and we don't even have a name for the client in the case."

"Call her Miss Deficit then," Mason said. "That will serve until we have a better name."

"Perhaps," Della mused, "it could be Miss Deceit."

"She hasn't deceived us," Mason said. "At least we don't know that she has. What we need is information. She has diagnosed her own case, prescribed her own remedy, and she may be wrong on both counts."

Della Street picked up her shorthand notebook and pencil. "Well," she observed, "we're only starting the day two hundred dollars worse off than when you sat down at the desk."

Chapter Three

The next day Perry Mason was in court all day defending a young Negro lad who had been accused of robbing a pawnshop.

The identification by three eyewitnesses who had seen the robber running madly down the street, jumping into a parked car, and making off at high speed was absolutely positive.

In vain Mason tried to shake the identification of the witnesses.

At three o'clock the Deputy District Attorney concluded his opening argument and Mason had an opportunity to address the jury.

"Contrary to popular belief, gentlemen, circumstantial evidence is about the strongest we have, and eyewitness evidence is about the weakest.

"Here is a tall, young Negro lad with a mustache, carrying a paper bag.

"The place in question was held up by a tall, young Negro lad, wearing a mustache, carrying a paper bag.

"It is the theory of the prosecution that the defendant made his escape, hid the money somewhere, put half a dozen packages of cigarettes in the paper bag, and then, when he was arrested, explained that he had been running short of cigarettes; that he went to a coin-vending machine in the neighborhood, bought the six packages of cigarettes, put them in a paper bag he had taken with him, and was returning to his modest apartment when he was apprehended by the police.

"I ask you, if he had disposed of the money so that he could conceal the evidence against him, why, in the name of reason, didn't he also dispose of the paper bag?

"A tall, young Negro with a mustache and carrying a paper bag was like a magnet to the police within a matter of minutes after the holdup when the alarm had been broadcast on an all-points bulletin.

"People get a fleeting glimpse of an individual. They remember the salient points. In this case, that he was a tall, young Negro with a paper bag and a mustache. That is all they really remember.

"Later on when they try to cudgel their recollection into producing additional facts at the insistence of the police officers, they hypnotize themselves into believing there are other things which they remember clearly. Later on they are given photographs to look at, the so-called mug shots of the police. They are asked to study these photographs carefully. They study them until they see the defendant in a line-up and promptly pick him out as the man they saw running down the street, carrying a paper bag.

"It is a case of self-hypnotism.

"It is incumbent upon the prosecution to prove its case beyond all reasonable doubt. I ask you to return a verdict of not guilty."

Mason returned to his seat.

The Deputy District Attorney in his closing argument resorted to sarcasm.

"The defendant robs the store. He puts the money in a paper bag. He is seen running down the street by three witnesses. He tries to fabricate the evidence after he has hidden the money by putting some packages of cigarettes in the paper bag so that it will look like an entirely innocent transaction.

"Three reputable eyewitnesses identify this man positively. Perry Mason, who is one of the shrewdest cross-examiners in the country, has resorted to every arrow in his legal quiver to weaken the testimony of these men. They remain unshaken.

"Don't be hypnotized by eloquence. Don't by swayed by spurious reasoning. Don't be conned out of your just convictions. Go out and find this man guilty."

It was after five o'clock by the time the judge had finished his instructions, and the jury retired immediately.

It was expected there would be a quick verdict, but the jury was taken out to dinner at six-thirty, returned at eight, and resumed deliberations. By nine o'clock the buzzer sounded and the jury announced they had agreed upon a verdict.

The courthouse grapevine promptly transmitted the news.

The jury had found the defendant guilty.

The judge took his place on the bench, the defendant was brought into court. All was in readiness for the jury to be received when a plain-clothes officer hurriedly pushed his way through the swinging doors of the courtroom, dashed down the central aisle, approached the bench, and said something in a whisper to the judge.

The judge frowned, leaned forward for a whispered colloquy. Then the Court said to the bailiff, "You will keep the jury waiting for a few minutes. I will ask counsel for both sides to join me in chambers."

When the judge had retired to chambers, he kept on his judicial robes, seated himself in the creaking swivel chair back of his desk, and said, "Gentlemen, there has been a surprising development in this case.

"The police have apprehended a man in the act of holding up a store. They found a cache of money containing one of the hundred-dollar bills taken from the store in the robbery which is being presently tried before this court.

"You gentlemen will remember that the proprietor had taken the numbers of those hundred-dollar bills. The culprit has confessed to the holdup. It appears that the defendant in this case is innocent."

"What!" the Deputy District Attorney exclaimed.

The judge nodded.

"But they've agreed on a verdict," the prosecutor blurted. "It's 'guilty.'"

"We can't let that verdict be received in court," the judge said, "and there is a legal point. Having agreed upon the verdict, I don't know offhand exactly what the legal status of the case is. I could, of course, call the jury into court, explain the circumstances to them, and instruct them to return a verdict of 'not guilty'. But it is my present idea that the best thing to do is to tell the jury that circumstances have occurred which necessitate their discharge before any verdict is formally received in court."

"Explaining the circumstances to them, of course," Mason said.

"Certainly not! " the Deputy District Attorney objected.

"Why not?" the judge asked.

"Because this would tend to weaken the whole fabric of identification evidence," the Deputy protested.

"Otherwise," Mason said, "the twelve people on that jury are going out and criticize the judge and the administration of justice. It's a lot better to have the people lose a little faith in too confident, too cocksure eyewitness identification than it is to lose confidence in the administration of justice."

"I think so, too," the judge said, pushing back his swivel chair and getting to his feet.

"Gentlemen, we will return to court. I will call the jury in, and before I ask them if they have agreed upon a verdict, I will make a brief statement to them advising them of recent developments and discharge the jury. At that time you, Mr. Deputy District Attorney, can ask for a motion dismissing the case. It will be granted."

The Deputy District Attorney accepted the judge's decision with poor grace. They returned to the courtroom, and the judge made a brief statement to the jurors as to what had happened.

Mason enjoyed watching their astounded expressions as they realized the significance of what the judge was saying.

Then the lawyer shook hands with the jurors. The jurors, after some hesitancy, shook hands with the defendant, and Mason said to his client, "Go home and shave that mustache off and never wear one again. Also never carry a paper bag."

The defendant laughed. "Tall Negro boy with a mustache. Tall Negro boy with a paper bag, yes, *sir*. I am going back home and shave off that mustache just as soon as I can get my hands on a razor, and I'm *never* going to carry anything in a paper bag again!"

Mason, tired after the long trial, nevertheless stopped in at his office on the way home.

Della Street had left a note for him:

8:45 P.M. COULDN'T WAIT ANY LONGER, BUT WANTED YOU TO SEE THE AD IN THE EVENING PAPER. IT'S ON YOUR DESK.

Mason picked up the folded paper, looked at the ad which had been circled.

The ad read:

36-24-36. WANT TO AVOID ANY TRAPS.
WILL BE AT HOTEL ENTRANCE IN TAXICAB
AT EXACTLY NINE O'CLOCK TONIGHT.
CONTACT ME THERE. NO WITNESSES,
PLEASE. U NO HOO.

Mason regarded the ad thoughtfully, then dialed the number of the Drake Detective Agency.

"Perry Mason talking," he said. "Is Paul Drake in?"

"No, he isn't. Mr. Drake's out working on a case. He said he didn't know when he'd be back."

"Anyone there know what job he's working on?" Mason asked.

"I'm afraid not," the secretary said. "Mr. Drake said it was extremely confidential."

"Thank you," Mason said. "I guess that's all we can do tonight."

The lawyer hung up the phone, closed the office, went to his apartment, and sank into deep sleep.

Chapter Four

Paul Drake was already at his office at nine o'clock the next morning when Perry Mason, leaving the elevator, detoured into the office of the Drake Detective Agency.

The girl at the switchboard smiled, nodded, pointed down the corridor toward Drake's private office, and returned to the telephone conversation she was holding at the switchboard.

Mason walked down a veritable rabbit warren of cubbyhole offices where Drake's operatives prepared reports on their various cases, and then entered Drake's personal office at the end of the passageway.

This also was a tiny office with a desk and a battery of telephones.

Drake looked up at Mason, grinned, yawned, said, "You and your mysterious client!"

"How come?" Mason asked.

Drake passed him over the newspaper containing the ad which Della Street had left on his desk the night before.

"Some of your work?" the lawyer asked.

"My work," Drake admitted.

"Do any good with it?"

"Yes and no."

"What happened?"

"Well, I had to take certain chances—that's one of the things you have to figure on in this game. I'm playing it blind. The other side has all the numbers.

"Now, either this party had already contacted the person she wanted, or she hadn't. I couldn't tell which."

"Wait a minute," Mason said. "You're using a female pronoun. Why?"

"Because she is a female."

"Go on."

"Well, as I said, either she had contacted the person or she hadn't. Then I had another horn of the dilemma. Either she knew the person by sight or she didn't. The fact that she put that ad in the paper indicated the probabilities were that she didn't know the party by sight.

"Of course, I had one other chance to take. Either the party was a man or a woman. I was in a position to hedge a little bit on that by taking one of my women operatives with me.

"I put that ad in the paper, stating that I would be parked in front of the hotel entrance in a taxicab at exactly nine o'clock."

Mason said, "I presume you had made other efforts to find her identity?"

Of course. I went to the office of the newspaper which had run her ad. A five-dollar bill got me the information that she was a young woman, good figure, blonde, blue eyes, a little bit diffident.

"I went to the Willatson Hotel and wasted five dollars. I couldn't get any lead there.

"So I decided to take a chance and put this ad in the paper. Then, with my female operative, I went to the hotel and sat in front in a taxicab."

"Why the taxicab?" Mason asked.

"So she couldn't trace the license number."

Mason nodded approvingly. "What happened?"

"Promptly at nine o'clock she walked past the car, but so did a lot of other people. However, I had it fixed so she couldn't get a real good look at either my female operative or myself. I was wearing a cap pulled down over my forehead and dark glasses. The operative was wearing a coat with a high collar and dark glasses. . . . It was all real cloak-and-dagger.

"With all those people walking past we couldn't spot her the first time, but when she turned at the end of the block and walked back we had her spotted. She did that three times, never giving us the faintest tumble; no signal, no recognition, no attempt to come up and engage us in conversation. She just walked past four times. And she was clever enough so she didn't indicate any particular curiosity. She kept her eyes straight ahead each time she passed the cab."

"And so?" Mason asked.

"So," Drake said, "we didn't press our luck. We had the cab drive away."

"You didn't try to shadow her?"

"Of course, we shadowed her. I had one operative in an automobile parked behind me, and when the girl walked past the cab the second time he spotted her the same way we did. When we moved on I gave him the signal to follow her.

"After our cab drove off she went back to the Willatson Hotel. She's registered as Miss Diana Deering of San Francisco. She's in room seven-sixty-seven."

"Good work, Paul," Mason said.

"Wait a minute," Drake told him, "I'm not finished. We put some more five-dollar bills to work with the bellboys and the phone operator. Her luggage is stamped D.D.

"Now, when a person assumes an alias they quite frequently use their own first name, and, of course, with initials on the baggage they want to get a name that tallies with the initials. So Diana Deering could well be Diana——, of San Francisco."

Mason raised his eyebrows.

"So," Drake went on, "we did a little leg work. We found that our subject telephoned a San Francisco hospital from time to time to inquire about a patient, one Edgar Douglas.

"Edgar is employed by the Escobar Import and Export Company of San Francisco. He was in an automobile accident a few days ago, has a fractured skull, and is still unconscious.

"So we took the initials of Diana D. and tried Douglas as the last name. We phoned the Escobar Company and asked about Edgar Douglas, were told about the automobile accident, and asked about Diana Douglas.

"We were told she was his sister, that she was also an employee of the company, was upset about the accident, and had been given a leave of absence for a few days so she could be near him.

"We got a description. It checks. We also found out there are no other members of the family."

"Arouse any suspicion?" Mason asked.

"Not a bit. We said we were a finance company checking on Edgar's employment and credit standing, made the questions as routine as possible and asked them in a somewhat bored tone of voice."

"Then what?" Mason asked.

"So then we did leg work in San Francisco," Drake went on. "The Escobar Company doesn't seem at all alarmed, but they're having a 'routine' audit of their books. We found that out more or less incidentally."

"What's the prognosis on the brother?" Mason asked.

"Probably going to be all right, but may be unconscious for as much as two weeks," Drake said. "The guy was all set to take a business trip somewhere—that is, suitcase all packed; drove to a service station to get the car filled up; was clobbered by a car which drove through a red light and knocked him unconscious."

"Any question that it was his fault?" Mason asked.

"None whatever. Not only did the car that struck him come through a red light with several witnesses willing to testify to that effect, but the driver was pretty well potted. The police took him to jail to sober up and he's facing a citation for drunk driving."

Mason was thoughtful for several seconds. "Why should all this cause Diana to leave her brother, critically ill, come to Los Angeles, and start putting ads in the paper?"

Drake shrugged his shoulders and said, "If you want us to keep on we'll find out. Probably it's some form of blackmail which involves the family in some way."

"You say there are no other members of the family?" Mason asked.

"That's all. The parents are dead. Diana and her brother, Edgar, are the only survivors at the present time. Diana has never been married. Edgar is a bachelor, but the rumor is he's going to announce an engagement to a wealthy heiress—although that's just rumor."

"How old?" Mason asked.

"Diana?"

"No, Edgar."

"A little over twenty-one."

"Younger than Diana," Mason said thoughtfully.

"A couple of years."

"She could try to mother him a little," Mason said.

"It has been done," Drake conceded. . . . "How about you giving a helping hand?"

"To whom?"

"To me, and, incidentally, to yourself," Drake said. "If you can tell me about Diana's case and why you're interested I may be able to help both of you. At least I can save you a little money."

Mason shook his head. "I can't, Paul. I'm bound by professional ethics."

"Do you want me to keep on the job?" Drake asked.

"For a while," Mason said.

"Want me to put a tail on her?"

Mason said, "I'd like to know where she goes and who she sees, but that's a pretty ticklish job because I don't want her to feel that she's being shadowed. If that happened it might alarm her and cause her to take steps which would be against her own best interests."

Drake said, "Then you'd better let me make a very casual shadow job of it, because on a tight shadow job the subject is quite frequently aware of the tail. It's a pretty difficult job to put on a real shadow and guarantee that the subject is completely unaware of it."

"Then make it a loose shadow job," Mason said.

"Of course," Drake went on, "where money is no object, we can use enough operatives to—"

"We haven't an unlimited expense account here, Paul, and I don't know that it's absolutely imperative that we know where this young woman goes and what she does, but I would like to keep in touch with her and I would dislike very, very much to have her become alarmed and take a powder."

"Okay," Drake said, "I'll see what can be done. We'll make a loose tail job of it. When do you want a report?"

"Whenever you have anything worthwhile," Mason said, put his hand briefly on Paul Drake's shoulder, and walked down to his own office.

Chapter Five

The Willatson Hotel was a commercial hotel which operated on a basis of live-and-let-live. Very little attention was paid to people who came through the doors, crossed the lobby, and walked directly to the elevator.

Perry Mason, however, felt it better to follow the procedure of being a total stranger.

He went to the desk, caught the eye of the clerk, and said, "Do you have a Miss Diana Deering registered here?"

"Just a moment."

The clerk looked through a file and said, "Seven-sixty-seven."

"Will you announce me, please?"

The clerk seemed bored. "What name?"

"She won't know the name," Mason said. "It's in connection with a social-security inquiry. Tell her it has to do with thirty-six, dash, twenty-four, dash, thirty-six."

The clerk said, "Very well," picked up the phone, rang Room 767, and said, "A gentleman is here to see you in connection with an inquiry about a number. I believe it's a social-security number.

. . . What's that? . . . Very well, I'll tell him if that's your message."

He turned to Mason, said, "She is having no social-security problems. You'll have to give me a name or—"

Mason raised his voice and said, "You didn't give her the number: thirty-six, twenty-four, thirty-six."

The receiver suddenly made squawking sounds.

The clerk said, "It's quite all right. She wants to see you. She heard you give the number over the telephone. You may go on up."

The clerk hung up the telephone and returned to the task of bookkeeping with a manner of bored indifference.

Mason took the elevator to the seventh floor and knocked on the door of Room 767.

The young woman who had been in his office earlier in the week opened the door quickly, then fell back in amazement. "Good heavens!" she exclaimed. "You!"

"Why not?" Mason asked.

"How . . . how did you know where I was? . . . How did you know who I—"

Mason pushed his way into the room as she fell back, closed the door, walked over to a chair, and seated himself.

"Now, let's talk a little sense for a change," he said. "Your real name is Diana?"

"Yes."

"Diana what?"

"Diana Deering."

"Let's try doing better than that," Mason said.

"That's my name, Mr. Mason. You ask down at the desk if you don't believe it. That's—"

"That's the name you're registered under," Mason interrupted. "But that's not your name. How about Diana Douglas of San Francisco? Would that do any better?"

For a moment her eyes showed dismay, then her face flushed. "I retained you as *my* attorney," she said. "You're supposed to help me, not to go chasing around trying to uncover things about my past, trying to cooperate with . . ."

Her voice trailed into silence.

"With the police?" Mason asked.

"No, not with the police," she said. "Thank heavens, I haven't done anything that violates the law."

"Are you sure?"

"Of course I'm sure."

"Look here," Mason said, "I'm an attorney. People come to me when they're in trouble. I'm supposed to help them. You came to me and sneaked up on my blind side. I didn't do a very good job of helping you. I'm sorry about that. That's why I decided I'd better find you before it was too late."

"You're mistaken, Mr. Mason. I'm not in any trouble. I'm trying to—to protect a friend."

"You're in trouble," Mason said. "Does the Escobar Import and Export Company know where you are?"

"I don't know. . . . They know that I'm away on personal business."

Mason reached across her lap, picked up the black handbag.

"You leave that alone!" she screamed, grabbing his arm with both hands.

Mason kept his grip on the bag.

"Full of money?" he asked.

"That's none of your business. I want to fire you right now. I wanted an attorney to protect me. You're worse than the police. Let go of that bag. You're fired!"

"Where did you get the money that's in this bag?" Mason asked.

"That's none of your business!"

"Did you, perhaps, embezzle it from the company where you worked?" the lawyer asked.

"Good heavens, no!"

"You're sure?"

"Of course I'm sure!"

Mason shook his head. "Would it surprise you to know that the Escobar Import and Export Company called in an auditor to go over its books?"

Her face showed surprise, then consternation. Her grip on his arm weakened. "Why, why in the world—good heavens . . . they couldn't."

"That's the information I have," Mason said. "Now suppose you do a little talking and try telling the truth for a change. What's your capacity with the Escobar Import and Export Company? What do you do?"

"I'm a cashier and bookkeeper. I have charge of foreign exchange and foreign payments. I . . . Mr. Mason, there *must* be some mistake."

Mason said, "Let's look at basic facts. You come to my office. You have a bag that's loaded with money. You—"

"How did you know about what's in this bag?"

"My receptionist had a chance to see the inside of it," Mason said. "It was loaded with bills."

"Oh," she said, and then was silent.

Mason said, "You put an ad in the paper indicating that you were here to pay off a blackmail demand. So, let's put two and two together. You take an assumed name. You come to Los Angeles. You put an ad in the paper. You are dealing with a blackmailer. You have a large sum of money with you in the form of cash. The company where you work evidently feels some money is missing. It calls in an auditor."

Diana sat silent. From the open window came noises of traffic from the street.

"Well?" Mason asked, after a while.

"It's absolutely fantastic," she said, removing her hands from Mason's arm. "There's—there's nothing I can do."

"I'm trying to help you," Mason reminded her. "You've made it rather difficult for me so far. Perhaps if you tried telling me the truth I could put in my time helping you instead of running around in circles trying to cut your back trail. . . . Now, *did* you embezzle that money?"

"Heavens, no!"

"How much money do you have in this bag in the form of cash?"

"Five thousand dollars."

"Where did you get it?"

She was silent for a moment, then said, "I'm going to tell you the truth."

Mason settled back in his chair, said, "You're a little bit late with it and I don't know how much time we have, but go ahead."

She said, "The whole thing happened when my brother was injured in an automobile accident. After they took him to the hospital I went to his room to get some things for him—shaving things and things of that sort that I thought he'd need in the hospital, and I found his bags all packed and a letter addressed simply 'DEAR FUGITIVE.' The letter said that the writer was fed up with waiting around; that either he should receive five thousand dollars by Tuesday night or other action would be taken."

"How was the letter written?" Mason asked.

"In typing. It was all typed, even the signature."

"And the signature was 36-24-36?"

"That's right."

"And the postmark?"

"Los Angeles."

"So, what did you do?"

"Mr. Mason, my brother was unconscious in the hospital. I couldn't let him down. I arranged to put an ad in the paper, just as the letter said I was to do, and came down here."

"And the money?"

"My brother had the money in a briefcase in his apartment. He was all ready to go. Apparently, he was going to drive down. He had the briefcase with the money, a suitcase and an overnight bag."

"And where did he get the money?"

"Mr. Mason, I . . . I don't know."

"Your brother works in the same company you do?"

"Yes."

"Could he have embezzled the money from the company?"

"Mr. Mason, in the first place Edgar wouldn't ever do anything criminal. In the second place, he wouldn't have had access to the money. The cash is kept in a money safe in the vault. Only the top executives have the combination."

"But you have it?"

"Yes, it's my job to check the books on the cash—not every day, but twice a month I have to add up the withdrawal slips and see that everything balances."

"Tell me a little more about Edgar," Mason said.

"He's young. He's a year and a half younger than I am. He . . . our parents were killed five years ago. I've tried to help Edgar every way I could. He's a sensitive individual who—"

"You're both working for the Escobar Export and Import Company. Who got the job there first?"

"I did"

"What about the company?"

"It engages in exports and imports just as the name indicates."

"What kind of a company?"

"What do you mean?"

"A big company, a little company, a—"

"No it's pretty much of a one-man concern."

"Who's the big wheel?"

"Mr. Gage—Franklin T. Gage."

"How many employees?"

"Oh, perhaps ten or fifteen altogether. There are five working full time in the office and an auditor and tax man."

"Do I understand then there are others who work outside of the office?"

"Yes, there are scouts and buyers."

"But nevertheless they are employees?"

"In a sense, yes."

"How old a man is Franklin Gage?"

"Forty-something or other. Perhaps forty-five."

"He runs the company?"

"Yes. He's the big shot."

"Who's next in command?"

"Homer."

"Homer Gage?"

"Yes."

"His son?"

"His nephew."

Mason's eyes narrowed thoughtfully. "How long after you started work there did your brother, Edgar, start work?"

"About six months."

"And what was he doing during those six months?"

"He was doing nothing. He had been let out at the place where he was working. He became involved in a lot of office intrigue and— It's too long a story to tell you."

"Who supported him?"

"I did."

"So then after six months, you got a job for him there at the company where you work. . . . Who gave him the job, Franklin Gage or Homer?"

"Franklin."

Mason regarded her shrewdly. "You didn't talk to Homer about it?"

"I talked to Mr. Gage. Mr. Franklin Gage."

"At the office?"

"No, I worked late one night and he said that I'd missed my dinner on account of working and that the company was going to buy my dinner."

"So in the intimacy of that little dinner party you took occasion to tell him about your brother and asked him if Edgar could have a job?"

"Yes. Only you make it sound so very . . . so very calculating."

Mason brushed her remark aside with a wave of his hand. "How did Homer react to that?"

"I didn't ask Homer."

"That wasn't my question," Mason answered. "I wanted to know how Homer reacted to it."

"Well," she said, "I think that Homer felt that we really didn't need to take on Edgar at the time."

"And what are Edgar's duties? What does he do?"

"He's a liaison man."

"Now then," Mason went on, "Edgar had been out of work for six months and you had been supporting him?"

"I'd been helping out. He had unemployment insurance and—"

"So where," Mason interrupted, "did he get five thousand dollars in cash?"

"I—I just don't know."

"Not from you?"

"No."

"Do you have five thousand dollars?"

"I . . . yes, I do."

"More than that?"

"A very little more."

"Where is it?"

"In savings banks."

Mason took mental inventory of the situation, then said abruptly, "This Homer Gage, what's his attitude toward you?"

"Friendly."

"Very friendly?" Mason asked.

"I think he'd like to be."

"Married or single?"

"Married."

"Ever met his wife?"

"Not formally. She's been at the office a couple of times to get checks cashed or something like that. She's smart-looking . . . you know, very much on the ball. They say she's a witch."

"Her husband steps out?"

"I wouldn't know. I do know his married life isn't happy."

"You see him looking at the other girls in the office. Doubtless you've discussed him with the other girls. Does he keep them after hours?"

"I don't know. I think perhaps . . . well, I just don't know."

"Does he step out?"

"I told you I don't know."

"Does he step out?"

"All right, if you're going to be insistant about it, I think he does, but I wouldn't know."

"And Homer's had you stay after hours more than once?"

She hesitated, then said, in a low voice, "Yes." Then added quickly, "You see the business is very, very unconventional. It's a complicated deal of buying and selling in large lots, and quite frequently the deals are made on a spot-cash basis.

"This is particularly true in connection with Oriental goods. You see, we have to have a Certificate of Origin on goods which are taken out of Hong Kong, for instance, and . . . well, sometimes matters have to be handled with a great deal of diplomacy."

"So sometimes you work late?"

"Yes."

"And Homer has had you work late?"

"Yes."

"And taken you out to dinner?"

"Twice."

"And propositioned you?"

"What do you mean by that, Mr. Mason?"

"You know what I mean."

"If you mean has he ever come out cold turkey with a proposition, the answer is 'no,' but all men proposition you. They size you up.

They look you over. They make a remark occasionally with a double meaning. They tell a story that's a little broad. They are quick to follow up any opening. . . . Mr. Mason, I don't need to tell you how men are. They're always on the lookout in an aggressive way, and if they get an opening they follow up and just keep pushing."

"And Homer Gage has been like that?"

"He's been like that. He isn't going to come right out in the open and make any proposition and get rebuffed and perhaps have his uncle know what is happening and—"

"The uncle likes you?" Mason said.

"Yes, he does."

"Married or single?"

"He's a widower."

"And how about him? Does he have the aggressive, masculine mannerisms?"

"No, no, Mr. Mason. Mr. Franklin Gage is very much of a gentleman. He is courteous and considerate and—well, he's an older, more mature man and his attitude is . . .

"Fatherly?" Mason ventured, as she hesitated.

"Well, not exactly fatherly. More like an uncle or something of that sort."

"But he likes you?"

"I think so."

"Very much?"

"I think so. You see, I am pretty good at adjusting myself in a business way and I have tried to do a good job there at the export and import. And Mr. Gage, Mr. Franklin Gage, knows it.

"In a quiet way he's very nice to—to all of the girls who work in the office."

"How many others than you?"

"Three."

"Names?"

"Helen Albert, a stenographer; Joyce Baffin, a secretary-stenographer, but her duties are mostly of a secretarial nature—for Homer Gage; and Ellen Candler, who has charge of the mail and the files."

"Suppose a person wanted to embezzle money from the company?" Mason said. "Would it be easy?"

"Very easy—too easy for those who had the combination to the cash safe. The company keeps large sums of money on hand. Occasionally it's necessary to make deals on a completely cash basis with no voucher of any kind ."

"Bribery?" Mason asked.

"I don't think so."

"Smuggling?"

"I don't think it's anything like that."

"And how do you keep your books under those circumstances?" Mason asked.

"Well, there's a certain amount of juggling with the cash so that the books are regular, but sometimes there are transactions which— well, it would be a little difficult to trace them."

"So your brother could very easily have embezzled five thousand dollars to go to Los Angeles and pay off a blackmailer?"

"Mr. Mason, I tell you Edgar wouldn't do that, and even if he had wanted to he couldn't have done it. He doesn't have the combination to the cash safe."

"Who does have the combination?"

"Franklin Gage, Homer Gage, Stewart Garland, our income-tax man, and myself."

"You found five thousand dollars in cash in Edgar's apartment?"

"Yes. I've told you that two or three times. It's the truth."

"And you knew Edgar hadn't had an opportunity to save that much out of his salary since he'd started work?"

"Well, yes."

"Where did you think he got it?"

She said, "My brother is—well he has friends. He's very likeable, very magnetic, and I think he has friends who would help him out in a situation of that sort. . . .That's what I thought."

"All right," Mason said, "let's face it. You're in a jam. You've come to Los Angeles under an assumed name. You've got five thousand dollars in cash. You're mixed up with a blackmailer. Suppose the accounts at the Escobar Import and Export Company show a five thousand-dollar deficit?"

Her hand went to her throat.

"Now, you're getting the point," Mason told her. "There's only one thing for you to do. Get a plane back to San Francisco. Get into your office tomorrow morning.

"Now, do exactly as I say. If it turns out an auditor says there's a five-thousand-dollar shortage, just laugh and say, 'Oh, no, there isn't.' Tell the auditor that your brother was working on a company deal at the time of the accident; that you took out five thousand dollars to finance that deal; that Edgar asked you not to make an entry until he had had a chance to discuss the deal with Franklin Gage; that he thought it was going to be a good deal for the company but that you knew all about the five thousand dollars that he had and knew that it was company money.

"You go to a local bank this afternoon, deposit the five thousand, buy a cashier's check payable to you as trustee. As soon as your brother recovers consciousness, you'll see him before anyone else does. . . . Make certain of that. As a member of the family you'll have the right-of-way.

"Then you can use your own judgment."

"But Mr. Mason, this thing is coming to a head. It isn't going to wait. This blackmailer—or whatever it is—this letter that my brother had was most urgent, imperative, demanding."

"What did you do with that letter?"

"I burned it."

Mason said, "There was an ad in the paper for you to make contact with a cab passenger as—"

"Heavens, how did you know about that?" she asked.

"We make it a point to read the personal ads," Mason said. "Why didn't you contact the man in the taxicab?"

"Because I didn't like the looks of the thing. There were two passengers, a man and a woman. It was night, yet they both were wearing dark glasses. I thought it was a trap of some kind. I . . . well, I decided to pass it up. When I made contact I wanted it to be where there were no witnesses."

"I see," Mason said thoughtfully, then abruptly he walked over to the telephone, asked the switchboard operator for an outside line, and got Paul Drake's office.

"Paul," he said, "I want a female operative—blonde, twenty-two, twenty-three, or twenty-four, with a good figure—to come to the Willatson Hotel and go to Room Seven-sixty-seven.

"She can't carry anything with her except a handbag. She can make purchases and have them sent in from the department stores where she buys. She'll take the name of Diana Deering, which is the name of the present occupant of the room."

"I know," Drake said.

"She'll masquerade as Diana Deering. She'll make it a point to get acquainted with the bellboys, with the clerks as they come on duty. She can ask them questions. Inquire about a monthly rate on the room. Do anything which will attract attention to herself as Diana Deering. And quit tailing the real Diana."

Drake said, "It happens that I have a girl who fits the description in the office right now, Perry. She's Stella Grimes. She's worked on one of your cases before, although I don't know if you've seen her personally. The only thing is she's a little older."

"How much older?" Mason asked.

"Tut, tut," Drake said, "you're asking questions."

"You think she can get by?"

"I think she can get by," Drake said.

"Get her up here," Mason told him.

"But what about me?" Diana asked when Mason hung up.

"You're going to get that cashier's check payable to you as trustee and then go back to San Francisco."

"And what about my baggage?"

"You'll have to wait for that."

"How will I get it out of the hotel? Don't they check people when you leave with baggage?"

"Sure they do," Mason said, "but we'll fix that."

"How?"

"I'll rent a room here in the hotel. I'll try to get one on the same floor. We'll move your baggage into that room. Then I'll check out, carrying the baggage with me, go right to the desk, and pay the bill on that room. They'll have no way of knowing that one of the suitcases I'll have with me was taken from Room Seven-sixty-seven."

"And what about this girl who is going to masquerade as me?"

"She'll deal with the blackmailer."

"And if I've turned the money in for a cashier's check, what will we pay him—or her?"

"We won't," Mason said. "It's against the policy of the office to pay blackmailers."

"But what are you going to do? How can you avoid payment?"

"I don't know," Mason told her. "We'll play it by ear. I wish to hell your brother would regain consciousness so we could find out what it's all about. . . . Get your suitcase packed."

Tears came to her eyes. "Edgar's a wonderful boy, Mr. Mason."

Mason said, "I'm going down to a baggage store and get a suitcase. I'll stuff it full of old paper, come back, and check into the hotel—somewhere on the seventh floor, if possible. I want you to wait right here. Promise me you won't go out until I get back."

"I promise."

"And don't answer the phone," Mason warned.

"I . . . all right, if you say so."

"I say so," Mason told her.

The lawyer walked to the door, turned, smiled, and said, "You'll be all right, Diana."

Her eyes started to blink rapidly. "You're wonderful," she said. "I wish I'd told you all about it when I first came to your office."

"You can say that again," Mason told her, "We might have headed off that damned auditor. As it is now, you're hooked."

"What do you mean?"

"Figure it out," Mason said. "We're starting a little late. You've come to Los Angeles, registered in a hotel under an assumed name. You have a bag containing five thousand dollars in currency. And if the company where you work *should* happen to be short five thousand dollars, and if your brother *should* happen to die, and if you're arrested before you get that cashier's check—figure where you'll be."

Mason walked out as her mouth slowly opened. He closed the door gently behind him.

Chapter Six

The lawyer took the elevator to the lobby, went to a baggage store two doors down the street, selected a suitcase, paid for it; then he crossed to a secondhand bookstore.

"I'm looking for some books dealing with the history of early California and, particularly, with the discovery of gold," he said.

The clerk led him to a shelf.

"Do you," Mason asked, "have paperback books?"

"Oh, yes, we have quite a selection."

"I also want to get some of those books for lighter reading," Mason said. "I'll pick out some."

Ten minutes later Mason presented himself at the checking-out desk with an armful of books.

The cashier scanned the penciled prices marked on the title pages, gave Mason the total figure, $27.85.

"All right," Mason said, "I'll . . . why not put them in this suit-case?"

The clerk, his attention drawn to the suitcase, leaned forward to pick it up and make sure it was empty, then smiled and said, "That's quite all right. Put them in there if you want."

Mason put the books in the suitcase, paid the bill, walked back to the Hotel Willatson, said, "I'm going to be here probably overnight. I'd like to have a room somewhere above the fifth floor. I don't like traffic noises."

"I can let you have eleven-eighty-four," the room clerk said, "if you're only going to be here one night, Mister . . . uh . . . ."

"Mason," Perry Mason said. "I prefer to be a little lower than the eleventh floor. What have you got on the eighth?"

"We're all taken up."

"The seventh?"

"I have one room on the seventh floor—seven-eighty-nine. It's a slightly larger room than our average and a little more expensive. . . ."

"That's all right, " Mason said, "I'll take it. I'm likely to be here only one night."

The lawyer registered, gave a bellboy a dollar to take his bag and escort him up to the room, waited until the bellboy had withdrawn; then put the room key in his pocket and walked down the hall to 767.

He tapped gently on the panels.

Diana Douglas opened the door.

"Mr. Mason," she said, "I've been thinking over what you said. It's—I'm afraid I'm in a terrible position."

"It'll be all right," Mason told her, "I'll take charge."

"You're going to—to need more than the money I gave you."

"Unfortunately," Mason said, "I spent a large amount of the money you gave me trying to check up on you and get back of the falsehoods you had told me. As it is now . . ."

The lawyer broke off as a knuckle tapped gently on the door.

Diana Douglas raised inquiring eyebrows.

Mason strode across the room, opened the door to confront an alert-looking young woman with blonde hair, blue eyes, and that something in her bearing which radiated competency and ability to look after herself under any circumstances.

The woman smiled at him and said, "I recognize you, Mr. Mason, but you probably don't know me. I'm from—well, I'm Stella Grimes."

"Come in, Stella," Mason said.

The lawyer closed the door and said, "Stella, this is Diana Douglas.

She's registered here as Diana Deering. You're going to take over."

"Who am I?" Stella asked. "Diana Douglas or Diana Deering? . . .
And how do you do, Diana. I'm pleased to meet you."

"As far as the hotel is concerned you're Diana Deering," Mason
said. "I'll let you read an ad which appeared in the paper."

Mason handed her a copy of the ad which Diana had inserted in
the paper and which was signed "36-24-36."

"I see, Mr. Mason," Stella said, reading the ad carefully. Then she
looked at Diana, looked at Perry Mason, and said, "Precisely what
do I do?"

"You identify yourself here as Diana Deering," Mason said. "You
sit tight and await developments and you report."

"Report on what?"

"On everything."

"Can you give me any line on what is supposed to happen?" she
asked. "I take it that I'm supposed to be here to make a cash payment.
Suppose someone turns up and wants that cash?"

"Then you stall," Mason said.

She nodded, took a card from her purse, scribbled something on it,
and said, "You'll probably want one of my cards, Mr. Mason."

The lawyer took the card she had given him. On the back was
scribbled, *"I've seen her before. I was the operative in the taxicab
with Paul Drake last night."*

Mason slipped the card in his pocket. "Exactly," he said, "I'll call
you by name if I have to, but in the meantime I want you to impress
upon the clerk that if someone calls and asks for you by the code
numbers of thirty-six, twenty-four, thirty-six that the call is to be
put through. You think you can make up a good story?"

"I can try," she said.

"What do you have in the way of baggage?" Mason asked.

"Just this purse that I brought in with me. I was instructed not to
attract attention by coming in with any more than this."

"You can buy what you need at the department stores and have it
sent in," Mason said.

"Any idea how long I'll be here?"

"It may be only a day. It may be three or four days. Just sit down
and make yourself at home. I'll be right back."

"I'll take your suitcase down to Room Seven-eighty-nine, Diana," he said. "Later on I'll check out with it and give it to you in San Francisco. In the meantime, you take this key, go on down to seven-eighty-nine, and wait. Take that black bag and your purse with you. I'll be seeing you in seven-eighty-nine in a few minutes. You use that room until you're ready to get the cashier's check and leave for the airport. Don't come back to this room under any circumstances and don't try to leave Room Seven-eighty-nine until I give you the all-clear sign."

"Any idea when that will be?" she asked.

"When I think the coast is clear."

"Suppose the banks close before you say it's okay for me to leave?"

"Then you'll have to keep the money with you until you get to San Francisco. Get the cashier's check there, but don't enter the office tomorrow until you have that check. When the office opens tomorrow I'll be on hand to help. We'll fix up the details before we leave Room Seven-eighty-nine. In the meantime, I want you out of here."

She nodded, said, "I want to get a couple of things from the bathroom."

Stella Grimes said to Mason, "You'd better brief *me* a little more. What happens if someone calls on me by this number, wants me to meet him with a sum of cash?"

"Stall it along and notify Paul," Mason told her.

"And if there isn't time for that?"

"Make time."

"Am I to have any idea what it's all about?" she asked.

"Nothing that I can tell you," Mason said.

"Am I the party that's being blackmailed?"

"No," Mason said, "you're a girl friend, an angel who's going to put up the money, but before you put up the money you want to be absolutely certain that you're getting what you're paying for. You're a fairly wealthy young woman, but you're rough, you're tough, you're hard-boiled. You know your way around. . . . Got a gun?"

By way of answer she reached down the V of her blouse and suddenly produced a wicked-looking, snub-nosed revolver.

"I'm wearing my working bra," she said as Diana emerged from the bathroom, her hands filled with toilet articles.

"Good enough," Mason told her. "I hope you don't have to reach for it, but I'm glad you've got it. We don't know with whom we're dealing."

"Have there been—other payments?" she asked.

"That we don't know," Mason said. "The present demand is for five grand. The probabilities are there's been one earlier payment and this is—you know, the old story, the guy hates to be a blackmailer. He wants to begin life all over again. He had intended to collect a thousand or so every few months, but he just can't live with himself on that kind of a deal. If he can get five grand he's going to buy a little farm way out in the sticks and forget all about his past and turn over a new leaf.

"In that case he'll tell the sucker he'll be done with payments forevermore, and all that sort of talk. . . . You know the line."

"I know the line," she said, smiling. "I've heard it."

Mason took Diana's suitcase and said, "We're taking this down to seven-eighty-nine, Diana. You take that black bag. Be sure to follow instructions."

"And I'll see you in San Francisco?"

"That's right. I'll get in touch with you. Put your phone number and address here in my notebook. But stay in seven-eighty-nine until I give you an all-clear."

The lawyer handed her his open notebook. Diana took it and carefully made the notations Mason asked, picked up the black bag, gave Stella her hand, said, "Thanks, sister. Be careful, and keep wearing that bra."

She turned to Perry Mason and said, "You're all right. You're good. . . . Let me carry my suitcase. I'll wait. I have the key to seven-eighty-nine." Impulsively she kissed him on the cheek, picked up the suitcase, the black bag and purse, crossed swiftly to the door, opened it, and was gone.

Mason settled himself in a chair, motioned for Stella to be seated, said, "I'm playing this pretty much in the dark myself, Stella. The blackmailer will be expecting the pay-off will be made by a man. You'll have to act the part of the financial angel, probably related to the sucker. However, you're skeptical, hard-boiled, and—"

The lawer broke off as knuckles tapped on the door.

"This may be it," he said. "Gosh, I hope Diana got down to seven-eighty-nine and out of sight."

The knuckles sounded again.

The lawyer went to the door, opened it, and said, "Yes, what is it?"

The man who stood on the threshold was a small man in his early thirties. He had black hair which was very sleek and glossy, parted in the middle and curled back from his forehead at the temples. He was wearing dark glasses and well-pressed brown slacks with a darker brown sport coat. His shirt was tan, and an expensive bolo tie furnished ornamentation.

"How do you do?" he said. "I called in response to an ad in the paper. I . . ." He broke off as he caught sight of Stella Grimes.

"That's all right," Mason said. "Come in."

The man hesitated, then extended a well-manicured hand, the nails highly polished, the skin soft and elaborately cared for.

"Cassel," he said, smiling, "C - A - S - S - E - L. I had hardly expected you would come down in person, Mr.—"

Mason held up his left hand as he shook Cassel's right hand.

"No names, please."

"All right, no names," Cassel said.

He regarded Stella Grimes appraisingly, as a cattle buyer might size up a prime heifer. There was a puzzled frown on his forehead which speedily gave way to an oily smile.

"We'll dispense with introductions," Mason said abruptly.

Cassel said, "As you wish. However, we don't put on our best performances in front of an audience, you know." He made a deprecatory gesture. "I confess *I* get stage fright," he said. "I may not be able to recall my lines at all."

Stella said, "Perhaps you two would like to have me go in the bathroom and close the door."

"No, no, no," Cassel said. "Nowhere in the room, please. I am *very* self-conscious."

Mason laughed. "Mr. Cassel and I have some very private business to discuss, Stella. I'm sorry that you and I didn't have more of an opportunity to talk, but it follows that we'll get together sometime later. I dislike these interruptions as much as you do, but that's the way things go. . . . Mr. Cassel and I are going to have a business talk, and *following* that I'll be in and out for a while, but I'll give you a ring whenever I'm at liberty. However, don't wait for my call. Just *follow* your own inclinations."

Stella Grimes regarded Mason thoughtfully for a few seconds, then said, "I think I've got it," to Mason, and, turning to Cassel said, "Good-by, Mr. Cassel."

She walked casually over to Perry Mason, put her lips up to be kissed as in a pleasant but often-repeated salutation of affection, then left the room.

"Nice babe," Cassel said, eying Mason.

Mason shrugged. "I like her."

"Known her long?"

Mason smiled. "Not long enough."

"You're not handing me *that* line," Cassel said.

"I'm handing you nothing."

"You can say that again."

There was a brief period of silence.

"Okay," Cassel said, "let's quit stalling around and get down to business. You brought it with you?"

"Brought what?" Mason asked.

"Now, let's not get cagey about this," Cassel said irritably. "I don't think that you'd be guilty of a breach of faith by trying to blow the whistle but . . . to hell with this stuff, let's take a look."

Cassel strode to the bathroom, jerked the door open, looked around inside, surveyed the walls of the room, moved a couple of pictures looking for a concealed microphone.

"Don't be simple," Mason said when he had finished.

Cassel's eyes were suspicious. "I don't like the way you're going about this," he said.

"What's wrong with the way I'm going about it?"

"You want me to make statements," Cassel said. "I'm not making statements. I'm here. You're here. It's your move."

Mason said. "I'm the one that should be suspicious. What took you so long to show up?"

"I had other matters which took me out of town for a while," Cassel said. "I called as soon as I came back and got free. . . . By the way, there was an ad in one of the evening papers. Do you know anything about that?"

Mason said, "I know enough about it to know that I wasted a lot of time giving the occupants of a taxicab an opportunity to give me the double take."

"And you received no signal?"

"No."

Cassel shook his head. "I don't like that. I don't like that at all. It means some third party is trying to chisel in on the deal."

"*You* don't like it," Mason said. "How do you suppose I feel about it? What the hell are you trying to do?"

Cassel thought for a moment, glanced at Mason, looked away, looked back at Mason again, frowned, said, "There's something familiar about your face. Have I ever met you before?"

"I don't think so."

"Well, every once in a while you—Wait a minute, wait a minute . . . I've seen your picture somewhere!"

"That's not at all impossible," Mason conceded.

"Hell's bells," Cassel said, "I've got it. Why dammit, you're a lawyer. Your name is Mason."

Mason didn't let his face change expression by so much as the flicker of an eyelash.

"That's right," he said, "Perry Mason."

"What are you trying to pull?" Cassel asked. "That wasn't part of the deal. I don't want to have any business dealings with any damn lawyer."

Mason smiled affably. "I'm not any damn lawyer," he said. "I'm a particularly special, high-priced lawyer."

"I'll say you are," Cassel said, edging toward the door. "What the hell's the matter with you, Mason? Are you crazy? You act as though you've got the room bugged. You know as well as I do that if you're trying to blow any whistles you're cutting your client's throat. You're acting just as if this was kind of a shakedown."

Mason said nothing.

"You know the proposition," Cassel said. "It's a business proposition. Your client doesn't have any choice in the matter but, under the circumstances, he can't have any protection. Any agreement that's made isn't worth the powder and shot to blow it up."

Mason said, "That doesn't prevent me from representing my client."

Cassel sneered. "It means that we've had our sights too low," he said. "If your client has got money enough to pay a high-priced lawyer a fat fee in a deal of this kind we've been too naïve. I don't blame you, I blame us. We aren't asking enough."

"Keep talking," Mason said. "I'm listening."

Cassel, annoyed now, said, "This isn't a payoff. This is something your client owes. . . . I'm not going to argue with you, Mason, have you got it or haven't you?"

"If you're referring to the money," Mason said, "I don't have it, and if I did have it I wouldn't pay it over on the strength of any proposition you've made so far."

"What's wrong with my proposition?" Cassel asked.

"You said it yourself. Any agreement is worthless. You could come back tomorrow and begin all over again."

"I wouldn't be foolish enough to do that," Cassel said.

"Why not?"

"Well, it wouldn't be . . . ethical."

Mason laughed.

Cassel's face darkened. "Look, Mason, you're supposed to be high-powered. You're supposed to be the last word. But all you're doing so far is making it tough for your client. He had a chance to get off the hook at a bargain price. Now, things are going up."

"Don't say that," Mason said, "or prices may go down."

"You think you can pull a rabbit out of a hat?" Cassel asked sneeringly.

Mason said, "That's what I'm noted for, pulling rabbits out of hats and coming up with another ace when it's least expected."

Cassel started angrily for the door, turned, said, "Look, Mason, let's be businesslike. Your client pays five grand and that's all there is to it."

"And what does he get in return for the five grand?"

"Immunity."

"What about the proofs?"

Cassel's face showed surprise. "What are you talking about, the proofs?"

Mason recovered easily. "The proofs of your integrity, of the fact that my client has immunity."

"Draw up an agreement," Cassel said.

"You said yourself it wouldn't be worth anything."

"Not in court," Cassel said, "and not if the right party brings the action. But it closes a lot of doors—all the doors your client needs to worry about."

"I'll think it over," Mason conceded.

"Think it over, hell! You haven't got a lot of time to think things over. This is a hot deal. If you're going to go for it, you've got to move and move fast."

"Where can I reach you?" Mason asked.

Cassel surveyed him thoughtfully. "You're asking a lot of questions."

"All right," Mason said, "where can I leave the money—if I decide to leave the money?"

Cassel said, "Look, your phone number is listed. You have an office. I don't know what you're doing here in the hotel. I'll give you a call from a pay station at your office."

"When?"

"When I get damned good and ready," Cassel said. He opened the door and walked out, slamming the door behind him.

Mason went to the telephone, put a call through the switchboard to Paul Drake's office.

"Perry Mason talking, Paul. Did Stella Grimes phone in for an operative to do a tailing job?"

"Haven't heard from her," Drake said. "The last I knew she was in the Willatson Hotel. Weren't you with her?"

"I was," Mason said. "I had a man I wanted followed. I tried to give her a signal."

"If you gave her a signal, she got it all right," Drake said. "She's a bright babe. Was there any reason why she couldn't do the tailing job herself?"

"The only trouble is, the subject knows her," Mason said. "A stranger would have been better."

"Well, she probably didn't have time to phone in. What was it, a rush job?"

"It was one hell of a rush job."

"You'll be hearing from her," Drake predicted.

Mason hung up the phone, walked casually around the room, again picked up the telephone, said to the hotel operator, "Ring Room Seven-eighty-nine, please."

It was some time before Diana Douglas answered the phone.

"Yes?" she asked.

Mason said, "It took you a while to answer, Diana."

"I didn't know whether I should answer or not. How's everything down your way? I thought you were coming to—"

"We were interrupted," Mason said. "The other party to the transaction showed up."

"You mean . . . you mean the blackmailer?"

"Yes."

"What happened?"

"We stalled around for a while," Mason said, "and, unfortunately, he made me."

"What do you mean by that?"

"He knew who I was. He recognized me from the photographs he had seen in the papers from time to time."

"Is that bad?" she asked.

"It may be good," Mason said. "I think he was just a little frightened. . . . I just wanted to tell you to sit tight until you hear from me. It's *very* important that you keep under cover."

"I should be—well, shouldn't I be getting my ticket back to San Francisco? And the banks will be closed here."

"We can't hurry this now," Mason said. "There may be developments. Wait a few minutes—or up to an hour—until I have a chance to join you. Don't try to leave that room until I give you a signal that everything's in the clear."

Chapter Seven

Mason stretched out in Room 767 at the Willatson Hotel. Despite himself he couldn't refrain from glancing at his wristwatch every few minutes. Twice he got up and paced the floor.

The phone rang.

Mason snatched up the instrument. "Yes?" he said.

Diana Douglas' voice said, "Mr. Mason, I'm frightened. Can I come down there and wait where I can be with you?.

"Definitely not," Mason said. "Sit where you are. I'll have instructions for you soon."

"What do you mean by soon?"

"I hope within a few minutes."

"I'm getting the heebie jeebies sitting here all by myself, Mr. Mason, just looking at the walls and . . . well, I feel that we aren't accomplishing anything this way."

"We're accomplishing a lot more than you realize," Mason said, "and it's imperative that you follow instructions. Just sit tight."

The lawyer hung up the telephone, walked over to the window, looked down at the street, came back to his chair, settled himself; then abruptly got up and started pacing the flooring.

The doorknob suddenly turned. The door opened and Stella Grimes walked into the room.

"Any luck?" Mason asked.

"Lots of it," she said, tossing a cardboard box on the bed.

Mason raised his eyebrows.

"Clothes," she said. "I picked up a few necessities at the department store because I felt I might have to ride herd on this room. I just snatched up some things and had them wrapped up because I didn't want to keep you waiting."

"What happened?"

"Well," she said, "I got your signal all right. You wanted him followed."

"That's right."

"Well, of course, he knew me by sight. That complicated the job. I felt that the chances that he was living here in the hotel were rather slim. So I went down to the curb, hired a taxicab, and told the driver to just sit there until I told him I wanted to take off.

"Well, it was absurdly simple, so simple in fact that I feel that perhaps it may have been a frame."

"What happened?"

"Our man had his own car, a Cadillac. He had given the doorman a substantial tip to park it for a few minutes in the loading zone. It must have been a pretty good-sized tip because when he came out the doorman was all attention. He ran over and held the car door open for Cassel and bowed his thanks as Cassel drove off."

"You followed?"

"That's right."

"Get the license number?"

She took a notebook from her pocket and read off the license number, "WVM five-seven-four."

"Could you tail him?" Mason asked.

"It was easy. He went to the Tallmeyer Apartments. Drove right into the garage in the basement of the apartment house and didn't come out."

"So what did you do?" Mason asked.

"I had my taxi driver drive three blocks to where a car was pulling out from the curb. I said, 'Follow that car but don't let him know he's being followed.'"

"Good work," Mason said.

"Well, of course, this driver got mixed up in traffic. We lost out on a traffic signal and I shrugged my shoulders and said, 'Well, that's the best we can do.' Paid off the cab and took another one and came back here to the hotel. I didn't want the cab driver giving me a double cross and tipping Cassel off, and, as it is, he thinks I'm some sort of a nut. At least, I hope he does."

Mason picked up the phone, said to the operator, "Give me an outside line," then gave the number of the Drake Detective Agency.

"Paul in?" he asked the switchboard operator.

"He just came in, Mr. Mason," she said, recognizing his voice.

"Put him on, will you please?"

Drake's voice came on the line, "Hello."

"Perry Mason, Paul."

"Where are you?"

"At the Willatson Hotel with Stella Grimes. She's back now."

"Doing any good?"

"I think we've struck pay dirt. I want to find out the owner of a Cadillac automobile, license number WVM five-seven-four, and if the owner lives at the Tallmeyer Apartments I'd like to try to find out a little bit about him without doing anything that would arouse suspicion."

Drake said, "Della was asking if it's all right to call you."

"She'd best not," Mason said. "I'll call the office from time to time and see if there's anything important. Was there something in particular on her mind?"

"I don't think so, except that you had a few appointments she had to get you out of with a story about you being called out of town on important business."

"I think that's just what's going to happen," Mason said.

"On the square?"

"On the square. . . . How long will it take you to find out about that car registration?"

"I can have that right quick."

"I'll call back," Mason said. "Get on it as fast as you can."

"How's Stella doing?" Drake asked.

"Fine," Mason said.

"Okay, if you want anything, just put in a call. It'll cost you money, but you'll get the service."

"Will do," Mason said, and hung up.

"Gosh, that guy was mad," Stella said. "You really must have pinned his ears back!"

Mason grinned. "How did you know he was mad, Stella?"

"The way he walked, the way he looked, and the way he left himself wide open."

"I guess he was disappointed," Mason said. "He was expecting a soft touch."

"I'll bet he thought he'd run full speed into a brick wall instead," she observed. "He certainly was one very mad citizen."

The lawyer looked at his wristwatch. "Hold the fort a minute, Stella," he said. "I'm going down the hall. If anything should happen that would complicate the situation hang the DO NOT DISTURB sign on the outside of the door. If Paul Drake phones while I'm down there tell him to call me in that room."

Mason walked down to Room 789 and tapped on the door.

Diana Douglas threw the door open.

"Don't do that!" Mason said.

"Do what?"

"Be so eager," Mason said. "Don't open that door until you find out who it is."

"I'm all on edge," she said. "I sit here and thoughts are running through my head. I just can't take this waiting game, Mr. Mason."

Mason said, "Listen very carefully, Diana. How much money do you have?"

"I told you, five thousand dollars."

"That isn't what I meant. I want to know how much you have outside of that."

"I drew out six hundred dollars from my savings account when I left. I wanted to have enough to give you a retainer and—"

"The money that you gave me didn't come out of the five thousand dollars then?"

"No."

"You don't have any idea on earth what this is all about? I want you to be frank, now."

She lowered her eyes. "Well, I suppose it's some kind of an indiscretion that Edgar—well, something he got himself mixed up with. . . . Oh, you know how those rackets go, some kind of a badger game or photographs or—Why do you ask me these questions, Mr. Mason?"

"Because," Mason said, "I think we may be following a wrong trail, barking up a wrong tree. Tell me as much as you can about Edgar, only condense it."

"Well," she said, motioning for him to sit down, and seating herself on the edge of the bed, "Edgar is naïve. He's—I won't say he's weak, but he is easily influenced, and I suppose I haven't been of too much help to him trying to make things a little easier for him. I guess life wasn't meant to be that way, Mr. Mason. I guess a man has to develop himself by having things made a little difficult at times instead of having someone whom he looks up to who can smooth things out and take some of the load off his shoulders."

"That's what I was coming to," Mason said. "Do you think there's anything in Edgar's past that would have caused him to come to you with a sum of money and ask you to bail him out?"

"I just don't know, Mr. Mason."

"He could have been coming to you?"

"He could have been, but everything indicates he was going to come here to Los Angeles and try to deal with this thirty-six-twenty-four-thirty-six situation."

"And you have no clue as to what that situation is?"

"No."

"Your brother gambled from time to time?" Mason asked.

She chose her words carefully. "Edgar was impulsive."

"He gambled from time to time?"

"Don't all men?"

"He gambled from time to time?"

"Yes," she flared. "You don't need to cross-examine me like that. He gambled from time to time."

"Where?"

"Where do men usually gamble? Sometimes he put two dollars on a horse. Sometimes he put ten dollars on a horse.

"Las Vegas—Reno?"

"He would go to Las Vegas once in a while."

"How much did he ever win?"

"I don't know. I don't think he won much."

"What was the most he ever lost?"

"Eight hundred dollars."

"How do you know?"

"He told me."

"Why did he tell you?"

"Because I'm his sister."

"Why did he tell you?"

"I told you," she blazed back at him. "I'm his sister. What are you doing, trying to break down my story?"

"Why did he tell you?" Mason asked.

"All right," she haid, lowering her voice, "I had to bail him out. He only had two hundred and I had to make good to the extent of six hundred dollars. He had given a check in Las Vegas and—well, you know how they are."

"How are they?" Mason asked.

She shrugged her shoulders. "I don't know, but the story is that if you gamble on credit with professional gamblers you have to make good or else."

"And Edgar was frightened?"

"Terribly frightened."

"In other words," Mason said, "I'm trying to establish a pattern. When Edgar gets into real trouble, he comes to you. You've been something of a sister and a mother to him."

"Well," she said thoughtfully, "I guess that's right."

"So, if Edgar was in some trouble where he had to raise five thousand dollars, the assumption is he would have told you."

"Unless he—well, it might have been something that he wouldn't have wanted to talk to me about. You know, men can get into scrapes of that sort where they wouldn't want their family to know just what had happened."

"Who told you that?" Mason asked.

"Why, I . . . I've read it."

"Ever talk with Edgar about anything like that?"

"No."

"Know anything about Edgar's sex life?"

"Virtually nothing."

Mason regarded her thoughtfully. He said, "There's a United Airlines plane leaving here for San Francisco at six twenty-seven. I want you to be on that plane.

"I'm going to escort you to the elevator. When you get to the lobby, walk across the lobby casually. Don't look around as though you might be afraid someone was trying to follow you. We'll walk two blocks down the street. There's a taxi stand down there. I'll put you in a cab. Go to the Union Station. When you get to the Union Station, try to make sure that you're not being followed. Then go out, get a cab, and go to the airport. When you get to the airport, wait."

"For what?"

"I'll try to meet you just before you get on the plane. I'll have your baggage. I'll check out of the hotel within an hour or so. That'll give me time to get to my apartment and pack a bag. I'll take my bag and your suitcase and join you at the airport."

"But what about this bag that has the—you know, the money in it?"

"The banks are closed now," Mason said. "You've got to take a chance with that because I want you to be sure and have a cashier's check made to you as trustee when you walk into the office in the morning.

"The minute the banks open in San Francisco, get that cashier's check. Then go to the office just as if nothing out of the ordinary had ever happened. I'll meet you there when you come in. That should be about ten-thirty. Let's have that as the deadline. Don't arrive before ten-thirty. Don't be any later than that if you can avoid it."

The telephone rang.

Mason said, "I think that's for me."

He picked up the instrument, said a cautious, "Hello."

Drake's voice, cheerfully routine, came over the line, "Hi, Perry. Got most of the information you want. It was like rolling off a log."

"What is it?"

"The Cadillac you wanted is registered under the name of Moray Cassel, nine-o-six Tallmeyer Apartments. I've got that much. I haven't been able to find out much about Cassel's habits as yet, but he's been a resident there for something over a year."

"Well, I'll be damned," Mason said in an undertone.

"Something wrong?"

"The guy gave me his right name," Mason said. "You could certainly have fooled me. I had him sized up as a blackmailer, a damned good, prosperous, shrewd thief."

"And he isn't?" Drake asked.

"That I'll have to find out," Mason said.

"You want him tailed?"

"No. The guy is either too dumb to be true or too smart to be trapped, and I want to find out which it is before I get my feet wet."

"Okay, let me know if there's anything else you want."

"Will do," Mason said, and hung up.

Diana, watching Mason with anxious eyes, said, "Is something wrong?"

Mason, frowning thoughtfully, let the question go unanswered for a few seconds, then said, "I don't know. I seem to have made a mistake in sizing up a situation."

"In what way?"

Mason said, "Thanks to good detective work on the part of the Drake Detective Agency, we have run the blackmailer to ground. His name is Moray Cassel. He drives a Cadillac automobile. He lives in the Tallmeyer Apartments, apartment nine-o-six. But when he came to call on us he gave us his real name. He had his Cadillac right in front of the door, having given the doorman a good tip to see that it was left where it would be readily accessible in the parking space reserved for incoming guests with baggage."

"Well, what's wrong about that?" Diana asked. "A lot of people who are on brief errands give the doorman a good tip to keep an eye on their cars. That's the way the doormen make a living. They—"

Mason shook his head. "It isn't that, Diana," he interrupted. "The man simply wasn't that kind of a citizen."

"How do you know?"

Mason said, "Well, I have to admit that this is a time when I may have led with my chin, but I sized the man up as a criminal."

"How, for heaven's sake?"

"His appearance. His manner. Everything about him."

"Mr. Mason, do you mean to tell me you can just take a look at a man like that, have a quick conversation with him, and know that he's . . . well, what you called him?"

"No," Mason said at length, "I won't go that far, Diana. And remember when I say the guy's a criminal, I don't mean that he's actually engaged in criminality, I mean he's that type of citizen. He's one who would make his living out of representing a woman in a blackmail scheme."

"But how in the world can you possibly tell? What is there about a man of that sort, the way he dresses, that . . . I just don't get it."

"It's not any one particular thing," Mason said. "It's a combination of things. You take a man who's making his living directly or indirectly out of women, and he knows there's something wrong inside. He tries to cover it up. He tries to square himself with himself. He tries to put the best possible veneer on top of what's underneath in order to hide the rotten part.

"So he goes in for a faultless personal appearance. His shoes are always shined. His trousers are sharply creased. He wears expensive shirts and ties. His nails are always well manicured. The skin of his hands is well cared for. His hair is cut, combed, and brushed so that it makes a flattering appearance in the mirror.

"Then there's his voice. There's something about it. A voice that isn't used to carrying weight with the world in general but is sharply authoritative in dealing with a situation which he thinks he can handle. It lacks tone and timbre. You have the feeling that if he became enraged and flew off the handle his voice would rise to a sharp falsetto."

"And this man, Cassel, had those points?"

"He had those points," Mason said.

"What did he want?"

"He wanted money."

"Did he say how much?"

"He wanted the bundle, five grand."

"And what did you tell him?"

"I stalled him along."

"Did he go for it?"

"He didn't like it."

"Did he feel that you were—?"

"As I told you, he recognized me," Mason said. "I've had my picture in the newspapers too often. He knew that he was dealing with Perry Mason, an attorney, and he didn't like any part of it."

"And you never did find out what he wanted, what he had on my brother, Edgar?"

Mason shook his head. "It evidently isn't the ordinary kind of blackmail deal," he said.

"You think it was something . . . well, worse than what you call the ordinary blackmail?"

"It could have been," Mason said. "He acted as though he really had the winning hand."

"What's he going to do next?"

Mason shrugged his shoulders, said, "That's something we'll have to wait for."

"Mr. Mason, suppose it could be something—well, *real* serious?"

"You don't make a pass at a guy for five thousand bucks on squaring for parking in front of a fire hydrant," Mason said. "Whatever it is, it's something serious."

"Look, Mr. Mason, I've . . . I could raise money if . . ."

Mason said, "Forget it. It's against my policy to pay off blackmailers. To hell with them. Come on, Diana, we're going to leave here casually. We won't be carrying anything except your purse and that black bag with the money in it. I'm going to walk with you through the lobby and out the front door. As we cross the lobby, be talking and laughing. You know, the quick, nervous laugh of a woman who realizes that she's embarking on an adventure which may have romantic overtones. I don't want anyone to think that you may be surreptitiously leaving the hotel.

"Now, after we've walked across the lobby, we're going down the street a couple of blocks to a taxicab stand. You remember and follow instructions. Get in a taxicab and pull away from the curb. Go to the Union Depot. Mingle around with the crowds. Switch cabs. Go to the airport and get that plane for San Francisco. . . . Hold everything. I'll see if I can get reservations."

Mason picked up the phone and asked for an outside line. He gave the number of United Airlines, got the reservations desk, and asked for two tickets to San Francisco on the flight leaving at six twenty-seven.

The lawyer nodded his satisfaction, said, "We'll pick up the tickets at the airport. Put them both under the name of Perry Mason. . . . That's right, Perry Mason, the lawyer. I'm listed in the phone books. I have an Air Travel Card and— That's fine! I'll pick up one ticket myself. Give the other one to a Miss Diana Douglas. Hold them right up until plane time, if you will.

"Thank you very much!"

Mason hung up the telephone, said, "Everything's all set, Diana. Ask for a ticket that's held in the name of Perry Mason. I'll see you aboard the plane. I'll have your suitcase with me when I check out of the hotel here. Now, remember that if anything happens to that bag of money you're carrying, you're stuck. You're behind the eight ball. You're in trouble."

"I know," she said. "I've been carrying it with me and I . . . I can hardly sleep worrying about it. I know that if anything happens to it I'm never going to be able to work things out. But I've got by so far and, after all, Mr. Mason, who knows I'm carrying five thousand dollars?"

"Too many people by this time," Mason said grimly. "Come on, Diana, put on your best smile and we're going to go down to the lobby, out the front door, and down to the taxicab stand. You're going to be laughing and talking and I'll try a wisecrack now and then. . . . Come on, let's go. I've got an idea this hotel may be a darn poor place for you from now on. . . . You'll have some time to wait at the airport, but try to be as inconspicuous as possible and get aboard the plane just as soon as the doors are open for boarding."

Chapter Eight

Mason returned to Room 767 at the hotel, knocked at the door, and when Stella admitted him said, "Well, I got rid of the bait in the case. She'll join me at the airport. Let's hope nothing happens until we get off."

"You think she's in danger?"

"Not danger exactly, but this guy Cassel worries me. He may be smarter than I had him pegged. I've had an uneasy feeling about Diana ever since I arrived here at the hotel. She left too wide a back trail and—"

The lawyer paused as the sharp rap of knuckles sounded on the door. He turned back and said to Stella Grimes in a low voice, "Those are masculine knuckles and they sound imperative."

"Cassel coming back?" she asked.

Mason shook his head. "He's a soft, sneaky knocker. These are the knuckles of authority—either the house detective, or—"

He was interrupted by another knock and a voice said, "Open up, please. This is the police."

Mason said to Stella Grimes, "Let me do as much of the talking as possible."

Mason opened the door.

Two plain-clothes men, standing in the hallway, showed surprise as they recognized the lawyer.

"Perry Mason," one said, "what you *you* doing *here?*"

"The question," Mason said, "is what *you* are doing here."

"We prefer to discuss it inside rather than in the corridor," the spokesman said, and pushed his way into the room, holding in his hand a leather folder displaying a badge. "Los Angeles police," he said.

"And what brings you here?" Mason asked.

The officers ignored him temporarily, looked at Stella Grimes. One of the officers nodded at the other. "Age twenty-two, five-feet-two, a hundred and sixteen pounds, blonde, blue eyes, good figure," he said.

The other nodded.

The two officers helped themselves to chairs, and one said, "We want to ask a few questions."

"Very well," Mason said, "go ahead."

"Is your name Diana Douglas?" one of the officers asked Stella Grimes.

"Now, just a minute," Mason said. "Let's do this thing in an orderly manner. Why do you come here?"

"We don't have to tell you that."

"No, but you have to tell the young woman that. Do you suspect her of a crime?"

"We're acting on telegraphed instructions from the San Francisco police. We're trying to get some information. We want to ask some questions, that's all."

"Do you suspect this young woman of any crime?"

"We don't know. We haven't the faintest idea."

"You're acting for the San Francisco police?"

"Yes."

"Do the San Francisco police suspect her of any crime?"

"We're not mind readers. We don't know."

"Then," Mason said, "since you're acting for and on behalf of the San Francisco police, and since you don't know whether the San Francisco police suspect her of any crime, before she answers *any* questions you had better advise her as to her constitutional rights."

"As if she didn't know them," the officer said.

Mason smiled. "Tell that to the Supreme Court."

"All right, all right," the officer said. "We want you to answer a few questions, Miss. We're not making any specific charges. We're not here to take you into custody, but we do want to ask you some questions.

"You are entitled to remain silent if you wish. You don't have to make any statement. You are entitled to have an attorney represent you at all times. If you don't have money enough to secure an attorney, we will secure one to act on your behalf. However, we want it understood that anything you do say may be used against you. Now then, do you wish an attorney?"

Stella started to say something when Mason motioned her to silence. "She's got one," he said.

"You're representing her?"

"Yes."

"What are you doing here—Miss Douglas, is it?"

"She's here on business," Mason said.

"What sort of business?"

"Personal business."

"Miss Douglas, were you aware that a relatively large sum of cash was being kept in the vault at the Escobar Import and Export Company where you work in San Francisco?"

"No comment," Mason said.

"Now, wait a minute," the officer said. "You're injecting yourself into this thing and you're just making it worse for this young lady. All we're trying to do is to elicit information."

"Why?"

"Because San Francisco wants that information."

"I take it there's a crime involved?"

"We're not sure. San Francisco isn't sure."

"I think, under the circumstances, my client doesn't care to answer any questions until the situation is clarified," Mason said.

"You're forcing us to report to San Francisco that there's every likelihood that your client is guilty of a substantial embezzlement."

"Indeed!" Mason said. "How much of an embezzlement?"

"The audit hasn't been completed," the officer said, "but it's a substantial amount—over twenty thousand dollars."

"How much?" Mason exclaimed, surprise showing in his voice.

"You heard me, over twenty grand."

"That's a lot of money to embezzle from one company," Mason said.

"There *have* been embezzlements involving larger sums," the officer said.

"Then there has been a crime committed in San Francisco?"

"If you're referring to the embezzlement, it looks that way."

"And San Francisco suspects my client of embezzling the money?"

"I haven't said that—yet."

"But you want to ask questions about it?"

"Listen, Mason, you're making things rather difficult and you're getting mighty hard to get along with. All we want to do is ask your client some questions about how the cash is kept in that company, about who has the authority to draw out cash, and, generally, things about the bookkeeping end of it. For your information, that company seems to keep perfectly huge sums of liquid cash available, and we'd like to know why.

"We'd also like to know how many people have the combination to the vault and how it is possible for a company to run up a shortage of that sort without somebody checking it earlier."

"It's been going on for a long time?" Mason asked.

"We don't know," the officer said. "That's what we're trying to find out. We're simply trying to get information."

"But you think my client *may* have embezzled that money?" Mason asked.

"Not exactly," the officer said. "I'll put it this way. We won't say that we've uncovered any evidence which makes it appear that it's a physical impossibility for her to have been guilty of embezzlement, but, on the other hand, we haven't uncovered any evidence which points to her—as yet."

"Except in a circumstantial way," the other officer said.

"Well, yes," the spokesman conceded.

Mason smiled and said, "That makes it very plain, gentlemen. My client is entitled to the advice of counsel."

"That's right. We told her that. There's no question about that."

"And, as her counsel," Mason said, "I advise her to say absolutely nothing."

"You won't even let her talk about the methods of bookkeeping, about the business background of the company?"

"Not a word," Mason said. "Not even to admit her identity."

The two officers looked at each other in frustration and disgust.

"That may not be a very smart thing to do," the spokesman said to Mason.

"Perhaps so," Mason conceded. "I'm not infallible. I make mistakes every so often. . . . How did San Francisco know enough about the situation to send you two hot-footing to the hotel here?"

The officer grinned. "On the advice of counsel, I decline to answer, Mr. Mason."

The lawyer was grave. "You're absolutely entitled to adopt that position. It's a constitutional privilege. You don't need to say a word."

The officers got up, looked belligerently at Stella Grimes.

The spokesman said, "Okay, sister, it's up to you, but let me tell you, you're not being very smart. When we walked in we just wanted information."

"What do you want now?" Mason asked.

"At least twenty grand," the officer said, and then made a parting shot at the lawyer. "Remember it won't do *you* any good to collect a fee out of embezzled money. It can be traced and impounded. . . . I guess that's all."

"See you later," Mason said.

"In court," the officer promised, and walked out.

Mason motioned for silence, said to Stella Grimes in a low voice, "Be careful what you say. They sometimes wait just outside the door."

They were silent for more than a minute; then Mason tiptoed to the door, abruptly jerked it open, and looked up and down the hall.

When he saw there was no one there, the lawyer closed the door and said, "Well, that's a fine kettle of fish."

"Twenty thousand dollars," Stella Grimes said.

Mason shook his head. "I don't get it," he said, "but I'm on my way to the airport. I'll take the baggage out of my room which has Diana's stuff in it and be on my way. I'm catching that six-twenty-seven flight to San Francisco."

"You're going to see Diana at the airport?"

Mason nodded, said, "She'll join me there. Hold the fort, Stella, and play it by ear. Keep in touch with Paul Drake. . . . Better have your meals sent up to the room for at least twenty-four hours. If you leave the room they may bug it."

She said, "I can get by all right now. What about the switchboard?"

"You'll have to take a chance on that," Mason said. "But don't scatter information around like birdseed. Be cryptic when you call your office, but be sure you get the idea across."

The lawyer left Room 767, walked down to 789, picked up his suitcase and that of Diana Douglas, and called the desk for a boy to assist him.

"Please ask the cashier to have my bill ready," Mason told the desk clerk. "I've received an unexpected long-distance call and I've got to leave at once."

Mason waited until the boy arrived, gave him the bags and a tip, hurried down to the cashier's desk, and explained the situation. "I'm Mr. Mason in Room Seven-eighty-nine. I wanted to stay for a day or two, but I've received a call which makes it imperative that I leave at once. Now, what can we do about the room? I've only been in it a short time. I've used a couple of towels, but the bed hasn't been occupied."

The cashier shook her head. "I'm sorry, Mr. Mason, but we're going to have to charge you for one full day."

Mason made a point of protesting the charge. "But you can put in two new towels and rent the room again."

"I'm sorry, but maid service is cut down at this time of the afternoon and—well, we have a rule, Mr. Mason. I'm sorry."

"All right," the lawyer yielded. "Give me the bill."

He paid in cash, nodded to a bellboy, said, "I want a taxi."

"There's one right outside," the boy said.

Mason gave the boy a good tip, settled himself in the cushions of the taxicab, said in a loud voice, "Take me to the Union Station. Take it easy because I've got a couple of telegrams to read and I want to catch the train to Tucson."

Suddenly Mason, folding the papers which he had taken from his pocket, said, "Hold everything, driver. That telegram really does it."

"You don't want the station?" the driver asked.

"Hell, no," Mason said, "I've simply got to get the plane that leaves for Phoenix and Tucson, so get me to the airport just as fast as you can."

"It's a bad time of day to hit the airport."

"I can't help it, we'll do the best we can."

"When's your plane due out?"

"Five forty-eight," Mason said.

The cab driver threaded his way through traffic, found a through boulevard, and started making time.

Mason sat forward on the edge of the seat, looking at his watch from time to time, occasionally complimenting the cab driver on the time he was making.

The lawyer got to the airport. The cabby honked the horn for a porter.

Mason whipped the door open, said to the porter, "Get those two suitcases on the plane for Tucson."

The lawyer handed the cab driver a ten-dollar bill. "Get going, buddy, before some cop catches up with you. That was a swell ride."

The driver grinned. "This is all for me?"

"Pay the meter and the rest is yours," Mason said.

The driver threw the car into gear.

When he was out of earshot, Mason hurried after the porter.

"I made a mistake," he said, "I was thinking about Tucson. Darn it, I want to get in one of those suitcases. Let me have them." Mason handed the porter a couple of dollars.

"You've got your plane ticket?" the porter asked.

"I've got it," Mason said.

The lawyer went into the waiting room and made a quick survey; then went to the airline counter, picked up one of his tickets, paid for both, checked in Diana's baggage, then walked down to survey the waiting room again. Following this, he strolled casually around, then settled himself comfortably after checking the dummy suitcase in a storage receptacle, and bought a drink.

Five minutes before departure time the lawyer walked in a leisurely manner to the gate and presented his ticket.

"You'll have to hurry," the attendant told him. "The last of the passengers is getting aboard now."

"I'll walk right along," Mason promised.

Mason walked through the door, signaled to the guard, and got aboard the plane just before the portable passageway was pulled back into place.

The hostess at the door looked at him chidingly. "You almost didn't make it," she said.

Mason smiled. "I almost didn't, but it's too hot to hurry."

"There's a seat toward the rear."

"Thank you."

Mason walked the length of the plane, glancing at the faces of the passengers.

After ten or fifteen minutes he walked forward to the lavatory and again took an opportunity to study the faces of the passengers on the plane.

Diana Douglas was not on board.

Mason rode to San Francisco on the plane, took a taxi to a hotel, registered, had dinner, then called the Willatson Hotel, asked for Room 767, and when he heard Stella Grimes' cautious voice on the telephone said, "Recognize the voice, Stella?"

"Yes. Where are you?"

"San Francisco. Did you hear anything from your double?"

"Not a word."

"She was to have taken the same plane I did, but she didn't show up. She didn't leave any message with you?"

"Not a word. I haven't heard a thing."

"Anything from anybody else?"

"Nothing."

Mason said, "I think we've been given a complete runaround on this case, Stella. I'll keep my appointment at ten-thirty tomorrow morning and if nothing happens then we'll wash our hands of the whole business."

"Okay by me. Do I report to you if anything happens?"

"Keep in touch with your employer and I'll contact him. Do you still have your working bra?"

"I have it."

"Keep it," Mason said, "and sleep tight."

Chapter Nine

The Escobar Import and Export Company had its offices in the United Financial Building.

Mason found from the registry list that the firm had offices on the sixth floor, then retreated to a point near the door where he could watch the people coming in.

The time was 10:20.

At 10:25 Diana Douglas walked through the door.

Mason stepped forward. "Where were you last night?"

She raised tear-swollen eyes; then clutched at his arm as though she needed his physical as well as his mental help.

"Oh, Mr. Mason," she said, "Edgar passed away at three twenty-five this morning."

"I'm so sorry," Mason said, putting his arm around her shoulders. "He meant a lot to you, didn't he?"

"A lot. I was very, very fond of him."

She suddenly buried her head against Mason's shoulder and started to cry.

Mason patted her back. "Now, don't let yourself go, Diana. Re-

member we have a job to do. You'll have to get your chin up and
face the facts."

"I know," she sobbed, "but I . . . I just don't feel that I can take
it. . . . If it hadn't been that I'd promised you I'd meet you here
I . . . I wanted to telephone Homer Gage and tell him not to
expect me. I . . ."

"There, there," Mason said, "we're attracting a lot of attention,
Diana. Move over here to the corner and try to get control of
yourself. You've got a job to do. You're going to have to go up
and face the music."

"How much music?"

"Lots of music."

"What do you mean?"

Mason said, "I'm afraid you're being sucked into a game which
is as old as the hills. Someone embezzles a thousand dollars from a
company and skips out. Somebody else, who knows what has been
going on, calmly reaches in and takes another four thousand out
of the till. The man who has absconded with the one thousand
dollars gets credit for having embezzled five thousand."

Her eyes, red with crying, widened as she looked at him. "You
mean that. . . ?"

"I mean," Mason said, "that the Escobar Import and Export Company is now claiming there's a shortage of twenty thousand dollars."

"*Twenty* thousand dollars!" she repeated, aghast.

"Exactly," Mason said. And then after a moment went on, "How
do you come to work? Do you drive or . . . ?"

"No, I take a bus."

"What about arrangements for your brother? Were there any
other relatives?"

"No, I got up early this morning and made arrangements."

"Why didn't you take that plane last night as you were instructed?"

"Because I thought someone was following me. Mr. Mason, I felt
certain that a man in an automobile followed my taxicab all the
way to the Union Depot and then tried to follow me. I tried to
lose myself in the crowd, but I don't think I was very successful. I
kept having that horrible feeling that this man was spying on me
and was where he could see me all the time, so I went into the

women's restroom, stayed for a long time, then came out and took a lot of what I suppose you would call evasive tactics. I started through the gate for a train, then doubled back and then, by the time I got to the airport, it was ten minutes too late. The plane had taken off. So then I decided to have dinner and come in on a later plane."

"Why didn't you telephone Paul Drake's office or somebody?"

"I—I never thought of it. I knew you were coming up on that plane and I knew I'd meet you here this morning and—well, I never thought of anything else.

"Then when I got in I telephoned the hospital and found out that my brother was worse and I went up there and—I was with him—when—"

"There, there," Mason said. "You've had a pretty hard row to hoe. Now, what I want you to do is to catch the next bus, go back to your apartment, and try to get some sleep. Do you have any sleeping medicine?"

"Yes, I have some sleeping pills."

"Take them," Mason said. "Go to sleep and forget about everything. . . . Do you have that cashier's check?"

"Yes."

"Give it to me," Mason said. "I probably won't use it, but I'd like to have it. And here's your suitcase."

"What are you going to do?" she asked, giving him the cashier's check.

"I'm going up to the Escobar Import and Export Company and throw a little weight around. At least, I'm going to try to."

"Mr. Mason—twenty thousand dollars. Good Lord!"

"I know," Mason said. "It's a shock."

"But what can we do?"

"That," Mason said, "remains to be seen. The game is old but it's almost infallible. Some poor guy gets to betting on the horses, gets in over his head, takes two or three thousand dollars and skips town, and the smart guy who remains behind cleans out all the cash available and the embezzler is stuck with the whole thing. If they never catch up with him, he's supposed to have taken it all, and if they do catch up with him and he denies that he took anything above two or three thousand, no one believes him. He goes to prison for the whole thing."

Mason put the check in his wallet, then guided her gently toward the street door. "Get on your bus," he said. "Go back to your apartment and go to sleep. Leave the Escobar Import and Export Company to me. . . . Do you have a private phone or does it go through the apartment switchboard?"

"It goes through the apartment switchboard."

"Leave word that you're not to be disturbed," Mason said. "Get some sleep. I have your phone number. Tell the operator that only calls from me are to be put through. This is Friday. I'll go back to my office this afternoon. You can reach me through the Drake Detective Agency if you need me. . . . I'm sorry about your brother's death. You poor kid, you've had a lot to put up with during the last few days. Take it easy and call on me if you need me. . . . Where does your bus stop?"

"Right here," she said, "at this bus stop. And I owe you for my plane ticket, Mr. Mason. I remembered you had ordered two tickets to be charged to you. When I got to the airport I made a rush for that plane, thinking it might have been a few minutes late taking off. I was going to pay for the ticket with my credit card, but I couldn't find it. I must have lost it, and the girl at the ticket counter said that the ticket was all paid for, and—"

"That's all right," Mason said. "Forget it."

He guided her to a wooden bench at the curb. "Take the first bus home. I'm going up to the office and see what can be done."

She flung her arms around the lawyer and kissed him impulsively.

"Mr. Mason, you're *so* wonderful!" she said.

Chapter Ten

Mason stood in the hallway on the sixth floor surveying the offices of the Escobar Import and Export Company.

There was a display showing Oriental art goods, carved ivories, and cloisonné.

On the other side of the entrance door the display showed figurines which had a Toltec or Aztec look about them.

Double plate-glass doors opened into a rather shallow showroom in which there were glass shelves containing further specimens of art. The entrance doors had the legend ESCOBAR IMPORT AND EXPORT COMPANY, *Wholesale Only*.

Mason pushed the doors open and entered the display room. A girl seated at a switchboard smiled mechanically. "May I help you?" she asked.

Mason said, "I'd like to see Mr. Gage, please."

"Which one? Mr. Franklin Gage or Mr. Homer Gage?"

"Franklin Gage."

"He isn't in. He's out on a business trip."

"Then I'll see Homer Gage."

"What's the name, please?"

"Perry Mason."

"Did you wish to see him about a purchase, Mr. Mason, about some art goods, or. . . ?"

"It's a more personal matter than that," Mason said.

"May I ask what firm you represent?"

"I don't represent any firm," Mason said. "My name is Perry Mason. I'm an attorney from Los Angeles. I happen to be here at the moment to discuss an employee by the name of Diana Douglas."

"Oh, oh!" she said. "Oh, yes . . . yes, indeed. Just a moment!"

She plugged in a line and Mason saw her lips moving rapidly, but the connection of the telephone was so arranged that he couldn't hear her words.

A moment later a door in the back part of the room opened and a heavy-set, chunky individual came striding out, a man in his late thirties, with dark hair which had receded well back from his temples, bushy black eyebrows, keen gray eyes, and tortoise-shell glasses. His mouth was a straight line of thin determination.

"Mr. Mason?" he said.

"Right."

"I'm Homer Gage. What did you wish to see me about?"

"Diana Douglas."

"What about her?"

"She's an employee of yours?"

"Yes. She is, but she's not here at the moment. Her brother was seriously injured in an automobile accident and I am afraid she is rather upset. If it's a matter of credit rating or integrity, I can assure you that she has a fine reputation."

"It's neither," Mason said. "I wanted to talk to you about her."

"Well, I'm here."

"All right," Mason said, "if you want to talk here, we'll talk here. I'm representing Miss Douglas. What was the idea of telling the Los Angeles police that she had embezzled twenty thousand dollars from this . . ."

Gage interrupted, throwing up his hands, palms outward. "Stop right there, Mr. Mason. We never said any such thing."

"Then you intimated it."

"Mr. Mason, this is hardly the time or the place to discuss a matter of this sort."

"What's wrong with the time?" Mason asked.

"Why . . . I hadn't anticipated . . . you didn't telephone . . . I had no warning."

"Did you need warning?"

"Not necessarily."

"Then what's wrong with the place?"

"It's public."

"You picked it," Mason reminded him.

Gage opened a gate in the counter. "Won't you please step into my private office, Mr. Mason?"

Mason followed him down a thick carpet where there were further showcases on the sides, past two young women, who very frankly stopped the work they were doing to gawk at the lawyer as he walked past.

Gage held the door of his private office open, then, when Mason had entered, said, "Please be seated, Mr. Mason. I'm sorry you brought this up where the girls in the outer office could hear it."

"You left me no choice," Mason said.

"Well, perhaps I didn't . . . I'm sorry. I didn't appreciate the importance of your visit."

"I hope you appreciate it now."

"Well, Mr. Mason, the fact remains that an audit of the books shows that there is a very substantial shortage in our cash, and, of course, under the circumstances, we wanted to check on any of our employees who are absent."

"Diana Douglas was one?"

"Yes."

"Your uncle, Franklin Gage, is another?"

"Well, he's hardly an employee. He virtually owns the business."

"And Edgar Douglas is another?"

"Yes. He's in the hospital with a fractured skull. He has never regained consciousness since the accident. I'm afraid the prognosis is not good."

"Did you check on him, too?" Mason asked.

"We were hardly in a position to check on him. You can't question a man who is unconscious."

"So Diana Douglas was the only one you asked the police to check on?"

"Now, Mr. Mason, you're getting the cart before the horse. With a shortage of that sort showing up we quite naturally wanted to talk with Miss Douglas. That was our right. She's an employee of this company. We had assumed that she was absent from work because of the condition of her brother and was spending all of her time in the hospital with him, but inquiry disclosed that she had left rather suddenly for Los Angeles."

"And you asked the Los Angeles police to check on her?"

"The Los Angeles police were asked to try to get some information from her."

"You intimated that she might be an embezzler?"

"Certainly not, Mr. Mason. Don't try to put words in my mouth. We simply asked for a check-up."

"And how did you find out where she was staying in Los Angeles?"

"I'm afraid that's a confidential matter that I don't care to go into at the present time, Mr. Mason."

"All right," Mason said, "I just wanted you to know that I'm representing Miss Douglas; that we feel that her reputation has been damaged because she was accused of embezzlement, at least by inference, and because you asked the Los Angeles police to look her up. . . . Here is my card, Mr. Gage, and if you have any further matters to take up with Miss Douglas you can take them up with me."

"You mean she is finished working here?" Gage asked.

"That is something I'm not prepared to discuss," Mason said. "I am referring only to the case she has against you for defamation of character. I would suggest you get in touch with me if you have any further activities in mind."

"Come, come, Mr. Mason. There's no need to be belligerent. You don't need to come up here with a chip on your shoulder. Did you come up all the way from Los Angeles to tell us this?"

"Why not?" Mason asked.

"It seems so futile, so— Good heavens, we don't know where the money is. All we know is that there's a shortage."

"You're sure of that?"

"Apparently so. An amount of something over twenty thousand dollars seems to be missing from the cash."

"You keep an amount of that sort on hand in the form of ready cash?"

"Yes, indeed. We have a lot more than that."

"May I ask why?" Mason asked.

"I don't know why not," Gage said. "A lot of our deals are for cash, and a great many of them are made on weekends when the banks are closed."

"And on some of them you don't want any question of having left a backtrack?"

"No, no, no, it isn't that. It's simply that we've followed a policy of buying many times for cash and then, when the deal is completed, getting . . . well . . . establishing—"

"I'm afraid I don't understand," Mason interposed.

"It's rather difficult to understand, Mr. Mason, but there are various embargoes in various countries which must be—well, taken into account. For instance, in Mexico it is illegal to export ancient artifacts, yet there is a very brisk demand for such artifacts in this country."

"And these Mexican figurines have been smuggled out of Mexico?"

"I didn't say that, Mr. Mason. I was very careful *not* to say that. I was telling you something about the reasons that we have to have large supplies of cash in our business. There are certain questions we do not ask. And when you do not ask questions, cash does the talking."

"I'm afraid I don't understand," Mason said.

"Is it necessary that you should?"

"I think it is."

Gage flushed. "After all, Mr. Mason, I have explained to you as much of our business activities as I think is required under the circumstances."

"When you talk about using cash," Mason said, "in order to get figurines across the border, I take it that you are referring to bribery."

"Not at all," Gage said. "You're a lawyer. You should be able to put two and two together."

"Perhaps I have," Mason told him.

"Perhaps you put two and two together and came up with an entirely wrong answer," Gage warned.

"In that event," Mason told him, smiling affably, "you'll have a chance to explain in greater detail in court."

"Now, wait a minute, Mason, there's nothing to go to court about, and there's no reason for you and me to get at loggerheads."

Mason said nothing.

Gage took a deep breath. "Let me explain it this way, Mr. Mason. Mexico has an embargo on shipping ancient artifacts out of the country. On the other hand, there is no embargo in the United States on importing ancient artifacts. Therefore, if someone shows up with a station wagon full of figurines from Mexico, we don't have to determine at the time we complete the transaction whether the figurines are genuine or whether they are copies.

"You must realize that there's quite an industry in Mexico in copying ancient figurines and selling some of the copies to tourists, who quite frequently think they're getting a genuine prehistoric artifact."

"That still doesn't explain the cash," Mason said.

"Well," Gage went on, "put yourself in the position of the man who is driving the station wagon. He wants to sell the artifacts. He wants to get what he considers a good price for them. He knows how much he had to pay for them. He wants to make a profit. But when a man has a station wagon filled with figurines of this sort, it's only reasonable to suppose that he's in business. It isn't merely an isolated transaction.

"Under those circumstances he prefers to have no official record of the transaction. He prefers to deal on a cash-and-carry basis.

"Then there's the other end of things, the export of goods from Hong Kong where it is necessary to have a Certificate of Origin. Here again there are situations which require cold, hard cash, which is transferred by wire.

"Now, it's not necessary to make any more detailed explanation than that. We . . ."

Gage broke off as one of the secretaries entered the door.

"I beg your pardon," she said, "but Mr. Franklin Gage has just returned."

"Ask him to come in, please," Homer Gage said. "Tell him that Mr. Perry Mason, an attorney of Los Angeles, is here and that it may be we will have to consult our own legal department."

"Why don't you do that?" Perry Mason said. "I'd much prefer talking with an attorney."

"No, no, no, not yet. I simply wanted Mr. Franklin Gage to understand the situation. He . . . here he is now."

Mason turned. The tall, distinguished-looking gentleman who stood in the doorway wore an affable smile on the lower part of his face, but his eyes were appraising and unsmiling. They were eyes which were wide and round and somehow seemed to dominate the face.

He was in his late forties, wore rimless spectacles which seemed somehow to emphasize the rather wide eyes. The mouth was large, the lips rather thick, and the smile was that of a man who is accustomed to using suave tactics in getting what he wants out of life.

"Mr. Mason, Mr. Franklin Gage," Homer Gage said.

Mason stood up.

Franklin Gage gave him a hand which seemed cushioned with flesh, as though the man's body had built up a layer of insulation in the right hand.

"Ah, yes, Mr. Mason," Gage said, "I've heard a great deal about you. Your reputation is not confined to Los Angeles by any means. It's a pleasure to meet you. What can we do for you, Mr. Mason?"

Homer Gage was quick to answer that question. "Mr. Mason is calling about Diana Douglas," he said. "You'll remember she's been absent for the last three or four days.

"We weren't particularly busy at the time and I gave her some time off. Her brother was seriously injured in an automobile accident and has been unconscious."

"I understand he passed away early this morning," Mason said.

The two Gages exchanged glances.

"Good heavens!" Homer said.

"The poor kid," Franklin muttered sympathetically.

"I'm glad you told us," Homer Gage said.

Franklin Gage turned to his nephew. "The firm must send flowers, Homer."

"Certainly. I'll attend to that."

"And contact Diana and see if there's anything we can do. We must express our sympathies."

"I'm afraid Mr. Mason doesn't want us to have any direct contact with Diana," Homer Gage explained. "And even if he had no objections, I don't think it would be wise—not until we consult our lawyers."

"Nonsense!" Franklin Gage snapped. "We can certainly be guided by the humanities and plain decency."

"I think you'd better listen to Mr. Mason," Homer said.

"And why should that make any difference?" Franklin inquired, his voice now losing its tone of cordiality.

Homer rushed in with a hurried explanation. "Well, it seems that Diana Douglas made a quick trip to Los Angeles for some reason and somehow word got out that she had traveled under an assumed name.

"Then Stewart Garland, in checking the cash, said that there seemed to be quite a discrepancy—a rough estimate fixed this discrepancy at some twenty thousand dollars. Quite naturally, I wanted to find out about it and I wanted to interrogate Diana Douglas."

"You mean you interrogated her about the cash shortage?" Franklin Gage asked.

"Well, not directly," Homer said. "I may have acted rather hastily, but when I found she was registered at a hotel under an assumed name, I asked a very close friend of mine on the police force what to do about it and he said he'd arrange to have her interrogated by some friends of his in the Los Angeles Police Department.

"Mr. Mason seems to feel that what we did amounted to an accusation of embezzlement against her and constituted a defamation of character."

"Tut, tut," Franklin Gage said to Homer, "you shouldn't have jumped at conclusions. A lot of people have access to that cash drawer—the way we do business, you know. I, myself, had ten thousand dollars which I took from the cash drawer in order to complete a deal I was working on. Unfortunately, the deal fell through. I returned the cash a few minutes ago."

"That would seem to leave us with a shortage of only ten thousand dollars then," Homer Gage said, his manner greatly deflated.

"You can't tell if there's been any shortage until you check everything," the older man replied. "You know how that cash vault is. We keep large sums there and whenever any of the executives need money they simply take out what they need and then leave a note stating what they have taken out. And sometimes those notes aren't up-to-date. That is, if a man's in a hurry he won't bother to leave a note.

"In my case I was negotiating for a deal which, unfortunately, fell through. I took out ten thousand dollars and didn't leave any note stating I had done so. I had no idea that there was going to be all this talk of embezzlement. . . . The way we're organized, Homer, you should have waited until you got all of us together before you even had any idea of embezzlement or let any talk of that sort get started."

"I'm sorry, but Diana Douglas used an assumed name, went to Los Angeles, and registered in a hotel as Diana Deering. Under those circumstances I felt that we—"

"How did you find out about all this?" Franklin Gage asked.

"Well, frankly, *I* didn't find out about it," Homer Gage said, now quite apparently on the defensive and somewhat flustered. "I wanted to ask Diana about the cash and whether she had any slips that had been taken from the cash safe which she intended to post. . . . Well, I found she wasn't in her apartment. She wasn't at the hospital with her brother, although she had been there faithfully for some two or three hours right after the accident. Then she seemed to have disappeared.

"Well, I had this friend on the police force and I asked him how a man would go about locating a young woman under those circumstances and he said he'd run down a couple of leads.

"Well, of course, he used common sense, something which I could have done if I'd only thought of it. He knew that Diana was concerned about her brother, so he went to the hospital, interrogated the telephone operator, and found that calls had been coming in regularly from Los Angeles to find out about Edgar Douglas' condition. A number had been left to be notified if there was any change. The officer found that number was the number of the Willatson Hotel in Los Angeles and that a Diana Deering had put in the calls. By checking her description he soon had it pretty well established that Diana Deering was Diana Douglas, so then he suggested that it would be a good plan to question her because—well, you can see the position I was in."

"I'm not going to make any comment at this time," Franklin Gage said, "but Diana Douglas has been a very loyal employee and I have the utmost confidence in her integrity. I'm sorry that Mr. Mason has adopted the attitude that there has been any defamation of character. I also feel that we had better check up rather carefully on that cash situation before we talk about *any* shortage. . . . You will understand, Mr. Mason, that at times there is as much as a hundred thousand dollars in our cash safe."

Mason raised his eyebrows.

"I know that seems large to you," Franklin Gage went on, "but it seems small to us because this is a very unusual type of business. This isn't like dealing in automobiles where there is a registration number and a pink slip. In this business the person who has possession of the articles is to all intents and purposes the owner—unless, of course, he has stolen the articles—and that is a chance we have to take.

"However, we have a regular clientele with whom we do business, and we have been very fortunate in dealing in property which was not stolen."

"But smuggled?" Mason asked.

"I wouldn't know," Franklin Gage said, shaking his head. "I wouldn't want to know. And, of course, smuggling is only a minor crime. There are embargoes against exportation. If a shrewd operator ships a dozen figurines out of Mexico without alarming the Mexican authorities, and then presents them at the United States border as copies which he has picked up for a nominal consideration in a Tijuana curio store, nobody is going to bother about it because there *are* curio stores selling copies of ancient figurines.

"Then when they get to this country, if it should turn out that the figurines are actually genuine, ancient figurines, we certainly aren't going to ask how it happened that they were released from the embargo in Mexico. We simply say, 'How much?' And if the price is right and if we are satisfied as to the quality of the merchandise, we close the transaction."

"Then these ancient figurines in your display windows are copies?" Mason asked.

Franklin Gage shook his head. "We don't deal in copies, Mr. Mason. We deal in genuine, authentic articles."

"But they come across the border as copies?" Mason asked.

"We have no idea how they come across the border, Mr. Mason. . . .

"Now, may I say that we are genuinely concerned about Diana's misfortune, the loss of her brother. I know that they were very close. I take it that this is a poor time to communicate with her, but, after the funeral, Mr. Mason . . . I think you will agree with us that this whole discussion should be postponed until after the funeral?

"Personally, I don't see how any good can come of trying to intensify the feeling of grief, on the one hand, or of injured feelings on the other. Mr. Mason, I ask you please, as a favor to the company, as a personal favor, to hold this matter in abeyance for a few days. This is the end of the week and, as you say, Diana's brother has passed away. That will mean funeral arrangements, and the poor girl has— Homer, see if you can get her on the phone and ask her if she wants any money. Ask her if she needs an advance."

"Don't try it today," Mason said. "I have advised her to take sedation and shut off the telephone."

"Yes, yes, yes, I see," Franklin Gage said, "and, of course, tomorrow is Saturday, but— I think it might be a little better, Homer, if you had one of the other girls in the office—surely someone must know her intimately and have a friendship with her, someone who could ring up in a few hours and express our sympathy in a perfectly natural way."

Homer Gage shook his head. "Not Diana. She's something of a loner as far as the others are concerned, but I'll see what I can do."

Franklin Gage arose and again held out his flesh-cushioned hand to the lawyer. "So nice to have met you, Mr. Mason, and thank you so much for dropping in to tell us what you had in mind. I am quite certain that it won't be necessary for us to adopt any adversary position—not that I agree with you in any way, but—well, we'll work out something somewhere along the line.

"And please don't get the idea that we are engaged in an unusual type of business. I can assure you that every importing and exporting business these days has problems, Mr. Mason, and I think everyone has contacts."

"What do you mean, contacts?" Mason asked.

"Well, brokers," Franklin Gage said with a wave of his hand. "You know, Mr. Mason, we don't give money to every Tom, Dick, and Harry who shows up with a load of curios. But we have certain people with whom we deal, and those people, in turn, deal with other people and . . . well, it's not at all unusual for me to walk out of here, picking up five, ten, or perhaps fifteen thousand dollars in cash and contacting one of our brokers who will have a shipment of curios that we feel we can dispose of at a profit—Mexican figurines, carved ivories, or good jade.

"We know that the broker is only a middleman, and, of course, he is making a profit on the deal. We try to see that his profit is not exorbitant, but, on the other hand, we want him to make a fair profit because in this business everyone has to make a fair profit. . . . Well, you can understand how it is."

"I see," Mason said.

Homer Gage did not offer to shake hands. He stood somewhat aloof and dignified.

Franklin Gage held the door open for Mason. "Thank you again for coming in, Mr. Mason. It's nice that you felt free to come and explain the situation to us. I feel that it can be worked out. Good day, Mr. Mason."

"Good day," Mason said.

The lawyer walked across the office and, on his way out, paused momentarily at the counter to look at a piece of the carved ivory which claimed his attention. A small slip of folded paper had been placed by the carved ivory figure. The slip of paper had Mason's name typed on it.

Mason leaned forward to study the figure more closely. As he did so his right hand unostentatiously closed over the paper. When he straightened he placed the folded paper in the right-hand side pocket of his coat.

Mason went through the gate to the outer display room and paused again to look at some of the figurines in the outer cases.

"They're really very beautiful," the girl at the switchboard said, smiling at him.

"Indeed they are," Mason said. "They grow on you."

The lawyer left the office, walked out to the corridor, and half-way to the elevator removed the small piece of paper from his pocket. A typewritten message was in his hand when he unfolded the paper.

The message read:

> Don't let them pull the wool over your eyes.
> Diana is on the level and tops. There are
> things going on here that they don't want you
> to know about. Be sure to protect Diana.

The message was unsigned.

Mason folded the typewritten slip of paper, put it back into his pocket, went to his hotel, and checked out.

Chapter Eleven

On Monday morning Mason fitted a key in the lock of his private office and swung back the door.

"Well, hello, stranger!" Della Street said.

Mason smiled. "It isn't *that* bad!"

"Pretty close to it, what with running up and down to San Francisco and working with detectives. What do you know?"

"Not a darn thing," Mason said, "except that this Diana Douglas is a problem. I feel like throwing her out."

"Why don't you?"

"Well," Mason said, "I have a professional obligation."

"She's lied to you all the way along the line," Della Street said. "And when she hasn't been lying, she's tried to conceal things."

"I know," Mason said, "but the poor kid certainly was all wrapped up in her brother."

"The one that had the automobile accident?"

"He died early Friday morning," Mason said. "I guess the funeral is this morning. I told Diana to take some sleeping pills Friday; to go to sleep and forget the whole mess."

"And you went to see the Escobar Import and Export Company?"

"I met a couple of very interesting men," Mason said. "I'd like to know something about the inside operation of that company. I met Homer Gage and Franklin Gage and there you have a couple of real characters."

"Smooth?"

"Puzzling. . . . Homer Gage has to control himself with an effort every once in a while. Franklin Gage is synthetically suave. He gives you the impression of having tried all of his life to keep from showing his real feelings. When he shakes hands with you you feel there's a cushion of flesh on his hand, a sort of sponge-rubber insulation that he uses to keep any magnetic current from penetrating."

"From him to you?" Della asked.

Mason thought for a moment, then smiled and said, "Both ways. . . . We're getting into a deep subject, Della, but somehow when you shake hands with a man you can tell a lot about him from his grip. There's a certain magnetic something you can feel."

"I know," she said. "Some hands are firm and sincere and others are—well, sort of evasive; it's hard to describe."

Mason was thoughtful. "Shaking hands is a peculiar custom. It consists in clasping a part of two bodies together so that a vibration or magnetism or whatever you want to call it is exchanged from one to the other. . . . Well, we'd better go to work."

Della Street shook her head. "You had two appointments for this morning, and when I didn't hear from you Friday afternoon I canceled them."

"I should have let you know," Mason said, "but I got up there and had this session with the Escobar Import and Export Company and I had a peculiar experience."

"What?"

"One of the stenographers left this note with my name on it beside a piece of carved ivory I had been looking at."

"Oh, oh," Della Street said. "So that's why you stayed over in San Francisco Friday night!"

Mason grinned. "It wasn't that kind of a note. Take a look."

The lawyer took the note from his notebook. Della Street looked at it, said, "I think it was done on an electric typewriter. Did you notice which of the secretaries had electric typewriters?"

"I didn't," Mason said. "I was noticing the decorations in the office—figurines, carved ivories, jade. They must have had half a million dollars' worth of stuff on display."

"Did they offer you anything at a discount?"

"Wholesale only," Mason said thoughtfully. "I'd like to know something about who their customers are and I'd like to know a lot more about where they get their stuff. . . . You say you canceled all my appointments for this morning?"

"That's right. They weren't important, and I rang up Friday afternoon and canceled."

Mason said, "After I got out of the Import and Export Company I went out to Fisherman's Wharf and had a good crab lunch—or I guess you'd call it dinner—and then went down to the airport. . . . Friday afternoon at a San Francisco airport. I was lucky to get home at all. I didn't get in until five-fifteen and then I didn't want to bother you. . . . I'm going down to Paul Drake's office and see if our stakeout has heard anything."

"Our stakeout?"

"Stella Grimes," Mason said, "the operative who's registered under the name of Diana Deering at the Willatson Hotel. Somehow I have an idea we may be a bit behind on developments.

"For your information Franklin Gage seemed to adopt a rather casual attitude toward a shortage of twenty thousand dollars. Actually it was only ten thousand, because Franklin had taken out ten thousand to use in a business deal that he hadn't consummated, and he had put the money back when he came in the office Friday morning."

"But he reported what he had done?"

"Yes, as soon as his nephew told him there was a shortage."

"Well, that was opportune," Della Street said.

Mason nodded. "The way they keep their cash is certainly cool and casual. I have an idea that Franklin Gage would a lot rather absorb a reasonable loss than have the matter come into court where he would be cross-examined about the reason they keep such a large amount of cash on hand and what they do with it. . . . There could be an income-tax angle there, too . . . and I'm willing to bet there's a lot of customs regulations that are being by-passed."

"You think they're smuggling?"

"I think people with whom they deal are smuggling, and there's an atmosphere of complete irregularity about the whole thing. . . . Some of those art objects they have on display are *really* beautiful. . . . I'm going down and have a chat with Paul Drake for a minute, Della. I think he's in this morning. Then I'll come back and get my nose ready for the grindstone."

"You have three rather important appointments this afternoon," she reminded him.

"Okay," Mason said, "I'll take a quick look; then back to the salt mines. . . . I guess Edgar Douglas' funeral is this morning. After that we may hear from Diana. And then again we may never hear from her again. I have an idea our Franklin Gage will be at the funeral, and he may tell Diana the whole embezzlement idea was a false alarm.

"Diana certainly looked a wreck. She had taken a plane up from Los Angeles, gone to the hospital, was with her brother when he died about three o'clock in the morning; then had to make funeral arrangements and meet me at the Escobar Import and Export Company at ten-thirty and—say, wait a minute, I told her to get a cashier's check. She had it for me."

Mason took the leather wallet from his inside coat pocket, pulled out several papers, and said, "Well, here it is. A cashier's check made by the Farmers' Financial Bank of San Francisco to Diana Douglas as trustee in an amount of five thousand dollars. She may have cut corners with us, Della, but she followed instructions on that check at a time when her heart must have been torn to ribbons. She was really fond of that brother of hers. I guess she's sort of been a mother to him as well as a sister. . . . If anything turns up in the next ten minutes, I'll be down at Paul Drake's office."

"No hurry," Della Street said. "I'll call if there's anything important."

Mason walked down the corridor to the offices of the Drake Detective Agency, said hello to the girl at the switchboard, and jerked his thumb in the direction of Paul Drake's office.

She smiled in recognition, nodded, and said, "He's in. He's on the phone at the moment. Go on down."

Mason opened the spring-locked gate in the partition which divided the waiting room from the offices and walked down the long corridor, flagged by little offices in which Drake's operatives made out their reports, until he came to Drake's office.

Paul Drake was sitting in his little cubbyhole behind a desk on which were several telephones. He was just completing a telephone conversation when Mason opened the door.

The detective indicated a chair and said, "Hi, Perry. This is intended as a place of command from which to direct multitudinous activities, not as a place of consultation."

Mason settled himself in the chair. "What have you got on those phones—a hot line to police headquarters?"

"Darned near," Drake said. "We handle a lot of the stuff at the switchboard, but on delicate assignments when we have cars cruising with telephones in them, there are lots of times when there just isn't time to go through a switchboard. I give the operatives an unlisted number. They can call me direct and be absolutely certain that they're going to get me here."

"But suppose you're not here?" Mason asked.

"Then there's a signal on the switchboard and the switchboard can pick it up, but I'm usually here. When you run a job like this you have to sit on top of it, and that's particularly true with men who are cruising with cars that have telephones. . . . What's on your mind, Perry?"

"This thirty-six-twenty-four-thirty-six case," Mason said. "Diana Douglas is the sort of girl who will go to a doctor to get medicine for the flu; then go home, take the advice of the janitor, take two aspirins with a hot lemonade, and throw out the doctor's medicine. Then a friend will drop in who'll tell her that what she needs is a lot of vitamin C and whiskey; so she'll take five hundred units of vitamin C and a hot toddy. Then somebody will tell her she needs hot tea and quinine and she'll take that. Then when the doctor comes to see how she's getting along she'll push the whiskey bottle and the teapot under the bed so he won't know she's taken anything on her own and say, 'Doctor, I feel terrible!' "

Drake grinned. "You're just describing human nature, Perry. What's she done now?"

"Nothing," Mason said. "She was very, very much attached to her brother who was in that automobile accident. He passed away early Friday morning. But up to that point our little Miss Douglas did all kinds of things, or rather didn't do all kinds of things. She was supposed to go up to San Francisco with me on the plane, but she didn't make it. She said she had a feeling that someone was following her.

"Ordinarily I'd have accepted that as the gospel truth, but in view of her record I'm inclined to doubt it. Anyway, Paul, we'd better get our double out of the Willatson Hotel, and then we'll sit tight on the case for a while."

"Can you tell me any more about it without violating ethics?" Drake asked.

Mason shook his head. "Remember, Paul, I was your client in this case and all that you found out about Diana Douglas came from the detective work you did.

"Let's give Stella Grimes a jingle. Tell her to pack up and come on home."

Drake picked up the telephone, said, "Call the Willatson Hotel and get Room Seven-sixty-seven for me."

A moment later he said, "Hello, Stella. I guess the job's over. You'd better pack up and— What's that? . . . Are you sure. . . ?

"Hold on a minute, Stella."

Drake looked up at Mason and said, "Stella thinks there's something funny going on. She went out to get breakfast and a man followed her. She's pretty certain there's a man on duty at the end of the seventh-floor corridor keeping an eye on the elevator."

Mason looked at his watch. "Tell her we're on our way down there, Paul."

"Gosh, Perry, I can't get away. I can send an operative if—"

"I can handle it," Mason said. "I just thought you might like to go along. I'm free this morning, and if our friend Moray Cassel has got one of his little larcenous friends waiting to throw a scare into the occupant of Room Seven-sixty-seven, it'll be my great pleasure to tell the guy where he gets off."

"Take it easy, Perry," Drake warned. "Some of these guys are vicious."

"I'm vicious myself," Mason said, "when some s.o.b. starts shoving a woman around."

Mason left Drake's office, said to the girl at Drake's switchboard, "Ring my office, will you please, and tell Della Street that I'm out on an errand for an hour, that I'll be back then."

"An errand?" the girl at the switchboard asked. "Just that?"

"Well," Mason said, grinning, "you can tell her it's an errand of mercy. Also, if she gets inquisitive, tell her that I've had to sit in a position of command and let the troops do the fighting for so long that I'm getting rusty. I think I need to get out on the firing line myself."

"You want me to tell her that?"

"On second thought," Mason said, "you'd better not. Tell her that I'll be back in an hour."

The lawyer took the elevator to the ground floor, picked up a taxicab, gave the address of the Willatson Hotel, went up to the seventh floor, and noticed a man with a hammer and chisel doing some work at the end of the hall. Otherwise he saw no one.

The lawyer walked down to Room 767, tapped gently on the door, and said, "Oh, Diana."

Stella Grimes opened the door. "Come in, Mr. Mason. And don't ever give me any more assignments like this one."

Mason said, "You mean you're alarmed because somebody is following you?"

"Heavens, no," she said, "I'm bored stiff. Did you ever sit in a hotel room hour after hour waiting for something to happen and nothing happens? You turn on the radio and have a choice of two stations. You listen to a lot of inane jabbering until you get tired. You move from one chair to another. You have meals served in your room, and don't leave the phone because you're afraid that someone may want you on something important. You don't dare to call up anyone because you don't want to tie the telephone line up in case the boss wants you. I'll bet I've slept enough in the last two or three days to last me for a month. I went out this morning for the first time in days. The chambermaid was getting suspicious, so I phoned the office switchboard that I'd be out for forty-five minutes and went out for some air.

"Next time I hope you can give me a job that's got some action to it."

"Where you'll have a chance to use your official bra?" Mason asked.

She smiled and said, "I never have had to actually *use* it. I've pulled it a couple of times when the going got tough. I . . ." She broke off as knuckles sounded on the door.

"Don't tell me nothing ever happens," Mason said. "We're calling things off too soon. Even money that's our friend Moray Cassel."

"And if he finds me here again?"

"Look guilty," Mason said. "Be the party of the second part in a surreptitious assignation. . . . And then be very careful. The guy will want to sign you up as a part of his stable of girls."

Knuckles sounded heavily on the door again. Mason nodded to Stella Grimes. "It's your room," he said.

She crossed over and opened the door.

Two men who were standing on the threshold pushed their way into the room. They were not the same officers who had called previously.

"Is this your credit card?" one of the men said. "Did you lose it?"

He handed Stella Grimes a BankAmericard credit card, then saw Mason and said, "Who's your friend?"

"Better ask your questions one at a time," Stella Grimes said. "Which comes first?"

One of the men turned belligerently to Perry Mason, said, "Who are you?"

The other man kept pushing the credit card at Stella Grimes. "All right," he said, "*is* it your credit card or *isn't* it?"

Stella Grimes glanced at Mason, said, "This seems to be a Bank-Americard credit card issued to Diana Douglas."

"Is it yours or isn't it?"

"I . . ."

"Don't answer that," Mason said, his voice sharp as the crack of a whip.

"Now, just a minute, Mac," the man said, "you're sticking your nose into a . . ."

"Wait a minute, wait a minute, Bill," the second man warned, "this is a lawyer. I recognize him now. This is Perry Mason."

"What the hell are you doing here?" the man asked.

"What are *you* doing here?" Mason countered.

"We're trying to find out whether this credit card is the property of this young woman."

"A credit card made out to Diana Douglas?" Mason asked.

"That's right. Diana Douglas."

Mason, suddenly thoughtful, said, "If you are investigating any crime it is incumbent that you warn the suspect and tell her of her constitutional rights."

"All right," the man said, "we're plain-clothes police. Homicide squad. Here are our credentials."

He took a leather folder from his pocket, opened it, and displayed a badge and an I.D. card. "Now then, young lady, you're entitled to remain silent if you want to. If you answer questions anything you say may be used against you. You're entitled to have an attorney at all stages of the proceedings."

"She has an attorney," Mason said. "I'm her lawyer. Now, tell her the specific crime of which she is accused."

"She isn't accused of anything yet," the man said, "but we're following a hot lead. For your information we want to question her about the murder of Moray Cassel, who lived in the Tallmeyer Apartments in Apartment Nine-o-six. Now then, you want to talk or don't you?"

"Just a minute," Mason said, "let me think."

"You'd better think fast," the man said. "We're not out to frame anything on anybody, but unless this young lady can explain what her credit card was doing in the apartment with the murdered man she's in trouble. If she can explain it, we're perfectly willing to listen and to check on any leads she gives us."

Mason said, "When was this man, Cassel, murdered?"

"Now, *you're* asking questions," the man said. "We're the ones who are asking questions, and we want some answers fast."

Mason said, "If you want some answers fast, you'd better grab that man at the end of the hall who's working down there with a hammer and chisel and find out where *he* fits into the picture."

The man grinned and said, "Don't worry, buddy, he's one of our men. We've had this room under surveillance since early this morning, hoping that somebody would come in. We were sort of looking for a male accomplice. You triggered our visit."

Mason said to Stella Grimes, "Show him your credentials, Stella."

Stella Grimes reached for her purse.

"Now, take it easy, you two," one of the officers said, "nothing fast or there's going to be a *lot* of trouble. Just hand *me* your purse, sister, and I'll look in it first."

She handed him the purse. He looked through it, then handed it back to her and said, "Okay, pull out your credentials."

Stella Grimes pulled out her license as a private detective.

Mason said, "For your information, I'm baiting a trap myself. Stella Grimes is a private detective, an employee of the Drake Detective Agency, and she's been here masquerading as Diana Deering from San Francisco."

The officer regarded the credentials thoughtfully. Then said, "And Diana Deering is an alias for Diana Douglas?"

"I didn't say that," Mason said.

"You didn't have to."

There was a moment of silence. Mason said, "I believe I have a professional obligation as an attorney and as a citizen to cooperate with the police in investigating serious charges.

"Since you apparently thought this was Diana Douglas I advised you as to her true identity and occupation. That's as far as we're going."

"Why did you want a double?" the officer asked.

"No comment."

"Anything to do with Moray Cassel?"

"No comment."

"Now, look," the officer said, "if this Diana Douglas happens to be your client—oh, oh, that's the angle, Bill. . . . Or is it?"

The officer addressed as Bill disgustedly pushed the credit card back in his pocket. "Well," he said, "we've tipped our hand now."

The other officer said to Mason, "Any attempt on your part to communicate with Diana Douglas will be considered as a hostile act by law-enforcement officers and may make you an accessory."

Mason said to Stella Grimes, "Take the phone, Stella, put through a call for Diana Douglas."

The officer called Bill threw a shoulder block and pushed her out of the way of the telephone. He picked up the phone, said to the operater, "This is a police emergency call. Get me police headquarters in San Francisco immediately."

The second officer stood guard, protecting the telephone.

A moment later the officer at the telephone said, "This is the Los Angeles police, Bill Ardley talking. We want you to pick up a Diana Douglas for questioning. She works for the Escobar Import and Export Company. She has a BankAmericard credit card issued in her name. . . . You folks gave us a tip that she was in Los Angeles at the Willatson Hotel, registered as Diana Deering. That's a bum steer. She's probably in San Francisco at the present time. Pick her up for questioning, and then notify us in Room Seven-sixty-seven at the Willatson Hotel. . . . You got my name okay? This is Bill Ardley of—Oh, you know me, eh? . . . That's right, I worked with you a year ago on that Smith case. . . . Well, that's fine. I'll appreciate anything you can do. Get on this immediately, will you? And when you pick her up ask her first rattle out of the box where her BankAmericard credit card is. If she says she lost it, find out when she lost it. . . . Okay. G'by."

The officer depressed the connecting lever with his finger rapidly several times until he got the hotel operator. Then he said, "This is the Los Angeles police, operator. Put this phone out of service until we stop by the switchboard and give you instructions to the contrary. We'll take all incoming calls. No outgoing calls, no matter who makes the call, unless it's identified as being police business. You got that? Okay."

The officer hung up the telephone, settled himself spraddle-legged across one of the straight-back chairs. "Okay, my lawyer friend," he said, "now suppose *you* start doing a little talking."

"On the other hand, suppose I don't," Mason said.

"We wouldn't like that," the officer said.

"Start not liking it, then," Mason said. "I'm leaving."

"Oh, no, you aren't! Not for a while."

"Do I take it," Mason asked, "that you're intending to hold us here?"

The officer smiled affably, nodded. "I'm going to do the best I can."

"Now, that might not be very smart," Mason said. "If you put me under arrest you're laying yourself open for suit for unlawful arrest, and this young woman is—"

"Take it easy," the officer interrupted. "I'm making this play for your own good. You may thank me for it later—both of you."

"That credit card," Mason said, "is that a clue in the murder?"

The officer said, "What do you think of the Dodgers' chances this year?"

"Pretty good," Mason said.

"Now then," the officer went on, "we'd like to know when was the last time you saw Diana Douglas, what you talked about at that time, and what you told her."

"You know I can't betray the confidence of a client," Mason said. "What do *you* think of the Dodgers' chances?"

"Pretty good," the officer said. He turned to Stella Grimes. "You don't have any professional immunity," he said. "You're a private detective, you have a license. You have to cooperate with the police. What brought you here?"

Stella Grimes looked helplessly at Mason.

"He's right," Mason said, "tell him."

She said, "Mr. Mason telephoned the Drake Detective Agency where I work and asked for me to come over here and to go under the name of Diana Deering, and if anyone asked for me at the desk using the code figures thirty-six twenty-four thirty-six I was to answer."

"Anybody come?" the officer asked.

Again she looked at Mason.

"Tell him," Mason said. "You're a witness. He's investigating a homicide."

She said, "A man came here and acted rather peculiarly."

"In what way?"

"He acted as if he might be trying to put across some sort of a blackmail scheme."

"And what did you tell him?"

She said, "I didn't tell him anything. I let Mr. Mason do the talking."

"And what did Mr. Mason tell him?"

"I wouldn't know. I left the room. I got a signal to act as Mr. Mason's girl friend who had been enjoying a rendezvous in the hotel and I went over to him, kissed him, and walked out."

"Leaving Mason and this man alone?"

"Yes."

"What did the man look like?"

"He was about—well, in his middle thirties. He had slick, black hair and was—well groomed. His trousers were creased. His shoes were shined, his nails manicured."

The officer frowned. "Did that man give you any name?" he asked.

Again she looked at Mason.

Mason nodded.

"He said his name was Cassel."

"I'll be damned," the officer muttered.

There was silence for several seconds. Then the officer said, "So, you left the room and left Mason and this man alone here?"

"That's right."

"Where did you go?"

"Tell him," Mason said.

She said, "Mr. Mason gave me a coded signal to follow the man who left here. I found it was absurdly easy. He had parked his Cadillac automobile right in front of the entrance and had tipped the doorman to take care of it for him. I got the license number of the automobile. It was WVM five-seven-four. I hopped in a taxicab, and when this man came out and got in his Cadillac automobile I told the cab driver to follow."

"And you followed him?"

"Yes."

"To where?"

"To the Tallmeyer Apartments."

"Then what?"

"Then I used a few evasive tactics so I didn't lay myself wide open to the taxi driver so he could pick up a good fee by tipping off the driver of the Cadillac that he had been followed."

"Then what?"

"Then I came back and reported."

The officer looked at Mason. "Take it from there, Mason," he said.

Mason said, "I'm an attorney, acting in a professional capacity, representing a client. I have no information in which you would be interested except that I have no comment on what this young woman has said."

"But," the officer said, "you immediately traced the license number of that automobile, did you not?"

"No comment."

"And found out it was registered to Moray Cassel in Apartment Nine-o-six at the Tallmeyer Apartments?"

"No comment."

"And," the officer went on, "if it appears that you passed that information on to Diana Douglas we've got just about the most perfect, airtight murder case you ever encountered. Even the great Mason isn't going to beat this one."

"Still no comment," Mason said.

The officer took out a pack of cigarettes, selected one, offered a smoke to Stella Grimes, then to Mason, and last to his brother officer.

"Well," he said, "we seem to have uncovered a live lead."

They smoked in silence, the officer quite evidently thinking over the information Stella Grimes had given him.

There was more desultory conversation for some twenty minutes. Then the phone rang. The officer answered the phone. A slow smile spread over his face.

"Okay," he said.

He turned to Mason and waved toward the door. "You and this young woman are as free as the air," he said. "Go any place you want."

Mason held the door open for Stella Grimes. "Bring your things," he said. "We've finished. That means they've picked her up in San Francisco."

Chapter Twelve

Perry Mason sat on the edge of the seat of the taxicab counting the minutes until the driver reached his office building. Then he tossed the driver a five-dollar bill, said, "Keep the change, cabbie. Thanks for speeding it up as much as possible."

The lawyer sprinted across the foyer of the building into the elevator, then hurried down the hallway to his office.

"Well, hello!" Della Street said as he made an explosive entrance into his private office. "What's the rush?"

"Heard anything from Diana Douglas?" Mason asked.

She shook her head.

"Any collect call from San Francisco?"

Again she shook her head.

Mason sighed his relief, picked up the telephone, said to Gertie, "If any call comes in from San Francisco reversing the charges, I'll take it. Put the call right through to me."

The lawyer settled back in the swivel chair at his desk, took a deep breath, and said, "If we don't hear within the next fifteen minutes, we'll call the San Francisco police and make a demand on them, and if that doesn't do the trick we'll start a writ of *habeas corpus* in San Francisco."

"What's happened?"

"They've arrested Diana Douglas."

"On the embezzlement?"

Mason shook his head. "The embezzlement is a minor matter," he said, "although they *may* try to arrest her on the embezzlement so they can hold her up there in the hope that she'll talk. If they do that I'm going to have to get right back to San Francisco in a hurry. . . . The charge they are putting against her is the murder of Moray Cassel."

"What!" Della exclaimed.

Mason nodded. "Somebody got into Moray Cassel's apartment, killed him, and made an exit."

"And the police think it was Diana Douglas?"

Mason nodded.

"When was this done?" she asked.

"There's something of a problem. The police will probably try to show it was done Thursday afternoon. The body probably wasn't discovered until today. That's going to make a ticklish problem with experts giving various opinions, contradicting each other, and all of the stuff that goes with it."

Della Street was thoughtful for a moment, "And our client was to have met you on the plane Thursday night at six twenty-seven and didn't show up?"

Mason nodded.

"Do you suppose there's any chance she could have been—But no, she isn't that kind of a girl."

"How do you know she isn't?" Mason asked.

"You have ideas?" Della Street asked.

Mason said thoughtfully, "When I saw her in San Francisco she told me that when she got to the airport she didn't have her credit card which she intended to use to pay for her ticket. Then she remembered that I had ordered two tickets charged to my account, so she picked up one of those tickets and said she'd adjust with me."

"And?" Della Street asked, as Mason hesitated.

"And," Mason said, "two officers from homicide showed up at the Willatson Hotel, barged in on Stella Grimes, shoved a BankAmericard credit card made out to Diana Douglas at her, and asked her to please identify the card."

"Did she?"

Mason said, "I stepped into the picture, told her to keep quiet, and then it suddenly developed we were playing for much bigger stakes than the embezzlement. This was a murder investigation and I didn't dare to carry on the deception any longer. So I had Stella Grimes identify herself to the officers, and then they rushed through a call to San Francisco as soon as they got the sketch and left orders to pick up Diana Douglas immediately on a charge of homicide."

"And you're expecting she'll telephone you?"

Mason nodded. "If she'll just follow instructions for once, keep her head, and keep her mouth shut—but they're going to bring her down here and really try to work her over."

"And so we enter into the picture?" Della Street asked.

"We enter into the picture," Mason said. "We—"

He broke off as his phone rang, and, motioning to Della to monitor the conversation in shorthand, Mason picked up the receiver and said, "Perry Mason talking."

A harsh voice said, "You're attorney for Diana Douglas, an employee of Escobar Import and Export Company?"

"Right."

"She's under arrest and is asking for an opportunity to communicate with you. We've given her that opportunity."

"Put her on," Mason said.

"It's a collect call," the official voice reminded.

"Quite right," Mason said.

A moment later Diana's frightened voice said, "Mr. Mason, I don't understand. They're charging me, they claim that—"

"Shut up," Mason said. "Don't talk. Listen!"

"Yes, Mr. Mason."

Mason said, "They're going to charge you with the murder of Moray Cassel. They will offer to take you before a magistrate in San Francisco before taking you to Los Angeles. I want you brought down here. Keep your mouth shut. Don't say anything to anyone about anything. Just use two words, 'No comment', and then add, 'I answer no questions. I make no statements except in the presence of my attorney, Perry Mason.' Can you remember that?"

"Yes."

"Can you do it?"

"I think so."

"Let me talk to the officer in charge," Mason said.

A moment later the official voice came on the line once more.

Mason said, "I'm attorney for Diana Douglas. I have instructed her to make no statement except in my presence. We waive any hearing in San Francisco in favor of a hearing before a magistrate in Los Angeles County. We make no objection to being transported from San Francisco to Los Angeles. Aside from that we make no stipulations, no admissions, no concessions, and as attorney for Miss Douglas I insist that I be present at all interviews and at all questioning. I wish to be notified the moment she arrives in Los Angeles."

"If you'd let us talk things over with her, we might be able to straighten this out," the officer said. "We don't want to bring her down to Los Angeles unless there's some real reason for it. If she can explain some of the circumstantial evidence in the case, and I certainly hope she can because she's a very nice young woman who seems to have had a lot of trouble lately, we'll turn her loose."

"That's certainly nice of you," Mason said. "It's a wonderful line. It's caused a lot of people to talk themselves into prison. For your information, I have instructed Diana Douglas not to talk unless I am present, and I am instructing you not to interrogate her except in my presence. I don't want her interrogated by anybody unless I am there. I am making a record of this conversation so that any further attempts to get information from Miss Douglas will be a violation of her constitutional rights. I think you understand the situation."

"Well, as her attorney, will you explain certain things that we'd like to clear up?" the officer asked.

"I explain nothing," Mason said.

"Do you know when your client first noticed that her Bank-Americard credit card was missing?"

Mason laughed into the telephone.

"What's so funny?" the officer at the other end of the line asked.

"You are," Mason said, and hung up.

Chapter Thirteen

In the consultation room at the County Jail, Diana regarded Mason with tear-swollen eyes.

"Have you had any trouble with the police?" Mason asked.

"They've been wonderful to me," she said, "just so kind and considerate and—Mr. Mason, it wouldn't hurt to tell them certain things, would it?"

"What things?"

"Well, about finding the money and about Edgar and about why I put the ad in the paper and—"

"And where would you stop?" Mason asked.

"Well, I suppose I'd have to stop somewhere. I suppose you'd want me to."

"Of course," Mason said, "you wouldn't want to talk yourself right into the gas chamber. You'd want to stop sometime before you got there, but the trouble is you wouldn't know where to stop."

"Yes," she said, "I suppose I'd have to, but they've been so nice and considerate and—"

"Sure," Mason said, "that's part of the technique. With some

108

people they're nice and considerate. With some women they're perfectly gentlemanly and fatherly. Then, if that doesn't work, they try the other tactic. They become hard-boiled and try all sorts of things.

"In recent years the courts have frowned on some of these police tactics, and the result is that they try to work up a case by getting the evidence rather than forcing the defendant to incriminate himself. But if anyone is willing to talk they're always willing to listen and many a person has talked himself right into the penitentiary, and I mean many an innocent person. He's made statements without knowing all of the facts."

"But I know all the facts," she said.

"Do you?"

"Yes."

"Who killed Moray Cassel?"

She winced at the question.

"Did you?" Mason asked.

"No."

Mason said, "Look here, Diana, you can be frank with me. I'm the only one you can be frank with. It's my duty to see that you have a defense whether you're innocent or guilty.

"Now then, you were to meet me on that six twenty-seven plane Thursday night. You didn't do it. I saw you the next morning and you had quite a story about having been followed by someone whom you couldn't shake off, someone who frightened you so you resorted to all sorts of evasive tactics and got there too late to catch the plane.

"Actually, you didn't even try to catch that plane. That story that you made up about someone following you was a lie to account for what you had done with your time.

"I gave you the information that the blackmailer was Moray Cassel. I gave you his address. You decided that I was never going to pay off a blackmailer and that might not be the thing that your brother wanted. So, you took it on yourself to second-guess my play. You took a taxicab to the Tallmeyer Apartments. You went up to see Moray Cassel. While you were up there something happened. You opened your purse, perhaps to take out a gun. When you opened your purse, your BankAmericard credit card fell out and you didn't miss it at the time.

"Later on you went to the airport. You wanted to buy your ticket to San Francisco and pay for it yourself, and that was when you missed your BankAmericard credit card for the first time.

"Now then, the police either know this much or surmise this much or can get evidence which will come pretty close to proving this much."

She shook her head.

"Yes, they can," Mason said. "The police are unbelievably clever. You have no idea what dogged footwork will accomplish in an investigation. They'll find the cab driver who took you to the Tallmeyer Apartments."

She gave a sudden, quick intake of her breath.

"Oh, oh," Mason said, "that hurt. . . . You little fool, do you mean that you took a cab directly to the Tallmeyer Apartments and didn't try to cover your tracks?"

"I was in a terrible hurry," she said. "I wanted to see him and then catch that plane with you. I thought I had time enough to pay him a quick visit and if . . . well, if . . . I was going to use my own judgment."

"In other words," Mason said, "if you felt that you could clean up the whole business with a five-thousand-dollar pay-off instead of putting that five thousand dollars into the bank and getting a check to yourself as trustee, you were going to pay him the five thousand dollars and try to make a deal with him by which your brother would be out of trouble."

"Well, yes . . ."

"Why didn't you do it?" Mason said.

"Because he was dead."

"Go on," Mason told her.

She said, "I got into the apartment house. It was one of those hotel-type apartment houses where they have a doorman on duty at the elevator, but he was busy parking a car for somebody and I slipped right on by him into the elevator. I went up to the ninth floor. I found apartment nine-o-six. I tapped on the door.

"Nothing happened, so I tapped again and when nothing happened I tried the knob. I don't know what in the world possessed me to do that but I did and the door opened and . . ."

"Just a minute," Mason said, "were you wearing gloves?"

"I . . . no."

Mason sighed and shook his head. "Go on," he said.

"I got in there and at first I didn't see him. I didn't see anybody, but I said, 'Who-whoo, is anybody home?' and walked in. And then I saw him lying there on his back on the bed. Oh, Mr. Mason, it was terrible, terrible. Everything was soaked in blood and . . ."

"Was he dead?" Mason asked.

She nodded.

"How do you know?"

"I picked up his hand and it was cold."

"Then what did you do?"

"I ran out."

"No, you didn't," Mason said. "You opened your purse. Why did you open your purse?"

"Heavens, I don't know, Mr. Mason. I . . . it's just . . . I suppose I was crying or something and wanted a handkerchief. . . . I can't begin to tell you how I felt. It was . . . I was almost nauseated."

Mason said, "You damn little liar. I have a notion to grab you by the shoulders and shake the truth out of you. Why did you open your purse?"

"I've told you, Mr. Mason. I've told you the truth."

Mason said, "You either opened your purse to take out a gun or to put a gun into it. Which was it?"

She looked at him with sullen resentment. "You always try to cross-examine me!"

"Because you always try to lie to me," Mason said. "Which was it?"

"I picked up the gun," she said.

"That's better," Mason told her. "Now, why did you pick up the gun?"

"Because it was Edgar's gun."

"How do you know it was?"

"I know it. He had a twenty-two revolver that he used to carry with him when he'd go out on his fishing trips on account of rattlesnakes and things of that sort. It had a polished wooden handle or grip, or whatever you call it, and a little piece was chipped out and . . .

"Mr. Mason, it was Edgar's gun. I know it when I see it. Edgar always wanted to teach me to shoot, and I've shot that gun hundreds of times."

"So you picked up the gun and put it in your purse?" Mason said. She nodded.

"And then what?"

"Then I tiptoed out of the room."

"And what did you do with the gun?"

"I'm all right on that, Mr. Mason. Nobody's ever going to find that gun. You can rest assured of that."

"They may not need to find it," Mason said.

"What do you mean?"

Mason said, "Every bullet which is fired through the barrel of a gun has certain distinctive striations or scratches that are made by peculiarities in the surface of the barrel. If the bullet that killed Moray Cassel was not deformed by striking bone and if the police can find where your brother had been target practicing, they can find some of the bullets which are embedded in a tree or a bank or whatever you used as a target. Then they can put those bullets in a comparison microscope and they may—mind you, I'm telling you they just *may*—be able to prove that the fatal bullet was fired from Edgar's gun without ever having the gun."

Her face showed dismay.

"However," Mason said, "with a small-caliber bullet there's not so much chance of that. Only you say you fired hundreds of shots. What did you use as a target?"

"Edgar had a target. He used to put it in the car. We'd put it up against a bank."

"What kind of a target?"

"He used a dart target," she said. "He had an old target that was made of some kind of a heavy cork, or something of that sort, and used it when he was shooting darts. Then after he quit shooting darts for pleasure, he put a backing of some kind of plywood on this target and then made some paper facings with a compass."

"He was a good shot?"

"A wonderful shot, and he trained me so I became a pretty good shot."

"Always with his gun?"

"Always with his gun. He was sort of a nut on wanting his women to be able to protect themselves. He wanted me to be an expert shot."

"You don't own a gun of your own?"

"No."

"You've never had a gun of your own?"

"No."

"Now, let's be sure about that," Mason said. "You've never made an application to purchase a revolver of any sort. Never had anyone give you a revolver?"

She shook her head in the negative.

Mason was silent for a while.

She said, "I don't think you need to worry too much about that revolver, Mr. Mason. They're never going to find it. Do you want me to tell you what I did with it so you can rest easy and—"

Mason help up his hand, "Keep quiet," he said. "Don't tell me. Don't tell anyone."

"But if I tell you, it's in confidence, isn't it?"

"Some things you can tell me are in confidence," Mason said. "But some things you can tell me would make me an accessory after the fact. I don't want to know where that gun is. I don't want anyone to know where that gun is. I don't want you to ever tell anyone anything about a gun or about being in that apartment. Just keep completely quiet. Say that your attorney doesn't want you to make any statement at this time, that a complete statement will be made sometime later.

"Then if they ask you how much later or anything of that sort you can tell them that it will be up to your attorney to fix the date.

"Where did Edgar keep this target that you mention?"

"I don't know. Somewhere in his garage."

"He had an individual garage?"

"Yes. The apartment house where he had his apartment was one of those where they had individual garages rather than a central basement garage."

"And his car?" Mason asked.

"That was all smashed up in the automobile accident and was towed away by the police, I believe."

"Did you see the car after the accident?"

"No."

"Did you look in the trunk?"

"No."

"You don't know whether this target might have been in the trunk?"

"No."

"It could have been?"

"Yes."

Again Mason was thoughtfully silent. Then abruptly he got to his feet. "All right, Diana," he said, "your future depends in large part upon keeping quiet and on an element of luck.

"You have taken it on yourself to disregard just about every bit of advice I've given you so far, and to try to substitute your own judgment in place of mine. Now you're in a jam."

"But I *had* to see Cassel," she said. "Don't you understand, Mr. Mason? You can't afford to take chances with a blackmailer. You say that you don't pay them and all that, but you know as well as I do that that's a high-risk game.

"I didn't want you to fight with this man and take a chance on doing something that would wreck Edgar's life. . . . And, of course, at that time I thought Edgar would recover."

"The way you planned it," Mason said, "would have been the high-risk game. You don't get rid of a blackmailer by paying him off. That simply makes him more eager. It postpones the time of the next bite for a few weeks or perhaps a few months, but eventually the blackmailer is always back. He regards his hold on his victim as a certain capital asset, just like owning a government bond or having money in the bank."

She shook her head. "I know that's what lawyers always say but you can't be sure. You don't know what he wanted. You don't know what his hold on Edgar was. It may have been something that . . . well, something that I could have protected him on."

"In what way?"

"By paying off, I could have had negatives and prints of pictures and all that."

"Negatives," Mason said, "can be duplicated. Pictures can be copied. When you take the word of a blackmailer that you're getting evidence, you're trusting the integrity of the blackmailer and, for the most part, that's a mighty poor risk."

The lawyer pressed a bell button, signaling that the interview was over.

"What's going to happen to me?" she asked.

"That," Mason said, "depends upon many things. But I can tell you one thing, if you start talking, if you try to explain your actions, if you start confiding in the police, you're either going to walk into the gas chamber or spend the better part of your life in the confines of a prison."

"Can't I be released on bail or something?"

Mason shook his head.

A deputy slid open the door. "All finished?" he asked.

"All finished," Mason said. He turned and waved a reassuring hand to Diana Douglas.

Chapter Fourteen

On his return to his office, Mason sent for Paul Drake.

"How does it look?" Della Street asked.

Mason shook his head. "The little fool!"

"What's she done now?"

"Lied to me. Used her judgment in place of mine. Probably left a back trail that the police can follow, but still thinks she's the smart little mastermind that can get away with it."

Drake's knock sounded on the door and Mason nodded to Della.

She opened the door.

"What is it this time?" Drake asked.

"I'm afraid," Mason said, "this is an end to your well-cooked restaurant meals, Paul. I'm afraid you're going back to sitting at the desk during long hours and eating soggy hamburgers which have been sent in from the drive-in on the next corner."

"What now?" Drake asked.

Mason said, "Diana Douglas."

"What's she done now?"

"I don't know," Mason said.

"Well, if you don't, I don't know who would."

Mason said, "I can tell you what the police think she did. The police think she went to the Tallmeyer Apartments on Thursday afternoon, that she went up to the ninth floor, had a conference with Moray Cassel, that Moray Cassel was trying to blackmail her, or perhaps her brother."

"But she paid off?" Drake asked.

"She paid off with a twenty-two-caliber revolver, shooting a particularly powerful brand of twenty-two cartridge."

"And they recovered the bullet?" Drake asked.

"Probably."

"Striations?"

Mason shrugged his shoulders.

"How many times? I mean, how many shots?"

"One, as I understand the facts," Mason said. "The man lived perhaps for some time, but he was unconscious and was unable to move. There was considerable hemorrhage."

"How do they know it's a twenty-two caliber?"

"Well," Mason said, "I'll amend that. They say it's a small caliber. I think probably they mean by that it's a twenty-two caliber. And the police claim that when little Miss Mastermind opened her purse and pulled out the gun she inadvertently jerked her BankAmericard credit card out."

"Which the police have?"

"Which the police have."

"And she claims the shooting was in self defense, or what?"

"She doesn't claim. She's silent."

"Anybody see her go into the apartment?" Drake asked.

"I don't know. She may have left a back trail that can be followed and proven. I'm only telling you what the police claim at the moment. The police claim that her BankAmericard credit card fell out of her purse on the floor without being noticed."

"Fingerprints?" Drake asked.

"I wouldn't know," Mason said.

Drake regarded him shrewdly. "A good possibility they do have fingerprints?"

"Could be."

"And you want me to find out?"

Mason said, "I want you to find out everything you can about the case, Paul. And particularly I want to find out about the victim, Moray Cassel."

"Personal habits, friends, contacts?" Drake asked.

"Everything," Mason said. "Paul, I sized that man up as some sort of a criminal. He's the sort who is making a living out of women or off of women some way and he's trying to disguise the rotten part underneath by a well-groomed exterior.

"Now, I'm particularly anxious to find out about his woman."

"Woman, singular?" Drake asked.

"Well, let's say women, plural," Mason said, "because the guy may have more than one of them. . . . And, of course, anything you can find out about the police case is something I want to know."

"How soon do you want to know?"

"At once. Relay information just as soon as you can get it."

"Costs?" Drake asked.

Mason said, "I *think* I can get costs out of my client, Paul, but I'm going to share the expense on this one, and if necessary I'll carry the whole load."

Drake raised an inquiring eyebrow.

Mason said, by way of explanation, "This case slipped up on my blind side, Paul. I gave a client the wrong advice right at the start."

"Forget it!" Drake said. "You never made a legal mistake in your life."

"I didn't make a mistake in advising her in regard to the law," Mason said, "but I made a mistake in letting her stick her neck way, way out; and then, notwithstanding the fact that I had been warned about her tendency to disregard a lawyer's advice and do things on her own, I let her out of my sight during the most critical period of all."

"When was that?" Drake asked.

"Confidentially," Mason said, "it was probably the time Moray Cassel was being murdered."

"Okay," Drake said, heaving himself to his feet, "we'll give you the usual trade discount and go to work, Perry."

Chapter Fifteen

Judge Charles Jerome Elliott looked down from the bench and said, "This is the time fixed for the preliminary hearing in the case of People versus Diana Douglas, charged with the murder of one Moray Cassel. The defendant is in court and is represented by counsel?"

Mason arose. "I am representing the defendant, if the Court please."

Judge Elliott nodded. "And the prosecution?" he asked.

Ralph Gurlock Floyd arose. "I am the trial deputy who will handle the prosecution, Your Honor."

"Very well," Judge Elliott said. "Now, I want to make a statement to both counsel. I am well aware of the fact that in the past counsel for the defense has made spectacular courtroom scenes in connection with preliminary hearings. I don't approve of trying a case at a preliminary hearing.

"The object of a preliminary hearing is to try to find whether there is a crime which has been committed and if there is reasonable ground to connect the defendant with the crime. In that event the defendant is bound over to the Superior Court for trial before a jury.

"Now then, gentlemen, I am *not* going to test the credibility of witnesses in this Court. I am going to take the evidence at its face value. Once it has been established that a crime has been committed and once evidence has been introduced tending to show the defendant is connected with that crime, this Court is going to make an order binding the defendant over regardless of how much evidence there may be in favor of the defendant.

"In other words, I am not going to try to decide the weight of the evidence or the preponderance of the evidence. Of course, it is understood that in the event the defendant can introduce evidence completely destroying the prosecution's case the situation will be different. But you gentlemen will understand that the chances of that are quite remote.

"Now that we understand the situation, you may go ahead, Mr. Prosecutor; put on your case."

Ralph Gurlock Floyd, a dedicated prosecutor, who had been responsible for more death-penalty verdicts than any prosecutor in the state, and was proud of it, apparently felt that this prosecution of a preliminary hearing was somewhat beneath his dignity. But, having been assigned by Hamilton Burger, the District Attorney, to prosecute the case, he went about it with the savage, vindictiveness which was so characteristic of his courtroom manner.

His first witness was a chambermaid at the Tallmeyer Apartments.

"Did you," he asked, "know Moray Cassel in his lifetime?"

"I did."

"When did you last see him alive?"

"On Tuesday, the tenth of this month."

"At what time?"

"At about four o'clock in the afternoon."

"When did you next see him?"

"On the evening of Sunday, the fifteenth."

"Was he alive?"

"He was dead."

"What did you do?"

"I notified the manager of the apartment house, who notified the police."

"Cross-examine," Floyd snapped.

"No questions," Mason said.

A police officer was called as a witness, then a deputy coroner. A diagram was introduced showing the position of the body on the

bed as of 9 P.M. on Sunday, the fifteenth, when the body was discovered and the position of the various articles of furniture in the
apartment.

Floyd next called William Ardley, the police officer who testified
to searching the apartment for significant clues.

"What did you find?"

"I found a BankAmericard credit card issued to one Diana Douglas
of San Francisco."

"What did you do with that card?"

"I marked it for identification by punching two small holes in it
in certain places which I selected."

"I show you what purports to be a credit card from the Bank of
America and ask you if you have seen that before."

"That is the identical credit card."

"You're positive?"

"The card is the same and the pin holes are in the exact location
that I placed them."

"Cross-examine," Floyd said.

"No questions," Mason announced cheerfully.

Floyd regarded him thoughtfully, then put a fingerprint technician on the stand who testified to finding quite a few latent fingerprints in the apartment. Some of them were the fingerprints of the
decedent. Some of them were the fingerprints of the maid who
cleaned the apartment twice a week.

"Any other fingerprints?" Floyd asked.

"There were some we couldn't identify."

"Any others that you could?"

"Yes, sir. Two of them."

"Where were they?"

"One of them was in the bathroom on the mirror of the medicine
chest. The other one was on a nightstand table by the side of the bed
where the body was lying."

"Did you determine the identity of these fingerprints?"

"We did, yes, sir. One of them is the middle finger of the defendant's right hand. The other is the thumb of the defendant's right
hand."

"You're positive?"

"We have more than enough points of similarity and several unusual characteristics."

"Anything else in the bathroom?"

"There was a towel with blood stains on it, a moist towel where someone had evidently washed—"

"Objected to as conclusion of the witness," Mason said.

"Sustained," Judge Elliott snapped.

"A bloody towel," the witness said.

"You have that here?"

"Yes, sir."

"Produce it, please."

The witness produced a sealed paper bag, opened it, and took out a hand towel with the words TALLMEYER APARTMENTS embroidered in the corner. The towel was stained a faint rusty color.

"We offer to introduce it in evidence as People's Exhibit B," Floyd said.

"No objection," Mason observed casually.

"You photographed the latent fingerprints?" Floyd asked.

"I did."

"Will you produce those photographs, please?"

The photographs of the latent prints were produced and introduced in evidence. The prosecutor then introduced a whole series of photographs, showing the decedent on the bed with blood which had saturated the pillow, dripped down to the floor, and spread over the carpet.

An autopsy surgeon was called as a witness. He testified that he had recovered the fatal bullet from the back of the skull; that the bullet was of a type known as a .22-caliber, long rifle bullet; that it had penetrated the forehead on the median line about two inches above the eyes; that there had been a very considerable hemorrhage.

"When did death occur?" the prosecutor asked.

"In my opinion, making all of the tests we could, death occurred sometime between two o'clock on the afternoon of Thursday, the twelfth and five o'clock in the morning on Saturday, the fourteenth."

"Was death instantaneous?"

"No, I don't think so. Unconsciousness immediately followed the shot, and there was probably no movement of the body. But, despite the fact the victim was unconscious, the heart continued to pump blood into the brain which accounted for the very extensive hemorrhage. Death may have resulted in a period of ten or fifteen minutes after the fatal shot, or it may have been an hour. I can't tell."

"You say you recovered the fatal bullet?"

"Yes, sir."

"What did you do with it?"

"I delivered it to the ballistics expert in the presence of two witnesses."

"Could you determine the weapon from which that bullet had been fired?"

"Not definitely at the moment. We knew that it must have been fired from one of several makes of guns and we rather suspected that it had been fired from a gun with a long barrel because of—"

"Move to strike out what the witness rather suspected," Mason said.

"It will go out," Judge Elliott ruled. "Stick to facts, Mr. Witness."

"Very well," Floyd said with a triumphant smile. "We'll withdraw this witness for the moment and put on other witnesses, then recall him. I will call Miss Smith, please."

Miss Smith turned out to be a neatly dressed young woman in her early thirties.

"What is your occupation?"

"I am employed at the ticket counter of United Airlines at the Los Angeles Terminal."

"Were you so employed on Thursday, the twelfth of this month?"

"I was."

"I will ask you to look at the defendant and tell us if you have ever seen her before."

"Yes, sir, I have."

"Where?"

"At the ticket counter on the evening of Thursday, the twelfth."

"At about what time?"

"It was exactly six-forty P.M."

"Did you have a conversation with her?"

"Yes."

"And what was that conversation?"

"She was very anxious to know if the plane which was due to leave at six twenty-seven had left on time or whether it would be possible for her to get aboard. I told her that the plane had left only about five minutes late, that she would have to wait approximately an hour and twenty minutes and take a flight leaving at eight o'clock."

"What did she do?"

"She asked for a ticket to San Francisco."

"And then?" Floyd asked, his manner triumphant.

"Then she produced her purse and said, 'I'll pay for it with a BankAmericard credit card.' Then she raised her purse so I could briefly see it and suddenly dropped it down out of sight."

"'You say, suddenly?"

"Suddenly and self-consciously."

"Was there any reason for such action?"

"She had a gun in her purse."

"What sort of a gun?"

"A long-barreled gun with a wooden handle."

"When you say a gun, you mean a revolver?"

"Yes, sir."

"Then what happened?"

"Then she fumbled around in her purse, keeping it below the counter so I couldn't see inside of it, and said, 'Oh, I seem to have misplaced my BankAmericard.' Then she thought for a moment and said, 'Did Mr. Perry Mason, the lawyer, leave a ticket here for me?'

"I told her that Mr. Mason had left two tickets which had been charged to his air-travel card. One ticket he had picked up, and the other one he had left to be picked up by Diana Douglas.

"Her face showed relief and she said, 'I am Diana Douglas. I'll take the ticket, please.' "

"So you gave her the ticket?"

"Yes."

"And then what?"

"Then she left and I made it a point to look at the purse she was carrying. The gun in it distorted the purse's shape and—"

"Move to strike out that it was the gun that had distorted the purse's shape," Mason said.

Judge Elliott hesitated, then said, "That may go out. The witness can state whether the purse was distorted."

"The purse was distorted by some object which had been thrust into the purse, an object so long that the purse was out of shape."

"Cross-examine," Floyd said.

"Did you," Mason asked, "ever pick the defendant out of a line-up?"

"No, I didn't."

"You didn't see her from the time you talked with her at the ticket counter until you went into the courtroom today?"

"I identified her picture."

"But you didn't pick her out of a line-up?"

"I did not. That wasn't at all necessary, Mr. Mason. After the manner in which my attention had been attracted to the defendant, I would have picked her out anywhere."

"That's all," Mason said.

Floyd put on his next witness with an air of triumph. He was a middle-aged individual who gave his occupation as part of a crew who cleaned up airplanes for the United Airlines.

"Are you familiar with the plane which left the Los Angeles Airport Terminal at eight o'clock on the evening of Thursday, the twelfth of this month, and arrived in San Francisco approximately an hour later?"

"Yes, sir."

"Did you clean that plane?"

"Yes, sir."

"Did you find anything unusual?"

"I did."

"What was it?"

"It was a gun."

"Where was that gun found?"

"The gun had been concealed in an opening underneath a pile of towels in one of the lavatories. I may state that these towels are placed in piles in the containers and are replenished from time to time. On this particular occasion I wanted to get at one of the connections for the plumbing, and in order to do that I had to remove the towels and insert my hand in the opening in back of the towels. When I did that I felt some foreign object in there and drew it out, and it was this gun."

"Did you take any steps to identify the gun?"

"I took it to my supervisor."

"And what did the supervisor do?"

"He notified the police and, at the request of the police, we took down the statistics on the weapon."

"What were the statistics?"

"This was a twenty-two caliber single-action revolver, having a nine-and-three-eighth-inch barrel and a wooden handle. On the gun was stamped Ruger twenty-two, with the words single six, the number, one-three-nine-five-seven-three and the name of the manufacturer, Sturm—S-T-U-R-M—Ruger—R-U-G-E-R—and Company, Southport, Connecticut. The initials E.D. had been carved in the handle."

"I'll show you a gun and ask you if that is the gun that you found."

Floyd came forward and handed the witness the gun.

Diana Douglas' hand clutched Mason's leg, the fingers digging in so hard that the lawyer surreptitiously lowered his own hand to loosen her grip.

Diana's face was tense, tight-lipped and chalky.

The witness turned the gun over in his fingers, nodded, and said, "This is the gun."

"What was the condition of the gun when you found it?"

"It was fully loaded except for one shell which had been discharged."

"This is a single-action gun, and, in other words, it has to be cocked and then the trigger pulled. It isn't the so-called self-cocking gun?"

"No, sir, it is what is known as a single-action gun."

"Cross-examine," Floyd said.

"You have no idea how long the gun had been in that receptacle?" Mason asked.

"No, sir. I know when I found it, that's all."

"Thank you," Mason said, "no further questions."

Floyd introduced in evidence the sales register of the Sacramento Sporting Dealers, Inc., showing that the Ruger gun in question had been sold five years earlier to Edgar Douglas.

His next witness was a young woman who identified herself as a hostess on the eight o'clock plane to San Francisco on the night of Thursday, the twelfth. She had noticed Diana, observed that she was a passenger, had observed the peculiar shape of the cloth purse she was carrying when she boarded the plane. She stated that Diana was carrying a sort of overnight bag as well as the cloth purse, and when Diana went to the lavatory she noticed that she carried both the overnight bag and the purse with her, which the stewardess thought was rather peculiar. Aside from that, however, she could contribute no evidence. She hadn't paid any particular attention to the purse after Diana had been in the lavatory.

Then Floyd pulled his trump witness, the ballistics expert who stated that the fatal bullet which had killed Moray Cassel had come from the gun which had been registered in the name of Edgar Douglas.

This expert was followed by the manager of the San Francisco apartment house, who stated that after the automobile accident which had rendered Edgar Douglas unconscious and had resulted in his going to the hospital, his sister, the defendant, had been given a key to her brother's apartment and had been in and out, straightening things up.

Next Floyd introduced the doorman at the Tallmeyer Apartments. He had, he admitted, not seen the defendant when she entered the apartments, but he had seen her when she left; he noticed she had been carrying a black type of overnight bag and a black cloth purse. The purse was stretched to the limit by some rigid object which was within it. He had noticed the purse particularly.

Floyd introduced a purse which was identified as the property of the defendant and asked the doorman if he recognized the purse. The doorman answered in the affirmative. It was either that purse or one that was an exact duplicate of it.

Judge Elliott glanced at the clock and cleared his throat. "Gentlemen, it is nearing the hour of adjournment and it would certainly seem there is no use in prolonging this inquiry further. There is undoubtedly evidence that a crime has been committed and an abundance of evidence connecting the defendant with the crime. In fact, the Court has been rather surprised at the amount of detailed evidence put on by the prosecution."

Floyd said, "The prosecution is all too well aware of the reputation of defense counsel and wishes to leave no possible loophole."

"Well, it would seem that you have left no loophole," Judge Elliott said, smiling. "I think, gentlemen, we can adjourn the hearing and bind the defendant over."

Mason arose. "If the Court please," he said with respect but very firmly, "the defense may wish to put on some testimony."

"Why?" Judge Elliott asked.

"Because I believe it is our right."

"You have a right to subpoena witnesses, that is true. But this Court is not called upon to judge the credibility of witnesses. This Court is not called upon to weigh questions of reasonable doubt. You certainly can't claim that a *prima facie* case has not been established."

"The question of whether a *prima facie* case has been established," Mason said, "depends upon the evidence at the conclusion of the case and any attempt to decide a case without giving the defendant a day in court would be—"

"Oh, all right, all right," Judge Elliott said impatiently. "We'll continue the case until ten o'clock tomorrow morning. I want to warn counsel, however, that we have a busy calendar and the Court does not take kindly to fishing expeditions or attempts to try a case on the merits at a preliminary hearing. The Court warns counsel that this Court will not weigh the credibility of witnesses and that any question of conflicting facts will be determined in favor of the prosecution as far as this hearing is concerned. However, the Court will try to do nothing which will preclude the defendant from having a fair hearing on the merits before a jury in the Superior Court, at which time the credibility of witnesses can be raised and the doctrine of reasonable doubt will apply.

"It is simply a case of differing procedures in different courts. Do you understand that, Mr. Mason?"

"I understand it," Mason said.

"Very well. The case is adjourned until ten o'clock tomorow morning."

Mason placed a reassuring hand on Diana's shoulder. "Keep a stiff upper lip, Diana," he said.

"They're going to bind me over to the Superior Court?"

"Probably," Mason said, "but I want to find out as much about the case as I can before the Court makes its order."

"And what happens when I get to the Superior Court?"

"You are tried by a jury. You have the benefit of any reasonable doubt."

Mason bent forward to say in a low voice, "Where did you get that gun?"

"Just as I told you, Mr. Mason. It was on the floor with blood on it. I took it in the bathroom and washed the blood off and then put the gun in my purse. I had a hard time getting it in, and I guess that's when I lost the credit card."

"And you hid it in the airplane?"

"Yes, I took out the towels and felt all around in the back of the towel compartment and found this little opening way in back. I thought they'd never find the gun in there."

Mason said, "Tell me—about the girls in the San Francisco office. Do you know who could have written that message to me?"

"It might have been any one of them."

"It was written on an electric typewriter."

"All the typewriters are electric," she said.

"All right," Mason told her, "keep a stiff upper lip. I'll see you in the morning."

The lawyer picked up his briefcase and left the courtroom.

Chapter Sixteen

Perry Mason, Della Street, and Paul Drake were huddled around a table in an Italian restaurant which was near the courthouse and where the proprietor was accustomed to devoting a small private dining room to the exclusive use of the trio.

"Well," Drake said, "it looks as if the judge has his mind made up, from all I could hear."

Mason nodded. "What have you found out, Paul?"

"Not a whole lot," Drake admitted, "a lot of detached bits of information. I don't know whether they'll do you any good. . . . As you, yourself, have remarked, your client is an awful liar."

"She is and she isn't," Mason said. "She lied to me because she wanted to save her brother's reputation. She thought there was something that was hanging over his head, something that he'd pay five thousand dollars to eliminate. She wanted to carry out his wishes.

"Therefore, she acted independently of my advice and she tried to deceive me, but when it came to a showdown I don't think she did try to deceive me. At least, I think there's a possibility she's telling the truth.

"That's a duty that a lawyer owes to his client. Regardless of how many times he has been lied to in the past, he always has to keep the faith. He always has to believe that in the final showdown, the client is telling the truth and putting the cards face up on the table."

Drake said, "She can't be telling the truth on this one, Perry. She went down there and tried to buy him off. She couldn't do it and she killed him."

"What have you found out?" Mason asked, detouring the subject.

"Well," Drake said, "you probably had Moray Cassel pretty well pegged. The guy lived a mysterious life, and no one knows his real source of income or how much his income was.

"This much I did find out. The man was always armed. He carried a thirty-eight-caliber, snub-nosed revolver in a shoulder holster under his left armpit. His clothes were tailor-made, and for years the same tailor had been making his clothes and making them so that there was an extra bit of room under the left armpit so the bulge made by the gun wouldn't be conspicuous."

"The deuce!" Mason said.

Drake nodded.

"And that gun was on him at the time his body was found?"

"It must have been," Drake said.

Mason's eyes narrowed. "Now, isn't it interesting that the police described everything in the room, showed photographs of the body lying fully clothed on the bed with a bullet hole in the forehead, the blood all over the pillow and down on the floor, and no one said anything about the gun?"

"Did you ask them?" Drake inquired.

Mason grinned. "I didn't ask them. I wouldn't have thought to have asked them about a gun, but I certainly should have thought to have asked them what was found in his pockets and whether anything significant was found in the room. . . . What about the source of income, Paul?"

Drake shook his head. "The guy did everything with cash. He wore a money belt. There were four one-thousand-dollar bills in the money belt. He had a leather wallet that was pretty well crammed with hundred-dollar bills. As nearly as can be found out he had no bank account. He bought that Cadillac automobile and paid for it with cold, hard cash."

"Women?" Mason asked.

"Women came to see him from time to time."

"The same woman or different women?"

"Different."

"What did you find out about the note that was placed on the display case in San Francisco where I'd pick it up?"

"The note was written on an electric typewriter," Drake said. "They're all electric typewriters, but this particular note, as nearly as I can determine, was written on the typewriter of Joyce Baffin.

"For your information, Perry, if it's worth anything, Joyce Baffin left the import-export office at noon, Thursday, pleading a terrific headache. She was, however, back on the job Friday morning, and Joyce was and is very popular with the officials and employees of the company and was at one time very friendly with Edgar Douglas. In fact, he had quite a crush on her. But so did lots of other people. Perhaps Franklin Gage, who is a widower, and Homer Gage, who has a predatory eye, would have liked to enjoy a closer relationship with Joyce Baffin."

Mason, sipping a cocktail, digested that information.

Drake went on. "I have some more odds and ends of various bits of information. I spent quite a bit of time and a fair amount of money with the telephone operator at Tallmeyer Apartments. I found out that Moray Cassel put through a lot of telephone calls to a local number. I found that number was the apartment of one Irene Blodgett, twenty-seven, blonde, Millsep Apartments, divorced, employed steadily during the daytime at the Underwood Importing Company. At night she's something of a gadabout but never anything spectacular. Quiet, refined, good-looking, popular—I've got operatives working quietly on her, but if there's anything phoney she's pretty well covered.

"The only thing is that this Underwood Importing Company does have some dealing or has had dealings with the Escobar Import and Export Company."

Della Street, watching Mason's face, said, "You have an idea, Chief?"

"Just this," Mason said. "At the time of his death, Moray Cassel was either standing by the bed or sitting on the edge of the bed. He was shot in the forehead by one shot from a high-powered, single-action, twenty-two-caliber revolver with a nine-and-three-eighth-inch barrel. The murderer must have been facing him."

"Well?" Drake asked. "What's so peculiar about that? Diana

Douglas went to call on the guy. She rang the bell. Cassel let her in. She tried to bargain with him, then he got tough with her. She knew at that time that blackmailers never quit. Once they get a hold on a victim they bleed him white. Diana was obsessed with the idea she had to protect her brother."

Mason held the stem of his cocktail glass, watching the liquid on the inside as he twisted the glass between his thumb and forefinger.

"You got into Cassel's apartment?" he asked the detective.

"Sure, after the police were through with it. That seemed to take an awful long while. They went over the whole place dusting for fingerprints, testing for blood stains, and all that."

"What about the fellow's wardrobe?" Mason asked. "Was he meticulous with his clothes as I thought?"

"Boy, you've said it," Drake replied. "It was a fairly large-sized apartment with lots of drawer space. The drawers were filled with monogrammed shirts. He even had monograms on his underwear, and the closet was pretty well filled with tailor-made clothes."

"You checked with his tailor?"

"Sure. The tailor told me that Cassel always paid him in cash, seldom wore a suit over six months, and was very fastidious. And, of course, there was that bit about tailoring the suits so the bulge didn't show where the revolver was carried under the left armpit.

"The tailor got quite friendly with me, said that he always had an idea Cassel was a gangster of some sort, and was very certain that Cassel was cheating on the income tax. But, of course, it was none of the tailor's business, and, believe me, the tailor loved to get that money in the form of cash. . . . I wouldn't be too surprised, Perry, if perhaps the tailor didn't do a little cheating on the income tax himself."

"What about overcoats?" Mason asked. "Were those tailor-made, too?"

"Everything," Drake said. "Now, wait a minute, Perry, there's one exception. There was one overcoat in there that Cassel had evidently used for rough-and-tumble stuff when he was loading or unloading things in an automobile."

"What makes you say that?"

"Well, it was an overcoat that wasn't tailor-made and the labels had been cut out from both the neck and the breast pocket."

"The deuce you say," Mason said. And then, after a while, "How did it fit, Paul?"

"How should I know?" Drake asked. "The corpse was being dissected in the medical examiner's office at the coroner's by an autopsy surgeon. I couldn't very well go in there and try on an overcoat. . . . He couldn't have had it on since late spring. It had been hot for the whole week of the murder. . . . What difference does the one coat make?"

Mason sat for a long moment in contemplative silence, then abruptly changed the subject. "You have the various telephone numbers of the personnel at the Escobar Import and Export Company?"

Drake nodded.

Mason said to Della Street, "See if you can get us a telephone, Della."

When a telephone had been brought into the room and connected, Mason used his credit card, saying, "This is a credit-card call. I want to talk with Franklin Gage at this number in San Francisco."

Mason took Drake's notebook and read the number of Franklin Gage's residence.

"It's a person-to-person call. No one else if he's out."

The lawyer drummed with the fingers of his right hand while he held the telephone to his ear. "Let's hope we're in luck," he said.

A moment later he heard the suave voice of Franklin Gage on the telephone.

"This is Perry Mason, the lawyer," Mason said. "I take it that you are somewhat interested in this case against Diana Douglas, who is working for you . . . for your company, that is."

"Well, in a way," Gage said cautiously. "It depends upon what you want."

"Has an audit been completed of the cash shortage of your import company?"

"Yes, it has."

"Would you mind telling me what it shows?"

"In round figures," Gage said, "it shows a shortage of ten thousand dollars."

Mason said, "Would you be willing to do something which might prevent a miscarriage of justice, Mr. Gage?"

"What?"

"I would like to see that Joyce Baffin is present in court tomorrow morning when the case against Diana Douglas is called up."

"Well, of course, if you want to pay her expenses down and back," Gage said, "I would give her a leave of absence."

"It's not that," Mason said. "She might not want to come."

"Well, I certainly can't force her to come."

Mason said, "She has been in your employ for some time?"

"Yes, all of the secretaries have been with us for quite some time. We don't have a turnover with help, Mr. Mason. Our business is highly specialized, and after we have trained a young woman to perform competent secretarial duties we try to keep her."

Mason said, "The reason I am calling you personally, Mr. Gage, is that it is tremendously important that Joyce Baffin be here. I can't begin to tell you how vital it may be. I am going to ask that you and your nephew, Homer Gage, come down to Los Angeles to the trial, that you personally get in touch with Joyce Baffin tonight and tell her that it is highly important that the three of you come down."

"The *three* of us!" Gage echoed.

"Exactly," Mason said. "I have reason to believe that if you ask her to come down by herself she might not come. She might even skip out. And, if only one of you is coming with her, she might again become suspicious. But if both you and your nephew are coming down ostensibly to see what you can do to help Diana Douglas—"

"If she's guilty, she's not entitled to any help," Gage interrupted sternly.

"But suppose she isn't guilty? You've had a chance to study the young woman. You've had a chance to know something of her loyalty. Do you think that she's the type of a woman who would commit a murder?"

"Well, of course," Gage said cautiously, "you never know what a person will do when they're hard pressed, and she always tried to protect her brother, but—Do you feel this is really important, Mr. Mason?"

"I feel that it is highly important. I feel that it is vital," Mason said.

There was silence at the other end of the line.

"If you can do exactly as I suggested," Mason said, "I feel that it will be possible to eliminate certain questions which might otherwise come up in court."

"What sort of questions?"

"Oh, about the Escobar Import and Export Company, the nature of its business, the large amount of cash that it keeps on hand, and all of those things that are business details which you *might* not care to have your competitors know about."

"Very well," Gage said quickly, "if I can have your assurance that you feel this will keep the business affairs of our company out of evidence, Mr. Mason, and if you assure me that it is vital to the case of your client, Homer and I will do our best to induce Joyce to come with us, and I feel that we can be successful. . . . Where and when do we meet you?"

"You take a plane tonight," Mason said, "so you will be sure to get in. You go to a hotel. All you have to do is to ring up the Drake Detective Agency and Paul Drake will send a car to escort you to the courtroom tomorrow morning, see that you are given admission, and properly seated."

"The Drake Detective Agency," Gage said.

"That's right," Mason said, and gave him Paul Drake's number.

"Very well. We'll do it."

"I can depend on you?" Mason asked.

"You have my word," Franklin Gage said with dignity.

"That's good enough for me," Mason told him, and hung up the telephone.

"Now, what the hell?" Drake asked.

Mason picked up the cocktail glass, drained it, and smiled. "I think," he said, "I'm beginning to see daylight. . . . A shortage of *ten* thousand dollars."

"The original figure was twenty thousand," Drake said.

Mason nodded. "Remember, however, that when Franklin Gage entered the office he said that he had been working on a business deal and had taken ten thousand dollars out, that the deal had fallen through and he was in the process of replacing the ten thousand dollars in the cash drawer."

"I don't get it," Drake said.

"If we can get those people in court tomorrow morning perhaps we'll get lucky," Mason said.

"But you assured them that those business matters wouldn't come out."

"I think they won't," Mason told him. "Now then, I'm going to have another cocktail and then we're going to order one of these fabulous Italian dinners and relax while we eat it."

Chapter Seventeen

Ralph Gurlock Floyd arose with something of a flourish when the case of the People vs. Diana Douglas was called.

"I think, if the Court please, we can rest the prosecution's case."

"I certainly would think so," Judge Elliott said. "In fact, I think this whole matter could have been disposed of yesterday afternoon. I take it there is no defense."

"Indeed there is a defense," Mason said.

"I want to repeat that this court is not interested in fishing expeditions, Mr. Mason. I am not going to preclude the defendant from putting on any legitimate defense, but it would seem virtually mathematical that there is no defense and can be no defense to the array of facts which have been marshaled thus far by witnesses."

"If the Court please," Mason said, "I would like to recall one of the officers for just one or two questions on further cross-examination."

"That's irregular," Floyd protested. "That motion should have been made earlier."

"Oh, come, come," Judge Elliott said, "one thing is certain. I'm not going to preclude this defendant from an opportunity to cross-examine any witness of the prosecution. I take it, Mr. Mason, there's some particular significance in connection with this?"

"There is, Your Honor."

"Recall the witness," Judge Elliott said.

Mason motioned to the officer. "Take the stand," he said. "Remember you've already been sworn. Now, you have the bag which has been identified as the cloth purse which the defendant had in her possession when the ticket seller at the airlines saw the gun in the purse, the same purse which the stewardess noticed on the airplane?"

"That's right."

"You have both the gun and the purse," Mason said. "Now, have you tried putting the gun in the purse?"

The officer smiled patronizingly. "Of course we have. It fits so snugly that the cloth is stretched tight and the purse is bulged out of shape. That's why it was so noticeable."

"Please put the gun in the purse," Mason said.

The clerk handed the two exhibits to the officer. He took the purse, opened it, inserted the muzzle of the gun, then gradually worked the gun into the purse, explaining as he did so, "You can see what a snug fit it is and how it is necessary to twist the cloth of the purse so it fits over the grip of the gun, which, of course," he added with a quick look of triumph at the Deputy District Attorney, "explains why the defendant lost the credit card out of the purse when she was taking the gun out."

"All right," Mason said, "you have the gun in the purse now."

"That's right."

"And you can close the purse?"

"Yes, you can barely close the purse, and," the witness went on, "when you open the purse anyone who looks in it can see a part of the gun . . . the wooden butt of the weapon."

"Exactly," Mason said. "Now, a gun has two outlines, the convex outline and a concave outline, does it not?"

"I don't understand what you mean," the officer said.

"Well," Mason said, "a gun is made generally on a curve so that when you hold the butt of the gun in your hand in a shooting position the barrel of the gun is elevated so that you can aim down it."

"Oh, certainly, that's right."

"And, by the same sign, when you turn the gun over, the position is reversed. That is what I would call the concave position."

"All right," the officer said.

"Now then," Mason said, "you have put the gun in the purse in a concave position. Could you reverse that position and put it in a convex position?"

"Not and close the purse," the officer said. "The fit is too snug. In fact, I don't know if you could even get the gun in the purse in what you refer to as the convex position."

"All right," Mason said, "now, it's taken you a little time to get the gun in the purse."

"It's a snug fit," the officer admitted.

"Now, take it out," Mason said. "Let's see how fast you can take it out."

"What do you mean, how fast I can take it out?"

Mason turned up his wrist and consulted the second hand of his wristwatch. "Let's see exactly how long it takes you to take the gun out."

"Oh, I see," the officer said, "one of those tests, uh?"

He started pulling frantically at the gun in the purse, managed only to jam it tighter against the cloth. To get the gun out, it was necessary for him to take the top of the purse and start pulling the cloth back a fold at a time.

"Five seconds," Mason said.

The officer fumbled frantically.

"Ten seconds," Mason said. "Twelve seconds. Now, you have the gun out. Now, it is in an upside-down position. If you wanted to shoot it you'd have to turn it around in your hand. Please do so."

The officer shifted the gun rapidly in his hand.

"Now, that is a single-action gun," Mason went on. "It can't be cocked and discharged by simply pulling the trigger. You have to pull back the hammer. Do that."

The officer did so.

Mason smiled. "Do you think you could beat that time?"

"Oh, sure, I could," the officer said, "now that I know what you're getting at I could beat it all to pieces."

"All right," Mason said, "put the gun back in the purse, close the purse; then get ready, pull the gun out of the purse, turn it to a firing position, cock the hammer of the gun, and pull the trigger. Start when I say 'ready', and we'll time it until the trigger clicks."

"I'm afraid I don't see the object of this test, interesting as it may be," Judge Elliott said.

"It is simply this, Your Honor," Mason said. "Moray Cassel, the victim, was shot in the forehead by one bullet. Moray Cassel was wearing a revolver in a shoulder holster at the time of his death. I understand that he habitually carried this weapon with him.

"Is it reasonable to suppose that he stood there inactive while the defendant fumbled with her purse and—"

"I see, I see," Judge Elliott said. "Go ahead with the test."

Ralph Gurlock Floyd was on his feet. "We object, Your Honor. It's not a fair test. It is not conducted in accordance with conditions as they existed at the time of the crime. How do we know that the defendant had the gun in what Mr. Mason calls a concave position in her purse when she entered Cassel's apartment. She might have stood outside of the door and done all of the fumbling before Cassel opened the door.

"In that event she would have had the gun in her hand, ready to fire."

"Nevertheless," Judge Elliott said, frowning thoughtfully, "it's an interesting hypothesis and the Court is not going to preclude the defendant the opportunity to advance it. Go ahead, let's make the test and take the time."

This time the officer, knowing what was required and working frantically, was able to cut the time down to approximately seven seconds.

Judge Elliott, who had been watching the performance, said, "The Court gets it at about six seconds."

"Between six and seven seconds," Mason said, "to the time of the click. However, that's good enough."

"Your Honor," Floyd protested, "this is absolutely meaningless. The defendant could have had the gun out of the purse, cocked and ready to shoot before pressing the buzzer so that Moray Cassel would have opened the door to find himself helpless."

"And what happened then?" Mason asked Floyd.

"Don't try to cross-examine me," Floyd snapped.

Mason said with a smile, "I will address my remarks to the Court. The idea of having the defendant ring the buzzer with a gun, loaded and cocked and ready to shoot, would necessitate that the decedent be shot while he was at the door. In place of that the decedent was shot at the far end of the apartment, either while he was standing by the bed or sitting on the bed, and he was shot from some distance since there is no powder tatoo around the edges of the wound."

"We'll argue the case at the proper time," Judge Elliott said. "You have made your point, Mr. Mason."

Floyd said, "The defendant could have had the drop on him and forced him back a step at a time."

"For what purpose?" Mason asked.

"In order to intimidate him," Floyd said. "Who else would have had her brother's gun and— Oh, this is absurd, too absurd to ever waste time on."

"Then why are you wasting it?" Mason asked.

"Don't try to question me," Floyd shouted irritably.

"I beg the Court's pardon," Mason said. "I was merely retorting to a retort."

Judge Elliott smiled. "Proceed with your case, Mr. Mason. Do you have any questions of this witness on further cross-examination?"

"I have one or two more questions of this witness, if the Court please," Mason said.

He turned to the officer. "You made a careful examination of the apartment?"

"I did. Several of us did."

"And you noticed the wardrobe of the decedent?"

The officer smiled. "I certainly did."

"It was rather elaborate?"

"That's an understatement. It was *very* elaborate."

"And did you notice that the clothes were tailor-made?"

"The outer garments, yes sir. The under garments were also, I think, custom-made, at least they were initialed."

"And in that collection of outer garments would you say that *all* of them were tailor-made?"

"Yes, sir, all of them."

"*All* of them?"

"All—Now, wait a minute. There was one overcoat in there that didn't have a tailor's label."

"And did you notice that overcoat, try it for size to see whether or not it would have fit the decedent?"

"Well," the officer said, "we didn't try it on the decedent, if that's what you mean."

"How long," Mason asked, "would it take to have this coat brought into court?"

"Oh, Your Honor," Ralph Floyd said in the tone of voice of one whose patience has been taxed to the limit, "this is absurd, this approaches the ridiculous. *I* don't know where this coat is. I suppose it's somewhere in the coroner's office. . . . The Court has said that it wouldn't encourage fishing expeditions and if this isn't a fishing expedition I don't know one when I see it."

Judge Elliott started to nod his head, then frowned thoughtfully and glanced at Mason. "Do you care to make a statement, Mr. Mason?"

"I care to make a statement," Mason said. "I would like to have that coat brought into court. I think it is a vital clue in this case. I have one more question to ask of this witness and then I am finished with my cross-examination. I will start to put on the defendant's case. The first witness will be Stella Grimes, a private detective. Before her testimony is finished, I think that coat should be in court. I also have subpoenaed the tailor who made all of Moray Cassel's clothes, who will testify that this overcoat was not made by him and would not have fit Moray Cassel."

"Go ahead, finish your cross-examination of this witness," Judge Elliott said, "and the Court will direct the prosecution to take steps to have the coat in question brought into court. . . . If this is a fishing expedition it is certainly using most unusual bait.

"Go ahead, Mr. Mason."

Mason said, "You were present in the laboratory when the gun which was recovered from the airplane was tested and examined?"

"Yes."

"For fingerprints?"

"Yes."

"Were there any fingerprints you could find?"

"Nothing that was identifiable. You must understand, Mr. Mason, that regardless of popular fiction stories, the finding of a fingerprint upon a gun—that is. an identifiable latent fingerprint—is not only the exception but it only happens once in a very great number of cases."

"I understand," Mason said. "Now, there are other tests to which that gun was subjected."

"You mean the ballistic tests?"

"No, I meant tests for blood."

The witness hesitated, then said, "Yes, there were tests for blood. There are very sensitive tests which show up blood even when the blood can't be classified."

"The benzidine test?" Mason asked.

"That is one."

"Was a benzidine test performed upon this gun?"

"It was."

"With what result?"

The witness hesitated, then chose his words carefully. "There were widespread reactions. Evidently the gun had been exposed to blood over almost its entire surface. More probably it had been exposed to a concentration of blood and then someone had attempted to wash that blood off very hastily with water or with a damp rag."

"That concludes my cross-examination," Mason said.

"Any redirect?" Judge Elliott asked Ralph Floyd.

"Certainly not," Ralph Floyd said. "We consider these so-called points completely extraneous."

"Now, you have a case to put on for the defense, Mr. Mason?"

"Yes, I will call my first witness, Miss Stella Grimes."

Stella Grimes came forward, gave her name, age, occupation, and residence.

"When did you first see the defendant in this case?" Mason asked.

"It was at night. Mr. Drake and I were in a taxicab. We both wore dark glasses. Mr. Drake had put an ad in the paper suggesting that the person who had money to pay could make the payment to a person in a taxicab at a certain place."

"Did you talk to the defendant at that time?"

"No, she walked past two or three times, but gave no sign of recognition, no indication that she wished to convey any message."

"When did you next see her?"

"The following day."

"Where?"

"At the Willatson Hotel."

"What room?"

"Room Seven-sixty-seven."

"And what happened while you were there?"

"I was instructed to take over as the occupant of that room."

"And the real occupant of that room was the defendant?"

"That's right."

"And what was done with her?"

"You had rented another room down the hall. You took the defendant down to that room."

"Then what happened?"

"Then there was a knock at the door and the decedent paid us a visit."

"By the decedent, you mean Moray Cassel?"

"Yes, sir."

"And what was the conversation?"

"It was very apparent that he was expecting a payment of money, that he expected this from a man, that when he saw that two people were in the room he became suspicious and thought that perhaps a trap was being laid for him."

"So, what did you do?"

"I followed a code signal from you, Mr. Mason. I pretended that I was simply a girl friend who was paying you a visit for purposes of affection. I gave you a casual kiss, departed, but, in accordance with your code signal, I rented a taxicab, watched the exit of the hotel so that I could follow Mr. Cassel when he left, and did so follow him to the Tallmeyer Apartments.

"I then reported to you, giving you the license number of the Cadillac owned by the decedent and the address to which he had driven."

"And then?" Mason asked.

"Then I returned, and continued to occupy the room, waiting for someone to get in touch with me seeking a blackmail payment."

"When the defendant was in the room did you see her purse?"

"I did."

"The purse which has been introduced in evidence and which I now hand you?"

"It was either this purse or a similar one."

Mason said, "I now put the gun which is supposed to have fired the fatal bullet into this purse and ask you if, in your opinion, that gun could have been in that purse at the time that the defendant left the room."

"It definitely could not have been in the purse, not that gun. I would have noticed the manner in which the purse was bulged out of shape."

"Cross-examine," Mason said to Ralph Floyd.

Floyd said, "The defendant could have had the gun someplace else, in her suitcase or concealed somewhere on her person and put it in her purse at a later date."

"Mr. Mason took her suitcase," Stella Grimes said, "to smuggle it out of the hotel. She was to take with her nothing but her purse and a black sort of overnight bag."

"And that gun could have been in the overnight bag?"

"It could not."

"Why not?"

"Because that bag was full of money with which to pay a black-mailer."

"How much money?"

"I didn't count it," she said, "but it was full of money. I saw that much."

Floyd hesitated a moment, then said, "I guess that's all."

"If the Court please," Mason said, "I notice that an officer has handed the bailiff an overcoat. I believe this is the overcoat that was taken from Mr. Cassel's closet, the one which didn't fit him?"

"*I* don't know that it didn't fit him," Floyd snapped.

"We'll very soon find that out," Mason said. "Mr. Ballard, will you come forward and be sworn, please."

Ballard, a very short, thick-set individual in his early forties, came to the witness stand, moving with surprising swiftness and agility for one of his build.

He gave his name, address, occupation, age, and then turned to face Mr. Mason.

"You knew Moray Cassel in his lifetime?"

"Yes, sir."

"How long had you known him?"

"About seven years."

"What is your occupation?"

"I am a custom tailor."

"Did you make clothes for Mr. Cassel?"

"I did."

"How many clothes did you make?"

"Heavens, I don't know. He seldom kept a suit over six months, and I know that he had a very extensive wardrobe. I made literally dozens of suits for him."

"And you kept his measurements on file?"

"Certainly. I didn't want to have to measure him every time he came in. He would pick out the material, tell me what he wanted, and I would have the clothes ready for the first fitting within a few days."

"I show you an overcoat which I will mark for purposes of identification as Defendant's Exhibit Number One and ask you if you made that overcoat."

The witness fingered the overcoat. "I certainly did not."

"I ask you if that overcoat could have been worn by Moray Cassel."

The witness pulled a tape measure from his pocket, made a few swift measurements, then shook his head. "Moray Cassel would have been lost in that overcoat," he said.

"Cross-examine," Mason said.

"I certainly have no questions about this overcoat of this witness," Floyd said.

Mason said, "In view of the fact that this overcoat which has been marked for identification as Defendant's Exhibit Number One is one that was produced by the prosecution as having been found in the closet in Moray Cassel's apartment, I now ask that this be introduced in evidence as Defendant's Exhibit Number One."

"Objected to as wholly incompetent, irrelevant, and immaterial," Floyd said.

"I would be inclined to think so," Judge Elliott said, "unless counsel believes it can be connected up. The Court would be glad to hear your theory of the case, Mr. Mason."

Mason said, "Before I give my theory of the case, I would like to have this overcoat tried on by someone who will fill it out. I have two witnesses here in court whom I expect to use. I think they will be willing to volunteer. Mr. Franklin Gage, will you step forward, please, and try on this overcoat?"

Franklin Gage hesitated, then got to his feet, came forward, took the overcoat, looked at it, and put it on. It instantly became apparent that the sleeves were too short and the overcoat too full.

"That won't do," Mason said. "Mr. Homer Gage, will you step forward please and put on the coat?"

"I see no reason to do so," Homer Gage said.

Mason looked at him in some surprise. "Is there any reason why you *don't* want to?"

Homer Gage hesitated for a moment, then said, "All right. It looks like it's about my size, but I've never seen it before."

He stepped forward and put on the overcoat. It instantly became apparent that the coat was a perfect fit.

"Now, then, Your Honor," Mason said, "I will give the Court my theory about the overcoat. . . . Thank you very much, Mr. Gage. You may take the coat off."

Homer Gage squirmed out of the overcoat as though he had been scalded.

Mason folded the overcoat and put it over his right arm.

"Now then, Your Honor," he said, "if a person approaches a man who is armed and dangerous and wants to be absolutely certain that he gets the drop on him, he must necessarily have a gun in his hand, cocked and ready to fire.

"The best way to do this without being detected is to have a folded overcoat over the right hand, which can hold the gun under the folds of the overcoat. . . . If you'll hand me the gun which is the exhibit in the case, Mr. Bailiff . . . thank you. I will illustrate to the Court how it can be done."

Mason folded the coat, placed it over his right arm, and held his hand with the gun in it just under the folded overcoat.

"Now then, if the Court please, I will make my opening statement. It is my belief that a young woman who was a friend of a girl who worked with Moray Cassel got into that condition which is generally known as being 'in trouble.' I believe that an executive for the Escobar Import and Export Company was responsible for that condition. I will refer to this man as Mr. X.

"Moray Cassel was a very shrewd, adroit blackmailer. He found out about what was happening and what company the man worked in. He wasn't too certain of some of the facts, but he saw an oppor-

tunity to make a few easy dollars. I believe the young woman had
no part in the blackmail scheme.

"She had gone to some other state to have her baby. But one of
Cassel's scouts learned of the facts in the case and probably knew
that the young woman used a code in communicating with her
lover. Mail was probably addressed simply to thirty-six-twenty-
four-thirty-six, Escobar Import and Export Company, and signed
the same way—and these may well have been the measurements of
the young woman in the case.

"So Moray Cassel took a chance on making some quick and easy
money. He wrote a letter to the Escobar Import and Export Company and probably said something to the effect that if thirty-six-
twenty-four-thirty-six wanted to escape a paternity suit it was
incumbent to have five thousand dollars in spot cash. He probably
said he was related to the young woman.

"Mr. X was married. He couldn't afford to have the true situation
come out. His marriage was not a happy one and he knew that his
his wife would sue for divorce and for large alimony if she could
find some good legitimate reason to prove infidelity.

"So Mr. X went to Edgar Douglas and persuaded him for a
financial consideration to pretend to be the man responsible for the
woman's condition, to go to Los Angeles and make the payment to
Moray Cassel. He furnished Edgar Douglas with five thousand dollars in cash with which to make that payment.

"It happened, however, that when Edgar Douglas was getting
his car filled with gas, preparatory to his trip to Los Angeles, he
became involved in an automobile accident which rendered him unconscious and he remained unconscious until the time of his death.

"Mr. X, knowing that Moray Cassel was getting impatient, didn't
dare to try to find another stooge. He took five thousand dollars in
cash, but he also took a gun, which as it happened, although he
probably didn't know it at the time, was a gun belonging to Edgar
Douglas. He went to Los Angeles feeling that he would make a
pay-off if he could be absolutely certain that there would only be
one pay-off. If he couldn't be certain there would only be one
pay-off, he intended to kill the blackmailer.

"He went to Moray Cassel's apartment. They had a conversation.
Mr. X was a man of the world. He knew a blackmailer when he

saw him, and Moray Cassel was a shrewd blackmailer who knew a victim who would be good for any number of payments when he encountered him.

"Very calmly, very deliberately, Mr. X killed Moray Cassel, left the gun on the floor in a pool of blood, and returned to San Francisco.

"The defendant entered the apartment some time later, found a gun which she recognized as her brother's on the floor in a pool of blood. She hastily washed off the blood, wiped the gun with a damp rag, put it in her purse, and returned to San Francisco."

Judge Elliott leaned forward. "How did this Mr. X get hold of the gun that belonged to Edgar Douglas?" he asked.

Mason looked at Joyce Baffin and said rather kindly, "Edgar Douglas was a nut on guns and on the protection of his women. He wanted any woman in whom he was interested to know how to shoot and loaned one young woman his gun for target practice. I think that Mr. X probably had some influence over the woman to whom Edgar Douglas had last loaned his gun. He may have seen it in her apartment. . . . Do you care to make any statement, Miss Baffin?"

Homer Gage got up and said, "I guess everybody's done with me," and started hurrying out of the courtroom.

Judge Elliott took one look at the white-faced Joyce Baffin, at Homer Gage, and said to the bailiff, "Stop that man! Don't let him out of the door. This Court is going to take a half-hour recess and the Court suggests that the Deputy District Attorney in charge of this case use that half hour to advantage—bearing in mind, of course, that the parties are to be advised of their constitutional rights in accordance with the recent decisions of the United States Supreme Court.

"Court will recess for thirty minutes."

Chapter Eighteen

Mason, Della Street, Paul Drake, Franklin Gage, and a starry-eyed Diana Douglas were gathered in the private dining room at Giovani's.

"How in the world did you ever get all that figured out?" Diana asked.

Mason said, "I had to put two and two together and then find another two that seemed to fit into the picture. A net shortage of ten thousand dollars in the revolving cash fund indicated that there could well have been two withdrawals of five thousand dollars each. With Edgar dead there was no need to explain the first five-thousand-dollar shortage. The explanation would be that Edgar was an embezzler and he might as well have been pegged for a ten-grand theft as for five thousand. . . . Actually, I don't think your nephew would ever have given himself away, Mr. Gage, if it hadn't been for your presence."

"It is a tremendous shock to me," Franklin Gage said. "I had no idea . . . no idea at all of what was going on."

"Of course," Mason said, "handling it as we did, Ralph Gurlock Floyd wanted to button the whole thing up quick. He didn't want to be characterized in the press as one who had prosecuted an

innocent person. Therefore, he was willing to make a deal with your
nephew for a plea of guilty to second-degree murder and call
everything square."

Diana said, "I know that my brother wouldn't have had anything
to do with getting this young woman— I mean, because of . .
well, the way you said."

Mason said, "But I couldn't count on that. I was working fast
and I didn't dare to share your faith without the evidence of that
overcoat.

"Apparently, Homer Gage was in a situation which could have
cost him his position, his social prestige, and a lot of alimony. Moray
Cassel found out about it and put the bite on him, but Moray Cassel
wasn't entirely certain of his man. He knew that he was an executive
in the Escobar Import and Export Company, that the woman in the
case prided herself on her perfect measurements and that the man
used to address her as 'Dear Thirty-six-twenty-four-thirty-six.' So
Cassel used those code words in putting the bite on his victim.

"And," Mason went on with a smile, "Diana tried to live up to
the description."

Diana blushed. "I did the best I could without seeming to
overdo it."

"So," Mason went on, "Homer Gage made a deal with Edgar by
which Edgar was to take the rap, so to speak. He was to go down
and identify himself as the culprit, state that he had no funds anywhere near the amount in question but that he had embezzled some
funds from the company and was going to try to make restitution
before the shortage was noticed.

"In that way, Moray Cassel would have very probably been con-
tent with the one payment. . . . Of course, if Cassel suspected that
his real target was a prosperous executive of the company, he would
have kept on making demands. And that is why Moray Cassel is
dead.

"When Edgar had his accident and nothing was said about the
five thousand dollars Homer Gage had given him, there was nothing
for Homer Gage to do except take another five thousand out of the
rotating cash fund and make a trip to Los Angeles to size up the
man with whom he was dealing. He very definitely intended to
make a payment if he felt he could make one payment and get out.

And he very definitely intended to commit murder if he couldn't make a deal.

"He had that overcoat with him and he became afraid he'd be noticed if he wore or carried an overcoat on a very warm, sunny day so he cut the labels out of the overcoat, and when he had finished with the killing, he simply hung the overcoat in with Moray Cassel's clothes and tossed Edgar's gun down on the floor."

"But what," Franklin Gage asked, "became of the five thousand dollars which was given to Edgar by my nephew?"

Mason said, "Diana recovered that, thought that the blackmail involved her brother's reputation, came to Los Angeles to pay off, and then, following my advice, deposited the money in cash in San Francisco, getting a cashier's check payable to Diana Douglas as trustee."

Franklin Gage thought for a minute, then said, "I think, under the circumstances, the best thing you can do with that check, Diana, is to endorse it over to Mr. Mason for his fees in the case."

There was a moment's silence, then Paul Drake pressed the button. "Hold still, everybody, we're going to have a drink to that," he said.

Diana Douglas smiled at Perry Mason. "You have the check," she said.

And Franklin Gage, producing a fountain pen from his pocket, said, "And I have the pen."

THE END

All Grass Isn't Green

1

The squeaky swivel chair in which Bertha Cool shifted her hundred and sixty-five pounds of weight seemed to share its occupant's indignation.

"What do you mean, we can't do the job?" Bertha asked, the diamonds on her hands making glittering arcs of light as she banged her palms down on the desk.

The potential client, whose card gave his name simply as M. Calhoun, said, "I'll be perfectly frank . . . er, uh, Miss Cool—or is it Mrs. Cool?"

"It's Mrs.," snapped Bertha Cool. "I'm a widow."

"All right," Calhoun went on smoothly, "I need the services of a first-class, highly competent detective agency. I asked a friend who is usually rather knowledgeable in such matters and he said the firm of Cool and Lam would take care of me.

"I come up here. I find that the Cool part of the firm is a woman, and that Lam is . . ." Calhoun looked at me and hesitated.

"Go ahead," I said.

"Well, frankly," Calhoun blurted out, "I doubt if you could take care of yourself if the going got rough. You won't weigh over a hundred and forty pounds soaking wet. My idea of a detective is a big man, aggressive, competent—heavy-fisted if the occasion requires."

Bertha once more shifted her weight. Her chair creaked indignantly. "Brains," she said.

"How's that?" Calhoun asked, puzzled.

"Brains is what we sell you," Bertha Cool said. "I run the business end. Donald runs the outside end. The little runt has brains and don't ever forget it."

3

"Oh, yes . . . ah . . . doubtless," Calhoun said.

"Perhaps," I told him, "you've been reading too many mystery stories."

He had the grace to smile at that.

I said, "You've had a chance to look us over. If we don't look good to you, that door works both ways."

"Now, just a minute," Bertha Cool interposed, her diamond-hard eyes appraising our skeptical client. "You're looking for a detective agency. We can give you results. That's our forte. What the hell do you want?"

"Well, I *want* results," Calhoun admitted. "That's what I'm looking for."

"Do you know what the average private detective is?" Bertha Cool rasped. "A cop who's been retired or kicked out, a great big, beefy, bullnecked human snowplow with big fists, big feet and a muscle-bound brain.

"People like to read stories about private detectives who shove teeth down people's throats and solve murders. You tie up with an agency that is run by people who are all beef and no brains and you'll just ante up fifty dollars a day for every operative they put on the case— and they'll manage to load it up with two or three operatives if they think you can pay the tab. They'll keep charging you fifty bucks a day per operative until your money runs out. You *may* get results. You may not.

"With this agency we have one operative—that's Donald. I told you before and I'll tell you again, he's a brainy little runt. He'll charge you fifty dollars a day plus expenses and he'll get results."

"You can afford to pay fifty dollars a day?" I asked, trying to get the guy on the defensive.

"Of course I can," he snorted. "Otherwise I wouldn't be here."

I caught Bertha's eye. "All right, you're here," I told him.

He hesitated a long while, apparently trying to reach a decision. Then he said, "Very well, this is a job that calls for brains more than brawn. Perhaps you can do it."

I said. "I don't like to work for a man who is a little doubtful right at the start. Why don't you get an agency which measures up more to your expectations?"

Bertha Cool glared at me.

Calhoun said thoughtfully, "I want to find a man."

"How old?" I asked.

"About thirty," he said. "Perhaps thirty-two."

"Give me a description."

"He's about five eleven, weighs a hundred and eighty-five or so. He has wavy hair, blue eyes, and has a magnetic personality."

"Picture?" I asked.

"No picture."

"Name?"

"Hale—H-a-l-e. The first name is Colburn. He signs his name C. E. Hale. I understand his close friends call him Cole."

"Last address?"

"Eight-seventeen Billinger Street. He had an apartment there, number forty-three. He left very suddenly. I don't think he took anything with him except a suitcase."

"Rent?"

"I believe it is paid up until the twentieth."

"Occupation?"

"I am given to understand he is a novelist."

"That location," I said, "is a bohemian neighborhood. There are lots of writers and artists living there."

"Exactly," Calhoun said.

"May I ask why you want to find Hale?"

"I want to talk with him."

"Just what do we do?"

"Locate the guy. Don't leave a back trail. Just give me the place where he is at present."

"That's all?"

"That's all."

"And Hale is a novelist?"

"I believe he is working on a novel. In fact, I know he is, but as to the nature of his writing I can tell you nothing. I know that he has a theory that when you talk about a story you either have a sympathetic or an unsympathetic audience.

"If the audience is unsympathetic it weakens your self-confidence. If the audience is sympathetic you are encouraged to talk too much and tell too much, which dissipates your creative energy in conversation rather than in writing."

"He is, then, secretive?"

"Reticent," he said.

I looked the guy over—casual slacks that were well pressed, a sports coat that had cost money, a short-sleeved Dacron shirt with a bolo tie. The stone in the tie guide was a vivid green.

He saw me looking at it. "Chrysocolla," he said proudly.

"What's chrysocolla?" I asked.

"A semiprecious stone which ounce for ounce is probably worth more than gold. It is very rare. I might describe it as being a copper-stained agate. That doesn't exactly describe it, but it gives you an idea."

"Are you a rock hound?" I asked.

"So-so," he said.

"Find the stone yourself?"

"No, I traded for it. It's a beautiful specimen."

"When did you last see this Hale?" I asked.

Bertha said, "Now, just a minute, before we get down to brass tacks, we'd better finish with the preliminaries."

"Preliminaries?" Calhoun asked.

"Retainer," Bertha said.

He turned from me to study her.

"How much?"

"Three fifty."

"And what does that buy me?"

"Services of the agency, Donald doing the legwork at fifty bucks a day plus expenses. I furnish the executive management."

"At another fifty bucks a day?" he asked.

"It's all included in the one package," she said.

He regarded Bertha, sitting there as stiff as a roll of barbed wire, and somewhere around sixty-five, give or take a few years.

"Very well," he said.

"Got your checkbook handy?" Bertha asked.

He didn't like being pushed. He hesitated again, then reached in his pocket and brought out a billfold.

No one said anything while he hitched his chair over to the corner of Bertha Cool's desk and started counting out fifty-dollar bills.

Bertha leaned slightly forward, trying to see the interior of the billfold and make an estimate of the amount of money it held. He shifted his position so she couldn't see the interior.

There was silence while he counted out seven nice crisp fifty-dollar bills and put them on Bertha's desk.

"Now then," I said, "when did you last see Hale?"

"Is that important?"

"I think it is."

"I have never seen him."

"You've told me all you know about him?"

"No, I've told you all a good detective should need to know."

"And," I went on, "we'd like to know a little more about *you.*"

He regarded me with uncordial eyes, then reached over to Bertha's desk and tapped the money with his fingers. "That money," he said, "gives you all of my background you're going to need."

He got to his feet.

"Where do we make reports?" I asked. "By mail or telephone? In other words, how do we reach you?"

"You don't reach me," he said. "I reach you. I have your phone number, you have my name. You know what I want."

"Just a minute," I said. "I want to take a look at a map of the city and get this location straight."

He hesitated halfway to the door.

I hurried down to my office and said to Elsie Brand, my secretary, "There's a man in slacks and sports coat just leaving Bertha's office, about thirty-one or thirty-two. I'd like to find out where he goes. If he takes a cab, get the number of the cab. It he has his own car, get the license."

"Oh, Donald," she said despairingly. "You know I'm a rotten detective."

"You're all right if you don't act self-conscious," I said. "Get out there in the corridor. Get in the same elevator he takes and try thinking about something else while you're riding down with him. If he acts suspicious, call off the job, but there's just a chance he'll be rather preoccupied and won't pay any attention to you."

I went back to Bertha's office just as Calhoun left the reception room. She was fingering the money. She looked up and said, "I don't like that smirking, supercilious s.o.b."

I said, "He's putting on an act."

"What do you mean?"

I said, "He knew more about us than he wanted to let on. All that business about being surprised that you were a woman and that I wasn't built like a professional wrestler was part of an act."

"How do you know?"

"I sensed it."

"Why would he put on an act like that?"

"To get us on the defensive."

Bertha rang for her secretary and handed her the money. "Take this down and deposit it," she said.

I played a hunch. "This man that was just in," I said, "Calhoun. What did he say when he entered the office?"

"He wanted to know if Mrs. Cool was busy."

"Then he didn't just see the sign on the door, COOL & LAM, and know nothing about the firm."

She shook her head. "He knew about Mrs. Cool because he specifically asked for Mrs. Cool."

"Mrs. Cool?" I asked.

"Definitely, Mrs. Cool."

I glanced over at Bertha.

Her diamond-sharp eyes were blinking contemplatively.

I said, "The guy was very careful to keep from telling us anything about himself."

"As far as that is concerned, his money talked," Bertha said. "We don't give a damn who he is. We'll use up the three hundred and fifty and then we quit until he puts some more money in the kitty."

"I don't like it at all," I told her. "Let's take a look in the phone book."

"Oh, Donald, we can't look through all the different districts in the city. Here, let's take a look at this one district and see how many Calhouns there are."

"M. Calhouns," I reminded her.

Bertha opened the phone book, found the proper page and said, "here are half a dozen of them right here. M.A. Calhoun, an M.M. Calhoun, a Morley Calhoun, an M. Calhoun and Company . . . the guy could be anybody."

Bertha had a reference book in back of her desk, *Prominent Citizens of California.* I pointed to it.

Bertha pulled the book down, opened it and said, "And here we've got a lot more Calhouns. Wait a minute, here's Milton Carling Calhoun who looks something like our man—Milton Carling Calhoun, the Second."

I looked at the picture. It could have been our client taken five years earlier. He was the son of Milton Carling Calhoun, the First.

His father, who was dead, had been a stockbroker. Our man had graduated from college with honors, majored in journalism and had married Beatrice Millicent Spaulding.

There were no children. There was a list of clubs as long as your arm. Apparently the guy had never done anything in his life except inherit money.

"Fry me for an oyster," Bertha said, reading the copy. "The s.o.b. sure held out on us."

"Well, we've got him pegged now," I told her.

"Pegged is right," Bertha said.

I went down to my office and waited for Elsie Brand.

Elsie came back with the report. "He took a cab," she said, "a yellow cab. I managed to get the number. He evidently had the cab waiting at the curb because the flag was down and as soon as the cabbie saw him coming he reached back and opened the door. Our man got in it and the cab drove away."

"You couldn't follow?"

"There was no cab I could grab in time," she said. "I told you, Donald, I'm a lousy detective."

"The number of the cab was what?"

"I got that all right. It was a Yellow Cab, number sixteen seventy-two."

"Okay, Elsie," I said. "You did a good job. I just wanted to make certain he was trying to give us a double cross. I'll take if from there and thanks a lot."

2

Eight-seventeen Billinger Street was an apartment house which had been converted from a three-story residence.

At one time that section of the city had been the site of imposing homes, but that had been many, many years ago.

The city had grown and engulfed the district. The luxurious homes had run downhill, then had been converted into rooming houses, or apartments with beauty parlors, small offices and nondescript stores on the ground floor.

I detoured a single-chair barbershop, found the stairs, climbed to the second floor, located Apartment 43 and stood for a moment at the door listening.

From Apartment 42, which adjoined it on the south, I could hear the steady clack of a typewriter, then an intermittent pause, then more clacking on the typewriter. From Apartment 43 there wasn't a sound.

I tapped gently on the door. There was no answer.

The typewriter in Apartment 42 was clacking away again.

I stood there in the semi-dark hallway, undecided. I put my hand on the doorknob of Apartment 43. The latch clicked back. I pushed gently on the door for an inch or two. The door opened soundlessly.

I closed the door again and knocked, this time a little more firmly. There was no answer.

I turned the knob, opened the door and looked inside.

It was a furnished apartment and someone had gone places in a hurry. There were a couple of empty cardboard cartons on the floor, and some old newspapers. Drawers had been pulled out, emptied, and left open. It was a one-room affair with a little kitchenette off to

11

my right and an open door to a bath at the far end. There was a curtained closet; the curtain had been pulled back, exposing a wall bed. Empty wire clothes hangers were swinging dejectedly from a metal rod.

I wanted to go in and look around, but I had a feeling that it wasn't wise. I backed out and gently closed the door.

The typewriter in 42 had quit clacking. I heard steps coming to the door.

I raised my hand and knocked hard and loud on the door of 43.

The door of Apartment 42 opened. A woman in her late twenties, or perhaps early thirties, stood there looking at me appraisingly.

I smiled reassuringly at her and said, "I'm knocking on forty-three," and with that raised my hand and knocked again.

"Are you Colburn Hale's publisher?" she asked.

I turned to regard her searchingly. "Why do you ask?"

"Because Cole is expecting his publisher."

"I see," I said.

"You haven't answered my question," she observed.

"Should I?" I asked.

"I think so."

"Why don't you ask Mr. Hale when he comes back?" I said.

"Because I don't think he's coming back—perhaps I could help you?"

"Perhaps you could."

"Will you kindly tell me what's going on?" she asked.

I raised my eyebrows. "Is something going on?"

"You know it is. People came here in the middle of the night. They opened and closed drawers, put things in cardboard cartons, carried them downstairs."

"What time?"

"Around one o'clock in the morning."

"Did you see them?" I asked.

"I couldn't stand it any longer," she said. "I couldn't sleep with those people tramping back and forth, and I finally got up, put on a robe and opened the door, but they'd gone by that time."

"What time?"

"About one-thirty."

"How many people were there?"

"Two, I think."

"Colburn Hale and a friend?"

"I didn't have a chance to hear what was said. I didn't recognize Cole's voice. It might have been two other people for all I know. Now then, I'll ask you again, publisher?"

"No, I'm not," I said, "but I'm interested in talking to him before he talks to his publisher."

"Then you're a literary agent?" she asked.

"Well, not exactly, but—well, I can't tell you any more than that I'd like to talk to Hale before he talks to his publisher."

"Maybe you're making him an offer for a motion picture contract," she said.

I moved my shoulders in a deprecatory gesture and said, "That's your version."

She looked me over and said, "Would you like to come in for a minute?"

I looked dubiously at Hale's door. "I guess he's not home," I said. "You don't have any idea when he'll return?"

"I think he moved out. I don't think he's coming back."

"Behind in the rent?"

"I understand he pays his rent in advance from the twentieth to the twentieth. You don't get behind with your rent in this place. You either come up with the money or out you go."

"Hard-boiled like that, eh?" I asked.

"Very hard-boiled."

I followed her into her apartment. It was a little more pretentious than the apartment next door. Doors indicated a wall bed. There were a table, a battered typewriter desk, a portable typewriter and pages of a manuscript.

"You're a writer?" I asked.

She indicated a straight-backed chair. "Please sit down," she said. "Yes, I'm a writer, and if you're a publisher . . . well, I'd like to talk with you."

"Frankly," I told her, "I'm not a publisher. I don't even know whether I could help you or not. Wht kind of material do you write?"

"I'm writing a novel," she said, "and I think it's a *good* one."

"How far along are you with it?"

"I'm a little over halfway."

"Good characters?" I asked.

"They stand out."

"Character conflict?"

"Lots of it. I have suspense. I have people confronted with dilemmas which are going to require decisions, and the reader is going to be vitally interested in what those decisions are going to be."

"That's very interesting," I said. "How well do you know Colburn Hale?"

"Fairly well. He's been here only five or six weeks."

"What made you think I was his publisher?"

"I knew he was expecting a visit from his publisher and he had been working terribly hard on his novel, pounding away on the typewriter. He was a very good hunt-and-peck typist."

"Any idea what his novel was about?"

"No, we just decided we wouldn't tell each other our plots. And I have a basic rule. I never tell the details of a plot to anyone. I think it's bad luck."

I nodded sympathetically. "You and Hale were quite friendly?" I asked.

"Just neighbors," she said. "He had a girl friend."

"So?" I asked.

"Nanncie Beaver," she said. "I'm going to run over and see her sometime this afternoon and see what she knows. You see, we don't have telephones."

"A neighbor?" I asked.

"Up on eight-thirty," she said. "That's just a few doors up the street. She has Apartment Sixty-two B. I hope—I hope she knows."

"Is there any reason why she wouldn't?"

"You know how men are," she said suddenly.

"How are they?" I asked.

She flared up with sudden bitterness. "They like to play around and then if there are any—any responsibilities they duck out. They take a powder. They're gone. You can't find them."

"You think Colburn Hale was like that?"

"I think all men are like that."

"Including publishers?"

Her eyes softened somewhat and surveyed me from head to foot. "If you're a publisher," she said, "you're different. And somehow I think you are a publisher regardless of what you say."

"I'd like to be a publisher," I said.

"A subsidy publisher?"

I shook my head. "No, not that."

"You haven't told me your name."

"You haven't told me yours."

"I'm Marge Fulton," she said.

"I'm Donald Lam," I told her. "I'll be back again to see if Colburn Hale has come in. If he does come in, and you happen to hear him, will you tell him that Donald Lam is anxious to see him?"

"And what shall I tell him Donald Lam wants to see him about?"

I hesitated for several seconds, as though debating whether to tell her, then I said, "I think I'd better tell him firsthand. I don't want to be rude, but I think it would be better that way."

I got up and walked to the door. "Thanks a lot, Miss Fulton. You've been very helpful."

"Will I see you again?"

"Probably," I said.

"I think I'm writing a honey of a novel," she said.

"I'll bet you are," I told her.

She stood in the doorway watching me down the stairs.

I had a secondhand portable typewriter in my car. It fitted snugly into its case, and I got this portable out, climbed the stairs at 830 Billinger Street and found Apartment 62B was on the second floor. I tapped on the door and got no answer. I tentatively tried the knob. The door was locked. I stepped back a few paces and knocked on the door of Apartment 61B.

The woman who opened the door was a faded blonde with traces of pouches under her eyes, but she was slim waisted and attractive. She was wearing a blouse and slacks, and I had evidently disappointed her because her facial expression showed that she had been expecting someone whom she wanted to see and I was a letdown.

I said, "You'll pardon me, ma'am, but I've got to raise some money in a hurry. I've got a typewriter here, a first-class portable that I'd like to sell."

She looked at me, then at the typewriter, and her eyes showed quick interest. "How much do you want for it?"

I said, "My name is Donald Lam. I'm a writer. I want money. I'd like to have you try out this typewriter and make me an offer. I'm desperately in need of cash. You can have this machine at a bargain."

She said, "I already have a typewriter."

"Not like this one," I told her. "This is in first-class shape, perfect alignment, and the work it turns out is—impressive."

I saw that interested her.

"Write a manuscript on this typewriter," I went on, "and it will stand out from the run-of-the-mill typing. Any editor will give it his respectful attention."

"How did you know I wrote?" she asked.

"I thought I heard the sound of a typewriter as I was walking down the corridor."

"Who referred you to me?"

"No one. I'm in a spot where I need cash, and I'm going to sell this typewriter to sombody before I leave the building."

"For cash?"

"For cash."

She shook her head and said, "Lots of people in this building use typewriters, but mighty few of them have the kind of cash that you would want."

I said, "Would it be too much to ask you to try out this typewriter? I might make a trade, taking your machine, giving you this one and taking some cash to boot."

"How much to boot?"

"I'd have to see your machine first."

She looked at her wrist watch. "Come in," she said.

The apartment was a two-room affair with a partial division screening off the kitchenette. A portable typewriter sat on a rather battered card table with a folding chair in front of it. There were pages of manuscript on the card table and the apartment gave evidences of having been well lived in. It wasn't exactly sloppy, but it wasn't neat.

"You're living here alone?" I asked.

Her eyes suddenly became suspicious. "That's neither here nor there. Let's look at your portable," she said, picking her portable up off the card table and setting it on a chair.

I opened my portable and put it on the card table.

She put some paper in and tried it out. She had the hunt-and-peck system, but she was good at it.

"What do you write?" I asked. "Novels, articles, short stories?"

"Anything," she said. "I am Annaemae Clinton."

I looked around a bit. There were writer's magazines and a book containing a list of markets. There was a pile of envelopes on a shelf which I surmised contained rejected stories which had been returned from the editors.

She swiftly picked up the pages of manuscript that were on the card table, took them over to the chair which held the typewriter and put them face down on top of the typewriter.

"This is a pretty good machine," she said.

"It's in perfect condition."

"What kind of a trade?" she asked.

"I'd want to take a look at your machine."

She went over to the chair, picked up the manuscript pages from on top of the typewriter, moved them over to a bookcase, brought the typewriter over, shoved my machine out of the way and put her typewriter down on the card table. Then she rather grudgingly handed me a sheet of paper.

The typewriter was an ancient affair which ran like a threshing machine and the type was pretty much out of line. In addition to which the type faces were dirty. The *e* and the *a* gave pretty poor impressions.

"Well?" she asked.

I said. "I'll take your typewriter, give you mine, and take forty dollars in cash."

She thought it over for a while, then said, "Let me try your machine again."

She did more typing this time. I could see she wanted it.

"Twenty-five dollars," she said.

"Forty," I told her. "This machine is like new."

"Thirty."

"Make it thirty-five and it's a deal."

"You're a hard man to do business with."

"I need the money, but I've got a good typewriter here. Your machine needs lots of work done on it."

"I know that."

She was silent for a while, then said, "Would you take fifteen dollars down and twenty dollars in two weeks?"

I shook my head. "I need money."

She sighed reluctantly. "I can't cut the mustard," she said.

"All right," I told her. "I'll try next door. Who's your neighbor in Apartment Sixty-two B?"

"There isn't any."

"Not rented?"

"It was, but she moved out, a woman by the name of Beaver, Nanncie Beaver. She spelled her first name N-a-n-n-c-i-e."

"A writer?"

"I guess so. She used to do a lot of clacking on the typewriter. I didn't ever see her by-line on anything."

"Sociable?"

"Not particularly—but a nice sort. She moved all at once. I didn't know anything about it until yesterday when she moved out."

"Boyfriends?"

"I wouldn't know. We live our own lives up here. There's a couple in sixty B, name of Austin. I don't know what they do. I think he has a job somewhere. I don't know if she writes. I never hear a typewriter over there. I think she's some sort of an artist. They keep very much to themselves. When you come right down to it, that's the way people live in this section."

She thought for a moment and then added, "And it's the only way to live."

"Did Miss Beaver give you any hint she was moving out?" I asked.

"No, I didn't know anything about it until she started moving out cardboard boxes and suitcases."

"Transfer man?"

"Taxicab," she said. "She made some arrangements with the driver to help her."

"That's strange about the cardboard boxes and the suitcases," I said.

"Well, she had cardboard cartons. There must have been a half a dozen of them that were sealed with tape and had stationary pasted on the side. She took those first and then in about thirty minutes came back and got the suitcases."

"Taxi driver helped her all the time?"

"Yes."

"A Yellow Cab?"

"Yes, at least I think so."

"Same taxi driver?"

"I wouldn't know. Heavens! *Why* are you so interested in Nanncie Beaver?"

"I'm darned if I know," I told her, "but I'm a great one to try and put two and two together and understand people. I regard everyone as a potential story. What you have told me just arouses my curiosity."

"Well, she's gone. You can't sell her a typewriter now."

"You don't think she'll be back?"

She shook her head. "Tell me, what's the best deal you'll make on a trade?"

I looked at her typewriter again. "I can't offer you very much encouragement. This is in bad shape. It needs cleaning, oiling, a general overhaul."

"I know. I keep putting things off, and when you're freelancing on articles and things, you don't have much money. I can't get along without the machine—and I don't have much money—so I can't afford to put it in the shop. Some of my checks I get for stories are for less than five dollars . . . the cheaper magazines, you know."

"Tough luck," I said. "Perhaps if your manuscripts looked—well, more professional, you could make better deals."

"That's what I was thinking. That's why I wanted to see what kind of a trade you'd make—but I can't go without eats, and rent is due in two weeks."

"I can't better the proposition I've made you," I said.

"You don't feel you could take fifteen dollars down and then come back in two weeks and get twenty dollars. I've had a story accepted. I'll have the twenty for sure."

"I'm sorry," I said. "I couldn't do it. Who else is in the building that you know that might be interested in typewriters?"

"No one," she said. "There are only four apartments on this floor. The fourth apartment is rented by some kind of a business woman. She's up and off to work every morning. I don't know anything about the people on the upper floor."

I put my typewriter back in its case.

"I'm sorry," I said. "I'll try the building next door. Do you know anything about it?"

She shook her head. "We don't pay much attention to our neighbors," she said. "We have our friends and that's that. I sure would like to have that typewriter."

"I wish I could afford to sell it on the basis of the offer you've made, but I have my own living to think of."

"Do you write?"

"Once in a while."

"You look prosperous. You look as if you didn't have trouble selling."

"Can you tell that by looking at me?"

"Yes, there's an incisive something about you, an atmosphere of assurance. You take us free-lance writers that get beaten down with rejections and after a while there's a general aura of frustration and futility which clings to us. I've seen it happen to others and I think it's happening with me."

"Tell you what I'll do," I told her. "You've been a good sport. I'll take a chance. Give me fifteen dollars and your typewriter, and I'll come back in two weeks for the twenty."

"Will you do that?" she asked, her face lighting up.

I nodded.

"Oh, that's wonderful! I've been thinking about the appearance of my work lately. It does look sort of—well, amateurish."

"A fresh ribbon wouldn't hurt any on your typewriter," I said.

"Fresh ribbons cost money," she said, "and money doesn't grow on bushes."

She went into a closet, fumbled around for a while, then came out with two fives and five dollars in one-dollar bills.

I handed her my typewriter, put her typewriter in its case, and said, "Remember, I'll be back in two weeks. I hope the new machine brings you luck."

"It will. It will! I know it will!" she said. "I'm feeling better already. You said your name was Lam?"

"Donald Lam."

"I'll have the money for you, Donald. I just know I will. I'm assured of that sale. I feel it in my bones. I would have done a little bit better on this first installment, only I have to eat and I'm saving out enough for hamburger. You can't do good work when you're *really* hungry.

"That's right."

She saw me to the door, then on impulse put her arms around me and kissed me on the cheek. "I think you're very wonderful," she said.

I took her battered-up typewriter and went back to my car, thinking over the information I had obtained about Nanncie Beaver.

Two trips in a taxicab. Cardboard cartons, one trip, which lasted less than half an hour; and then suitcases on the *second* trip, and she didn't come back after the second trip.

I went back to the directory and found the card that was marked MANAGER.

I went to the manager's apartment. She was past middle age, heavy and cynical. "Do you have a vacancy?" I asked.

"I'm going to have one, sixty-two B on the second floor. It's a nice apartment."

"Can I take a look at it?"

"Not right now. It isn't cleaned up yet. The tenant just moved out yesterday and left things in something of a mess."

"I'll make allowances for that."

"I can't go up with you now. I'm expecting a long-distance call."

"Let me have the key and I'll take a look," I said.

"What do you do?" she asked.

"I'm a writer."

She shook her head. "Writers are pretty poor payers. They mean all right, but they can't come up with the money when they don't have it, and there's lots of times when they don't have it."

"What do you want for the apartment?" I asked.

"Fifty-five dollars," she said.

I said, "I'm a little different from the average writer. I would be able to give you the first month's rent down and fifty-five dollars for the last month's rent. Anytime I didn't pay up you could take the rent out of that second fifty-five dollars."

"Well, now, that's something different," she said. "You must be a very successful writer."

"I'm getting by," I told her.

She handed me a key. "Remember, the apartment is in an awful mess. I'm going to have it cleaned later on today."

"Sure," I said. "I'll make allowances."

I went back up the stairs and into Apartment 62B.

It was in something of a mess. Papers were strewn around on the floor. Other papers had been hastily crumpled and thrown into the wastebasket. Some of the drawers were half open.

I smoothed out the crumpled papers. Most of them were the type of form letter that is sent out on direct mail advertising. One of the papers was typed and listed a series of articles, three books, with the title and the author, and then the list went on: half a package of first-page typewriter paper, a full package of copy paper, pencils, pens, erasers, typewriter ribbons, envelopes, writer's market data.

There was nothing to tell me why she'd pulled that piece of paper out of the typewriter, crumpled it up and thrown it in the wastebasket.

At the top was the name—NANNCIE ARMSTRONG, BOX 5.

I took the paper, folded it up, left the apartment, gave the keys to the manager and said I was thinking it over and that I'd like to see the apartment after it was cleaned up.

I drove to my apartment, got the classified telephone book, and looked under STORAGE.

There was a storage company, the International, which had a branch within about five blocks of Billinger Street, where Nanncie Beaver had lived.

I went back out to the car and drove over to the Yellow Cab Company. The dispatching operator said, "I had a cab yesterday that picked up some cardboard cartons at eight-thirty Billinger Street and took them to the International Storage branch that is about five blocks away . . . Was there trouble?"

"Quite the contrary," I said. "I found that cab driver very alert, very competent, very courteous. I have some other things I want done and I'd like to get him."

"That cab might be rather hard to locate," the operator said.

"Your cabs report in on what they're doing," I said. "This cab reported in that it was on Billinger Street and was taking a bunch of cartons to the International Storage Company; then the cab picked me up with my suitcases."

Since I knew that the cab drivers reported by address and not by customer, I knew the dispatcher had no way of knowing whether the customer had been a man or a woman.

I pushed a five-dollar bill through the wicket. "It's quite important to me," I said. "If a box of chocolates would help refresh your recollection, this would give the needed stimulus."

"That won't be necessary," she said.

"It might help," I told her.

She almost absent-mindedly reached for the five-dollar bill. "It might take a little while to look this up," she said.

"I'll wait."

"I . . . wait a minute, I've got it right here. It was cab two twenty-seven A. These drivers work in shifts, you know. The cabs keep busy all the time, theoretically twenty-four hours a day. One cab driver returns the cab to the garage, the next driver picks it up."

"I know," I said, "but this driver was on duty in the morning and . . ."

"Then he'd probably be on duty at this hour," she said.

"Could you locate him," I asked, "and have him go back to Eight-thirty Billinger Street? I'll be waiting there for him."

"You want to get this particular cab?"

"This particular *driver*," I said.

"All right," she told me, making a note. "I'll notify him. You'll be waiting there?"

"I'll be waiting there at the foot of the stairs."

I drove my car back to 830 Billinger Street and waited twenty-five minutes before a Yellow Cab drove up.

The driver got out and looked around.

"You did a job for me yesterday," I said, "moving some cartons to the International Storage Company."

He looked at me thoughtfully. "It wasn't for you," he said. "It was . . ."

"I know," I told him. "It was for my assistant, Nanncie Beaver, who was moving out of Apartment Sixty-two B. Now then, there's been a mix-up on some of the stuff that she took with her and some of the cartons that were left at the storage company. I'm going to have to check and you can help me. First, we'll go to the International."

He took the ten dollars I handed him and said, "Is this on the up and up?"

"Of course it's on the up and up. I'm just trying to get some stuff straightened out. I think Nanncie made a mistake in packing up in the apartment and put a manuscript in which I'm interested in one of the boxes that was stored."

"Okay," he said, "let's go."

He pulled down the flag and I rode with him to the branch of the International Storage Company.

"Just wait here," I said. "I won't be long."

I walked in and told the girl at the desk, "My assistant brought in a bunch of cartons from our apartment at Eight-thirty Billinger Street yesterday. The cab driver out there made the delivery. She signed the papers. There's been a mix-up in the number of boxes. I want to find the bill of lading, or whatever it is you issue, and check on the number of boxes."

She took it as a matter of course. "What name?" she asked.

"Nanncie Armstrong," I said taking a shot in the dark.

She ran down an alphabetical list, said, "Here it is. There were six cardboard cartons."

"Only six?"

"Only six."

"Then six A is missing," I said. "I'll have to try to locate it. Thank you very much."

I could see that there was just a faint hint of suspicion in the girl's eyes, so I didn't press my luck. I went back to the taxicab and said, "There's been a mix-up somewhere. We'll go back to Eight-thirty Billinger Street."

On the road back, I said, "You took my assistant and her suitcase after she had stored the boxes?"

"That's right."

"Airport?" I asked.

He turned around with sudden suspicion. "Not the airport," he said.

I laughed and said, "She's always trying to save money. I suppose she went by bus. I told her to take the plane."

"I took her to the bus depot," he admitted.

I didn't ask any more questions but paid off the meter when he stopped at Billinger Street and started for the stairs. "I've got to find that extra box somewhere," I told him. "I suppose Nanncie left it with the manager for me to pick up. We're giving up the apartment, you know."

"So I gathered," he said, then looked at the tip I had given him, nodded his head, said, "Okay," and then drove away.

I got in my car, drove to my apartment and picked up a cardboard carton, took some old newspapers and three or four books that I didn't care much about, sealed everything in the box and typewrote a sheet, NANNCIE ARMSTRONG, Box 6A.

I made up a detailed fake inventory and taped the sheet of paper on the carton.

I then went back to the International Storage Company and came in lugging my dummy box with a cheerful smile on my face.

"All right," I said, "I chased down the box that was lost. This is box number six A. Put it with the others if you will, please."

She took the box.

I said, "I presume there may be a little more to pay on the storage."

"It won't amount to much. We get two months' storage in advance on jobs of this sort. There were six packages and she paid for them—there'll only be fifty cents due on a package this size, which we'll put in with the others."

"Fine," I told her, handed her fifty cents, and started for the door, then checked my step as though struck by an afterthought.

I walked back and said, "I'm sorry, but I'm going to have to have a receipt."

"But Miss Armstrong has the receipt," she said.

"I know, for six cartons. Now there are seven, counting this one which is numbered six A."

She frowned a minute, then said, "All right, I'll make out a separate receipt."

She took a piece of paper, scribbled "One cardboard carton added to Nanncie Armstrong's account, General Delivery, Calexico, California," marked ".50¢ paid," signed the receipt with her initials and handed it to me.

"You can put this with the others and it'll be all right," she said.

I thanked her and walked out.

Nanncie Armstrong had taken a Greyhound Bus. She had given an address, General Delivery, in Calexico. She didn't have a car of her own. Colburn Hale hadn't left the faintest sign of a backtrack, but putting two and two together, it was a good bet that he and Nanncie Beaver were planning a meeting.

I drove back to my apartment, picked up a suitcase, threw it in the back of the agency heap and started for Calexico.

3

I drove through the Beaumont and Banning Pass with the San Gorgo-
nio Mountains on my left and San Jacinto towering high on my right.

We made a charge to clients of fifteen cents a mile for the agency
car, and as the miles clicked off I wondered how Bertha and the client
were going to react to the expense account.

Bertha was always screaming to keep expenses down because that
meant more of a fee for the agency, and driving down to Calexico was
going to put a big nick in the client's three hundred and fifty bucks—
by the time I charged mileage and my living expenses on top of that.

There was still snow on the north side of San Jacinto, which towers
more than two miles above sea level, but it was hot down in the valley, and by the time I had left Indio behind and the road dropped
down to below sea level it was too hot for comfort. Bertha would
never listen to having an agency heap with air conditioning. She
claimed all of our driving was around the city and air conditioning
was more of a nuisance than a benefit there.

I hadn't reported to the office or told Bertha where I was going. I
knew she'd have a fit. But the Calexico lead was the only one I had.

It was late afternoon when I reached Calexico.

Calexico and Mexicali are twin cities. Calexico on the north, Mexicali on the south, and the international boundary fence between the
United States and Mexico is about all that separates the two cities.

Now, Nanncie had no car. She had taken a bus. She evidently
wasn't too flush with money. I felt she wouldn't be staying at the
rather swank De Anza Hotel. In fact, I wasn't sure that she was in
Calexico at all. The only thing I had to go by was that address of

27

General Delivery. She could very well have crossed the border and gone into Mexicali.

I knew that I was going to have to do a lot of routine work.

I had a decoy envelope with me which I had addressed to Nanncie Armstrong at General Delivery, and I dropped it into the mail.

Unless you're a Federal officer, the post office will give out no information about its customers, but the decoy envelope is a good way to get you the information you want in a reasonably small town.

The decoy envelope is manufactured especially for that purpose. It is too big to be put in a pocket or in a purse. It has red and green stripes on it so it is as conspicuous as a bright-red necktie at a funeral. You mail the envelope, get a parking place where you can watch the door of the post office and keep an eye on the people who come and go, particularly at about the time the mail is being distributed.

If the subject calls for mail at the General Delivery window and gets the decoy envelope, he can't put it in his pocket if he's a man, or if it is a woman it won't fit in her purse. The subject comes out the door holding the decoy envelope and usually pauses on the sidewalk to open it.

The decoy envelope has an ad in it, a routine solicitation to buy real estate, and the subject thinks it's just part of a broadside mailing campaign.

The detective covering the post office gets a good look at the subject and a chance to follow.

After I mailed my envelope I drove up and down the street, listing the motels and rooming houses. I didn't have too much hope here because I had a feeling the subject had crossed over to Mexico but would continue to get mail at Calexico.

However, having made out a list of the motels, I got to a public telephone and started making calls.

With each one I said, "This is the Acme Credit Agency. You have a woman who is registered with you who doesn't have an automobile but who came in a taxicab. Her name is Debora Smith. Can you tell me what unit she's occupying?"

I got a turndown in three places and then at the Maple Leaf I struck unexpected pay dirt.

"We have a woman such as you describe," the voice said, "who came here by taxicab carrying two suitcases, but her name is not Debora Smith."

"What unit does she occupy?" I asked.

"Unit twelve."

I said, "The party I want is about sixty-two years old. She comes from New York City. She's about five feet six, rather slender, and—"

"No, no, no," the voice interrupted me. "This person is around twenty-six with auburn hair. She's medium height, has a good figure and . . ."

"That's not the one I'm after," I said. "My party is in the sixties and rather slender, a little above average height."

"I'm sorry, we have no one by that description."

"Thank you very much," I said, and hung up.

I got in the agency car, drove to the Maple Leaf, registered and was assigned to Unit 7.

It was a fairly good motel with a small swimming pool, a patio and some beach chairs around the pool.

It was getting late, but a couple of kids and a matronly woman were in the pool.

I put on my suit, went to the pool, hesitated about getting in, and then went to one of the beach chairs and relaxed, sitting where I could keep my eye on Unit 12.

It was no dice.

It got dark. The swimmers left the pool and I was getting chilled. I went in and dressed, sat in my parked car and kept my eye on Unit 12.

Nothing happened until twenty minutes to nine when my party came in.

I had her spotted as soon as I saw her, even before she fitted the key to the door of Unit 12. She was a nice looker. She arrived by taxicab and she looked dejected.

I waited until I saw she was headed for Unit 12; then I started the agency heap, overtook the taxicab, which was headed toward the border, and signaled him over to the curb.

The driver was an alert-looking Mexican.

"Is this a Mexican cab?" I asked.

He nodded.

"I want to go across the border," I said, "but I don't want to take my car. Can I park it here and go across with you?"

"It is illegal for me to pick up a fare on a return trip," he said.

"I came across from Mexicali with you," I told him. "Don't you remember?"

White teeth flashed in the dim light from the instrument panel. "Now I remember," he said. "Get in."

I parked and locked my car and got in the cab.

"We have to make a little detour to cross the border," he said, "but we make a flat rate. Where do you want to go?"

He looked at the five dollars I handed him.

"You just delivered a young woman at the Maple Leaf Motel," I said. "Where did you pick her up?"

"Oh ho," he said, "a detective!"

I grinned at him and said, "A caballero who is lonesome. I would like very much to pick up that young woman, but I don't think the usual approach would be any good."

"She came to me," the driver said, "from the Monte Carlo Café in Mexicali."

"And that is where you are taking me," I said.

Again his teeth flashed in a wide smile. "But certainly," he said.

Pedestrians can walk straight across the border of Calexico, but the automotive traffic has to make a detour around through a side street, then along a street which parallels the border, until it comes to the north and south road where it is stopped by a traffic signal, then has to make a right-hand turn in order to cross into Mexico.

This gave me time for a little conversation with the driver.

"You Mexican taxicab drivers are permitted to drive across and deliver fares in the United States?"

"*Si*, senor," he said. "And the American cab can cross into Mexico and deliver a fare in Mexicali, but we are not supposed to pick up a fare in Calexico to return to Mexico." He shrugged his shoulder. "Perhaps there is trouble. I do not know. If I am unfortunate I could have a fine."

I thought perhaps that was an approach for a touch so said nothing.

After a while he said, "That is peculiar, that case of the woman who goes to the Maple Leaf Motel."

"Yes?" I asked.

"Yes," he said.

There was a period of silence.

This time I interpreted the silence correctly and he had made the right approach. I produced another five-dollar bill.

He took it eagerly, said. "I have much trouble at home. I have four children, another is coming, and the cost of living is very high."

"The cost of living is very high for me," I said. "What is peculiar about the woman?"

"She does not speak Spanish," he said. "The waiter that she asked to call the cab called me. He told me he had a passenger for me to deliver in the United States. Then he told me she had gone to the café, she had ordered one drink. She had waited, waited, waited. Then had ordered another drink. She had waited, waited, waited. Then she ordered a meal and she ate very, very slowly, very slowly, indeed, senor . . . She was waiting for someone who did not come. Does that help, senor?"

"It may help," I said.

Then he said, suddenly stopping the car, "Get out, please, and walk the one block until you have passed the border. I will be waiting for you there and I will deliver you the rest of the way. It is better this way. I cannot afford the trouble."

I got out of the cab at the corner, walked down the street and crossed the border. I would not have been surprised if I had never seen the cab driver again, but he was there waiting to drive me the four blocks to the Monte Carlo Café.

The café was a fairly large restaurant, although the entrance was modest, a single room with a bar at the back and a few tables. There was a door leading into another room and then a door into still another room. These rooms had many tables and there was a good sprinkling of customers.

There was quite a bit of family trade. The restaurant was quiet, conservative, respectable, and the aroma of the food was so appetizing that I sat down and ordered a meal.

While the meal was coming I found a telephone and put through a call to Bertha's unlisted number at her apartment.

"Fry me for an oyster!" Bertha gasped. "You can disappear longer and make fewer reports! Where the hell are you now?"

"Mexicali," I said.

"Mexicali!" she screamed at me. "What are you doing down there?"

"Following clues."

"You'll use up all of the retainer money in expenses," she complained.

"I've used up plenty of it so far."

"That's the worst of you. You throw money away as though it grew on bushes. Why don't you ever make a report?"

"I didn't have anything to report."

"Well, our client has been chewing his fingernails as far as the elbow."

"You've seen him again?"

"Have I seen him again! He's been in once, and he's been on the telephone three times. He hung up about half an hour ago and told me if you reported before midnight tonight to let him know. I was to give you his number and you were to call him at once."

I said, "I'm following a lead that has taken me south of the border. That's all I can tell him. You call him and tell him I'm on a hot trail—and, by the way, if he's so worked up about things it might be a good plan to touch him for another hundred and fifty."

"He's worked up all right," Bertha said, "but he doesn't seem to be in a generous mood. He's in an anxious mood. You'll have to call him yourself. The number is six-seven-six-two-three-o-two."

"All right. I'll call him. I'm staying in Calexico. I followed a lead across to Mexicali, and I expect to have something definite by tomorrow."

"You're on a hot trail?"

"A hot trail."

"At fifteen cents a mile," Bertha said.

"We're making money at fifteen cents a mile," I reminded her.

"Not when it cuts into our retainer," Bertha said. "It's easier to sell personal services at fifty dollars a day than cars at fifteen cents a mile."

"All right," I told her. "This case has been more complicated than we had anticipated and there'll be a bill for expenses."

"Where are you going to be tonight, Donald? Where are you staying?"

"In Unit Number Seven at the Maple Leaf Motel in Calexico. I think that the man we want is going to show up within twenty-four hours. I'll give you a ring just as soon as I get anything definite."

"Well, call up and tell our client," Bertha said. "He's wearing holes in the carpet."

"All right. I'll call him," I paused, "but I don't want him messing into the play."

"Be sure to call him right away," Bertha said. "He said if I heard from you before midnight you were to call him. You have the number —six-seven-six-two-three-o-two. Now, play it cool, Donald, and keep the guy happy with what we're doing."

I promised her I would and hung up.

I called the number Bertha had given me.

Calhoun's voice came rasping over the line. "Hello, who is it?"

"Donald Lam," I said.

"Well, it's about time!" he exclaimed.

"About time for what?"

"About time for you to make a report."

"You didn't hire me to make reports," I said. "You hired me to find somebody."

"Have you found him?"

"No."

"Where are you?"

"At the moment I'm in Mexico."

"In Mexico!"

"That's right."

"What the hell are you doing in Mexico?"

"Looking for the person I'm supposed to find."

"Well, you're not going to find him down there."

"Are you sure?"

When he hesitated at that one, I said, "I've followed what I think is a live lead."

"What is it?"

"His girl friend," I said.

"His what?"

"His girl friend."

"Who?"

"I don't like to mention names over the telephone, but she lives not too far from where the man you want lived and she disappeared at about the same . . ."

"Don't tell me you've found her?"

"I've found her."

"The hell you have!"

"Why?" I asked. "Is that important?"

"I agree with you, Lam," he said his voice suddenly friendly. "That's a very, very live lead. Is she near where you are now?"

"Yes."

"Where?"

"I'm talking over a public telephone," I said, "on the south side of the international border. I dont want to go into details."

"Damn it, Lam," he said, his voice sharp with irritation, *"I'm* the one to take the responsibility. *I'm* the one who's paying you. Where is she?"

I said, "She's on the other side of the line at Calexico."

"Where?"

"At a motel."

"What's the name of the motel?"

I hesitated a moment, then said, "The Maple Leaf. She's in Unit Number Twelve, but I don't think our man is going to join her there. I think the rendezvous is going to be somewhere south of the border."

"Do you have any idea why?"

"Not at this time. I had quite a job locating her. She tried to cover her back trail and she's here under an assumed name."

"What name?" he asked.

I said firmly, "I'm not going to give that out over this telephone. What's your interest in the girl? You hired us to find somebody else."

"I'm interested in finding out what you're doing. When I spend money, I want to know what I get in return for it."

I said, "Hello, operator . . . operator . . . you've cut me off . . . operator."

Then I gently slid the receiver into its cradle and went back to enjoy my dinner.

It was a wonderful dinner. The sweet-meated lobsters of Baja California, a side dish of chile con carne, not the bean dish which is really a misnomer, but chunks of tender meat swimming in hot, red sauce.

There were also tortillas and *frijoles refritos*.

Just as I was finishing my meal a man came up to the manager at the cash register, which was directly behind the table where I was sitting.

"I was expecting to meet someone here," he said, "but I was delayed on the road. Did anyone leave any messages for me?"

"What's the name?"

"Sutton."

The manager shook his head. "No messages, Senor Sutton."

The man looked around the restaurant dubiously.

The manager said, "There was a senorita, an American girl, who came here and waited and waited, then had dinner and departed.

"But no message?" Sutton asked.

"I am sorry, senor, no message."

The man walked out.

I grabbed a bill, threw it at the cashier, didn't wait for the check or any change, but hurried to the door. I was in too much of a hurry. My waiter grabbed me. "The check, senor. You have not paid."

"I paid," I told him. "I put money on the counter at the cash register."

"It is not possible to pay without the check," he insisted.

Trouble in Mexico can be serious trouble, I lost precious seconds convincing the guy.

When I finally had him convinced, I brushed aside his apologies and made it out to the street. There was no sign of the man. He had turned the corner, but I couldn't tell which corner. I tried the one to the east. It was the wrong corner. It had started to rain while I had been eating.

It had been cloudy during the evening, but it rains very little there in the desert and I had expected the clouds would simply blow over. Now there was a steady drizzle of rain.

When it rains in the Imperial Valley it makes trouble.

The crops in that fertile soil are predicated upon moisture from irrigation and the ranchers don't want rain. The soil is largely silt from the prehistoric deposits of the Colorado River, and rain turns that soil into a slick clay that is as adhesive as wet paint. Automobile tires spread it over the pavement. It sticks to the soles of the shoes and, on certain surfaces, makes it as difficult to proceed as if one were walking on glare ice.

I went back into the restaurant.

"That man who was just in here saying someone was to have met him—do you know him?" I asked the manager.

"No, senor, I have never seen him before."

"Can you get me a taxi, quick?" I asked.

He went to the door, looked out, looked up at the clouds, looked up and down the street, and shook his head. "Not tonight, I am afraid, senor. This is not like across the border in the United States. Here we usually have one, sometimes two taxicabs. Tonight it is raining and there is none."

Mexico is a wonderful country, but there are some things Mexicans can't understand or don't want to understand. Our hurry and sense of urgency leave them cold.

My man had given me the slip, but I had had a good look at him. I wouldn't forget him.

I had to go to the place where I had left my car, and, it being a rainy evening, there was only one way to get there.

It wasn't too long a walk. I buttoned my coat and made the best of it, keeping under the protection of buildings, porches and awnings wherever possible, and hurrying across the intersections.

Soon I came to the line of cars that was waiting to clear United States Customs at Calexico.

It was a long line.

Overworked immigration men and customs inspectors were at the checking point far up ahead, asking motorists what country they were citizens of, whether they had anything they had bought in Mexico, occasionally putting a sticker on the windshield which meant the car had to pull over out of the line for a detailed search. For the most part, however, after a brief inspection, the cars were waved on.

I'd read up on smuggling and, statistics show that literally tons of marijuana come across the border with a goodly sprinkling of heroin and other contraband mixed in for good measure.

The customs inspectors are unbelievably skillful in sizing up drivers but they are snowed under by the sheer volume of numbers.

Do you know what is the leading tourist city in the world? Rome? Paris? London? Cairo? Guess again. The answer is Tijuana, Baja California, Mexico, and while there aren't nearly as many cars crossing at Mexicali as at Tijuana, the volume is still terrific.

Right now the cars were in a long line, the drivers waiting impatiently with motors running, the windshield wipers beating a monotonous, rhythmic cadence.

I saw a pickup carrying a small houseboat on a trailer and it aroused my curiosity.

Quite a few boating enthusiasts trail their boats down through Mexicali to the fishing port of San Felipe, a hundred and twenty miles to the south. There is a good surfaced road, and fishing and ocean adventure are at the end of it.

Other enthusiasts who are more venturesome go on another fifty-odd miles to the south of San Felipe to Puertecitos, a little gem of a bay, where there are a few dwellings, a few house trailers, supplies, and the warm blue of a gulf which is generally quite tranquil.

A houseboat, however, is something of a novelty.

This one was rather short and was mounted on twin pontoons powered with two outboard motors. The pickup which was pulling the outfit was powerful enough to snake it over roads all the way to Puertecitos if the driver had been so inclined.

My eyes came up to the driver and suddenly I snapped to attention. He was the man I was looking for, the one who had been in the Monte Carlo Café a short time before, asking if there was someone there waiting for him, saying that he had been delayed.

I could readily understand the reason for the delay. If he had been fighting his way up from San Felipe over pavement which had suddenly turned wet while he was dragging a pontoon houseboat on a trailer, a delay was to have been expected.

I moved on, just about keeping pace with the slow-moving double line of cars, studying the driver of the pickup.

I noticed that my party had a passenger with him, a male, but I couldn't see much of the man's face because he was on the side away from me and the shadow obscured his features.

Then I crossed the line of traffic and went through the border station myself, giving my citizenship, stating that I had purchased nothing in Mexico.

Again I tried for a taxicab but in vain. I hurried to the point where I had my automobile parked by the side of the road and drove back to the road that led from the border crossing. The pickup with its houseboat had gone. However, I had jotted down the license numbers of both the pickup and the trailer. I felt I could find my man again, although from the description I had of Hale, I knew this man wasn't the one I had been hired to find.

I couldn't be certain about the other man in the pickup, however. He could have been the man I wanted.

I gambled I could follow up the lead I now had.

The rain had got me good and damp.

I finally drove to the Maple Leaf Motel, got a flask out of my suitcase, had a good swig of whiskey and went to sleep.

4

Sometime in the night, when my senses were still drugged with sleep, I was half awakened by the sound of voices raised in what seemed to be an argument.

I rolled over, punched the pillow, went back to sleep again, then suddenly wakened to a realization that those voices *might* have been coming from Unit 12.

It took me a few moments to get my senses together, to jump out of bed and get to the window.

There was no light on in Unit 12.

The voices had ceased.

The motel lay silent under the stars, the night light reflected in the shimmering surface of the swimming pool in the patio.

I stood by the window until I began to feel chilled. Then I went back to bed, but it was a long while before I could get to sleep. I was lying there listening for the sound of voices, and listening in vain.

I arose at seven o'clock, showered, shaved, and started out to breakfast.

I had a desire for the Mexican dish of *huevos rancheros,* in which fried eggs, swimming in a sauce of onions, peppers and spices, are placed on top of a thin tortilla.

There is no place that makes *huevos rancheros* any better than the kitchen of the De Anza Hotel.

The rain had ceased. The sky was blue, the air clear. It was only a four-block walk to the hotel and I decided to make it, swinging along with shoulders back, inhaling the pure desert air in great, long pulls.

I entered the dining room at the De Anza Hotel, found an inconspicuous table, seated myself, gave my order and sipped delicious coffee while I waited for the eggs to arrive.

The waiter brought the *huevos rancheros*. I put down my coffee cup and looked up into the startled eyes of our client, Milton Carling Calhoun, who was seated three tables away, facing me.

He hadn't expected to see me. His facial expression was a dead giveaway.

I waved to him casually, as though seeing him there was the most natural thing in the world, and went on with my eggs, keeping an eye on him, however, to make sure he didn't sneak out.

He finished before I did and had the grace to come over to my table.

"Well, well, Lam," he said, "good morning. How are you this morning?"

"Fine, thanks. How are you?"

"A little sleepy but very well."

"I hardly expected to see *you* here this morning."

"As a matter of fact," he said, "I hardly expected to be here, but after talking with you over the phone last night I decided to come down so I could . . . could . . . have a chat with you personally. Talking over the telephone is so unsatisfactory."

"Isn't it?" I said.

"Indeed it is."

"Where," I asked, "are you staying?"

"Here in the hotel. It's a very nice place, air-conditioned and all that, and the food is very good."

"You get down here often?" I asked.

"Not often. Now, tell me, Lam, just *what* have you discovered?"

"Not very much more than when I talked with you on the telephone last night."

"But you must have *some* additional facts. You were so secretive last night. I knew I had to *talk* with you. You held out on me on the telephone. You know something else, don't you?"

"Yes."

"What?"

I said, "The young woman is waiting for someone to join her. I think it may be Hale."

"Now, this young woman," Calhoun went on, "you didn't want to mention names over the telephone—that's one reason I wanted to talk with you—just *who* is this young woman?"

"Her name," I said, "is Nanncie Beaver. She's registered here as Nanncie Armstrong. There's a trick spelling on her name. It's N-a-n-n-c-i-e."

"How in the world did you ever get a lead that brought you to her?" he asked.

I said, "I tried to find out all I could about Colburn Hale. I found out that Nanncie was his girl friend, and when I went to look for her I found that she'd mysteriously disappeared at about the same time Colburn Hale had disappeared. It was, therefore, a strong possibility that they were together."

"But how in the world did you ever find her down here?" he asked. "I couldn't—" He broke off suddenly.

"Couldn't what?" I asked.

"Couldn't imagine," he said.

"It was routine detective work," I said, "but quite a bit of work at that. What time did you get in here?"

"Around two-thirty or so this morning. It was a mean drive over wet roads."

I said, "Expenses are running up. We make a charge of fifteen cents a mile for the agency car."

"That's all right," he said hastily.

"So," I went on, "the question arises whether you want us to quit when the deposit is used up or whether you want to put up some more money to have us go ahead."

"Go ahead with what?"

"To find Hale, of course."

He took a pencil from his pocket and started playing with it, putting the point on the table, sliding his thumb and forefinger from the eraser down to the point, then upending the pencil and sliding his thumb and forefinger back again. He was thinking of what to tell me, or how to tell me.

I beat him to the punch. "Just why did you want to find Colburn Hale?" I asked.

He hesitated for two or three seconds, then said, "Somehow, Lam, I doubt if that's particularly important."

"It might help if I knew."

"And it might not."

I shrugged my shoulders. "It's your money," I pointed out.

He took out his wallet and extracted two new fifty-dollar bills.

"I'm going to add another hundred dollars to the deposit," he said. "That will take care of things for two more days."

"Not with traveling expenses," I said.

"Well, then, for one more day after the three fifty is used up."

"Okay," I told him, "you're the boss. When this is used up you want me to pack up and go home?"

"If you haven't found him by that time, yes. And make every effort to keep expenses down."

I started to say something, then paused as I regarded the door from the hotel.

The surprise must have shown on my face.

Calhoun, whose back was toward the door, whirled to see what I was looking at.

Sergeant Frank Sellers of the Metropolitan Police saw me at just about that time. His own face registered surprise, although he fought to control the expression. Then he was coming over toward us.

"Well, well, well," he said, "look who's here!"

"Hello, Sergeant, how are you?"

"What are you doing down here, Pint Size?" he asked me. "And who's your friend?"

I said, quickly so that Calhoun would get the idea, "Mr. Calhoun, shake hands with Sergeant Frank Sellers of the Metropolitan Police. Sellers is sort of a liaison man who gets around on cases where outside jurisdictions telephone in for help. Are you down here on official business, Sergeant?"

Sellers grinned and said, "Very neatly done, Donald."

Calhoun extended his hand. Sellers grabbed it, crushed it in his big paw and said, "Pleased to meet you."

"What was neatly done?" I asked.

"Telling Calhoun who I was and warning him that I might be on official business. The way you're acting Calhoun might be a client of yours."

I didn't say anything.

"I am," Calhoun said.

Sellers turned to me. "What's the pitch?" he asked. "What are you doing down here, Pint Size? What does Calhoun want down here?"

"Information," I said.

Sellers pulled up a chair and sat down. "Think I'll join you for a while. You two have had breakfast?"

I nodded. "The *huevos rancheros* here are very good, Sergeant."

"Can't eat 'em," he said. "Have to go pretty easy on spicy food. Now then, let's go back to where we were. You say Calhoun hired you to get information?"

"That's right."

"What sort of information?"

I smiled and said, "You're asking the wrong person. I can't betray the confidences of a client."

Sellers turned to Calhoun. "What sort of information?" he asked.

Calhoun was plainly flabbergasted. "Is this official?" he asked.

"It could be made official," Sellers told him.

Calhoun gave him a long look, then said somewhat coldly, "I fail to see how any stretch of the imagination would make my business with Mr. Lam of any possible interest to you, Sergeant."

Sellers didn't back up an inch. "Then you'd better stretch your imagination some more."

"I've already stretched it to the limit," Calhoun said.

"The name Colburn Hale mean anything to you?" Sellers asked.

Calhoun couldn't resist the slight start.

Sergeant Sellers grinned a triumphant grin.

"I see it does," he said. "Suppose you start talking."

"I don't know what I'm supposed to talk about," Calhoun said.

Sergeant Sellers said, "Now, Pint Size here is a fast worker and you can't underestimate the guy. If you do, you get into trouble. Now, take for instance the case of Marge Fulton who lives at Apartment Forty-two at Eight-seventeen Billinger Street. This man, Colburn Hale, or Cole Hale, as his friends call him had the apartment next door, Apartment Forty-three.

"Now, what do you think happened? Donald Lam shows up and knocks on the door of Colburn Hale's apartment. He gets no answer. So then he knocks again until finally Marge Fulton comes to the door of her apartment to see what the noise is all about and to tell Donald Lam that she doesn't think Hale is home.

"Now, that's where you can't underestimate this guy. He's ingenious. He leads Marge Fulton to think he's Colburn Hale's agent. He pumps her for all she knows—which is that Hale moved out in the middle of the night. Then Pint Size shows up down here."

Calhoun looked from Sergeant Sellers to me, then back to Sellers.

"And," Sellers went on, "Donald Lam somehow got information that put him on the track of coming down here to the border. So we'd like to know a little bit more about Hale and just what your interest is in the guy."

"Is he hot?" I asked.

Sellers measured his words carefully. "He may be hot and he may be cold—very cold."

I said, "The Calexico Police Department didn't telephone for help just because someone in Los Angeles is missing."

"That's logical," Sellers agreed affably.

"And," I said, "if you were looking for Hale and you knew I'd been looking for him, you must have uncovered a lead which brought you down here without knowing you were on my back trail because you were surprised when you walked into the dining room here this morning and saw me."

"Who says so?" Sellers asked.

"Your face said so."

Sellers said, "We're getting our roles mixed. I'm doing the questioning."

"Has any crime been committed?" I asked.

"Could be," Sellers said. "Hale is mixed up in a dope-running case. We don't know how deep."

I said to Calhoun, "In that case, if any crime has been committed and if there's any reason to suspect you of any connection with the crime, you don't have to say a word. Sellers has to warn you that anything you say can be used against you and that you're entitled to the advice of an attorney."

"But there *can't* be any crime involved," Calhoun said.

"Oh, sure," I said sarcastically. "Frank Sellers just came down here to sell tickets to the Policemen's Ball."

Sellers grinned.

After a few moments of silence, Sellers said, "Now I'll start telling both of you jokers something. I flew down here in a police plane. I didn't get in until about five o'clock this morning, but I had some pretty good leads. I went right to work.

"Hale was a writer. He did all sorts of things, little short articles, fiction, and, occasionally, he'd run onto some article that he could sell to the wire services.

"Now, somewhere along the line he found out something about the marijuana traffic. He had been investigating that quietly and under cover for some little time. He evidently stumbled onto something big because the night he disappeared he was pounding like mad on his typewriter.

"Then something happened. Some man came to see him. We want to know more about that. Who was that man, a friend or an enemy?

"Hale packed up and got out. He evidently didn't have too much junk, but what he had he threw into an automobile, and the guy vanished.

"Now, that could have meant either one of two things. Either he had a lot of red-hot information that he was going to spill in an article on marijuana smuggling, the word got around and some friend of his came to tip him off that the situation was hot and he'd better get out, so he got out, or he knew a shipment was coming across, and he came to the border.

"The fact that he took all of his things with him makes me think that it was a friend that gave him the tip.

"On the other hand, it could have been that it was an enemy, some member of the dope ring.

"Hale was busily engaged in typing out a story that was red-hot and there was a knock at the door. He went to open the door and found himself looking down the barrel of a gun.

"The man behind that gun just took Hale with him and wanted to be awfully careful that he didn't leave anything behind in the way of notes, so he and a couple of buddies cleaned out the apartment.

"Right now," Sellers said, "we're acting on the theory that Hale's move was voluntary, that he hadn't all of his article finished, that he suddenly realized he was hot, that some friend came and helped him and they moved in a hurry.

"Now then, we'd like . . ."

The door opened and a man who had police officer stamped all over him came into the dining room, looked around, saw Sellers, pounded over to him and touched him on the shoulder. "Can I speak with you a minute, Sergeant?" he asked.

Sellers looked up. "Why sure," he said.

The two officers walked over to a corner of the dining room where they were out of earshot. The local officer poured stuff into Sellers' ears and Sellers was jolted—there was no question about that.

Whatever the local guy told him was important enough so that Sellers never came back. The two men walked out of the room and Sellers didn't even so much as give us a backward glance over his shoulder.

Calhoun said, "Gosh, *that* was close!"

I watched the door through which the officers had disappeared. After a few thoughtful seconds, I turned back to Calhoun. "That brief interlude," I said, "gives you a chance to start talking."

"To whom about what?"

"To me about you."

"I don't think you need to know any more than you know already."

"Think again," I told him.

He hesitated for a moment, then said, "Colburn Hale really is nothing to me."

"Sure," I said sarcastically. "You toss three hundred and fifty dollars onto Bertha Cool's desk to try to find him and then you put another hundred into the kitty down here, but he's less than nothing to you."

Calhoun looked at me thoughtfully, then said, "I'm going to tell you the truth."

"It just might make a welcome change," I pointed out.

He said, "I'm not interested in Colburn Hale. I'm interested in Nanncie Beaver."

He jolted me with that one. "What?" I asked.

"That's right," he said. "I'm interested in Nanncie Beaver. She ran away with every evidence of having left in a panic. I tried to trace her. There wasn't a chance. So I went to see if Colburn Hale had anything to do with her disappearance and I found out that Hale had left very hurriedly. I figured they were together.

"I didn't want anyone to know I was interested in Nanncie Beaver. I didn't even dare to tell you and Bertha Cool, but I felt if you could locate Colburn Hale, that would give me all the information I needed to find Nanncie."

"Why be so secretive?" I asked.

Calhoun said, "Because I'm married. It's not a happy marriage. We're getting a divorce. My wife and I are working out a property settlement right now through our lawyers. I can't afford to play into her hands. If she knew anything about Nanncie Beaver the fat would be in the fire. Her demands for a settlement would go way up out of all reason."

I said, "If you had put the cards on the table with us you might have saved yourself a lot of time and a lot of money."

"Then, by the same token," he said, "you or Bertha Cool might have made a slip and it could have cost me two or three hundred . . ."

"Two or three hundred thousand?" I asked, finishing the sentence for him.

He thought for a moment, then said, "Could be."

I did a lot of thinking. "Look," I said, "you've lied to me about a lot of things. You drove down here and you went directly to Unit Twelve at the Maple Leaf Motel when you arrived. You had to talk with Nanncie. There was an argument. Things didn't go as smoothly as you expected."

"What makes you think that?" he asked.

"You forget that I'm in Unit Seven," I said. "I was awakened by voices last night, voices coming from Unit Twelve."

"You heard voices?" he asked.

"Voices."

"A man and a woman?"

"That's right."

"Did you hear what was being said?"

I said, "Suppose you quit asking me questions for a while and start telling me the facts. You may be in this thing a little deeper than you anticipate."

"I've told you the facts."

I shook my head. "No, you haven't."

"What do you mean by that?"

I said, "If you had really been anxious to locate Nanncie when I told you last night over the telephone that I'd followed her down here and that she was in Unit Twelve of the Maple Leaf Motel, you'd have said, 'Well, I've gone as far as I want to go with this thing, Lam. I've spent all the money I can afford to spend, and if you haven't located Colburn Hale by this time, you'd better come on home and call it a day.'

"Instead of that you jump in your car and come down here and when you see me this morning you fork over another hundred bucks first thing."

"Well, what does that prove?" he asked, trying to be belligerent.

I said, "It proves that your actions and your words don't fit together."

I pushed back my chair. "Come on," I said, "let's go see Nanncie."

"I . . . I don't want to see her now."

"You're going to see her now," I said.

"You're working for me," he pointed out.

"You're damn right I am, and there's more to this than meets the eye, otherwise Sergeant Sellers wouldn't be down here. Come on, we're going to see Nanncie."

"I don't want to see her now."

"I'm going to see her now. You can come along if you want to have it that way, or you can stay here."

"All right," he said, "I'll come along."

I paid the check and left a tip.

"Where's your car?" I asked.

"Parked out front."

"Let's go in it. Time may be a little more precious than we realize."

It was a big Cadillac and we purred the four blocks to the Maple Leaf Motel, found a parking place, got out and approached Unit Twelve.

The key was in the door on the outside.

"What does that mean?" Calhoun asked.

"It probably means that she's checked out," I said.

"She couldn't have."

"Why not?" I asked.

He was silent at that one.

I walked up to the door, bold as brass, and knocked on it. When I received no answer, I pulled the door open.

The bed had been slept in but hadn't been made. I went into the bathroom. There was a bathmat on the floor, but it was dry. The bath towels were folded on the rack. They were both dry.

We looked the place over. There wasn't any sign of baggage or any article of women's clothing.

"Okay," I said to Calhoun, "let's get out of here. We'll go to my place. Perhaps you can refresh your memory there and tell me a bit more."

🙋   **5**   🙋

Calhoun and I went into Unit 7.

The bed hadn't been made. I put a couple of pillows behind my back and sat on the bed, giving Calhoun the only comfortable chair in the place.

"Well?" I said.

"Well, what?"

"Some more talk," I told him.

He shook his head. He was worried. "Lam," he said, "I can't afford to have my name mixed up in this thing. Good Lord, if there's any publicity and my wife should get hold of it—that lawyer of hers is a vulture. He picks the last shred of meat off the smallest bone he can find. This little escapade alone could cost me a . . . well, plenty."

I said, "You don't need to talk to anyone except me."

"If I don't talk, they'll throw newspaper publicity all over me."

"If you do talk, what'll they do?" I asked.

He didn't like the answer to that one either.

We sat for a couple of minutes in silence. I was thinking and Calhoun was worrying.

The door pushed open and Sellers came in.

"Well?" he asked.

I tried to look innocent.

"Start talking," Sellers said.

"What happened to your friend?" I asked.

"He's a deputy sheriff," Sellers said. "He's been called away on business." He looked at me, grinned, and said, "Important business. Maybe you know what it is."

I shook my head.

"Talk," Sellers said.

I said, "Calhoun and I are going on a fishing trip down to San Felipe when you get done bullying us around. I did a little job for him and he was very grateful. He offered to meet me here this morning and we'd go down to San Felipe together and try to catch some fish. He's giving the party."

"And what was the little job you did for your friend here?" Sellers asked.

I said, "Calhoun is planning an expose on drug traffic from Mexico. Colburn Hale has some material he wanted to get. Hale left overnight. My client wanted to find him."

"And what brought you down here?" Sellers asked. "Go ahead, Pint Size, better think fast because you haven't time to think up a really good one and I'm going to trap you on any lies you tell. When that happens you and Bertha are going to be in serious trouble.

"We're investigating a crime. You know what happens to people who give false information to officers who are investigating a crime."

"What sort of a crime?" I asked.

"Murder one," Sellers said.

I came bolt upright on the bed. "Murder what?"

"Murder one, you heard me."

"Who's the victim? Is it Hale?"

"Nope," Sellers said, "it's a chap by the name of Eddie Sutton. The name mean anything to you, Pint Size?"

I shook my head. "Not a thing."

"Sutton," Sellers said, "is part of a smuggling ring. They're pretty slick.

"We hadn't found out just how they worked until this morning. Sutton posed as an enthusiastic yachtsman. He had a little houseboat on pontoons that he'd trail back and forth from San Felipe, sometimes down as far south as Puertecitos.

"Last night Sutton came back from San Felipe and checked through the border here a little after nine forty-five—perhaps as late as ten-fifteen—that's as nearly as we can place it. He got through the border without any trouble. He got out to the outskirts of Calexico here and pulled off to the side of the road.

"We think a scout car was waiting to join him. That scout car was to go ahead and make sure the coast was clear. It would have had a Citizen's Band radio.

"Last night there was a roadblock traffic check just this side of Brawley. The way we figure it, the scout car radioed back to Sutton.

"Sutton decided to hole up. He went back into the houseboat.

"He never came out."

"Why?" I asked.

"On account of a bullet through the heart," Sellers said. "We think it's probably a thirty-eight caliber."

"When was his body found?"

"About seven o'clock this morning."

"How long had he been dead?"

Sellers shrugged his shoulders. "Maybe three hours, maybe seven hours."

"Why tell us all this?" I asked.

"Because," Sellers said, "I think that perhaps you can help us, and, in case you can't, we'll give you the facts so that you'll know we're investigating a murder case. Then if you do uncover anything you'll know the consequences of withholding the information."

Sellers pulled a cigar from his pocket, ripped off the end with his teeth, shoved the cigar in his mouth, but didn't light it. He stood there looking at us with a sardonic gleam in his eye.

"Now then," he said, "you two are going to take a little ride with me."

"Official?" I asked.

"We can make it official."

I got up off the bed and said to Calhoun, "Let's go."

"Where are we going?" Calhoun asked.

"Down to the police parking lot," Sellers said.

"What for?"

"I want you to take a look at the scene of the crime."

I said, "I may be able to help you, Sergeant."

Sellers pulled the cigar out of his mouth, inspected the wet place and grinned. "I thought perhaps you'd break loose with a little information."

"It's not the kind you think," I said. "It has nothing to do with my reason for being here."

"No?"

"No."

"Well, tell me," Sellers said, putting the cigar back in the right-hand side of his mouth and twisting it over to the left side by rolling it with his tongue.

I said, "I was coming across the border last night on foot and I saw this outfit coming through, at least it's an outfit that matches the description you gave me—a small houseboat on pontoons being carried on a trailer."

"What time?" Sellers asked.

"I can't give it to you any better than you have it already. It was somewhere, I would say, between nine forty-five and ten-fifteen. When I last saw it, it was about ten o'clock."

"Anything else?" Sellers asked.

I said, "The man who was driving the car had parked the outfit someplace within easy walking distance of the Monte Carlo Café, went into the café and looked around to see if he could find somebody who was going to meet him there."

"The devil!" Sellers said.

I nodded.

"How do you know?"

"I was in the café."

"Anything else?"

"Yes," I said. "The guy wasn't alone."

"You mean someone was with him when he came in the café?"

"No, someone was in the car with him when he crossed the border."

Sellers' eyes narrowed. He bit several times on the end of the cigar, chewing it gently while he digested that bit of information.

"Description," he said.

"I can't give it to you."

"Why not?"

"It was dark. I was walking across the border. This car was in the line that was waiting to go across. I got a good look at the driver, but the man with him was on the side of the car away from me and was in the deeper shadows."

"Any idea how tall, how old, how heavy?"

"I'd say he was probably somewhere in his thirties, but that's just making a blind stab at it from the set of his shoulders and the way he

held his head. I don't know how tall he'd have been if he'd been standing up, but when he was sitting he was about average height."

"Come on," Sellers said. "I'm going to show you jokers something."

We followed him out to a police car. He took us to a parking lot by
the police station.

"This the outfit?" Sellers asked, when we got out and faced a pontoon houseboat mounted on a trailer pulled by a Ford pickup.

"That's the outfit."

"Well, you can't go in," Sellers said. "We're going through it with a
fine-tooth comb, looking for fingerprints and clues, but I want to show
you guys something."

He led us over to the rear part of one of the pontoons.

I could see this had already been processed for fingerprints. There
was dusting powder over it and a couple of good latents which had
evidently already been photographed.

Sellers said, "Just a minute." He picked up two metal bottle open-
ers that were on a stool by the end of the pontoon, fitted the two bent
ends to a little ridge on the pontoon and pulled.

The cap loosened.

Sellers took his handkerchief so he wouldn't leave any fingerprints
and took the end completely off.

The pontoon underneath was filled with dried marijuana that had
been stuffed in and packed until it was solid.

I gave a low whistle.

Calhoun said nothing.

Sellers said, "As you can see, we got a couple of good fingerprints
off the tip here. Now then, just to protect yourselves, I think it will be
a good idea if you'll just step inside the station with me and leave your
fingerprints."

"Why?"

"We just want to make sure that the latents we have developed
aren't the prints of either one of you."

I looked at Calhoun.

"I don't think you have any right to take our prints under the circumstances," Calhoun said.

"Probably not," Sellers said, "but I think we're going to take them
just the same—one way or another. What's the matter, you got any
objections?"

"None at all," I said hastily. "As a matter of fact, you've got mine on file. You've taken them several times."

"I know, I know," Sellers said.

Calhoun said, "This is an arbitrary high-handed procedure. If you had the faintest reason to suspect either one of us it would be different, but you're just on a general fishing expedition and—"

"And," Sellers interrupted him, studying him with a cold, speculative eye, "we've been looking you up, Mr. Milton Carling Calhoun.

"You and your wife are separated. Since the separation you have been living in the Mantello Apartments, a very swanky apartment out on Wilshire Boulevard.

"Around nine-thirty last night you got a call from Mexicali which came through the apartment switchboard. Right after that you phoned the apartment garage, told the attendant you had to have your car right away, that you were being called out of town on a business trip.

"Evidently the call gave you information which was important enough so you left immediately for the Imperial Valley. You must have arrived about two o'clock this morning. It must have been rather a tough trip because of the rain. I thought you looked a little tired when I met you.

"You know, you must have driven right past this houseboat where it was parked by the side of the road when you came into town. You might have recognized the outfit, I don't know. You may have stopped and gone inside. We're finding a few fingerprints on the inside as well as these on the outside on the cover of the pontoons.

"Now, Mr. Milton Carling Calhoun, would you like to step inside and have your fingerprints taken?"

Calhoun took a long breath. "How in the world did you find out about the telephone call and the time I left Los Angeles?"

Sellers grinned around the cigar. "Don't underestimate the police, son. I put through a long-distance call after I talked with you at breakfast and had the information I wanted within a matter of minutes. You are very law-abiding. When you changed your residence, you even notified the Department of Motor Vehicles of your new address—it's very commendable. That's the law, you know. Now, that Mantello Apartments is a swanky outfit. They have a twenty-four-hour switchboard service. The night operator didn't listen in on your call, but she remembers that it came from Mexicali. Do you suppose there's any chance that it was Eddie Sutton who was calling you to tell he'd reached the border okay with his shipment and you told him to park the outfit and wait until you got there?"

"You're crazy," Calhoun said.

Sellers pulled the soggy end of the cigar out of his mouth, inspected the frayed end which he had chewed, put the cigar back in his mouth, pulled out a lighter, snapped it into flame and held the flame at the end of the cigar until a cold, bluish-white whisp of smoke made its appearance.

"So far I haven't anything to go on except hunches," he said. "But I'm playing hunches. Come on in and we'll take your fingerprints."

We went inside and Sellers took our fingerprints.

It was evidently the first time Calhoun had had all of his finger-prints taken. He was a little awkward, and the fingerprint technician had to hold the tip of each finger firmly as he gently rotated the finger. He also fumbled around a little when it came to handling the paper tissue with the ink solvent on it which the technician handed him.

Sellers puffed on the cigar.

"All right, you two," he said, "I'll take you back to the motel. Be sure to let me know if you think of anything else."

6

When Sellers had driven away, I said to Calhoun, "Suppose you come clean with me."

"I'm already clean with you," he said irritably. "You talk like that damn Los Angeles cop."

I said, "All right, I'll ask a few questions. Why did you want to find Hale?"

"I've told you why. Because I wanted to look for Nanncie."

"And why did you want to find Nanncie?"

"Because I knew she was getting mixed into a very dangerous situation."

"This man, Hale, was a rival of yours?"

"With a girl as good-looking as Nanncie, everybody is a potential rival."

"And how did you know Hale was working on a dope story?"

"Because Nanncie told me."

"She betrayed Hale's confidence?"

"It wasn't his confidence. Nanncie was the one who had lined up the story for him in the first place."

"And where did Nanncie get it?"

"She got a tip from an operator in a beauty shop and followed up on the story."

"Why? Because she was interested in dope?"

"No, because she was interested in Hale. She knew he was looking for something that would make a sensational article and she thought this would be it. It was a man's story."

"Did she have details?"

"I don't know."

"Don't pull that line with me. You and Nanncie were pretty close. If she told you anything, she told you all. Did she say anything about a houseboat on a trailer?"

Calhoun didn't answer that question for a second or two then he said, "I'm not going to have you cross-examine me this way, Lam."

I said, "You damn fool, I'm trying to save your bacon. You've left a broad back trail. Don't underestimate the police. Frank Sellers is going after Nanncie."

"And we've got to go after her," Calhoun said.

"He'll pick her up somewhere," I said. "She didn't have a car. She probably didn't take a taxi. Somebody came and picked her up, probably about three or four o'clock this morning. That was shortly after you had arrived in Calexico. I think you did it."

"You think wrong," Calhoun said. "I only wish to heaven I had been the one. I'd have taken her and put her in a safe place."

"Safe for whom?" I asked. "You or her?"

"Her."

"I'm still not sure you didn't pick her up," I told him. "Now, we'll come back to the original question. Did she tell you anything about a houseboat that was used in the smuggling operation?"

"Well, generally."

"So when you drove into town in the wee small hours of the morning and saw a pickup with a pontoon houseboat on a trailer parked by the side of the road, what did you do?"

"All right," he said. "I thought—well, I didn't know what to think. I stopped the car and went across to try to get in the door of the houseboat."

"What did you do?"

"I knocked."

"And you left fingerprints."

"Knuckles don't leave fingerprints."

I said, "What were you intending to do if the guy had opened the door—ask him if he was the dope peddler that your girl friend, Nanncie, had been telling you about?"

"No, I was going to sound him out a bit, pretending I was a yachtsman and wanted information about launching facilities at San Felipe."

"At three o'clock in the morning?" I asked.

"I tell you I was worried sick about Nanncie," he said. "I wasn't thinking clearly."

"And you're not thinking clearly now," I told him, then I asked him abruptly, "Do you own a gun?"

He hesitated, then nodded.

"Where is it?"

"I . . . why, home, I guess."

"Where is home? Where your wife is living or in the Mantello Apartments?"

"In the . . . in the home, I guess."

"You sure?"

"No, I'm not absolutely certain. I haven't seen it for some time."

"What is it?"

"A thirty-eight-caliber revolver."

"You're sure you didn't bring it with you when you came down here last night?"

"No, certainly not. Why would I have brought it?"

"Sometimes people carry guns when they're traveling at night over lonely roads in an automobile."

"I don't. I'm law-abiding."

"All right," I said. "The best thing for you to do is to go back to Los Angeles."

"Are you crazy?" he asked. "I've got to stay down here and together we've got to look for Nanncie."

"Not together."

"I want to be kept posted. I want to know what you're doing. I want to work with you."

"You would simply clutter up the scenery," I told him.

"I have reason to believe she's in danger."

"If she is, I can help her a lot better if I'm alone than if you're hanging around. What are your feelings toward Colburn Hale? I want to know."

"I hate him," he said.

"Jealous?"

"I'm not jealous. I just tell you that the man dragged Nanncie into danger, fooling around with this article of his on dope smuggling."

I told Calhoun, "If you won't go back to Los Angeles, there's just one thing I want you to do."

"What?"

"Get in that Cadillac of yours, drive to the De Anza Hotel, go into your room, close the door, don't do any telephoning, and stay put."

"For how long—I'd go crazy."

"Until you hear from me," I said.

"How long will that be?"

"It depends."

"On what?"

"On when I can find some of the answers."

"Answers to what?"

I looked him straight in the eyes and said, "Answers to some of the things you've been doing and have lied about."

"What do you mean by that?"

"I mean that I have a feeling you're not being frank with me."

"I've paid you everything you've asked. You're working for me."

"That's right," I told him, "and if you want to keep me running around in circles like a trotting horse that's being trained at the end of a rope, that's your privilege. I'll trot around just as far as you want and as fast as you want at fifty bucks a day and expenses.

"On the other hand, if you want to take the rope off my neck and let me trot straight down the road so I can get somewhere, I'll try to get somewhere."

"Perhaps then you'd get to some place that I don't want you to be."

"There's always that chance."

"I can't take it."

"You can if you tell me where you *don't* want me to go," I said, "and why you don't want me to get there."

He shook his head.

I said, "Has it ever occurred to you that you could find yourself charged with murder?"

"With murder?"

"With murder in the first," I said. "Sellers is measuring you for size right now. A fingerprint or two or just some little bit of evidence and you'd be elected."

"Why, they couldn't . . . they wouldn't dare."

"And," I said, "there'd be nice, juicy big headlines in the papers. LOS ANGELES MILLIONAIRE ARRESTED IN DOPE-SMUGGLING MURDER."

He acted as though I'd hit him in the stomach.

"Think it over," I told him. "I'm trying to help you. Despite all the double crosses you've given me, I'm still trying to help, but there are certain things I can't do. I can't suppress evidence. And when I know that the police are investigating a murder case, I can't lie to them. After all, I'm a licensed private detective and I have certain obligations under the law.

"Now get out of here. Go to the De Anza Hotel. Shut yourself in your room and stay there."

He looked at me as a wounded deer looks at the hunter. Then he got up and walked out.

7

I didn't have much trouble finding where the houseboat had been parked. I drove slowly out of town, watching the road.

There was still a little crowd hanging around, enough people so that it was impossible to tell anything about footprints or wheel tracks. The police had apparently roped the place off earlier in the morning, and after they finished with their search and photography they had taken the ropes away, presumably when they moved the pickup and trailer. Then the people had moved in.

I looked the place over.

It was a real wide space on the west side of the road, which would be the left-hand side going north. It must have been a good fifty feet from the edge of the pavement over to a drainage ditch that was along the side of the road. On the other side of the drainage ditch was a barbed-wire fence and beyond that was an alfalfa field.

As the alfalfa field was irrigated, the surplus waters ran down into the drainage ditch, which was still moist with a base of muddy clay on the bottom.

I walked along the road, looking at the drainage ditch to see if I could see any footprints.

There weren't any in it, but there were lots of them along the side. The police, and presumably some of the spectators, had looked to see if anyone had crossed that ditch. It couldn't have been done without leaving a set of tracks.

I took off my shoes and socks and waded through the clay mud in the bottom of the ditch, climbed the bank on the other side, and crawled through the barbed-wire fence, holding my shoes and socks in my left hand, trying to act natural and unconcerned—just a loco gringo doing something that didn't make sense.

I walked about fifty yards along the bank, looking over in the alfalfa field; and then I walked back to where I had started and walked fifty yards in the other direction.

I started back, and then I saw it, a gleam of bluish metal reflecting the sunlight.

I glanced around. Everyone seemed to have lost interest in me.

I walked through the alfalfa field for about twenty feet.

The gun was lying at the foot of an alfalfa plant.

I studied it intently. It was a blued-steel .38-caliber, snub-nosed revolver.

I turned and walked slowly away from what I had found.

I had taken only a few steps toward the fence when a little ten-year-old, black-eyed, barefooted urchin came running across the muddy bottom of the drainage ditch.

"What did you find, mister?" he asked.

"Find?" I echoed, trying to look innocent.

"You found something. You moved over. You . . . I'll look."

He started to run back to where I had turned into the alfalfa.

"Wait!" I called after him.

He stopped.

"I found something," I said, "that is of great importance. I don't want the other people to know. Can I trust you?"

His face showed intense excitement. "Of course, sure," he said. "What do you want?"

I said, "I am going to wait here to see that what I found is not disturbed. I was going to call the police myself, but it is better this way. You have your mother and father near here?"

"I live in that house over there," he said, pointing. "The white house."

"Do you have a telephone?"

"Yes."

I said, "I'll wait here. Don't say anything to any of the people out there. Go to your house. Get your father if he is home, your mother if he isn't home. Telephone the Calexico police. Tell them to get out here right away, that Donald Lam has found some important evidence."

"A Lam?" he asked.

"Donald Lam," I said. "L-a-m. You think you can do that?"

"Oh, sure."

"And don't say anything to anybody except your parents."

"Only my mother," he said. "My father is at work."

"Then hurry," I told him.

I sat down on the bank of the ditch and waited while the kid wormed his way through the barbed-wire fence, spattered across the muddy bottom of the ditch, and, with his bare brown feet beating an excited tattoo on the ground, headed off for the big white house.

It took about fifteen minutes for Frank Sellers and a Calexico cop to get there.

The kid was waiting for them. He beckoned them eagerly and led the way across the ditch.

Sellers and the cop hesitated before getting in the mud, but finally they waded on through.

The people who had been aimlessly milling around suddenly became interested when they saw the cops' car and the ten-year-old kid leading the two men across the drainage ditch. Then they noticed me and one or two came trooping across, but the officer waved them back before they got into the alfalfa field.

Sellers and the officer came slogging down to me.

"This had better be good, Pint Size," Sellers said.

"Want to take a look?" I asked.

I led the way and stopped when I reached a point where they could see the gun.

"I'll go to hell!" Sellers said.

They looked at each other; then they looked at me. "Have you been over there?" Sellers asked.

"This is as close as I've been."

"I hope you're telling the truth," Sellers said. "How did you know that gun was there?"

"I didn't. I came out to look the place over."

"Lots of people have looked the place over," Sellers said.

"I reasoned that if a man wanted to get rid of a gun, he'd stand on the edge of that drainage ditch and throw it out into the field, just as far as he could throw it."

"Why not take it with him for a ways and throw it where it wouldn't be found?"

"He might not have had that much time. The gun was too incriminating. He wanted to get rid of it right then."

"All right, Pint Size," Sellers said, "you masterminded that, but what caused you to cross the ditch?"

"Because no one else had crossed the ditch," I said.

"How did you know that?"

"No one could have crossed the ditch without leaving tracks."

"And so?" Sellers asked.

"So I knew that no one had looked in the alfalfa field."

"And how did you know the gun was in the alfalfa field?"

"I didn't, but as a matter of good investigative technique I knew that all the terrain around the scene of the crime should be explored, particularly places where a weapon could have been thrown."

Sellers looked at the Calexico cop, took a cigar from his pocket and put it in his mouth, walked over to the gun, bent slowly down, took a fountain pen from his pocket, inserted it in the barrel and lifted the gun.

"The chances of latent fingerprints on a gun are pretty slim," he said, "but we'll just protect this evidence as much as we can and dust it for fingerprints."

"For my money," the Calexico cop said, "you'll find the fingerprints of this slick detective."

Sellers shook his head. "We may find it's been wiped clean of fingerprints, but he's too slick to pull a boob trick like that."

We walked back along the bank of the ditch, Sellers holding the gun up in the air, the fountain pen in the barrel, keeping it from falling.

He had some trouble getting through the fence and holding the gun, looking like a Japanese juggler trying to hold a ball aloft on a billiard cue.

By this time the crowd had gathered in a big semicircle, gaping at the officers and the gun.

The officers slogged across the muddy bottom of the drainage ditch. I walked across barefoot and over to where I had parked my car.

"Don't try to get lost," Sellers warned. "We may want you."

"You can always find me," I told him. "Unit Seven, Maple Leaf Motel, or somewhere in the vicinity."

"You're right," Sellers said, "we can always find you. I just hope it won't be too much trouble."

I got back in my car and tried to drive barefooted. It was too ticklish.

I stopped at the first service station, got out, and turned the water hose on my feet. The attendant looked at me with a baffled expression.

"I got my feet dirty," I told him.

He shook his head. "Now I've seen everything," he said.

I didn't try to put my socks on over my wet feet. I simply put my shoes on and drove back to the De Anza Hotel, found that Milton Carling Calhoun was in Room 36B, found the room and knocked on the door.

Calhoun opened the door eagerly.

His face showed disappointment when he saw who it was. "You again!" he said.

"Me again," I told him.

My feet were dry by this time. I walked in and sat down in a chair, pulling my socks from my pocket. I took off my shoes and put my socks on.

"Now what," Calhoun asked, "is the idea?"

"I went out to the scene of the crime," I said.

"You mean the murder?"

"What other crime is there?"

"Dope smuggling."

"It was the same scene," I said.

"What happened?" he wanted to know.

I said, "The cops pulled a boner."

"How come?"

I grinned and said, "Sergeant Sellers came down here from Los Angeles. He's the high-powered liaison guy, the expert on homicide investigation, and he pulled a boner right in front of all these local cops. I'll bet he feels like two cents right now."

"What did he do?"

"He failed to search the scene of the crime for a weapon."

"You mean they hadn't . . . ?"

"Oh, they'd looked the trailer over and they'd looked over the ground all around the trailer," I said, "but there was an alfalfa field and a ditch with a muddy bottom between the edge of the highway right-of-way and the field. If anybody had tried to cross over they'd have left tracks.

"The officers looked the place over, found there were no tracks, so assumed no one had been over to the alfalfa field and they could cross it off the books."

"And what happened?" Calhoun asked.

I said, "You should always search the premises, not only the immediate premises, but look at places where a person could stand and throw some object such as a weapon that he wanted to get rid of."

"You mean there was a weapon?" Calhoun asked.

"There was a weapon," I said. "A thirty-eight-caliber revolver, blued steel, snub-nosed—it looked to me like an expensive gun. The police took it into custody and, of course, got on the telephone right away.

"Within a matter of minutes they'll have found the sales record of the gun from the numbers. Then they'll process it for fingerprints— probably they won't have much luck with that. Latent fingerprints aren't usually found on a gun."

"But they can identify it from the numbers?"

"Sure," I said. "There's a sales record on every gun. Now, is there any chance this is your gun?"

He shook his head emphatically. "Not one chance in a thousand. I know where my gun is."

"Where?"

He hesitated, then said, "Home."

"Let's do better than that," I said. "You may not know it, but you're a poor liar."

He took a deep breath and said, "All right, Nanncie has it."

"How do you know?"

"Because I gave it to her. The poor kid was worried sick and she was scared. I didn't know she was going to try to run away. I thought she was going to stick it out . . . I told her, 'Nanncie, when you go to bed, keep your door locked and don't open it for anybody unless you know for sure who it is. Keep this gun under your pillow and if you have to use it, don't hesitate to do so.' "

"And then?" I asked.

"And then I showed her how to pull the trigger," he said. "You know, it's a self-cocking gun. It sometimes takes a little practice for a woman to pull the trigger so she can fire the gun."

"And you think Nanncie has hung onto the gun?"

"I know she has."

"What are the chances," I asked, "that Nanncie got involved in this thing and pulled the trigger on the gun out there in the trailer?"

"Not a chance in the world," he said. "Not a chance in a million."

I thought it over and said, "Well, maybe you're right. I'm basing my judgment on the fact that she didn't have an automobile and she'd hardly have hired a taxicab to follow the dope car up to the place where the crime was committed, then told the taxi to wait while she went in, pulled a gun and got rid of Eddie Sutton."

"You talk like a fish," Calhoun said impatiently. "Nanncie wouldn't have—"

Imperative knuckles sounded on the door.

I said, wearily, "You'd better open the door for Sergeant Sellers." Calhoun opened the door.

Sellers took one look at me and said, "Well, well, Pint Size, I see you hotfooted it up here to tell your client the news."

"I've told him the news," I said.

Sellers said to Calhoun, "You own a Smith and Wesson thirty-eight-caliber revolver with a one-and-seven-eighth inch barrel number one-three-three-three-four-seven. Where is it?"

"Go ahead and answer the question," I told Calhoun. "He's now suspecting you of a specific crime and asking you a specific incriminating question. He hasn't warned you of your constitutional rights, and anything you say can't be used against you . . ."

Sergeant Sellers resorted to profanity, fished the Miranda card out of his pocket.

The Miranda card is something that officers carry these days since the decision of the United States Supreme Court in the Miranda case. They have to give a series of warnings to anyone, either when they're making an arrest or when the investigation has quit being an investigation in general terms and has moved into a specific area where they are questioning a specific suspect about a specific crime.

Sellers started reading.

"You are," Sellers droned in a monotone, "under suspicion of having murdered one Edward Sutton. You are warned that anything you say may be used against you. On the other hand, you are advised that you do not need to make any statement at all. You are also advised that you are entitled to consult an attorney of your own choice and to have an attorney represent you at all stages of the investigation. If you are unable to afford an attorney, the state will get one to represent you."

Sellers put the card back in his pocket. "Now then," he said, "when did you last see this gun?"

I said to Calhoun, "You're entitled to have an attorney at all stages of the proceeding. Do you have a lawyer?"

"Not here," Calhoun said.

"Suppose you keep out of this," Sellers advised me.

"You mean he's not entitled to have an attorney?" I asked.

"I've already told him," Sellers said, "he's entitled to have an attorney."

I caught Calhoun's eye and surreptitiously put my finger to my tightly closed lips.

Calhoun said, "I have no statement to make. I want to consult a lawyer."

"You may call a lawyer," Sellers said.

Calhoun gulped, thought, then suddenly turned to me. "Lam," he said, "I want a lawyer."

"Don't you have one in—"

"Not one that would be any good in a situation of this sort," he said. "I want a local lawyer and I want the best lawyer in the county —the best *criminal* lawyer."

Calhoun reached in his pocket, pulled out his billfold and started counting out fifty-dollar bills; then he changed his mind, looked in the other side of the billfold and pulled out five one-hundred-dollar bills. He handed them to me. "Three hundred is for you," he said. "Two hundred is for a retainer for the lawyer. Get him to come to the jail and talk with me. I'll make arrangements for his fee then.

"In the meantime, you go ahead and keep working on this case. I'm well able to pay at the price we agreed upon."

"There will be expenses," I said.

"Incur them."

"Where do I stop?" I asked. "What's the limit?"

Calhoun pointed upward. "The sky is the limit."

Sellers said, "I hate to do this to you, Calhoun. If you would co-operate with us, it might not be necessary to take you into custody. After all, we simply are trying to find out about the gun and to trace your movements."

Calhoun looked at me. I shook my head.

"You aren't his lawyer, Pint Size!" Sellers said irritably. "You don't need to advise him."

"I'm his investigator," I said.

"Then you'd better be damn certain you keep your nose clean or we'll give you an adjoining cell. Then you can do all the yakety-yakking you want to."

"With both cells wired for sound," I said.

"You're damn right we'll have them bugged," Sellers said angrily. "How simple do you think we are?"

"You'd be surprised," I told him.

Sellers turned to Calhoun. "I'm not going to put handcuffs on you under the circumstances, but you're under arrest and don't make any mistake about it. Don't make any false moves. Come on, let's go."

They got to the door and we went out. Calhoun locked the door. I went as far as the lobby with them. Sellers put Calhoun in a police car where a local cop was waiting and they drove away. I went to the public phone in the lobby and called Bertha.

"I'm down here at Calexico," I said. "I'm still in Unit Seven at the Maple Leaf Motel. I'm probably going to be around here for a while. For your information, I just got some more money out of our client and instructions to go ahead . . ."

"Money out of our client!" Bertha yelled. "Where is he? And how the hell did you do that?"

"He's down here."

"How long's he going to stay?"

"Probably some little time," I said. "Frank Sellers and a local officer just arrested him for murder."

"Fry me for an oyster!" Bertha said.

"I'll take it from there," I told her, and hung up while she was still sputtering.

8

I found that Anton Newberry, with offices in El Centro, the county seat of Imperial County, had the reputation of being the best criminal lawyer in the county.

I didn't have any difficulty getting in to see him.

He took one of my business cards and said, "Cool and Lam, Private Investigators, eh?"

"That's right."

"And you're Donald Lam?"

"Right."

"What can I do for you, Mr. Lam?"

"I have a client in jail in Calexico. He'll probably be transferred to El Centro."

"What's he charged with?"

"Murder."

Newberry was a wiry, raw-hided individual in his late forties or early fifties, with high cheekbones, eyes spaced wide apart, a high forehead and a quick, nervous manner.

"When was he arrested?"

"About an hour ago."

"Who made the arrest?"

"A local officer accompanied by Sergeant Frank Sellers of the Los Angeles Police Department."

"What does Sellers have to do with it?"

"He was investigating the dope-running angle of the case. I think he's been working on it for a while.

"The victim is a dope runner named Eddie Sutton. He was killed last night or early this morning. The body was found in a houseboat on a trailer parked in Calexico."

"What's the name of our client?"

"Milton Carling Calhoun."

"Money?" he asked.

I took two hundred-dollar bills from my pocket. "This," I said, "is in the nature of a retainer. You're to see Calhoun and make arrangements for compensation with him, and you'd better be sure he gives you the true story. I think he'll try not to."

Newberry's long, thin fingers wrapped themselves around the money. "What's the story that he gave to you?" he asked.

I said, "The guy's evidently well fixed. He's married. It's been one of those cat-and-dog propositions. They're splitting up. Each one has an attorney. They're fighting over property."

"How much property?"

"Apparently a good deal."

Newberry folded and pocketed the two hundred dollars, then thoughtfully explored the angle of his jaw with thumb and forefinger. His face showed keen interest.

"Calhoun," I said, "is worried about publicity, particularly on a certain angle of the case."

Newberry twisted his lips in a wide grin.

"Funny?" I asked.

"Funny as hell," he said. "Los Angeles millionaire comes down to Calexico, gets himself arrested for murder. Los Angeles police are cooperating with the local authorities, and the guy would like to cut down on publicity.

"One thing I can guarantee," Newberry went on, "there'll be headlines all over the front page of the local paper tonight, and the story will be good enough to make the wire services. In all probability a feature writer for the Los Angeles papers will be down here by this time tomorrow looking for an interview."

Newberry picked up the telephone and said to his secretary, "Get me the chief of police at Calexico on the line—I'll hold on."

He sat there with the phone at his ear. I could hear the numbers click as his secretary worked the dial in the outer office.

Then Newberry said, "Hello, Chief, this is Anton Newberry, El Centro. . . . How's with you? . . . Good, eh? . . . You've got a

client of mine down there by the name of Calhoun . . . How's that?
. . . Oh, I see . . . Well, thanks a lot. I'll catch him up here."

He held on for a minute, then shook his head. "No comment," he said, "but thanks a lot for the information."

He hung up the telephone, turned to me and said, "The guy was brought up here an hour ago. He'll be in the jail here by this time. I'd better go over."

"Sounds like a good idea," I said.

"You're a professional licensed private detective?"

"Right."

"How much assistance from you can I count on?"

I said, "I'm going to investigate the case, but I'm going to do it my way."

"I'd like to have you work under me."

"Probably you would, but I've had experience in this game. I want to use it."

"I've had quite a bit of experience myself."

"Doubtless you have. Perhaps you'll have more before we get this case buttoned up."

"You've done some work so far?"

"Yes."

"Can you tell me about it?"

"Calhoun can tell you about it."

"But you'll keep in touch with me?"

"I'll keep in touch with you."

"And give me information as you get it?"

"I'll pass on the things I think you should know."

He thought that one over, then asked, "What evidence do they have against Calhoun?"

"I think Calhoun owned the murder weapon, a thirty-eight Smith and Wesson revolver.

"The dead guy came across the border last night, driving a Ford pickup with a pontoon houseboat on a trailer behind. The pontoons were cleverly made so that a cap could come off the ends and they could be stuffed with dried marijuana. They took quite a load.

"He got across the border all right, then parked the car by the side of the road. How's your coroner here?"

"Pretty good."

"You'll need a really good medical examiner, one who's a real expert in forensic medicine."

"Why?"

"I have an idea the time of death may be one of the most important bits of evidence in the whole case."

"How come?"

I said, "The evidence shows that Sutton had crossed the border by ten-fifteen at the latest. I think he picked a good parking place off the highway. He either had a scout car waiting there or one joined him there. The scout car went on ahead and found a roadblock. The driver radioed back for Sutton to wait it out. Sutton was tired. He got out of the pickup, went back to the trailer, climbed up, opened the door of the houseboat, and went in to take a rest.

"It's a small houseboat but, apparently, equipped with a gas stove for making coffee, a table, chairs, a bed and probably a water tank and some of the conveniences. While it's small, it looked pretty swank to me."

"You saw it?"

"I saw it."

"When?"

"When it came across the border."

"Did you see this man, Sutton, when he was driving the pickup?"

"I saw him when he was driving across the border and I saw him ten or fifteen minutes before that."

"Where?"

"In a restaurant in Mexicali."

Newberry looked at me thoughtfully. "You know," he said, *"you* could be involved in this case."

"Were you thinking of involving me?" I asked.

Newberry chose his words carefully. "I will be representing my client, Calhoun," he said, "and if it should appear—well, now, mind you, I'm saying that if it should appear from the evidence that there would be any chance of taking the heat off him by directing suspicion toward you, I won't hesitate for a split second."

"Thanks for telling me," I said.

Newberry had a habit of blinking his eyes rapidly when he was thinking, and from the way he was blinking I had an idea he was giving the situation a lot of thought.

"The more I think of it," he went on slowly, "you are in a rather vulnerable position. Where were *you* at the time of the murder?"

"Probably in Unit Seven at the Maple Leaf Motel in Calexico."

"How far from the scene of the murder?"

"Not far."

"And you saw the driver at a restaurant in Mexicali?"

"Yes."

"Talk with him?"

"No."

"Had you seen him before?"

"No."

"Did you know who he was?"

"No."

"When did you next see him?"

"When I was walking across the border. The Ford pickup and the trailer with the houseboat on it were waiting in line to get across."

"So you probably crossed the border just before he did?"

"Probably."

"Anybody who can back up your story?" he asked.

"I sleep alone," I told him.

Newberry shook his head. "It may be a most unfortunate habit, Lam."

He pushed back his chair. "I'm going over and see my client. Where can I reach you if I want you?"

"At the Maple Leaf Motel in Calexico, for the moment."

"Will you keep in touch with me as you move around?"

I shook my head. "There probably won't be time."

He said, "Why do you think the time element of the murder is so important?"

"Because Calhoun was just leaving Los Angeles at about the time Sutton was crossing the border with the houseboat. Sutton ran into some delay. His scout car hit a roadblock, so Sutton went back to the houseboat to wait it out. If that roadblock was on all night, that's one thing. If it was off before midnight, that's another thing. It may be important. If Sutton didn't go on after the roadblock was lifted, it could mean he was dead at that time."

Newberry asked, "What was the condition of the houseboat when the police discovered the body? Was there a light on or had the battery that furnishes juice for the lights been run down? Had the bed been slept in? Was there a dirty coffee cup? Was there—"

"The police," I said, "are singularly uncommunicative. They wanted to get Calhoun's story before they gave out any facts."

"They didn't get Calhoun's story?"

"No."

"Why not?"

"I advised him to see a lawyer before he talked," I said.

"Anything else?" Newberry asked.

I said, "Eddie Sutton had a companion with him when he crossed the border."

"Male, female?"

"Male."

"Description?"

"Can't give it. He was on the far side of the pickup and the light was such that I could only see the figure of a man."

"Do the police know that?"

"They know it."

"And they know that you saw this companion?"

"They know that."

"We would, of course, like to know who that companion was."

"We would all like to know who he was."

"Any ideas?"

"Nothing I can talk about."

Newberry was thoughtful. "You know, Lam," he said, "I think I can use you."

"One way or another," I said.

Again he grinned. "One way or another—no hard feelings if I try to pin this on you?"

"No hard feelings."

"And you'll let me know if you uncover anything that will help my client?"

"Probably."

"But you won't confer with me and cover the case under my directions?"

"No, I play a lone hand."

"All right," he said. "I'm going over to the jail and see my client."

He shook hands, a strong, sinewy hand that gripped mine hard.

"And you were in Calexico at the time the murder was committed?"

"Apparently."

"Good luck, Mr. Lam," he said. "You may need it."

He went out. I stopped at the desk in the outer office to get his secretary to give me one of his cards with telephone numbers on it; then I got in the agency car and drove back to Calexico.

9

I did a lot of thinking on the road back.

Nanncie had left the Maple Leaf during the early morning hours. She had gone either north or south. She wasn't apt to have gone either east or west. She had gone by taxicab or in a private car.

I had more legwork to do.

It didn't take me long to cover the taxicabs in Calexico. I drew a blank.

If Nanncie had gone south, she could have gone to San Felipe. Someone must have taken her in a private car. If she went north, she probably would have returned to Los Angeles by bus. But that wouldn't have been smart under the circumstances.

If Calhoun had been the one to call on her there at the motel, he couldn't have taken her very far. He had driven down from Los Angeles. He was tired. He might have taken her to the north as far as El Centro, or he might have taken her south—across the border.

I decided to check the really modern hotel in Mexicali as being the most logical place to look.

The Lucerna is an up-to-the-minute hotel with a patio, swimming pool, cocktail lounge and luxurious rooms.

I parked my car and walked out to stand by the pool, looking over the people who were basking in the Baja California sunlight.

I thought some of quizzing the hotel clerk as to whether some young woman had checked in early in the morning, but I thought better of that when I took stock of the situation.

The Mexican is an innate gentleman. If I had been able to get a Mexican police officer to go with me I could have secured the information; but to try to get it out of the clerk cold turkey was out of the question. The senorita's business would have been her own business and money wouldn't have changed the situation very much.

I was trying to think what Calhoun would have done—what he had done—what he had told Nanncie.

It had been some emergency which had caused her to check out and . . .

Suddenly I stiffened to attention. Nanncie, in a two-piece suit that showed a bare midriff, carrying a towel over her arm, came out and seated herself in one of the sunning chairs around the swimming pool.

I had a chance to take a good look at her. Then I went to where I had parked the car, unlocked the trunk, took out my baggage, and registered in the Lucerna Hotel.

Ten minutes later I was in my trunks and dunking in the pool. I came out, picked a chair which wasn't exactly the right style to suit me, got up, moved around and finally dropped into a vacant chair next to Nanncie.

I debated whether to make a pickup and get acquainted the slow way or whether to hit her right between the eyes.

I decided to hit her right between the eyes. There wasn't time for the slow way.

I looked straight ahead at the people in the swimming pool and said, "Nanncie, why did you check out of the Maple Leaf this morning?"

She jumped as though I had jabbed her with a needle, sucked in her breath as though to scream, then thought better of it and looked at me with wide, startled eyes.

I watched her out of the corner of my eyes but kept my face straight ahead.

"Who . . . who are you?"

"Donald Lam," I said, as though that explained everything.

"No, no, I don't mean your name. I mean who . . . how do you know who I am and what is it you want?"

I said, "I'm looking for Colburn Hale."

"What makes you look here and why ask me?"

"Because I'd like to have your help."

"Why do you want him?"

"I want to talk with him."

"About what?"

"Dope smuggling."

Again she caught her breath.

There was an interval of silence. "You're a detective?" she asked.
"Private," I said.

She thought for a few moments, then said, "I'm afraid I can't help
you, Mr. Lam."

"I think you can. How did you get over here, Nanncie? You left the
Maple Leaf Motel this morning, but you didn't have any car and you
didn't come by taxi."

"A friend drove me over."

I made a shot in the dark. "You came here with a man who is
driving a Cadillac automobile," I said.

"Lots of men drive Cadillac automobiles. If you must know, I'm
hiding out."

"But you were waiting for Hale at the Monte Carlo Café last
night."

She said, "He was supposed to meet me there right around seven
o'clock. He said if he didn't show up within an hour I wasn't to wait
but was to start protecting myself."

"Why did you check out of your apartment in Los Angeles, putting
all your things in boxes and taking them to the storage company?"

"Because I'm in danger. We're both in danger."

"Meaning you and me?"

"No, meaning Colburn Hale and myself."

"On account of that dope information you gave him? The information you got from the hairdresser?"

"I'm afraid Cole is in trouble. He was to have met me last night and
would have unless something terribly urgent had prevented him.

"He was to have followed that dope shipment up, getting the license number of the automobile and all that, and then he was to look
me up. The dope runner was to go to the Monte Carlo Café to see if
the coast was clear. He was to meet a confederate there, so Cole said I
was to go there at seven and wait. While I was waiting I could look the
situation over. After last night he'd have all the information he needed
to file his story. He had some editor who was waiting for it."

"Now, let's get this straight," I said. "You picked up the tip origi-
nally in a beauty shop?"

"Yes, my hairdresser is very friendly and she was going with a man
whom she didn't care too much about, but he was a good spender and

she was playing along with him. Then suddenly she found out that he was smuggling dope across the border. She didn't know exactly how, but she had enough proof so that she didn't want any part of it. The guy was not only smuggling it across but he was pushing it, particularly with school kids."

"All right," I said, "she told Colburn Hale?"

"No, she told me. She didn't intend to tell me all the details but she let the cat out of the bag enough so that I could put Colburn Hale on the track of a beautiful article."

"What did he do?"

"He picked up the trail of the dope smuggler in Los Angeles."

"Eddie Sutton?" I asked.

"Uh-huh. How did you know?"

"I've been working on the case for a while myself."

"Well, he picked up Eddie's trail and followed him around, getting some surreptitious pictures of him near some of the high schools, and I think he even got a picture of a delivery being made. You know, one of those deliveries where they slip a person an envelope while they're brushing against each other casually and things like that."

"Then all of a sudden Colburn cleared out of his apartment and you cleared out of yours?"

"We got in trouble," she said.

"How come?"

"Hale was a little careless, a litt—well, I guess you'd say a little unskillful. The man he was tailing followed *him* and found out where he lived."

"Then what happened?"

"My beauty-shop operator hadn't broken off with the guy. She was still playing along with him, and he told her that some guy—he thought it was a hijacker—had moved in on him; that he was going to take care of the fellow, and he asked the operator if she knew me. So my friend knew that . . . well, anyway, I knew we were both in danger."

"So you told Hale?"

"I told Hale."

"Who else did you tell?"

"No one. We just both got out without leaving any back trail."

"But why come to the border?"

"Because Colburn Hale knew that this shipment was due to come across and he wanted to find out just how it came across. The smuggler was to pick up an accomplice—what they call a scout car—at the Monte Carlo Café. Cole Hale was to meet me there right after that had been done. I was to try to get a line on the accomplice and then Cole would join me."

"After they'd already found out about him, didn't he realize he was taking desperate chances?"

"He did, and he didn't. It would be risky, of course. But he thought he could follow the shipment up and find out just how it was coming across."

"That was a crazy thing to do," I said. "You're both a couple of rank amateurs and you're playing this like rank amateurs."

She said nothing.

"Now," I said, "Hale will be in trouble. Did the shipment come across last night?"

"I don't know, but I think it did."

"Why did you check out this morning?"

"I . . . I thought it was dangerous staying where I was there in the Maple Leaf."

"Who told you it was dangerous?"

"I . . . I just felt it."

"Try again," I told her.

"How's that?"

I said, "Try again and this time try to make it a little more convincing."

She flared up and said, "I don't have to account to you for everything."

"You don't have to," I told her, "but you'd better. Now, suppose you tell me about Milton Carling Calhoun."

"What about him?"

"Everything about him."

She said, "I'll tell you about that because I have nothing to conceal. Milt and I are good friends, and that's it."

"How good?"

"As friends, very good."

"You knew he was married?"

"Of course I knew he was married. Now, you listen to me. I don't like the tone of your voice and I don't like the look on your face.

"You've heard a lot about married men who string a girl along,

telling her they're going to get divorced and when they're free they'll
marry her and all that stuff.

"Nine times out of ten even if they *think* they're telling the truth,
they aren't.

"The situation is different with Milton Calhoun. I met him at a sort
of bohemian party. He was getting a kick out of talking with the people on the—well, on the other side of the tracks. He's very wealthy,
you know."

"Is he?"

"I'll say he is."

"All right, so you met him at this party, and then what happened?"

"He and I sort of struck it off. He asked me if I'd go out to dinner
with him some night during the week and I told him I would.

"So then he came out like a gentleman and told me that he was
married, that he was having trouble with his wife, that they had separated, that he was living in a separate apartment, that he had moved
out of the big house and left that to her, that there were no children,
and that was that."

"And you've seen quite a bit of him since?"

"Quite a bit of him."

"And you're also friendly with Colburn Hale?"

"I am very friendly with Colburn Hale and I have half a dozen
other men friends. I'm gregarious and I move around with a crowd
that is gregarious. We like to live. We like to laugh—and I don't see
where all this is any of your business."

I said, "We've got to do something about Colburn Hale. He was
getting an article on this dope smuggling."

"That's right."

"And he told you he was going down to San Felipe and follow the
shipment up?"

"Well, not in so many words, but I gathered that was what he was
going to do. He told me to meet him last night at the Monte Carlo
Café. He said he was due there around seven o'clock; that if he didn't
show up right on time to wait for him for an hour."

"So you waited two hours?"

"Not quite two hours, but pretty close to it."

"Did it ever occur to you that he might be in danger?"

"Of course it occurred to me. Why do you suppose we checked out the way we did and didn't leave any back trail? We're dealing with people who are playing for keeps."

"Hale had his own car?"

"Yes."

"Anything distinctive about it?"

"No, it's just an ordinary black . . . Now, wait a minute, there is too. The left front fender has been struck and pushed up. He's been going to have it fixed but . . . Well, he's been busy and he hasn't had too much money."

"You don't have a car?"

"I don't have a car."

"All right, how did you get from the Maple Leaf Motel down here?"

"Milt drove me across."

"You mean Milton Calhoun?"

"Yes."

"And how did he find you?"

"I don't know. He came to the window and called my name about . . . I don't know, it was along in the night. He asked me to open the door so he could talk with me."

"And you did?"

"I opened the door and I was a little bit annoyed. I told him that I didn't appreciate being called in the middle of the night that way and that he didn't have any claims on me and that I was annoyed.

"Then he told me to keep my voice down, to get my things packed up; that I was in danger and he was going to move me to some other hotel. He finally convinced me and I packed up and got in the car with him and he drove me across here, registered, and paid for the room for three days in advance."

"What are you going to do at the end of that three days?"

"I don't know, but I presume that by that time the story will have broken and there'll be no further danger from those dope smugglers."

"You sound to me like a bunch of amateurs trying to climb a perpendicular rock face," I said. "You just don't know what you're getting into. You're dealing with professionals."

"What would you suggest doing?" she asked.

"The first thing we'd better do is to try to find Colburn Hale. He's evidently somewhere between here and San Felipe. Get your clothes on and we'll take a ride."

She said, "I think he can take care of himself all right. He . . . he had a gun."

"What kind of a gun?"

"A thirty-eight-caliber revolver."

"Where did he get the gun?"

"I gave it to him."

"And where did you get it?"

"I got it from Milton."

"Now, wait a minute," I said. "Let's get this straight. Milton Calhoun gave you a thirty-eight-caliber gun?"

"That's right."

"When?"

"A couple of days ago when he first learned that I was working with Cole on a deal involving some dope smuggling. He told me that I could get in a lot of trouble that way and that he wanted me to be protected."

"So he gave you the gun?"

"Yes."

"His gun?"

"Of course it was his gun, if he gave it to me."

"And then you gave that gun to Colburn Hale?"

"That's right."

I did a lot of thinking. Then I said, "Come on, we're going to drive down the road to San Felipe and keep our eyes open on the side roads."

"Why?"

"Because," I told her, "we may find a car with a front right fender that's been bent up and a dead body in it."

"A dead body!"

"Your friend, Colburn Hale."

"But he . . . they . . . they wouldn't dare . . ."

I said, "You're dealing with a professional bunch of dope smugglers. Their deals run into the thousands of dollars. A murder now and then is more or less of an incident. Get your clothes on and meet me here in as close to five minutes as you can make it."

She hesitated for a moment, then got to her feet and said, "Well, perhaps that's the best way, after all."

The road from Mexicali to San Felipe runs for some distance through a territory where there are occasional roadside restaurants selling ice-cold beer to the thirsty traveler together with a few of the more simple Mexican dishes.

There are some houses along this section of road before it crosses a barren stretch of desert to climb through a mountain pass. The Gulf of California is on the left, the barren desert on the right, and to the south the heat-twisted volcanic mountains where the hot desert winds have blown the sand high up on the rocky slopes.

I had settled for a long run and we had gone some distance in silence. Then Nanncie said to me, "I don't want you to get me wrong. I don't play my boyfriends one against the other. I am gregarious. I'm fond of people. I'm a writer. I don't want to give up my career so I can be a housewife and raise squalling babies. I'm not cut out for that kind of work. I'm ambitious."

"You're living your own life," I told her.

"And," she went on, "I want you to know that I didn't have anything to do with breaking up Milt's home. He and his wife had separated before I ever met him, and I never did furnish a shoulder for him to cry on about how she didn't understand him or how cold she was . . . But I will admit I gave him a taste of the sort of life he had never seen. A taste of bohemian life, a taste of associating with people who were living by making their minds work. A rather precarious living, I'll admit. But that's not because of any lack of talent on the part of the people who are doing the writing. It's on account of editorial policies."

"What's wrong with editorial policies?" I asked.

"Everything," she said. "The good magazines have a tendency to close the doors against free-lance writers. They have more and more adopted a policy of staff-written contributions.

"And then the bigger magazines cater to the big names, the people who are well established."

"And how do you get to be well established in the literary world?" I asked.

"By having your stuff published."

"And how do you get your stuff published?"

She smiled and said, "By getting to be a big name. You can't . . . Donald! Donald, there's Cole's car!"

"Where?"

"Over in that roadhouse restaurant parked right by the open-air kitchen. See that fender?"

I swung my car off the road and we came to a stop by a somewhat battered old-model car that was parked against the rail of an open-air dining room.

There was no one in this dining room, but I opened a door which led to a rather cramped interior and suddenly Nanncie was flying past me with outstretched arms. "Cole! Oh, Cole, oh my God, how glad I am to see you! Tell me, are you all right?"

The man who had been sitting at the table drinking beer got stiffly to his feet.

He and Nanncie embraced, completely oblivious of me.

"I made it," he told Nanncie, "but it was touch and go."

"Cole, you've got a black eye and there's blood on your shirt!"

"And my ribs are sore and I've taken a beating," he said.

She remembered me then. "Cole, I want you to meet Donald Lam. Donald, this is Colburn Hale."

Hale backed away suspiciously, ignoring my outstretched hand. "Who's Lam?" he asked.

"A detective," she said. "A . . ."

Hale started to turn his back.

"A private detective," she said. "A private detective who has been looking for you."

Hale turned back. He regarded me with suspicious eyes, one of which was badly swollen and had turned purple, the eye being bloodshot underneath the discoloration.

"All right," Hale said, "start talking."

I said, "I know just about everything there is to know. When Nanncie told me that you were going to meet her at the Monte Carlo Café at seven o'clock last night and didn't turn up and when I knew that the shipment of dope you had been tailing had crossed the border, I thought it might be a good idea for us to drive down the road toward San Felipe and see if we could find some trace of you."

"Well, you waited long enough," Hale complained.

"There were other matters claiming attention," I told him. "Why don't we go outside where we can talk? Bring your beer along and perhaps you can give me some information and perhaps I can give you some information."

"Perhaps," Hale said, but he picked up the bottle and glass of beer and carried them along with him.

He was a suspicious individual. He didn't wear a hat and had a shock of wavy, dark hair. I estimated him at about a hundred and eighty pounds, about five foot eleven or so.

The guy had surely been in trouble. In addition to his black eye he had evidently had a bloody nose and some of the blood was still on his shirt.

He hadn't shaved for a couple of days and his skin had that oily look which comes from extreme fatigue.

We sat down at a table in the outdoor dining room. There was no one else in the place. I ordered a couple of bottles of ice-cold beer.

"You seem to have had a beating," I told Hale.

He said, ruefully, "I thought I was smart, but I was dealing with people who were smarter than I was."

"Who gave you the beating?"

"Puggy."

"Who's Puggy?"

"Hell, I don't know his last name. All they called him was Puggy."

"And how did Puggy happen to meet you?"

"I was following a dope shipment."

"We know all about that," I said.

"No, you don't," he said. "Nanncie may have told you what she knows, but she doesn't know all the details. The—"

"She does now," I said. "The little houseboat on pontoons that makes regular trips up and down from San Felipe on a trailer drawn by a Ford pickup. The pontoons are made with a removable cap on the rear, so cunningly fitted that it looks like a welded job. But the cap slides off and the interior of the pontoon is filled with dried marijuana."

"And how do *you* know all this?" Hale asked.

"The authorities know it now," I said.

"The hell they do! Then my story has gone out the window."

"Perhaps not," I said. "There are other angles which may make your story newsworthy, provided it's dramatic enough."

"Well, it's dramatic enough," he said.

"What happened?"

He said, "Nanncie got wind of what was happening. She tipped me off to the dope smuggling and the people who were doing it, but I needed to have some firsthand information. I couldn't do it all on hearsay. I had to know just how the stuff came across.

"Anyhow, I got pretty much of the first part of the story together and was typing it like mad when Nanncie got in touch with me late at night and told me we had to run for cover fast."

"Why?"

"The beauty operator who had told her had let the cat out of the bag and Nanncie was in danger, and if she was in danger, I would be, too. They had followed me when I was tailing them."

"So what did you do?"

"I didn't want to have a bunch of dope runners on my trail. These men are desperate. I decided to move and not leave any back trail. I also decided to bust that gang of dope runners and not disclose my identity until after they had been captured and were serving a term in prison.

"So I packed up everything in my apartment. I got a friend of mine to help me and we moved out, stored my stuff, and I drove to Mexicali where I knew that these dope runners made their rendezvous."

"Go on," I said.

"I knew who was doing the dope running and I knew they were smuggling it in at Calexico, but I didn't know all of the details and I wanted to get a story based on firsthand observation.

"Anyhow, I picked up this dope runner, a man they called Eddie. If he's got another name I don't know what it is. He was driving a Ford pickup. I thought at first the stuff came up in that pickup, but I followed him down to San Felipe and saw that he hitched onto a houseboat that was mounted on a trailer, a small houseboat on pontoons.

"I knew that the shipment was due to cross the border at seven o'clock last night. I knew that much because I heard Eddie talking about the second car that was to pick him up at Calexico."

"The second car?" I asked.

"The second car," he said, "equipped with Citizen's Band radio. That's the way they work. After the stuff gets across the border at Calexico, they send a scout car on ahead. The scout car is absolutely clean. Anybody could search it all day and couldn't find even a cigarette stub that had any pot in it.

"That car goes on ahead, quite a ways ahead. If there's a roadblock of any kind, or if the border patrol has a station where they watch the road, this scout car sends a message back to the car with the dope by Citizen's Band radio. So then the dope car turns off or may turn clean around and go back.

"You understand, Lam, I'm telling you this in confidence. I want the exclusive story rights to it. You also understand that we're dealing with something big here. This isn't any little two-bit dope-smuggling outfit that brings in a few pounds at a time. This is big stuff. They're dealing with many thousands of dollars."

"Go ahead," I told him.

"Well," Hale said, "I knew that the scout car with the Citizen's Band radio was to be waiting just north of the border so that it could pick up the dope car, but I didn't know it was being followed by a muscle car that was to come along behind. I suppose I should have. I guess I was dumb."

"What happened?"

"I started trailing that Ford pickup with the houseboat on the trailer from San Felipe. I didn't have any trouble until we got almost up here, then suddenly the muscle car closed in on me."

"What happened?"

"Some fellow wanted to know who I was following and who the hell I thought I was. He was abusive and the first thing I knew he'd slugged me."

"What did you do?"

"I slugged him back, and that was the mistake of my life. This guy was evidently an ex-pugilist. I think that's where he got the name of Puggy. The driver of the car called him Puggy, anyway."

"And what did they do?"

"I took a shellacking," Hale said, "and then I had a gun and I made up my mind I wasn't going to take any more. I jumped back and pulled the gun, and that's where I made my second mistake. I found myself looking down the barrel of a sawed-off shotgun that the driver of the pickup had produced out of nowhere."

"So what?"

"So," Hale said, "they took my gun away from me. They put me back in my own car which Puggy proceeded to drive. They went down a side road which they knew and they tied me up good and tight, stuck a gag in my face, and warned me that the next time I wouldn't get off with just a beating. In fact, the driver of the car wanted to kill me, but Puggy said the Mexican drug ring didn't like murders and they wouldn't commit one unless they had to."

"Go on," I said.

"I stayed trussed up in that confounded car all night," Hale said. "Then this morning about eight o'clock a fellow driving along the side road from some ranch saw the car parked there, stopped to look it over, and found me, bound and gagged in the rear of the car. By that time my circulation had stopped. I was as stiff as a poker and so sore from the beating I'd taken I could hardly move."

"Keep talking," I said.

"Well, he was shocked, of course, but he untied the ropes and . . ."

"Untied them?"

"That's right."

"Go ahead."

"He untied the ropes and took the gag out of my mouth, put me in his car, took me to a ranch house, and he and his wife gave me hot coffee, then some kind of a Mexican dish of chile and meat, some tortillas, and the native kind of white cheese and some sort of fish.

"They were awfully nice people."

"How far from here?" I asked.

"Oh, ten, fifteen miles, something like that. I don't know exactly. Right down where a side road turns off and goes around the head of the Gulf."

"Can you find the place again?"

"I guess I could, yes."

"You'd better find it," I said.

"Why? And who the hell are you to be quizzing me like this?"

"I'm doing it," I told him, "because you're going to have to collect all the evidence you can get."

"Why?"

"Puggy took your gun away from you?"

"Yes."

"And where did you get that gun?"

He hesitated and looked at Nanncie.

Nanncie nodded her head. He said, "Nanncie gave it to me."

"Where did Nanncie get it?" I asked.

He shook his head. "She didn't tell me. She said she had it for her protection and she thought I needed it more than she did."

I said, "For your information, Eddie, whose last name was Sutton, accompanied by another man who was probably Puggy, crossed the border with the load of marijuana about ten o'clock last night. It had started to rain and they were two hours late—and I guess the fact that Puggy had to take care of you threw them off schedule a bit.

"Anyway, Sutton pulled off to the side of the road to wait for the scout car to go ahead and report a clear road. He and Puggy evidently got in some kind of an argument over the division of the profits or perhaps over the fact that they hadn't killed you to silence you and—"

"Wait a minute, wait a minute," Hale said. "I'll bet they sent a car back to finish the job."

"What makes you think so?"

"After I'd been lying in that car what seemed like ages another car came down the road and seemed to be looking for something. It came down the road and went back two or three times."

"You were close to the road?"

"I was close enough to the road so I could be seen by daylight, but a man coming down on a dark night, trying to find me by the headlights on a car, could very well have missed the car . . . I'll bet that was what it was all about. I'll bet they came back to take care of me, probably to drive me out someplace where they could load me aboard a boat, take me out in the Gulf and throw me overboard with weights tied to my neck and feet. It had started to rain. The night was as dark as pitch and the guy couldn't find me.

"I was desperate at the time. I tried to make noises to attract the attention of the driver. I realize now it's one hell of a good thing that I didn't."

"All right," I said, "that's probably true."

"What happened after that?" he asked. "You said Puggy and Eddie got in a fight about something?"

"Puggy and Eddie got in a fight about something," I said. "I imagine that Puggy started putting pressure to bear on Eddie about the fact that you needed to be taken care of on a permanent basis. Anyway, they got in a fight and Eddie got killed."

"Got killed?" Hale said.

"Got killed," I said.

"How?" Hale asked.

"One shot from a thirty-eight revolver," I said, "and I wouldn't be at all surprised if the revolver that fired the fatal shot wasn't the gun Puggy had taken away from you, the one that Nanncie had given you so you could protect yourself, and the same gun that had been given Nanncie so that she could protect herself."

Hale looked from me to Nanncie, then from Nanncie to me, then back to Nanncie. "Did Milt give it to you?" he asked Nanncie.

She nodded her head.

Hale reached an instant decision. "Don't tell anybody about where you got that gun," he said. "Let Calhoun explain it. He's got plenty of money, plenty of pull, and he'll get the best lawyers in the country. Don't let them drag you into it. Let's let Calhoun shift for himself."

11

I paid for the beers at the outdoor restaurant and said to Hale, "Come on, you've got to pilot us down to the place where you spent the night. What happened to the ropes they tied you up with?"

"They're in the back of my car."

"Did you get the names of the people?"

"Jose Chapalla," he said.

"They talk English?"

"Oh, yes."

I walked over to look at the ropes in his car. They were a heavy fishing twine. When a knot is tied in this stuff it can become very tight indeed.

I picked up the ropes and looked at the ends.

"What are you looking for?" Hale asked.

I said, "It's a shame your Mexican friend didn't know more about police science."

"What do you mean?"

"A good police officer," I said, "never unties a rope that a person has been tied up with. He cuts the rope and leaves the knots intact."

"Why?"

"Sometimes you can tell a good deal about a person from the type of knot he ties."

"Oh, you mean a sailor and all that stuff."

"A sailor, a packer—and sometimes just a rank amateur. Come on, let's go. You'd better get your car and we'll follow you. How far is it?"

"I would say around ten miles. But let me go with you, if you will, so I can stretch out. Nanncie can drive my car. I've had a real beating and I'm sore. My muscles are sore, my ribs are sore."

"I know," I told him. "I can sympathize with you. I've had several beatings."

He climbed slowly, laboriously into the back of the car. "Gosh," he said, "I'd love to have some hot water and a shave and get cleaned up."

"In a short time you will," I told him. "This is going to be my party from now on. I'm going to take you to the Lucerna Hotel in Mexicali. You can get a good hot bath and crawl into bed. Then you can get out in the swimming pool and float around and gradually exercise those muscles until you get the stiffness out of them."

"That sounds good," he said. "Boy, I'd sure love to get in a warm swimming pool and just relax and take all the weight off of myself and just float."

"It can be done," I told him.

We drove down to La Puerta where the road turns off to the east to go around the head of the Gulf.

"This is the road," Hale said.

We drove down the road for some distance; then Hale said, "This is where they left the car."

I got out and looked around.

I could see tracks where a car had been driven off the road, then where it had been standing perhaps a hundred yards from the edge of the road. There were footprints all around where the car had stood, lots of footprints.

We went back to the road and drove on . . .

"That's the place," Hale said, "that adobe house over there."

It was an unpretentious adobe house with an old dilapidated pickup in front of it.

I stopped the car and got out to knock on the door. Nanncie pulled up behind us and parked.

Hale eased his way out of the car and shouted, "Oh, Jose—Maria. It's me. I'm back."

The door opened.

A Mexican, somewhere in his fifties, with a stubby black mustache and a shock of black hair, attired in overalls and a shirt that was open at the throat, stood in the doorway, smiling cordially.

Just behind him, peering over his shoulder, I could see the intense black eyes of the man's wife.

"Amigo, amigo!" he called. "Come in, come in!"

Hale hobbled along and introduced us. "Jose and Maria Chapalla," he said. "They are my friends. And these two are my friends, Miss Nanncie and . . . What did you say your name was?"

"Lam," I told him.

"Mr. Lam," he said to the Mexicans.

"Please to come in," the Mexican said.

We entered the house, a place which had been designed to shut out much of the powerful sunlight, a place that was comfortable with the smell of cooking.

There was a fireplace with bricks built up so that a big iron pot could rest between the bricks. Underneath this iron pot was a small bed of coals, and by the fireplace were some sticks with which to keep the fire going.

To the left of the fireplace was an oil-burning stove with a battered tin coffeepot and a covered cooking pot in which a Mexican dish was simmering slowly, the cover lifting from time to time to let out a little spurt of steam.

The aroma of rich cooking filled the place.

Hale said, "My friend here wants to know about how you found me. Can you tell him the story?"

Chapalla said, "Sit down, sit down," and then became embarrassed as he realized there weren't enough chairs for all of us.

"Please to be seated," he said. "I prefer to stand when I tell the story."

We seated ourselves.

His wife, Maria, a heavily built Mexican woman with a chunky frame and a smile of good-natured hospitality, busied herself at the stove.

"Would you perhaps have coffee?" Chapalla asked.

"We haven't time," I said. "We're fighting against minutes. If you could just tell us how you found the car, it would be of great help."

"It is *muy mala*," Chapalla said. "Bandits have hurt this man very bad and left him tied up."

"How did you find him?"

"I am going to get some food," he said. "Our trips to the store are not many. When we go we take the pickup and we get much stuff.

"I am driving. I see this car off the road. At first I think nothing of it. I drive by it.

"Then I say to myself, 'Jose, why should that car go over there and be left. If there is trouble with the motor the car would be on the road. If it is driven over there, what is there to make the driver go to that part of the country to stop his car?'

"I drive on.

"But I think. I think. I do more thinking. Then I stop, I back up, I turn around. I go over to the car. At first I see nothing. Then I look inside. I see something that is light. It is the cloth that has been tied in your friend's mouth.

"I say, *'Caramba,* what is this?' I try the door of the car. It is not lock. I open it. Your friend is inside. He has been tied with a fishing cord in which knots are very tight indeed."

"You turned him loose?"

"I turned him loose."

"Did you cut the cords?"

"No, I am afraid. The cords are tied too tight. Maybe a slip of my knife and there is blood."

"Did you have a hard time untying the knots?"

"Not too hard. My fingers are very strong, senor. I have been a fisherman. I work much with lines. I know knots."

"And you took out the gag?"

"The gag?"

"The cloth in the mouth," I said.

"Oh *seguro,* sure. I take out the cloth and he speaks to me, but after some difficulty."

"What does he say?"

"He says he has been held up."

"And then?"

"So then the man is suffering. I invite him to come to my house."

"Does he drive his car?"

"No. He goes with me. He cannot get in the driver's seat of his car because he is sore in the sides of the stomach and his nose has bled and his eye is black.

"He has had a beating, that one!"

"And then what?" I asked.

"So we came to my *casa* and Maria she makes the hot food—tortil-las, some *chile verde* that we have cooking, some *frijoles refritos,* some cheese . . . He eats much, this man. He is sore, but he is hungry."

"And then?"

"Then we have him lie down on that bed. He lies still and he sleeps. Then he gets up and he leaves. I drive to his car."

"How long ago?"

Jose shrugged his shoulders. "I do not have the watch—maybe one hour, maybe two hours."

"And that is all you know?"

"That is all I know."

I nodded to Hale, "All right," I said, "we're going to Mexicali and I'm putting you in a good hotel. I'll bring you a sports shirt and . . . Where's your razor?"

"In my bag in the back of the car. It was in the back of the car. My God, do you suppose they took it?"

"Let's look."

He got the car keys and unlocked the trunk. A big bulging bag was in there, together with a smaller suitcase.

"Everything okay?" I asked.

"Apparently so," he said with relief. "You won't need to get me a new shirt. I have clean clothes in my bags, thank heavens."

"All right," I told him, "let's go."

"But there is a matter of money," Hale said. "I am a writer and . . . I had gambled much on this story and . . ."

"Pay it no mind," I told him. "The party is on me from here on."

The expression of relief struggling with his black eye was ludicrous.

Maria continued to busy herself over the stove, smiling a farewell and saying simply, "Adios."

I handed her a ten-dollar bill. "I make my thanks to you for the help you have given," I said.

They didn't want to take it, but it was apparent the money meant much to them. Maria finally took it with fervent thanks.

Jose Chapalla came to the door. He shook hands with all three of us. *"Via con Dios*—go with God," he said.

12

We stopped at a service station where there was a hose with running water. Hale washed the most noticeable bloodstains off his shirt and washed his face.

Nanncie tooted the horn of Hale's car and waved as she passed us on her way to the hotel.

Hale was doing some thinking en route.

When we stopped he said abruptly, "You're working for Milton Calhoun?"

"I'm working for him."

"I'm not," Hale said. "To be perfectly frank, I don't like the s.o.b."

"I'm working for him," I repeated.

"And," Hale said, "I'm not going to go out of my way to give him any help. He's got money, he can hire lawyers and . . ."

"He's already hired a lawyer. I want you to talk with him."

"I don't know whether I'll talk or not," Hale said.

"Suit yourself," I told him, "only don't forget one thing."

"What's that?"

"I'm working for Calhoun."

"Okay by me," he said. "You can work for anybody you damn please."

We entered the hotel. I escorted Hale to the desk.

The clerk smiled and shook his head, put his hands on the counter palms up. "I am so sorry, senors, but there are no vacancies. We are full and . . ."

103

"He is a friend of mine," I explained. "He has been in an automobile accident."

The clerk became all smiles. "Oh, in that case, *seguro,* yes, but certainly, we will take care of him."

He pushed a pen and a card in front of Hale and Hale registered. I noticed that he gave his address as 818 Billinger Street.

I saw that he was fixed comfortably in his room, got the bellboy to bring in his big bag and suitcase from his car and said, "You don't want these ropes that you were tied up with any more, do you?"

"I never want to see them again," he said.

"I'll get rid of them for you," I told him.

I took the ropes and put them in the trunk of the agency heap, drove across to Calexico, telephoned the office of Anton Newberry and asked the secretary if Newberry was in.

"He's just leaving for the day," she said.

"This is Donald Lam," I said. "Tell him to wait until I get there. I've got news for him."

"What kind of news?"

"It may be good news."

I could hear the mumble of off-the-telephone conversation; then the secretary said, "He'll wait. Try to get here as soon as possible."

"It won't be long," I told her. "I'm already across the line."

I made time to El Centro, was fortunate to find a parking place, and climbed the stairs to Newberry's office.

The secretary ushered me to the inner office where Newberry was waiting for me.

He twisted his thin lips in a smile which lacked cordiality.

"I hope it's good news, Lam," he said, "and it must be important."

"It is."

"Just what is it?"

"Sit down and get your notebooks," I said. "You'll want to take notes."

"I have a tape recorder and I can put you on tape."

"I'd prefer to tell you the story and have you make notes."

"Why?" he asked.

"For various reasons."

"All right," he said, "tell me why you think it's good news."

I said, "It's about the gun that did the fatal shooting."

"Tut, tut, we don't know what gun did the fatal shooting."

"But the police have found it—a thirty-eight-caliber revolver that's registered to Milton Carling Calhoun."

"How do you know it is the murder weapon?"

"I'll bet ten to one."

"I never bet against a client. They haven't done the ballistics work yet, and . . . I believe they have traced the registration. The gun was purchased some time ago by Mr. Calhoun, but that isn't necessarily conclusive."

I said, "I can account for the gun."

"Without involving Calhoun?"

"Without involving Calhoun."

His face lit up. This time the smile was cordial. "Well, well, well," he said, "tell me how it happened."

I said, "Calhoun gave the gun to a girl."

He shook his head and said, "We can't have any of this, Lam. We can't have any women brought into the case. Not at all, do you understand that?"

"I understand it. You are the one who decides what's going to be brought into the case. I'm the one who gives you the facts so that you know what to keep out of the case."

He nodded his head emphatically. "Very smart of you, Lam," he said, "very smart. Now, tell me about the gun."

"The girl," I said, "gave the gun to a fellow by the name of Colburn Hale. He's a writer. He was working on a story dealing with dope smuggling and—"

"Yes, yes," Newberry interrupted, "I've talked with my client. I know all about Hale."

I said, "No, you don't."

"What don't I know?"

"Lots of things. That's what I'm here to tell you."

"Go ahead."

"Hale," I said, "was given the gun for his protection. He went down to San Felipe and started playing around with this bunch of dope runners. I don't know when they made him, but probably about as soon as he left San Felipe on the trail of the shipment.

"They let him get as far as the vicinity of La Puerta; then the tail car closed in on him."

"The tail car?" he asked.

"There were two cars," I said. "The dope was in the lead car, a Ford pickup. It had Citizen's Band radio communication. The man who was driving it could communicate with the car behind."

"Why the tail car?" Newberry asked.

"The muscle car," I said.

"I see."

"In the vicinity of La Puerta, they used the Citizen's Band radio to instruct the muscle car to close in."

"And what happened?"

"The muscle car closed in. They worked Hale over pretty well and then Hale made the mistake of pulling his gun. He's very lucky that he isn't dead today. But down there in Mexico the people who run the drug shipments don't like to have murders. Drug shipments can be explained as a matter of course, but a corpse is something else again and the Mexican authorities don't like it.

"The Mexican dope rings want to be as inconspicuous as possible."

"Go ahead."

"So the dope shipment came to a stop and the guys moved in on Hale.

"Hale got beaten up in the process. Then they tied him up and left him in his own car."

"What about the gun?" Newberry asked.

"They took his gun. The point is, it wasn't his gun. It was Calhoun's gun, one that he had given his girl friend for her protection, and the girl friend, thinking Hale was in the greater danger, had passed the gun on to him.

"Now, that's the story. You can take it or leave it."

"Where's Hale now?"

"I've got him stashed."

"You found him when he was tied up?"

"I found him after he had been untied and set loose. A Mexican rancher by the name of Chapalla found the car with Hale in it and untied the ropes."

"What kind of ropes?"

"A fishing cord—heavy fishing cord."

"Then there must have been at least three men in the dope ring," Newberry said thoughtfully.

"Not necessarily. Sutton could have been driving the dope car. A man named Puggy could have been the one driving the muscle car. They left the muscle car south of the border and Puggy could have got in with Sutton when they came across. Puggy could have been the man I saw sitting beside Sutton in the pickup."

"And then there was a man driving a scout car," Newberry said.

I shook my head. "Puggy was probably the one to drive the scout car. They left the muscle car parked south of the border, then they came across and went to the point where they had a third car stashed, and Puggy was to take that and drive ahead and make sure the coast was all clear. So Puggy came to a roadblock and radioed back to Sutton that he'd better lie low for a while."

"There was a roadblock near Brawley last night. The Highway Patrol was checking cars from about eight o'clock until midnight," Newberry said.

"That explains why Eddie Sutton waited in Calexico," I told him. "He was waiting for the coast to clear. Puggy found the roadblock, radioed the alarm, and then drove back to join Eddie. They had an argument. Eddie got shot."

"It sounds very nice," Newberry said, and then added, "the way you tell it. However, there are certain facts which are very significant."

"Such as what?"

"Such as the fact that you were the one who found the fatal gun. You said it had been thrown in a field. No one saw it thrown in the field. You could have carried the fatal gun across with you and dropped it. You could have been intending to go away and leave it there until someone found it, but a sharp-eyed, ten-year-old kid followed you over and wrecked your plan.

"You're a private detective. You are pretty smart. You were tailing a dope shipment that was worth many thousands of dollars and a dope ring that was worth a lot more money. You could very easily have decided to cut yourself in for a piece of cake. Sutton wouldn't go for it.

"I don't think you'd kill Sutton in cold blood like that, but if you had this gun you might very well have beaten Sutton to the punch."

"And where would I have got the gun?" I asked.

"That," Newberry said, "is something my client insists is not to be brought out no matter what the provocation. That's your ace in the hole. It gives you a chance to beat the rap if anyone moves in on you."

"And I have a good lawyer, of course."

"And you have a good lawyer, of course," he said, smiling.

"You've had a talk with your client?" I asked.

"I've had a very comprehensive and satisfactory talk with him. I think I know more of the case than you do—unless, of course, you did the killing.

"Now then, my technique is to have a preliminary hearing just as soon as possible. I don't intend to call any witnesses or put on any defense. I want to get that over with fast. I want them to bind my client over for trial in the Superior Court. Once we get to the Superior Court, we'll really tear this case upside down.

"However, I am going to subpoena you as a witness at the preliminary because I may want your testimony perpetuated before you change it. I may tip the prosecutor off to you as a witness."

He grinned.

Newberry opened a drawer and whipped out a subpoena which he handed to me. "The preliminary hearing starts tomorrow morning at ten o'clock," he said. "This is your subpoena to be there."

"What about Colburn Hale? Do you want him there?"

Newberry said, "I don't care about Colburn Hale tomorrow. I'm going to use that boy in the Superior Court hearing. Have you seen the El Centro papers?"

"No, why?"

He walked over to a table, picked up a newspaper, and handed it to me. There were screaming headlines across the front page.

LOS ANGELES BILLIONAIRE ARRESTED FOR MURDER HERE—and then in smaller headlines, ATTORNEY NEWBERRY INSTRUCTS CLIENT TO SAY NOTHING.

I read the newspaper account. There wasn't much in it, but what they had had been stretched way, way out. A sergeant of the Los Angeles Police Force, on the track of a big dope ring, had come to Calexico and joined forces with the police there. The shipment had been brought across in the pontoons of a small houseboat on a trailer. The body of Edward Sutton, presumably a dope smuggler, had been found in the houseboat. He had been shot with a .38-caliber revolver.

Police had later found that .38-caliber revolver where the murderer had sought to dispose of it by throwing it into an alfalfa field some little distance from the scene of the crime.

While I was reading the article, Newberry was busy looking at my face, blinking his eyes all the while.

All of a sudden he said, "This Colburn Hale, he's positive that he had the gun the night of the shooting and they took it away from him?"

"That's right."

"And there was another man named Puggy who was in on the deal?"

"Right."

"And you saw two men in the pickup when it crossed the border?"

"Correct."

Newberry's face broke into a slow grin. "On the other hand," he said, "I think I'll make a grandstand. I may want this man, Hale, in court so I can get a statement. Can you get him to come to court?"

"Give me a subpoena for him and I'll try."

"What's the name?" he asked.

"Colburn Hale."

"It won't do any good to serve this subpoena across the line," Newberry said.

I grinned at him and said, "Do you suppose Hale knows that?"

Newberry matched my grin. "Not unless somebody tells him," he said.

"All right," I told him, "give me the subpoena. If you want him there, I'll try to have him there. He is not very pretty. He's got a beautiful shiner, and . . ."

"Wonderful, wonderful!" Newberry said. "Certainly we want him there. We want his picture in the paper—a mysterious witness who will clear my client in the Superior Court. We can let the newspapers get the story—pictures—black eye—wonderful!"

"There is one thing *I've* got to have," I said, "if I'm going to get Hale in court."

"What?"

"The opportunity to see Calhoun—now."

He shook his head. "It's too late. Visiting hours are . . ."

I pointed to the telephone. "You can fix it up," I said.

"It might be a little difficult."

I said, "Calhoun is paying you to smooth out difficulties."

He picked up the telephone, put through a call to the Sheriff's Office, talked a while in a low voice, hung up the phone, turned to me and nodded.

"It's all fixed," he said. "You'll have to go right away."

"On my way," I told him.

He was watching me speculatively as I left the office.

13

Milton Calhoun had the best quarters in the Detention Ward. I don't know whether money had fixed it or whether Anton Newberry had pull, but the place wasn't too bad as jails go.

He was glad to see me.

"How do you like the attorney I got for you?" I asked.

"I think he's all right," he said.

"He's arranged for a quick preliminary hearing," I said, "tomorrow morning at ten o'clock, I understand."

Calhoun nodded and said, "But the preliminary hearing means nothing. We're not going to do anything except ride with the punch. That's what Newberry thinks should be done."

I said, "Have you talked to anybody?"

"Newberry, that's all."

I said, "Sit tight. Don't talk to anybody. Don't give anyone even the time of day. Refer them to Newberry."

"That's what my attorney has told me."

"All right," I said. "Now I'm going to tell you a few things. Get over closer."

"Why closer?" he asked.

"So you can hear me better," I said.

I sat on one side of the toilet and motioned Calhoun to the other side.

I flushed the toilet, put my lips close to his ear, and started talking about Colburn Hale.

When the toilet ceased to make noise, I quit talking, waited for a few seconds, then flushed it and began all over again.

"What's that for?" Calhoun asked.

"That," I said, "is because the place is bugged and I don't want other people to hear what we're talking about. Why didn't you tell me that you knew where Nanncie was?"

"I didn't want anyone to know."

"You act like a clumsy fool," I said. "You can't hold out information on me any more than you can on your lawyer."

"I haven't even told him all you know," Calhoun said.

"Then don't. I'm going to take care of Nanncie. Be sure that you don't ever mention her name. They'll ask you about the gun and . . ."

A man appeared at the barred door. "What the hell is all this water running down the toilet about?" he asked.

I grinned at him and said, "How did you know water was running down the toilet?"

He looked at where Calhoun and I were seated on opposite sides of the toilet, shook his head, and said, "Come on, wise guy. Get out. Your visit is over."

"That was a short visit," I said.

"Wasn't it?" he agreed.

"Why cut it so short?" I asked.

"Because," he told me, "we don't like to waste water. We're out here in the desert. Come on, let's go."

I shook hands with Calhoun. "Remember what I told you," I said.

I followed the deputy sheriff on out.

The deputy had me check out on the visitors' register, looked me over and said, "Sergeant Sellers told us about you."

"Do you," I asked, "want *me* to tell *you* about Sergeant Sellers?"

He had the grace to grin. "That won't be necessary," he said.

After I got out of the jail I bought the El Centro evening paper. Seated in the agency car, I read about Calhoun. Evidently he was a real big shot in Los Angeles.

Then another item caught my eye.

Headlines read: ROADBLOCK NEAR BRAWLEY NETS MANY CARS WITH DEFECTIVE EQUIPMENT.

I read about the forty-two cars with defective lights, and then I read: "Peter L. Leland, a former pugilist, was also apprehended at the roadblock at 10:45 P.M. An alert officer spotted Leland waiting on the outskirts of the roadblock, communicating over a Citizen's

Band radio with some unknown individual. Inquires developed that Leland was wanted, having jumped bail in Los Angeles on a charge of dope smuggling. He was taken into custody."

I tore this out of the newspaper and put the item in my billfold. This could be Hale's "Puggy." I debated whether to call the matter to Newberry's attention, but decided to wait until I saw him at the preliminary hearing.

I drove across to the Lucerna Hotel and found Colburn Hale sitting fully clothed by the side of the swimming pool, talking with Nanncie. Nanncie was in a bathing suit.

"What's the matter?" I asked Hale. "No swim?"

He shook his head. "Just too plain sore to even think of it."

"It'll take the soreness out of you. Relaxing in water is one of the best ways there is to get your muscles unwound."

"I suppose so," he said, "but it's—it's just a problem even getting my clothes on and off. I managed a hot bath. I almost fainted. I'll wait a couple of days before I swim."

I said, "I have a little missive for you."

"What is it?"

I handed him the subpoena.

"Why, that's tomorrow morning at ten o'clock!" he said.

"That's right."

"In El Centro."

"That's right."

"Well, I suppose if I have to be there, I'll have to be there."

I said, "I've got one just like it."

"What about me?" Nanncie asked.

I shook my head and said, "You don't have anything to contribute to the situation at the present time, at least nothing that anyone knows about.

"And," I went on, looking pointedly at Hale, *"I know that no one will say anything that would drag your name into it.*

"It's getting late. I'll buy you folks a drink."

Hale eased himself up out of the chair.

"I'll shower and dress," Nanncie said. "It'll take me a few minutes."

"You can join us in the cocktail lounge," I said.

Hale started staggering and hobbling toward the cocktail lounge. I said, "Oh, just a minute, I forgot something."

I went back to where Nanncie was just getting up.

"Get your things all packed," I said. "You've got to get out of here."

"Why?"

"To keep your name out of the papers."

"But how am I going?"

"I'm taking you."

"Where am I going?"

"To a place where no one will ever think to look for you. Say nothing to anyone. Join us in the lounge for a drink, then make an excuse to get to your room. I'll give you a buzz."

I rejoined Hale. We went into the cocktail lounge and had a Margarita, one of those beautiful Mexican drinks with frosted salt around the edge of the glass and a cool balm of liquid delight inside.

Nanncie joined us. We had another drink.

Hale would have sat there and pinned one on, but I said I had some work to do and left.

Nanncie said she never cared for more than one drink before dinner, and we left Hale sitting there.

Things worked out like clockwork. Nanncie was packed all in one suitcase and a bulging bag. She had made a record for speed.

I tipped a bellboy, and while Hale was still in the bar we were on our way.

"Where," Nanncie asked, "are we going?"

I said, "You are going to go to a primitive place."

"Where?"

"Ever hear of El Golfo de Santa Clara?" I asked.

She shook her head.

"This," I said, "is a place down on the Gulf on the Sonora side. It's clean, it's nice, it's quaint, it's picturesque. There's a motel there that is fairly livable, and there are some very good restaurants where you can get perfectly fresh seafood and prawns that are almost as big as a small lobster.

"There's only one thing you'll have to put up with."

"What's that?"

"The water in the shower," I said, "is at what they call room temperature."

"And what is room temperature?"

"Pretty damn cold if you take it in the morning," I said.

"How long do I have to stay there?"

"Until I come and get you."

"Can't you telephone the . . ."

I shook my head. "I told you," I said, "I was taking you to a place that's isolated. No reporter is going to find you there. No one is going to find you there, not even Sergeant Frank Sellers of the Los Angeles Police Force, who is probably going to be looking for you."

We started out. We had a long, long drive ahead of us, but if they found her at El Golfo de Santa Clara, they could get rich finding needles in haystacks.

14

Even taking a shortcut by way of Puertecitos and Riito, it's a long way from Mexicali to El Golfo de Santa Clara, but one thing was certain—no one was going to be looking for a missing witness at El Golfo.

From the time the road passes Riito, it runs down as a straight and virtually deserted ribbon through barren desert country until it comes to the place where it drops down from the higher country and comes to the alluvial deposit of the Colorado River near the Gulf.

Then, after a few miles, one comes to El Golfo de Santa Clara, a little fishing village, beautifully picturesque, where a fishing fleet is tended by an ancient amphibious "duck" which goes from boat to boat as a sort of water taxi, bringing in fish and passengers.

The fish are used to supply the local restaurants and are the overflow of the cargoes which the fishing fleet keep iced for commercial deliveries.

Here also is where the supply of clams for the California markets comes from. Miles and miles and miles of tideflats are literally filled with clams. Clammers take light boats with outboard motors, drive them up over the mud flats, wait until the tide goes out, then start gathering clams. By the time the tide comes back in high enough to float the boat, the clammers will have a load of clams which, when brought to the United States, will command a fancy price.

Aside from that and the few tourists who know of the fishing and the clamming, El Golfo basks serene and deserted in the sunlight of the Gulf.

The motel there is clean with indoor plumbing and showers in the

Mexican style which tend to flood the floor of the bathroom whenever a shower is taken, and the water, as I had remarked, was at "room temperature."

Nanncie was a good sport and I felt she could put up with things and be happy.

On the way down I had a chance to get acquainted with her.

"You must think I'm something of a tramp," she said.

"Why?"

"Well, I have done so much for Cole Hale and I'm friendly with Milt Calhoun and I'm—I have quite a few friends."

I could see she wanted to talk so I just devoted my attention to driving the car.

She said, "It's hard for an outsider to understand the way we live— us writers."

Again I kept quiet.

She said, "It's sort of a society of its own, a freemasonry. We have very close friendships, but we're not prepossessed with sex the way some people think. It's more like an organization where everybody is just a close friend, as though we were all men or all women. We have so many things to think of, so much to do, so much to keep us occupied.

"Life is something of a struggle. We have to support ourselves and it's a grim fight, but it's a lot of fun.

"We watch the mail for envelopes, rejection slips with the returned manuscripts, and now and then a check.

"For the most part, we hit the smaller markets, the religious magazines, the trade magazines. We sell fillers, little articles, sometimes a short story of fiction.

"We all seem to keep just about one jump ahead of the landlord, and after you get to be a real part of the gang you can make a touch once in a while if a person has sold two or three good articles in succession and you're up against it for the rent. You can make a small touch to tide yourself over. But woe to you if you don't pay back at the first opportunity you have. The deadbeat is completely ostracized.

"It's hard to tell you how we work out there on Billinger Street. It's something like—well, from all I can hear, it's like Greenwich Village in New York used to be many, many years ago."

"And Milton Calhoun fits into that picture?" I asked.

"He emphatically does not fit into that picture," she said, "and that's why I'm afraid of him. Milt wants to be received as a friend, but you know instinctively that he isn't one of us. If I married him I'd be jerked out of the environment I love so well. We'd be on the French Riviera, or cruising in yachts. If I wanted to have my friends visit me in that environment I'd be uncomfortable and so would they.

"Right now Milt tries hard to be one of the gang, but despite the act he puts on he's an outsider."

"Do you mean he's a hypocrite?" I asked.

"No, no, no, I'm afraid you don't know what I mean. You don't understand what I'm trying to tell you.

"Milt thinks that is a poor life. He would like to rescue me from that life. That's the way he thinks of it, as a rescue. He would like to marry me when he becomes free and give me a big house and servants and a yacht and all the stuff that still goes with extreme wealth."

"And you don't want it?"

"I don't want any part of it, not the way I feel now. I like Milt. I'm tremendously fond of him. I could probably fall in love with him if I'd let myself, but I love this life that I'm living, this being just one jump ahead of the landlord, this studying the magazines, the writer's magazines, looking for tips on what can be sold and where it can be sold.

"Sometimes I'm a little behind in the rent, sometimes I've even been short on postage, but I'm one of the gang. We all of us sort of pull together. It's a great life and I like it."

"Perhaps," I said, "you're getting the cart before the horse."

"What do you mean?"

"Perhaps you ought to rescue Calhoun."

"Rescue him from what?"

"From the same thing he's trying to rescue you from."

"I don't get it."

"From the life he leads," I said.

"Oh," she said, then laughed. "He'd like that!"

"Here's a guy with money running out of his ears. He puts in his day turning to the financial column of the papers, reading the stock listings, giving orders to his brokers, having all the accessories of wealth including a dissatisfied wife. You could save him from all that."

"Yes," she said, laughing. "I've even thought of that. Suppose I did marry him and had all the glittering embellishments of wealth. Pretty quick he'd be burying his nose in the financial page at breakfast and

then hurrying away to give orders to his brokers. I'd be sitting there—
I won't say a bird in a gilded cage because it's too damn much of a
cliché, but you know what I mean."

"I know what you mean," I said.

"Why not tell Calhoun that if he'll cut himself off from his bank
account and move down on Billinger Street, take up writing and support himself by his earnings, you'll feel different about it?"

She laughed gleefully. "It would be a great gag at that. I'd like to
see his face when I pull that on him."

"And Hale?" I asked. "What about Hale?"

"Hale," she said, "is one of the gang. He's a friend.

"Good Lord, I run onto a chance of a real first-class article on dope
smuggling, but it's something that a man has to do—a woman can't
do it.

"So I pass the tip on to Cole Hale and do everything I can to make
the story jell."

"And what will you get out of it?"

"It depends upon what Cole gets out of it. He'll cut me in for a
percentage."

"And you'll take it?"

She looked at me in surprise. "Sure, I'll take it," she said. "What do
you think I'm doing this for?"

"I thought perhaps it was from a sense of devotion."

"Don't be silly," she said. "I like Cole, but I have a living to make
just as he has a living to make."

"So you're in this thing together?"

She nodded.

"And in deep," I said.

Again she nodded.

After a while she said, "You're the one I don't get. I don't get the
sketch."

I said, "I'm a private detective. I have loyalty to the person who
employs me. I don't have all of the immunities that an attorney would
have. As a result I have to protect myself and my client.

"For instance, I can't hold out evidence on the police if the police
demand that evidence, and I can't conceal evidence that would tend to
solve a case on which the police are working. If I did I'd be in
trouble."

"But you're concealing me."

"No, I'm not," I told her. "I'm just taking you where you're not going to be disturbed by a lot of newspaper reporters."

"Newspaper reporters?"

"That's right. Have you seen the evening papers?"

"No, I guess I haven't."

"Well," I said, "the evening papers are making a big feature of the Los Angeles millionaire who was arrested for murder."

"But he hasn't said anything about me, has he?"

"He hasn't said anything about you, but don't underestimate the skill of the reporters."

"But how could the reporters find anything that would lead to me from the fact that Milt Calhoun has been arrested?"

"They'll talk with Calhoun's attorney," I said. "His attorney will be very mysterious. He won't mention any names, but the name of Colburn Hale will be brought into the case. Then the reporters will start talking with Hale."

"Do you think he will talk?" she asked.

"Do you think he'll keep quiet?" I countered.

She thought that one over and said, "Then why don't you spirit him away?"

"Because," I told her, "Hale is a witness. He enters into the case. The police wouldn't like it if a private detective spirited Hale away. And don't get the idea that I'm spiriting you away. I'm just taking you to a place where you won't be disturbed and where you can get a good rest."

"All right, we'll let it go at that," she said, laughing.

We let it go at that.

By the time we got to El Golfo I felt that I knew Nanncie very well indeed and she was one nice kid. I could see her viewpoint. I didn't know how long she'd have it. I knew that sooner or later some guy would sweep her off her feet and I knew that it might well be Milton Carling Calhoun once he learned the proper approach, but I didn't think it was my duty as his private detective to give him the proper approach. It was up to him to find that out for himself.

We got into El Golfo in time to get two rooms in the motel. I told Nanncie, "There's a bus service out of here that you can take if you have to, but you won't be hearing from me, you won't be hearing from anybody, unless someone comes to get you."

"And suppose someone comes to get me?"

"Then," I told her, "you'll have a nice long ride."

"Will we have breakfast together in the—"

"I'll be long gone by breakfast," I told her. "I have work to do."

I filled up the agency heap and took Nanncie over to the little restaurant café. It was late, but they still had some fried prawns and I saw the surprise on her face at the quality of the food.

"Just watch that you don't get fat," I warned.

"What am I going to do for money?" she asked.

"How much do you have?"

"Damn little."

I laughed and said, "You have no objection taking money from me which came from Milton Calhoun as expense money?"

"Get this straight, Donald. I have no hesitancy whatever in accepting money from you for anything."

I handed her a hundred dollars.

She looked at the money with wide-eyed surprise.

"This," I said, "is going to have to last you for a while. Don't try to account for it. Just put it in as a hundred dollars' expense money, and if you have any left when you get home, just forget about it."

"But this is your money."

"There's more where that came from."

She hesitated, then folded the money and put it in her purse. I had an idea it was more money than she'd had at one time in quite a spell.

We finished our dinner. I got her a couple of bottles of Tehuacan mineral water and a bottle opener to keep in the room, told her it was better to drink Tehuacan, the mineral water of Mexico, than it was to take a chance on drinking tap water.

When I started to say good night, she reached and kissed me.

"Donald," she said, "I don't know whether anyone has ever told you, but you're a very wonderful person."

"Are you telling me now?" I asked.

She said, "I'm telling you now," and kissed me again.

I was up before daylight and on the long, lonely road north, leaving the tideflats behind me, climbing up into the higher desert, then driving for mile after mile.

The east lightened into a glorious orange, then into blue, and the sun burst over the mountains to throw long shadows from the greasewood and the desert plants.

Finally I came to the turnoff.

By this time it was broad daylight.

It was a job getting to El Centro in time for the preliminary hearing, but I made it.

The deputy district attorney was a man named Roberts, Clinton Roberts, and he took himself rather seriously.

He started out by making a speech to Judge Polk who was holding the preliminary hearing.

"The purpose of this hearing, if the Court please, is not to prove the defendant guilty of a crime, but simply to show that a crime has been committed and that there is reasonable ground to believe the defendant is connected with the commission of that crime."

Judge Polk frowned slightly as though he objected to being educated by a much younger man.

"This Court understands fully the scope of a preliminary hearing, Mr. Prosecutor," he said. "You don't need to explain it."

"I am not explaining it, if the Court please," Roberts said. "I am trying to set forth the position of this office. Because of the prominence and social standing of the defendant we are going to go further than would ordinarily be the case. We are going to introduce enough

123

evidence to show fully what the prosecution will rely on at the time of trial. And if the defendant can explain that evidence we will be only too glad to have such explanation made so that the case can be dismissed at this time."

Anton Newberry, twisting his thin lips into a grin, said, "In other words, you are inviting the defense to show its hand at this preliminary hearing?"

"Not at all," Roberts said angrily. "We are simply trying to show that the prosecution will conduct its case according to the highest standard of professional ethics and that if the defense can explain the evidence we will be only too glad to join with the defense in asking the Court for a dismissal."

"And if the defense makes no explanation?" Newberry asked.

"Under those circumstances," Roberts snapped, "we will ask that the defendant be bound for trial in the Superior Court on a charge of first-degree murder."

"Go ahead with your evidence," Judge Polk said to Roberts.

Roberts called the county surveyor to the stand to introduce the diagram he had made showing a section of the road between Calexico and Imperial.

There were no questions on cross-examination.

Roberts introduced the testimony of a Calexico police officer who was on patrol duty on the night of the nineteenth and the morning of the twentieth. He had noticed the pickup with the houseboat trailer parked at a wide space in the road very near the northern boundary of the city limits of Calexico. He had seen it earlier in the evening of the nineteenth and he saw it shortly after midnight on the morning of the twentieth. He decided to leave the occupant of the houseboat alone until morning and then waken him to tell him that there were laws against camping there by the roadside and that, while he didn't want to be arbitrary, he would have to insist that the occupant move on.

The officer had knocked on the door repeatedly. There was no answer, so he tried the handle of the door. The door was unlocked. He opened the door and looked inside and saw a body sprawled upon the floor.

He came to the conclusion that the man had been shot. He immediately backed away and closed the door, being careful as he closed the door not to leave any more fingerprints.

He had then radioed headquarters and they had sent out a team of investigators and had notified the sheriff in El Centro, who had sent deputies.

The officers had moved the pickup and houseboat to police head-quarters at Calexico where there were facilities for a scientific investigation.

An expert fingerprint man from the Sheriff's Office had taken over and, within a short time, Sergeant Frank Sellers, an expert in homicide from the Los Angeles Police, who was frequently engaged in liaison work in outlying communities, had joined forces with the other officers.

Newberry said shortly, "No questions on cross-examination."

An officer identified on the diagram, which had already been introduced, the place where the pickup and trailer had been located just within the city limits.

Again there was no cross-examination.

A Sheriff's Office fingerprint expert was called to the stand. He testified to painstakingly powdering the inside as well as the outside of the pickup and houseboat, searching for fingerprints.

Had he found any?

Indeed he had. He had found many latents that were smudged. He had found some seventy-five latents that couldn't be identified and he had found some latents that could be identified.

"The latents that could be identified," Roberts asked, "where did you find them?"

"I found five prints of a left hand that had been placed against the aluminum side of the houseboat just to the left of the door handle. One of the fingerprints, presumably the thumb print, was smudged. The other four latents were identifiable."

"Do you have photographs of the fingerprints?"

"I do."

"Will you produce those photographs, please?"

The witness produced the photographs.

"Now then, you say that those were identifiable. Have you identified those four fingerprints that were clear and unsmudged?"

"I have."

"Whose fingerprints are they?"

"The fingerprints of Milton Carling Calhoun, the defendant in this case."

There was a startled gasp from the spectators, and Newberry's eyes were blinking several times to the second, but his face was a wooden poker face.

Calhoun was the one who showed emotion. He looked incredulous and then chagrined.

This time Newberry made a perfunctory cross-examination.

"You don't know when those fingerprints were made," he said.

"No, sir, I do not. All I know is that they were made at some time before I was called on to go over the houseboat for fingerprints, and that was on the morning of the twentieth."

Was the expert absolutely certain these were the fingerprints of the defendant?

"Absolutely."

"Each print? Or was it the cumulative effect of the several prints?"

"No, sir," the expert said. He had identified each and every fingerprint. There had been enough points of similarity in each fingerprint to make an identification positive.

Newberry let the guy go.

A medical examiner summoned by the Sheriff's Office testified that he had journeyed with the county coroner to Calexico; that the body had been observed in place on the floor of the houseboat; that then the body had been removed to the mortuary and there had been a post-mortem. Death had been caused by a .38-caliber bullet which had penetrated the chest, severed a part of the heart, and lodged near the spine on the right-hand side of the body, traversing the chest at an angle. The bullet had been recovered. Death had been at some time between 9 o'clock at night on the nineteenth and 3 o'clock in the morning on the twentieth.

Newberry's cross-examination was perfunctory.

How had the time of death been established? The answer was that the witness had used body temperature and the development of rigor mortis and of post-mortem lividity, had taken into consideration the outer temperature that night, estimated the temperature inside the houseboat, etc.

"What about the stomach contents?" Newberry asked. Had not the contents of the stomach given a definite idea as to how long after the last meal had been ingested before death occurred?

"The stomach contents would be of no help," the physician said. The last meal had been ingested quite a few hours prior to death.

I passed a note to Newberry. "Find out about conditions in the houseboat," I said. "Was an electric light on at the time the body was discovered? Was there a gas stove which had been used and which would have changed the temperature in the houseboat and thereby thrown off the calculation of the time of death? And ask if it isn't a fact that rigor mortis develops sometimes very slowly and at times almost immediately, particularly if death occurs during the height of an argument or quarrel which has raised the blood pressure."

Newberry read the note thoughtfully, crumpled it, tossed it into the wastebasket, and said to the witness, "No further questions on cross-examination."

The witness left the stand.

The prosecution introduced a certified copy of the State Firearms Records showing that Milton Carling Calhoun had purchased a certain Smith & Wesson .38-caliber revolver with a one-and-seven-eighths-inch barrel, number 13347, the cylinder of which held only five shells. The weapon had been purchased from the Sierra Sporting Company in March three years earlier.

A photostatic copy of the record was introduced, showing the signature of Milton C. Calhoun and his address.

Roberts said, "I am going to call Sergeant Frank Sellers, of the Los Angeles Police, to the stand."

Sellers took the oath with the bored manner of one who had testified thousands of times.

The prosecutor asked questions showing Sellers' professional qualifications and the fact that he was in Calexico on the morning of the twentieth.

"What brought you to Calexico?" Roberts asked.

"Our department was asked by the chief of police of Calexico to furnish some technical assistance in connection with a matter—"

"Just a minute," Newberry interrupted. "Unless that matter is connected with the present case, I object to it as incompetent, irrelevant and immaterial."

"It is indirectly connected," Roberts said, "but we will withdraw the question."

Newberry smiled as though he had actually accomplished something besides keeping me from getting some information I would have liked to have had.

"But you were in Calexico on the morning of the twentieth?"

"Yes, sir."

"At what time in the morning?"

"I arrived by plane about five-thirty in the morning."

"And what did you do?"

"I reported to the police."

"And then what?"

"Then later on I went to the De Anza Hotel for breakfast."

"And what happened when you arrived in the De Anza Hotel?"

"I found a private detective, one Donald Lam, whom I had known and with whom I had had dealings on several occasions, and he was then and there accompanied by one Milton Carling Calhoun, the defendant in this case."

"Did you have any conversation with them?"

"Oh, yes. I asked Lam what he was doing there and was given to understand that he was working on a case and that the defendant in this case was his client."

"Then what?"

"Then a Calexico police officer came and asked me to join him for a few minutes and told me that a murder had just been discovered on the outskirts of town."

"I accompanied this officer to the scene of the crime, a houseboat mounted on pontoons and being in turn mounted on a trailer behind a Ford pickup."

"Did you search the premises for a possible murder weapon?" Roberts asked.

"We did," Sergeant Sellers said.

"Was any weapon found?"

"Not at that time."

"What do you mean by that?"

"I mean that the murder weapon was found at a later time."

"By whom?"

"I believe," Sellers said, "the murder weapon was discovered by Donald Lam."

"Is Donald Lam in court?"

"Yes, he is. He's seated there in the front row."

"I ask permission to withdraw this witness temporarily and to call Donald Lam to the stand."

"For what purpose?" Newberry asked.

"For the purpose of showing the finding of the murder weapon."

"I don't think that is proper procedure," Newberry said.

Judge Polk shook his head impatiently. "We aren't going to try this case on technicalities, not at this time and in this court. The witness will stand down while Donald Lam is sworn. Stand up, Mr. Lam."

I stood up.

"Hold up your right hand."

I held up my right hand.

The clerk said, "You solemnly swear that all of the evidence you will give in this case now pending before this court will be the truth, the whole truth, and nothing but the truth, so help you God?"

"I do," I said.

They asked me for my name, address and occupation, and I gave that information for the court records and seated myself in the witness chair.

Roberts, who had evidently carefully rehearsed the questions and was following a well-thought-out campaign, said, "You went out to the scene of the murder?"

"I don't know," I said.

"What do you mean, you don't know?"

"There was no corpse there when I got there."

"But you went to the place where the pickup and trailer had been located?"

"I don't know."

"Well, you went to what you thought was the place?"

"Objected to," Newberry said. "What the witness thought doesn't make any difference."

"All right," Roberts snapped, "I'll withdraw the question. I call your attention to this map or diagram of the northern portion of the city of Calexico, Mr. Lam. Does that mean anything to you? Can you orient yourself on that map?"

"Generally."

"I call your attention to certain marks here which represent the place where the witnesses have said the pickup and trailer with the houseboat was parked. Did you go to that locality?"

"I did."

"When?"

"I don't know the exact time. It was during the morning of the twentieth."

"Did you look for a murder weapon?" Roberts asked.

"I looked around. I wanted to see what evidence had been over-looked," I said.

Sergeant Sellers had the grace to wince. The deputy sheriff, who was sitting in court, frowned.

"And what did you do?"

"I looked around a place where quite a few people were present and then I walked over to the extreme edge of a wide place by the side of the road."

"Can you show us on the diagram, People's Exhibit A, where you walked?"

I went over to the diagram and indicated the place marked "Drainage Ditch."

"I walked along the edge of this drainage ditch," I said.

"What were you looking for?"

"Any evidence that had been overlooked."

"You said that before."

"You asked me; I tried to tell you."

"And what evidence did you think might have been overlooked?"

"I wanted to see if anyone had taken the trouble to cross that muddy ditch and look in the alfalfa field on the other side."

"Did you find any footprints indicating anyone had crossed the ditch?"

"I did not."

"Therefore, you felt that no one had crossed that drainage ditch since the water had left a deposit of mud in the bottom?"

"That's right."

"And what caused *you* to cross that ditch?"

"That fact that nobody else had."

"If the murderer had not crossed the ditch, what led you to believe that there was evidence which might have been found on the other side?"

"A man who throws a baseball doesn't necessarily walk to home plate," I said.

Someone in the audience snickered.

Roberts cleared his throat authoritatively. "You don't need to be facetious, Mr. Lam."

"I wasn't being facetious. I was pointing out a physical fact."

"In any event, you decided to cross that ditch?"

"I not only decided to, I did."

"And what did you do when you crossed the ditch? By the way, how did you cross that ditch?"

"I walked."

"No, no. I mean, what did you do about your shoes and socks?"

"I took them off and carried them."

"And you crossed the ditch and climbed barefoot up the bank on the other side?"

"That's right."

"Then what did you do?"

"I walked up and down the bank."

"And what did you find, if anything?"

"When I had arrived at a certain place which I will try to indicate on the map, I saw something metallic gleaming in the field. I moved over far enough to find that it was a revolver."

"And what did you do?"

"I told a young boy, who had followed me across, to call the police."

"Was that the first time you had seen this gun?"

"Yes, sir."

"Now, let's not have any misunderstanding about this," Roberts said. "I am showing you a thirty-eight-caliber revolver with a one-and-seven-eighths-inch barrel being numbered one-thirty-three-three-four seven, and having five shots, or the places for five cartridges in the cylinder. Will you look at this gun, please, referring, if the Court please for the sake of the record, to People's Exhibit B?"

I looked at the gun and said, "This looks very much like the gun. I never did pick it up. I simply asked the young man to notify the police and to ask them to come at once. That is, I actually asked him to go to his parents and ask his parents to notify the police."

"Now, this young man, would you know him if you saw him again?"

"Yes, sir."

"Stand up, please, Lorenzo."

The ten-year-old kid, looking very bugeyed, stood up in court.

"Is that the person?" Roberts asked.

"That's the person."

"You may sit down," Roberts said to Lorenzo.

Roberts looked at me long and hard, "Mr. Lam," he said, "I suggest that you had that murder weapon in your possession when you went out to the place which has been indicated on the map."

"I did not!"

"I further suggest that you looked around to find where would be a good place to conceal the weapon. That when you saw no one had crossed the muddy bottom of that ditch, you decide that it would be a good plan to drop that weapon in the alfalfa field."

"I did not!"

"I suggest that you, therefore, went out into the alfalfa field; that you dropped the weapon; that you then intended to return to the bank on the other side and say nothing about what you had done, but that the presence of this young man, Lorenzo Gonzales, forced you to change your plan; that the keen eyes of this young man detected that you had something you were trying to conceal, and he asked you what it was, or words to that effect."

"That is not so."

"That because this young man was standing where he could, within a short time, and would undoubtedly have discovered this gun and, under the circumstances, the fact that you had planted the gun would have been immediately apparent, you changed your plans and pretended to have discovered the gun yourself and asked young Lorenzo to run to his parents and get them to notify the police."

"That is not true."

"I further suggest that you did this in order to protect your client, Milton Carling Calhoun."

"That is definitely not true."

"But you did very fortuitously discover this gun?"

"Yes."

"And by some stroke of reasoning, or perhaps I should say some stroke of genius, you were able to walk directly to the place where this gun had been dropped."

"That is not true."

"Why did you go there?"

"I was making a general survey of the terrain."

"And that survey caused you to take off your shoes and socks and wade across a very mushy, muddy ditch bottom in order to go to an alfalfa field where your keen mind suggested to you that the murderer might have been able to have thrown the gun without leaving any tracks in the bottom of the ditch?"

"I wanted to survey the territory. I crossed the ditch. I found the gun."

"And you had never in your life seen this gun before?"

"Oh, Your Honor," Newberry said, "I should have objected a long time ago, but I have let this farce go on because I thought perhaps Counsel had some definite objective in view.

"I object to this entire line of questioning on the ground that Counsel is attempting to cross-examine his own witness."

"The objection is sustained," Judge Polk said.

"And I now move to strike out the entire testimony of this witness on the ground that the testimony was improperly elicited and as the result of improper questions which were the result of an attempt to cross-examine the prosecution's own witness."

"The motion is denied," Judge Polk ruled.

Roberts said, "You wish to cross-examine this witness before I dismiss him from the stand and recall Sergeant Frank Sellers?"

"Certainly not," Newberry said. "I have no questions of this witness. Here is a man who came out to the scene of the crime and made an investigation which should have been made by the Sheriff's Office of this county and the police of the city of Calexico, to say nothing of the really great expert imported from Los Angeles."

And Newberry made a sarcastic bow in the direction of Sergeant Sellers.

Sergeant Sellers angrily half arose from his chair, but thought better of it.

"There's no need for any grandstand oratory at this time," Judge Polk pronounced. "You may stand down, Mr. Lam. And Sergeant Sellers will return to the stand."

"Now that we have the background of this murder weapon clarified somewhat," Roberts said, "will you please tell what happened as far as you know—of your own knowledge?"

"I was at the Calexico Police Station, talking with the Chief," Sellers said. "There was a phone call and I was advised by the Chief . . ."

"Just a minute, just a minute," Newberry said. "I object on the ground that any conversation that you had with the chief of police which was not in the hearing of this defendant is hearsay and incompetent, irrelevant, and immaterial."

"Sustained," Polk said somewhat wearily.

"Just tell us what you did following this conversation," Roberts said.

Sellers said, "I called to one of the police officers and asked him to drive me out to the scene of the crime."

"Was a deputy sheriff there at the time?"

"There were several deputy sheriffs at police headquarters, but they were working on developing latent fingerprints and doing other things. As a matter of fact, I didn't think much of this hurried tip . . ."

"Move to strike out everything after the words 'As a matter of fact.' " Newberry said.

Judge Polk said, "It may go out. Sergeant, you know that you are not to offer any opinion."

"I'm sorry," Sellers said. "That just slipped out. I was thinking of my reactions at the time and what I did, and how it happened that we didn't call any of the Sheriff's Office to go out with us."

"That's quite all right. That can come out in cross-examination, if at all," Judge Polk said. "Just go ahead with what you personally did and what you personally found, Sergeant."

Sellers, who was not enjoying himself in the least, shifted his position uncomfortably and said, "Together with this Calexico officer I went out to the scene of the crime. This young boy, Lorenzo Gonzales, was there waiting for us. He said something to us which, of course, I can't repeat because it was not in the presence of the defendant, but, as a result of what he said, this officer and I walked across the ditch to a point where Donald Lam was standing over—that is, almost over, that gun, which as it turns out, is the gun marked People's Exhibit B and introduced in evidence in this case."

"And what did you do?"

"I inserted a fountain pen in the barrel of the gun so as to keep any fingerprints which might be on the weapon from being smudged. I elevated the fountain pen, thereby picking up the gun, and using this means of holding the gun in a perpendicular position, I carried it back across the ditch.

"We then took the gun to police headquarters where fingerprint men dusted it to try to develop latent prints.

"There were no prints on the gun. I may state that we hardly expected to develop latent prints on metal of this sort."

"There were no prints at all?"

"Objected to as hearsay," Newberry said.

Sellers grinned at him and said, "I was present when the dusting was done, Counsel."

"And there were no fingerprints?" Roberts asked.

"There were some smudges, but nothing that was identifiable on the gun."

"What was subsequently done with this weapon?" Roberts asked.

"I took it to the office of the sheriff in this county where a ballistics expert and I fired test bullets from it and put them in a comparison microscope with the fatal bullet in this case."

"And what did you find?"

"We found a perfect match."

"Meaning what?"

"Meaning that this weapon, which has been introduced in evidence as People's Exhibit B, was the murder weapon, the weapon which fired the fatal bullet."

"I believe that I have no more questions at the present time of this witness," Roberts said. "You may cross-examine, Counsel."

"Newberry thought for a moment, then said, "I have no cross-examination at this time."

"Call Lorenzo Gonzales to the stand," Roberts said.

Lorenzo, looking suddenly badly frightened, came forward.

"How old are you, young man?" Judge Polk asked.

"Ten—going on to eleven."

"Do you understand the nature of an oath?"

"Yes, sir."

"What does it mean?"

"It means that you have to tell the truth."

"And what happens if you don't tell the truth?"

"You are punished."

"And you are afraid of punishment?"

"Everybody is afraid of punishment."

"Administer the oath," Judge Polk said to the clerk.

The clerk administered the oath.

Roberts said, "You are acquainted with Donald Lam, the witness who testified here a short time ago?"

"Yes, sir."

"And what was he doing when you first saw him?"

"He was walking around the place where all the people were standing."

"And then what did you see him do?"

"I saw him take off his shoes and socks and cross over the muddy bottom of the drainage ditch."

"How were you dressed at the time?"

"I had on my pants and a shirt."

"The pants were long pants?"

"No, sir, they were the kind of an overall pants that had been cut off a little below the knee."

"And what about your shoes and socks?"

"I don't have none. I never wear shoes—except at church and—like when I come in here. Shoes hurt my feet."

"So you were barefooted at the time?"

"Yes, sir."

"So it meant nothing to you to run across the drainage ditch."

"No, sir."

"Now, what caused you to cross the drainage ditch?"

Lorenzo, who evidently had been carefully coached, said, "I saw that this detective man had found something."

"Now, just a minute, just a minute," Newberry interupted. "That question calls for a conclusion of the witness and the answer is a conclusion of the witness."

Judge Polk was interested. He leaned forward. "The Court will ask a few questions," he said.

"Young man, was there something in the demeanor of this private detective, Donald Lam, which cause you to believe he had seen something?"

"Yes."

"What was it?"

"Well, he was walking along, walking along, walking along, and I was watching him, and all of a sudden he stopped still and then turned and started walking out into the alfalfa field; and then he stood with his back to me so I couldn't see what he was doing and then all of a sudden he turned and started back toward the bank of the ditch."

"And what did you do?"

"As soon as I saw that he had found something, I ran across the muddy bottom of the ditch, up the bank on the other side, and over in the alfalfa field to where he was standing."

"Did you run very fast?"

"Very fast indeed, sir. I have my feet very tough. I can run over rocks and the roughness in the ground just as though I had shoes on—better than if I have shoes on."

"So then what happened?" the judge asked.

"When this man saw that I knew he had found something was when he told me to go to my parents and have them call the police."

"Now that, if the Court please," Newberry said, "is purely a conclusion of the witness, incompetent, irrelevant and immaterial, calling for—"

"Just a minute," Judge Polk said. "The objection will be temporarily sustained, but I want to ask this young man a few more questions. Just what did Mr. Lam do which was out of the ordinary?"

"Well, he started walking toward the bank of the ditch. Then he had taken a couple of steps and saw me coming, running just as fast as I could to join him."

"So what did you do?"

"I asked him, 'What did you find, mister,' and he didn't answer me right away. He sort of thought things over for a little while and then he said, 'Never mind, but go home at once—do you live near here?'

"I told him I did.

"He said, 'Go home and tell your father to call the police and have them come out at once.'

"So then I said, 'What did you find?' and he didn't say anything, so then I did a little looking and I saw this gun."

"Was it in plain sight from where you were standing?"

"Not in plain sight, but I would have seen it even if he hadn't said anything. It was lying where the sun was glinting on the metal enough so that you could see there was something in the alfalfa."

"I think that tells the story in a manner which is admissible in evidence," Judge Polk said. "Do Counsel for either side wish to ask any more questions?"

"This covers the evidence that I expected this young man to give," Roberts said.

"Is there any cross-examination?" Judge Polk asked Newberry.

"Newberry shook his head emphatically. "No questions," he said. "I do move, however, to strike out all of the evidence of this witness on the ground that he is too young to understand the meaning of the oath."

"Motion denied."

"Upon the further ground that the testimony given by this witness is purely speculative, is not objective, and relates to conclusions formed by this witness."

"The motion is denied," Judge Polk said. "I will admit that some of the testimony given by this witness relates to conclusions which he formed in his own mind. But in each instance the basis of those conclusions is set forth objectively in the form of admissible evidence so that any interpolation of what the witness thought or conclusions he reached from what he had seen are immaterial. This is an interesting bit of evidence and I don't mind stating that the Court is impressed by it, although, of course, at the present time I don't understand just what it is leading up to.

"Is it your contention, Mr. Prosecutor, that this murder weapon was in the possession of Donald Lam, that it was taken out into the field by Donald Lam and surreptitiously dropped at the spot where it was found?"

"That is correct, Your Honor," Roberts said.

"Very well, go ahead with the case," Judge Polk observed, glancing thoughtfully at me.

Roberts called a man by the name of Smith who testified that he was a semi-pro ball player; that he played the position of pitcher; that he had been taken to the scene of the crime by Sergeant Sellers; that he had been given a revolver which was an exact duplicate of the gun introduced as People's Exhibit B; that it was a Smith & Wesson chambered for five shells with a one-and-seven-eighths-inch barrel; that he had stood by the ditch at the scene of the crime and had thrown the gun as far as he could; that he had thrown it not once but several times, and that he had never been able to throw the gun as far as the spot in which the gun had been found when the police officers arrived.

"Any questions on cross-examination?" Roberts asked.

Newberry shook his head.

"Just a minute, Your Honor," I said. "Since my integrity is being impugned here, I would like to ask one question, whether or not the man tried throwing the gun from a point farther down the bank or whether he stood right at the scene of the crime. There is no evidence that the person who threw the gun had to stand at the exact scene of the crime and—"

"Now, just a minute," Judge Polk said. "You are out of order, Mr. Lam, although I appreciate the point you are making. If Counsel for the Defense wishes to bring out that point, he certainly is entitled to do so. On the other hand, as far as this Court is concerned, it is a self-evident fact. The diagram now shows the alfalfa field and the spot where the gun was picked up. Quite apparently, by moving down the bank of the ditch, and throwing the gun straight across, instead of at a diagonal, quite a few feet could have been saved. That is a matter of simple mathematics."

"Just a moment, Your Honor," Roberts said. "It stands to reason that if the murderer threw that gun he wanted to get rid of it just as soon as possible. He would have left the trailer, run to the bank of the ditch, trying to dispose of the gun, seen the muddy bottom in the ditch, and so decided to throw the gun as far as he could."

"Are you," Judge Polk asked, "trying to argue with the Court?"

Roberts thought for a moment, then said, "Well, yes, Your Honor."

"Don't do it," Judge Polk said. "There is no more reason for the murderer to have run directly from the scene of the crime at a right angle than there is for him to have angled down so that he came to the bank of the ditch at a point that was right opposite from the place where the gun was found."

Roberts hesitated for a moment, then sat down.

"Call your next witness," Judge Polk said.

Roberts said, "I call Maybelle Dillon to the stand."

Maybelle Dillon was in her late forties, with a flat chest, sagging shoulders, and a general air of despondency, but her eyes were alert and she spoke with a rapid-fire delivery.

She gave her address as 895 Billinger Street, Los Angeles, and her occupation as a typist.

"For whom do you type?" Roberts asked.

"I am a free-lance typist. I type manuscripts and do minor editing. I advertise in the writer's magazines and get quite a number of manuscripts in the mail. I give these minor editing, type them in acceptable form, and send them back, together with one copy at so much per page."

"Are you acquainted with one Nanncie Beaver?"

"Oh, yes, yes indeed!"

"And where does Miss Beaver live?"

"At Eight-thirty Billinger Street, Apartment Sixty-two B."

"Have you had ocasion to see Miss Beaver in the last week?"

"Yes, sir."

"When?"

"It was—now, let me see, it was the fifteenth of the month."

"And where were you at that time?"

"I was in Nanncie's apartment."

"Do you do work for Nanncie?"

"No, sir, she does her own typing, but we're very good friends, and Nanncie occasionally comes up with a client for me, some beginning author who either doesn't have a typewriter or who can't think on a typewriter or who doesn't turn out good enough work for submission to the magazines . . . you see I work with amateurs."

"Was anybody else present at that time when you saw Miss Beaver?"

"No, sir, there were just the two of us."

"Now, at that time, did Nanncie show you a gun?"

"Yes, sir."

"I show you a gun, People's Exhibit B, and ask you if that looks like the gun that she showed you at that time."

The witness handled the gun gingerly and said, "Yes, sir, it looks very much like the gun."

"And what did Nanncie tell you?"

"She told me that she had tipped off one of her writer friends to a dope-smuggling racket and that he was about to write it up; that one of her friends, a Mr. Calhoun—"

"Just a minute, just a minute," Newberry interrupted, on his feet, his voice filling the courtroom. "This is improper and Counsel knows it. This is irrelevant, immaterial, and is hearsay. It is completely outside of the issues. Unless it can be shown that the defendant was there or unless the witness heard the words of the defendant, anything that this Nanncie Beaver told her about the source of the gun is completely irrelevant."

"I think that's right," Judge Polk said.

"May I be heard?" Roberts asked.

"You may be heard, but this conversation seems to me to be hearsay."

"Surely, Your Honor," Roberts said, "we have here a murder weapon. We have this weapon in the hands of the very close friend of the defendant. We have—"

"Object to that statement as prejudicial misconduct. I move it be stricken from the record," Newberry shouted.

"It will go out," Judge Polk ruled. "Now, try to confine yourself, Mr. Prosecutor, to the facts of this case as they are admissible in court."

"We expect to prove a friendship, Your Honor. We expect to prove that statements as to this gun are really part of the *res gestae.*"

Judge Polk shook his head. "You can't do it by hearsay."

"Very well," Roberts said, "we'll go at it another way. I'll excuse this witness from the stand and I'll call Mrs. George Honcutt to the stand, please."

Mrs. Honcutt was a matronly woman with square shoulders, big hips and a bulldog jaw. She came swinging up to the witness stand like a full-rigged ship plowing into the harbor.

"What is your name, address and occupation?" the clerk asked.

"Mrs. George Honcutt. I manage the Maple Leaf Motel in Calexico."

"I ask you if, on the early morning of the twentieth of this month, you had a tenant in your motel by the name of Nanncie Beaver?"

"I did."

"How was she registered?"

"Under the name of Nanncie Beaver, but she first tried to register under the name of Nanncie Armstrong."

"And what caused her to change her registration?"

"I said, 'Look, dearie, when a single woman comes in here I have to know something about her.' I said to her, 'Now, I want to take a look at your driving license.' So then she produced her driving license and said she was sort of hiding and didn't want anyone to know she was registered there, and I told her it was all right by me as long as she behaved herself; that I was running a decent, respectable place and that I'd expect her to behave herself, otherwise out she went."

"And she stayed on there?"

"Yes."

"Until what time?"

"Until some time late in the night of the nineteenth or early in the morning of the twentieth. When I went in to check her room on the morning of the twentieth, there was the key in the door on the outside and she had gone. All of her baggage—everything."

"Was the rent paid?"

"You bet the rent was paid," Mrs. Honcutt said. "With a woman like that I collect in advance, day by day."

"Thank you, that's all," Roberts said.

"Any questions?" Judge Polk asked Newberry.

The lawyer seemed puzzled. "No questions."

"Now then," Roberts said, "I'm going to call Mr. Herbert C. Newton."

Herbert Newton was a middle-aged individual with a quick, nervous manner and a wiry frame. He quite evidently enjoyed being a witness.

He gave his name, address and occupation to the clerk, then turned expectantly to Roberts.

Roberts said, "Where were you staying on the evening of the nineteenth and the morning of the twentieth?"

"At the Maple Leaf Motel in Calexico."

"At any time during the night did you have occasion to get up and look out of your window."

"I did."

"What was your unit?"

"I was in Unit One which is right next to the street and right across from Unit Twelve."

"And what happened, if anything?"

"It was around two or three o'clock in the morning when I heard voices across in Unit Twelve, and the light came on in Unit Twelve which threw a light in my bedroom. The voices and the light wakened me and kept me from sleeping. I became very irritated."

"And what did you do?"

"After a while I got up."

"And what did you see or hear?"

"I could hear a man's voice and a woman's voice. They seemed to be arguing. After I got up out of bed I heard the man say, 'You've got to get out of here. You're in danger. You come with me and I'll take you to another place where you won't get mixed up with this writer friend and be in danger.' "

"Anything else?"

"Yes. He said, 'Get packed and meet me out in the car and I'll take the gun. You can't keep it with you in Mexico.' "

"What was that last?"

"He said, 'I'll take the gun.' "

"And then what happened?"

"Then he said, 'Pack just as fast as you can.' "

"Anything else?"

"Yes. He said. 'You're foolish to have got mixed in this thing. Now, I'll take charge of things and get you off the hook, but you've got to quit being tied up with that crazy writer.' "

"Then what happened?"

"Then the door opened and this man came out."

"Did you get a good look at him?"

"I certainly did. The light from inside the apartment was full on his face."

"And do you see this man in the courtroom?"

"Certainly. He is the defendant."

"That's the man you saw emerging from the apartment?"

"That's the man I saw."

"That's the man who said, 'I'll take the gun'?"

"That's the man who said, 'I'll take the gun. You can't keep it with you in Mexico.' "

"Then what happened?"

"Then the door was closed, and after a very few minutes the light went out and some woman whom I couldn't see opened the door and put a bag and a suitcase on the threshold, and this man who had been waiting in a big car, parked at the curb, came and picked up the bag and the suitcase and put them in the car. Then they drove away."

"Any questions on cross-examination?" Judge Polk asked.

Newberry said, "I have just one or two questions of this witness.

"Can you give us the exact time of this conversation, Mr. Newton?"

"No, I cannot. I was aroused from sleep and I was annoyed and irritated. In fact, I was so angry I couldn't get back to sleep for I guess an hour. I know it was before three o'clock because I didn't get to sleep until after three o'clock. I finally got up and took a couple of Bufferin."

"There's no question in your mind that the man you saw was Milton Carling Calhoun, the defendant in this case?"

"Absolutely no question."

"Do you wear glasses?"

"I wear glasses when I read, but I can see without glasses at a distance and I saw this man just as plain as day, standing there in the doorway."

"I think that's all," Newberry said.

Roberts said, "If the Court please, that concludes our case. We ask that the defendant be bound over to the Superior Court on a charge of first-degree murder."

I said to Newberry, "Ask for a continuance."

Newberry shook his head. "It won't do any good. We aren't going to put on any defense. I never put on a defense at a preliminary hearing. It just tips your hand and—"

I interrupted him to say in a whisper, "They haven't proven anything except a bare case of circumstantial evidence and—"

"Don't be funny," Newberry broke in. "They've shown his fingerprints on the houseboat. They've shown his ownership of the fatal gun. They have evidence showing that he went to the Maple Leaf Motel at two o'clock in the morning to get the gun. He was going to take care of things to protect his light-of-love. He went out and took matters into his own hands. He killed the dope runner."

"That's not the kind of a man Calhoun is," I said. "For God's sake, move for a continuance!"

Judge Polk said, "Gentlemen, is there any defense?"

"A half hour's continuance," I said.

Calhoun looked at me and then looked at his attorney.

"A half-hour continuance won't hurt anything," he said to Newberry.

Newberry got to his feet reluctantly.

"There seems to be some question as to procedure," he said. "May I ask for a thirty-minute recess?"

Judge Polk looked at his watch. "The Court will take a fifteen-minute recess," he said. "That should be ample for Counsel to confer with his client."

Judge Polk left the bench and retired to chambers.

I grabbed Newberry's arm and pulled him and Calhoun over to a secluded corner of the courtroom under the watchful eye of the deputy sheriff who had Calhoun in custody.

"You lied to me," Newberry said to his client.

Calhoun said, "I only lied to you on an unessential matter. It was absolutely vital to me to keep Nanncie out of it.

Yes, I did go to the motel. I wanted to get the gun back because I had an idea that I was going to stay and protect Nanncie. But she told me she didn't have the gun, that she had given it to this writer, this Colburn Hale."

"And that made you mad?" I asked.

"It made me *very* angry. I had given her that gun for her own protection."

"So what did you do?"

"I took her over to the Lucerna Hotel in Mexicali, got her a room and paid for it. Then I came back across the border and registered at the De Anza Hotel."

I shook my head and said, "No, you didn't. You drove along the road to that place where the pickup was parked. Now, what caused you to go in that houseboat?"

"I didn't go in and I didn't go back to the houseboat," Calhoun said.

"All right, what did happen?"

Calhoun said dejectedly, "I have held out on you people. I shouldn't have done it, but I was trying to protect myself."

"Go on, go on," I said. "We haven't got all day. What happened?"

Calhoun said, "When I was driving into Calexico my headlights picked up this pickup and the houseboat on the trailer, and as they did I saw a man jump out of the door of the houseboat, hit the ground in a flying leap and start running just as fast as he could go over toward that drainage ditch. After he got a few yards over there on an angle, he got out of the range of my headlights."

"And what did you do?"

"It was around two o'clock in the morning. I stopped my car, went over to the houseboat and called out, 'Is everything all right?'

"There was no answer. I rapped with my knuckles on the door. There was no answer. I started to try the door. That was probably when I put my left hand against the side of the houseboat to brace myself. And then I thought better of it. After all, it wasn't any of my business. I called out again, 'Is everything all right in there?' I received no answer so I got back in my car and drove on to Calexico.

"I went at once to the Maple Leaf Motel and I did have the conversation with Nanncie that this man overheard. I took Nanncie across the border to a hotel where I thought she would be safer than in that Maple Leaf Motel. And I wanted to get her out of the clutches of that writer friend of hers."

"What about the gun?"

"I did tell her that I'd take the gun back because I knew it would make complications if she had a gun across the border in Mexico, and she told me she didn't have it, that she'd loaned it to Hale.

"I'll admit I became angry. I had given her that gun for her personal protection. Certainly not with the idea that she was going to pass it around to some down-at-the-heel writer friend."

I turned to Newberry. "All right," I said, "You're going to have to use heroic measures."

"What do you mean?"

I said, "They're going to bind him over for trial unless you pull a fast one."

"They're going to bind him over for trial in any event. I'm not even going to object. I'm not going to put up a whisper of an argument except that I'm going to put up the old song and dance that there's nothing in this case except circumstantial evidence; that they can show that the murder was committed with his gun and that there are fingerprints on the houseboat, but they can't tell when those fingerprints were made or who was holding the gun when it was fired. The fingerprints may have been made at any time."

"And your client is going to get bound over."

"He'll get bound over."

I looked at Calhoun. "Do you like that?"

"Good God, no!" Calhoun said.

"But you can't stop it," Newberry said. "He's stuck."

"Not if you play it right," I told him.

Newberry looked at me with sudden distaste. "Are you," he asked, "now trying to tell me how I should handle this case?"

I looked right back at him and said, "Yes."

"Well, don't do it," Newberry warned. "I don't know just how you fit into the picture, Lam, but I think you're in this thing up to your necktie. Are you sure that you weren't the man Calhoun saw running out of the houseboat trailer?"

"I'm sure I wasn't the man he saw," I said, "and if you use your head a little bit we may be able to knock this whole thing into a cocked hat right now."

"You're crazy," he told me. "It's an axiom of criminal law that you can't do anything on a preliminary examination. You cross-examine the witnesses, you get as much of the prosecution's case as you can, and then you just ride along with the punch."

"To hell with the axioms of criminal law," I said. "I'm talking about a particular case. This case. You let Calhoun be bound over and there will be headlines all over the country."

"We can't control the press," Newberry said. "We have a free press in this country. They can print the news any way they want to just so they confine themselves to the truth.

"Now then, a feminine angle has been introduced into this case and, believe me, that's going to give the newspapers a field day. MILLIONAIRE DEFENDANT IN SURREPTITIOUS MIDNIGHT RENDEZ-VOUS . . .'"

I said to Calhoun, "Do you want to put on a defense?"

"I want to get out of this," he said.

"It isn't what Calhoun wants, it's what *I* want," Newberry said. "I'm the lawyer and I don't brook any interference from a client. I'll tell you right now, Lam, I don't brook any interference from some smart-aleck private detective either."

"I'm not a smart-aleck private detective," I told him. "I'm a damn good detective."

Calhoun looked from one to the other.

"What do you want to do, Calhoun?" I asked. "Make up your mind."

"I guess there's nothing I can do," Calhoun said. "Newberry has reached a decision."

"And who is Newberry working for?"

"Why . . . I guess he's working . . . he's working for me."

"I don't work for anybody," Newberry said. "I'm a professional man. I'm an attorney. I permit myself to be retained in cases. I go to court and I handle those cases my way. Make no mistake about it, *my way.*"

Calhoun shrugged his shoulders and looked helplessly at me.

I said, "You want my judgment, Calhoun? I think we can spring you out of this. In fact, I'm pretty damn sure we can."

"I'll bet a thousand to one against it," Newberry said.

"I'll take a hundred dollars of that right now," I told him.

He said angrily, "I don't want to make any actual bet. I was just simply giving the odds. It wouldn't do any good to make an actual bet because I'm going to stand up and tell the Court that we consent to an order binding the defendant over."

I looked at Calhoun and said, "Fire him!"

"What?" Calhoun asked incredulously.

"Fire him!" I said.

Newberry looked at me and said, "Why, you smart-aleck son of a . . ."

I turned away from him and said to Calhoun, "He's your lawyer. You fire him and do as I say and you'll get out of this."

"So you're practicing law," Newberry said.

"I'm telling Calhoun what to do. Calhoun can be his own attorney. You do what I tell you to, Calhoun, and we'll be home free."

Calhoun looked dubious.

The door from chambers opened and Judge Polk came in. The bailiff rapped the Court to order. We all stood up, then were seated.

"Very well," Judge Polk said, "We will take up the case of People versus Calhoun. Is there any defense?"

"Fire him," I said to Calhoun. "Now!"

Calhoun reached a sudden decision. He got to his feet and said, "Your Honor, I want to be my own lawyer."

Judge Polk was startled. Roberts whirled around and looked at us as though we had all taken leave of our senses.

"You want to discharge your lawyer?" Judge Polk asked.

Newberry grabbed up his briefcase. "There's no need to discharge *me,*" he said. "I'm quitting the case."

"Now, just a moment," Judge Polk said. "You can't quit the case without the consent of the Court."

Newberry hesitated and said, "I don't want any more of this client. I don't want any part of him or of this smart-aleck private detective."

"Just control yourself," Judge Polk said. "Mr. Calhoun, what seems to be the situation?"

"I want to put on a defense and I want to conduct my own case," Calhoun said.

"You want to discharge your lawyer?"

"I want to discharge him."

"Judge Polk looked at Newberry. "You want to withdraw from the case?"

"I withdraw from the case. I have withdrawn. I do withdraw. I don't want any more to do with it."

Judge Polk sighed. "Very well," he said, "the order will be granted. The defendant will act for himself in *propria persona.*

"Now then, Mr. Calhoun, do you wish to put on any witness?"

"Call Colburn Hale," I whispered.

Calhoun looked at me, then looked at the indignant back of Newberry who was stalking out of the courtroom.

"I'll call Colburn Hale as my first witness," he said.

While Colburn Hale came limping forward and held up his right hand as though his entire body hurt, Calhoun whispered, "What the devil do I ask him?"

"Sit down beside me," I said, "and ask the questions as I feed them to you."

I whispered to Calhoun, while Hale was giving his name, address and occupation to the clerk, "Make your questions as short as possible and encourage him to do the talking.

"Now, your first question is whether or not he ever saw the gun, People's Exhibit B. Hand the gun to him and ask him if he ever saw it, and if he says, 'Yes,' ask him when was the last time he saw it. Encourage the guy to talk."

Calhoun was as awkward as a man trying to water-ski for the first time. He floundered around and said to the clerk, "Please show this witness the gun and I want to ask him if he ever saw that gun before."

"What is the object of this?" Judge Polk asked.

Calhoun looked at me.

I said, "We want to find out how the gun got into that field."

Calhoun passed my comment on to the judge.

"Very well," Judge Polk said. "I think that is probably a legitimate part of the defense, since the prosecution has made a point of it. Let the witness answer the question."

"I have seen the gun before," Hale said.

"Where? How? When? And what happened to it? When did it leave his possession?" I asked Calhoun.

"When did you see it?"

"I saw it—well, I guess it was about the seventeenth."

"How did you get it?"

"Nanncie Beaver gave it to me. She told me that—"

"Just a minute," Roberts said. "We object to any conversation between the witness and Nanncie Beaver."

"Sustained," Judge Polk said.

"When did you last have the gun?" Calhoun asked.

"I lost it on the evening of the nineteenth."

"How did you lose it?"

"Puggy took it from me."

Calhoun looked at me.

"Who's Puggy?" I whispered to him.

"Who's Puggy?" he asked. "Tell me all about it."

Hale said, "I was on the track of this dope shipment. I had this gun. I was following the dope shipment up from San Felipe. I thought I was being smart.

"I didn't know there was a tail car behind me. When we got almost to where the La Puerta road turns off, this tail car closed in on me and crowded me to the side of the road. Then the pickup with the house-boat trailer stopped.

"The man who was driving the tail car was evidently a pugilist, because the other guy called him Puggy. He started working me over. I tried to pull the gun on him and the man from the dope car—I guess that was Eddie Sutton—had me covered and said, 'Get your hands up or your brains will get spattered all over the side of your car.' "

I nudged Calhoun. "Tell him to go on."

"Go on," Calhoun said.

I whispered to Calhoun, "Every time he stops talking, just tell him, 'Go on.' "

Calhoun nodded.

"Well," Hale said, "they really worked me over. That's where I got this shiner, and I got a bloody nose and a cut lip. There was blood all over my shirt and I was pretty much of a mess by the time they got done with me."

"Go on," Calhoun said.

"They got me down and they kicked me and really gave me a beating. Then they put me in my car, tied me up with some kind of a thin, strong cord, sort of like a fishing line—that is, a heavy fishing line—and they drove me down the side road, put a gag in my mouth, parked the car and said, 'Now, stay there, you smart s.o.b. That'll teach you to interfere in things that don't concern you.' "

"Go on," Calhoun said.

"They took the gun. The man called Puggy took the gun."

"Go on," Calhoun said.

"Well, that's all of it," Hale went on, "Except the fact that about—

I don't know—seven o'clock in the morning—eight o'clock, I guess, this very fine Mexican gentleman by the name of Jose Chapalla came along and saw my car by the side of the road. He stopped to take a look and saw me tied and gagged and he untied the ropes and took the gag out of my mouth. I was about half dead by that time, and Jose Chapalla took me to his home and they gave me coffee and some eggs and tortillas and then I went to sleep, and then Jose took me back to my car and after a long while I drove away. I started for Mexicali and got as far as a roadside restaurant where I went in to get some beer, and that's where Donald Lam and Nanncie Beaver found me."

"Ask him if he's sore and stiff," I said.

"Are you sore and stiff?" Calhoun asked.

"Of course I am! My ribs are just about caved in. I'm more sore now than I was the day of the beating. I not only have this black eye, but I'm afraid my ribs are cracked."

"Tell him to show us the bruises," I whispered to Calhoun.

"Can you show us the bruises?" Calhoun asked.

Hale pointed to his eye.

"On his ribs, on his sides, on his torso," I said.

"The other bruises," Calhoun said. "Where are they?"

Hale put a hand tenderly to his side. "All over."

"Show us," I said.

"Show us," Calhoun echoed.

"What do you mean, show you?" Hale demanded.

"Pull up your shirt," I whispered.

"Pull up your shirt," Calhoun echoed.

Hale looked at us and suddenly there was panic in his eyes. "I'm not going to disrobe here in public," he said.

"Just show us a bruise," I whispered. "Show us a bruise on your arm. Show us a bruise anywhere on your torso—just one single bruise —one black-and-blue mark."

Calhoun stammered, "Show us your body, show us anything that's black and blue."

"I don't have to," Hale said.

Calhoun seemed to be at an impasse.

"Tell him he's a liar," I said. "Tell him he can't show us a single bruise, that he hasn't got a spot on his body. Ask that the Court appoint a doctor to examine him."

Calhoun ran his fingers through his hair and said, "How about having a doctor make an examination, Your Honor? This man hasn't got a bruise on his body."

"He'd have to have," Judge Polk said.

"He's lying," Calhoun said.

"Wait a minute," Roberts said. "You can't impeach your own witness. I don't like to be technical with a man who is putting on his own defense, but we have to protect the rights of the people. He can't impeach his own witness."

I said, "Ask the judge if he wants to get at the truth in the case."

Calhoun was good that time. He said, "Does Your Honor want to get at the truth of this case or not?"

Judge Polk looked at the uncomfortable Colburn Hale and hesitated.

"Just a minute," Roberts said. "Who's trying this case? What does this private detective think he's trying to do? Donald Lam isn't an attorney. He doesn't appear in the case. He has no standing in court."

It was too much for Hale. He jumped out of the witness chair and scurried like a rabbit for the side door of the courtroom.

"Stop that man!" Judge Polk yelled at the bailiff.

They couldn't stop him. Hale was long gone.

I looked at the judge and said, "He recovered from all that stiffness and soreness pretty fast, didn't he, Your Honor?"

Judge Polk looked down at me, started to rebuke me, then suddenly smiled and said, "He did for a fact.

"I would suggest that the Sheriff's Office put out an all points bulletin for this man. His black eye should make it very easy to pick him up."

"But this Donald Lam doesn't have any right to ask questions in this case," Roberts objected.

Polk smiled at him and said, "Quite right, Mr. Roberts, but this Court *does* have the right to ask questions and this Court intends to ask some very searching questions."

The officers caught Hale at the courthouse door and returned him to court.

Judge Polk said, "Young man, you are on the witness stand. Now, you get right back there in that witness chair and you listen to me.

"It appears that you may have committed a crime. The Court warns you that you don't have to make any statement whatever. If you feel it may incriminate you, you don't have to talk. Or, if you just want to keep quiet, you have that privilege. You are entitled to have an attorney represent you at all stages of the proceeding and if you don't have money enough to get an attorney, the Court will appoint one. But you aren't going to get up off that witness stand and run out of the courtroom the way you did a moment ago.

"Now then, do you care to answer questions?"

Hale shifted his position and said nothing.

"Do you want an attorney to advise you? The Court is going to call a doctor to examine you."

Hale said, "I may as well come clean. I haven't got any way out, and, after all, I acted in self-defense. If I keep on being as foolish as I have been, I'll wind up facing a murder rap."

"You can either talk or not talk, just as you want," Judge Polk said, "but you're going to be examined."

Hale started talking, the words just pouring out of his mouth. He said, "I knew that dope shipment was coming across the border. I knew that they intended to make a rendezvous with the driver of a scout car at the Monte Carlo Café at seven o'clock. I told my girl friend that I would meet her there at seven o'clock.

"It started to rain. The shipment was delayed. I followed it across the border. There were two men in the car. One of the men picked up the scout car and went on ahead. The pickup with the houseboat trailer parked by the side of the road.

"I had the story I wanted. It was one whale of a story, but I didn't have it all. I wanted to see where they took this houseboat. I sensed the scout car had found a roadblock or something that caused a delay.

"I stayed where I could keep the houseboat under surveillance. It was a rainy night. I waited and waited. The driver of the pickup had gone back into the houseboat. I had an idea he'd gone to sleep.

"I was overly confident. I was a plain fool. I couldn't resist trying to get one detail I hadn't been able to get and that was the license number of the pickup. Because of the houseboat that number was hard to see. I felt the man who was driving the pickup had gone to sleep in the houseboat. I sneaked up, hoping I could get the number I wanted—and I walked right into a trap. This man had spotted me and he suddenly opened the door, held a gun on me and ordered me to get into the houseboat.

"I knew it was either him or me. He wasn't sure just what I was doing there. I could tell from the way he acted he didn't think I was an officer. He wanted to know what I wanted and what I was doing snooping around. Well, he got just a little careless. I suddenly jerked out my gun and said, 'Stick 'em up.' I was nervous. I waited maybe a tenth of a second to see what he was going to do. I waited too long. He fired. If the officers will look in that houseboat, they'll find a bullet hole somewhere near the front of the boat.

"I fired at about the same time he did. He missed. I didn't.

"I got in a panic. I took his gun, put it in my pocket and threw it away a couple of hours later. I took the Calhoun gun and ran down toward the place where I had parked my car and then threw the gun across the ditch as far as I could throw it.

"Then, instead of going to the police the way I should have done, I drove down across the border and tried to think of some way out of the mess. I stayed in the car all night. Finally, when one of the stores opened up, I bought some fishline and tied myself up at a place where I felt certain I'd be discovered. If I went too long without being discovered I could untie myself, but I felt certain I could get away with my story.

"I hit myself a good punch in the eye, bloodied my nose, and I made up that story about having been beaten up and kicked. It hadn't occurred to me that people would be looking for black-and-blue marks on my body.

"Donald Lam kept trying to get me in the swimming pool at the hotel, and that was when I realized how vulnerable I was. My story wouldn't stand up if—Well, I don't want to get blamed for murder. I acted in self-defense."

Judge Polk looked down at Sergeant Sellers. "Did the officers," he asked, "make a careful examination of the front of that houseboat to see if there was a bullet hole in the boat?"

"There was no hole in the boat, Your Honor," Sellers said, "but there was a sofa pillow on the davenport that had a very small hole in it. We didn't take the pillow to pieces to see if there was a bullet on the inside of it."

"You'd better do that," Judge Polk said, and then added gratuitously, "It seems to me that the police work in this case has been slightly below par.

"The sheriff will take this man into custody. The case against Milton Carling Calhoun is dismissed.

"Court's adjourned."

Judge Polk left the bench and there was pandemonium in the court-room. A couple of newspaper reporters got jammed in the door as they ran simultaneously for the nearest telephone.

I looked over at Calhoun and said, "Congratulations!"

The guy grabbed me in an embrace. I was afraid he might try to kiss me.

It took us nearly half an hour to get past the newspaper reporters and out to my car. I managed to get Calhoun to say "No comment" often enough to make the newspapermen give up, but the television men kept hounding us with portable cameras.

Finally we got free.

I gave Calhoun a road map. "What's this?" he asked.

"A map of the road to El Golfo."

"What's at El Golfo?"

"Nanncie Beaver," I said.

"Why at El Golfo?"

"That's so you can go down and get her without any newspaper reporters tailing you—that is, if you're smart. Then you can come into our office the first of next week and settle up."

He looked at me with dawning comprehension, then he gripped my hand, hard.

Bertha Cool was in rare form. She teetered back and forth in her squeaky swivel chair; her eyes were as hard as the diamonds on her hands.

"Now, you listen to me, Mr. Milton Carling Calhoun," she said. "You're supposed to be a big businessman. You're supposed to know your way around.

"What the hell was the idea of coming in here and getting us to go on a wild-goose chase, looking for Colburn Hale when what you really wanted was to find his girl friend?"

Calhoun squirmed uneasily.

"I had heard that private detective agencies sometimes blackmailed their clients," he said. "So I tried to conceal my background. I simply couldn't afford to have my name associated with that of Nanncie Beaver. If I had told you what I really wanted . . . Well, I would have left myself wide open."

"So," Bertha Cool said, "you led with your chin. And what makes me sore is the fact that you came in here trying to put us on the defensive, pretending that you didn't know anything about the agency, pretending that Donald was too slight to do the work, and that I wasn't any good because I was a woman.

"Get out your checkbook, Mr. Milton Calhoun. I'm going to hit you between the eyes."

"You agreed to a certain per diem," Calhoun said weakly. "I will boost that, of course, but after all . . ."

Bertha came forward in her chair with a thump, leaned her elbows on the desk, glittered at Calhoun. "And what happened?" she said.

"You lied to us. You threw us off on a false track. You put Donald in terrific danger. You . . ."

"I know, I know. I'm sorry," Calhoun said. "I'm prepared to pay something extra."

"How much?" Bertha Cool asked.

"Bearing in mind that Donald Lam gave me the best legal advice I ever had," Calhoun said, "I had intended to add a gratuity to the amount of the bill."

"How much?"

Calhoun took a deep breath. "I want your complete silence," he said. "No word of what I wanted must ever come out of this. I must have complete secrecy."

"How much?" Bertha Cool asked.

Calhoun reached in his pocket and pulled out a checkbook. "I have made out a check for ten thousand dollars," he said, "which I hope will cover the per diem expenses and the gratuity."

Bertha's jaw sagged open for a minute. She blinked her eyes a couple of times.

"Fry me for an oyster," she said.

And then there was a flash of light as her jeweled hand reached for the check.

"And, for your confidential information," Calhoun went on, "I am completely changing my life. I am sick and tired of the artificial existence I have been living, thinking only of money, money, money.

"From now on I am going to try to develop my creative energy. In short, I am going to take up writing, and I have a new address. It is Eight-seventeen Billinger Street. I am moving into the apartment vacated by Colburn Hale."

And the guy positively beamed at us.

Bertha Cool folded the check and said, "Fry me for an oyster—no, damn it, poach me for an egg!"

Calhoun grinned. "Without breaking the yolk—sunny side up," he said.

I reached across and shook the guy's hand.

THE END